TRINITY STONES

The Angelorum Twelve Chronicles
Book 1

L.G. O'CONNOR

COLLINS-YOUNG PUBLISHING

Praise for Angelorum Twelve

TRINITY STONES, Book One.

"O'Connor tackles important world-building, while also kicking off the story with a bang." *~Publisher's Weekly*

WANDERER'S CHILDREN, Book Two.

"Combining a marvelous talent for emotional resonance with a naturally light, playful attitude towards sex and romance…Although set in a supernatural milieu, the emotions and situations these characters find themselves in ring with a clarity that is unforgettable. The WANDERER'S CHILDREN (4.5 stars) is a satisfying and nuanced read for series readers and newbies alike." *~IndieReader*

HOPE'S PRELUDE, Prequel Novella

"Unique twist of the angels vs. demons mythology with characters that grab you by the heart." *~Maria V. Snyder, New York Times Bestselling Author*

"At the center of this apocalyptic struggle, L.G. grounds us in a tender love story that humanizes all the rest and gives it an intimate scale that touches the heart… I was truly captured by the love between Hope in her worldly guise as Dr. Sandra Wilson, scientist, and Isa, her…guardian and mate. Their passion is both human and otherworldly, and Isa is one of the most sexy-powerful yet gentle lovers I've ever read. This story can stand alone, but I recommend starting the series from the beginning." *~Alice Orr, Author of A Year of Summer Shadows (The Riverton Road Romantic Suspense Series)*

"Let me begin by saying that this book is not in my preferred genre. That being said, I was very much intrigued by the blurb and the storyline, and I was very pleased with author LG O'Connor's wonderful writing. The author's vivid descriptions and her take on angels versus demons place HOPE'S PRELUDE on my keeper shelf. It was an enjoyable read and I recommend it." *~Kim R., Amazon Reviewer*

"Such an easy read and so suspenseful, I couldn't put it down. An excellent job bringing the other Angelorum books together. It made me even more excited for the next book in the series. Can't wait until it is released!" *~CM, Amazon Reviewer*

"Hope's Prelude will not disappoint fans of the paranormal! The richly layered plot, paired with intricately developed characters and will keep you turning pages and anxious for the next installment!" *~Nate Loves Books*

License Notes

Epigraph

"There is no such thing as chance, and what seems to us mere accident springs from the deepest source of destiny."
–Friedrich Schiller (German poet and philosopher, 1759–1805)

"The sin, both of men and of angels, was rendered possible by the fact that God gave them free will."
–C. S. Lewis (Irish novelist and theologian, 1898–1963)

Dedication

To my nieces, Taylor, Kayla, and Jenni, three brave young women destined to keep the balance tipped toward good, whose lives will touch humanity and make it better.

In memory of David J. Keyes, whose music and smile touched hearts around the world—*literally*. I know he's singing with the angels, playing bass, and teaching them blues guitar.

To my writer whippets: Chloe, the inspiration for Cara's canine companion of the same name, and Nevada, my sweet rescue boy who slept quietly beside me as I wrote the first books in this series. Their sweet spirits frolic with Dave and the angels across the Rainbow Bridge in Heaven's Elysian Fields... And to all my dedicated readers and author friends who have waited for the series re-release and willingly re-enter the world of the Angelorum.

And for the one soul who inspired this series.

There are no coincidences. Only destinies to fulfill.

Journey forth in peace and love.

Prophecy from the *Book Of Human Angels*—5 Enoch (Hidden) Translation: Essenes Aramaic papyrus text, scribed second century BC

"As it was so spoken and then written, much time has passed since Michael bound the Watchers, led by Semyaza, to the confines of darkness. Wrath has been meted upon the Nephilim spawn. Their bodies and souls ripped from their being, leaving them shades of darkness to wander the corridors between Hell and Earth without peace."

. . .

"A new breed of Watcher has come, three hundred strong, to live among and as man to understand their strife and to empathize with their pain. Protected now by the children of Uriel, these Watchers will balance the Fallen who have been cast down from Heaven."

. . .

"The forces of darkness unite to battle for their freedom, to reach the key that will deliver them from Judgment Day and remain forever free. To acquire their promised reward, the forces of both darkness and light must abide by the laws of balance under the ever-vigilant eyes of justice or be forever vanquished by their enemy."

. . .

"It is with the birth of the First of Holy Twelve that the prophecy begins. It is with the battle that the prophecy ends."

Prelude

San Francisco, California

DR. SANDRA WILSON gripped the steering wheel hard, letting it bite into her palms. Anything to keep her eyes open. She wrestled to focus on the stretch of misty road illuminated in her headlights while shadowy figures of parked cars and low industrial buildings sped by in her peripheral vision.

Ten more minutes and her head could rest safely on a pillow, sadly without Ishmael beside her. Almost three days had passed since her beloved mate and protector had been abducted, but thanks to a note from a mysterious ally, she knew he was alive.

The police had called this morning. The owners of a bar twenty miles south of San Francisco had reported Isa's SUV sitting in their parking lot unmoved for a third day in a row. That explained his cryptic text. He hadn't wanted her to know that he'd broken down and taken a drink. She berated herself for not noticing the toll this mission had taken on him and for not being there when he needed her most.

Between Isa's disappearance and her accelerated research schedule, she'd barely slept. The final vaccine was within their grasp. She was certain it would only be a matter of days before they finalized the protocol. After that, her obligation to the Angelorum would be satisfied, and she would find her mate.

Out of nowhere, a large figure darted from the shadows in front of her car. Sandra reflexively jerked the wheel as the figure disappeared into the mist. Then, the vehicle bucked violently, yanking her hard against the seat belt. Lurching twice, the car sputtered and coasted to a stop at the side of the road.

Gritting her teeth, Sandra smacked the wheel in frustration. Why hadn't she sold the "classic" 1980s Honda to her mechanic when he'd asked? Now, she regretted not taking his offer.

She rummaged in her purse for her cell phone. It sprang to life beneath her touch, displaying the time: 1:30 AM. She located a bar within walking distance that stayed open until two. She'd summon a Lyft from the bar. A tow truck could wait until morning.

Relieved she hadn't changed into her heels from the rubber-soled lab shoes, Sandra stepped into the cool, damp night and retrieved a rain poncho from the back seat. She slipped it on, tucking her braid beneath the hood. The coat fell short on her six-foot frame, but provided enough coverage to protect her from the drizzle, which smelled of ozone and pollution.

Sandra set off at a brisk pace. To pass the time, she contemplated a modification to the vaccine formula that would ensure the safety of the *One* called Cara.

A block from her final destination, a ripple of energy raised the hairs on her arms and sparked her senses. She scanned the deserted street, the energy growing black, oppressive, and . . . familiar.

Dread coiled in her middle. The shadow hadn't been a person.

Someone had sent a Hunter demon.

But who? Had her mother been right?

Was there a traitor in the High Council?

Sandra picked up her pace. A streetlight winked out as she passed, followed by another, then two more. All at once, the streetlamps ahead flickered and exploded. Shattered glass tinkled, raining down and hitting the pavement.

She ran, dodging the falling shards, her night vision cutting through the eerie darkness. Glancing over her shoulder, she saw the black haze of the disembodied demon heading straight toward her. She sprinted harder, her gaze darting between the industrial buildings, looking for a means of escape.

Without Isa's angelic weapons to protect her, the demon would be unstoppable. Her only chance was to outrun it and reach a place with people before it could fully manifest.

The demon's energy triggered a prey warning—a crushing pain in her skull—along with searing heat in the scars where her wings used to be. To stop would mean death. Ignoring the pain, she kept moving, running toward a dark path between two buildings, praying for egress onto an adjoining street.

Taking a hard left, she stumbled into an alley and grazed a building, ripping her poncho on the jagged brick exterior. Relief surged at the sight of bright lights at the end of the passageway, accompanied by the sound of late-night revelers.

Hooves scraping pavement signaled the demon taking physical form behind her, dashing her hopes of escape.

Death can't be cheated, she thought with bitter resignation.

The demon struck with inhuman force.

Pain radiated like a nuclear blast between her shoulder blades, lifting her from the ground and launching her twenty feet through the air. Her cheek met wet asphalt with the sickening crunch of shattered bone.

Sandra lay paralyzed with her eyes open, air whistling through parted lips. Blood, warm and sticky, warmed her ear and fanned into a spreading pool. Her spine severed, the scorching agony faded to numbness.

Demon. They had forgotten to add *demon* to the list of how the One could die.

The demon lowered its red-skinned face to stare into her eyes, its breath heating her hair in rank puffs. Drool hung in strings from razor-sharp teeth. She knew what came next. The creature anticipated feeding before destroying her completely.

But that wasn't going to happen.

As her lifeforce ebbed, Sandra invoked the language of angels in a silent summoning prayer.

In answer, a ring of white light spread between the buildings, engulfing her and blowing her scaly nemesis off its hooves.

Embryonic warmth surrounded her, infusing her with a sense of peace. Inside the glow, a male appeared dressed in a tunic as white as the wings unfurled behind him.

His intense purple eyes gazed upon her, unlocking her memory of him. "*Jonas,*" she whispered in her mind, addressing the iconic Angel of Death.

"*Old friend,*" he acknowledged with a head bow.

"*Who's going to save him?*" she asked. Without her, Dr. Tom Peyton, her research partner, would surely be next.

The angel's hypnotic purple gaze held compassion and a soothing pull. "*Worry not, Hope,*" he said. "*There are no coincidences. Only destinies to be fulfilled. The others will finish your fine work.*"

Expelling a final breath, she relaxed, and the silver cord severed, releasing the soul from her body. The veil of her humanity lifted, and then she understood everything, including how their work would save the one who would save them all. No longer bound to a corporeal form, she grew and expanded with indescribable joyous light.

Floating up and away, she glanced downward at the demon.

Enraged, it watched her ascent from below, unknowing she'd done it a kindness. Consuming her soul would have led to its blazing destruction.

Then, her gaze shifted and expanded outward, following the second silver cord tethering her to another. She followed it to Ishmael, where he sat, alive, in his prison cell beneath the earth's surface.

"Isa?" she whispered on the wind.

His eyes shot open in the dark. "Hope?" She couldn't be sure exactly what he saw, since she would appear in whatever form meant the most to him. Understanding spread across his face, and tears welled in his pale eyes.

"Isa, find Samuel, and protect Sara," she said.

"I don't understand," he said softly.

"You will." She sang.

"Please . . . don't go," he whispered, reaching for her.

"Take heart," she said, the pure joy of their love filling her with rapture. "I'm forever inside you, my love. We share the same soul."

She blew him a kiss that draped him in loving warmth and pulled him into a peaceful slumber. "I'll be waiting for you," she whispered in his ear and smoothed back his hair. With that, she severed the silver cord connecting them. They would reunite once he passed through Heaven's gate.

Restored to her former glory, white wings unfurled behind her. Smiling at the other angel, she offered an ethereal hand. *"Take me home, Jonas."* And together, they returned to Heaven's embracing light.

Chapter 1

One year later. New York City.

CARA

"HEAL ME," the man whispered.

What? Cara flinched at the intrusion and ignored the man pressing against her in the fast-moving subway car. Then she caught a whiff of his offensive cologne, crinkled her nose, and resorted to mouth-breathing.

For the love of Pete.

She surreptitiously stepped away to create some distance.

Hiding her face behind a curtain of auburn waves, she repositioned her grip on the overhead bar and scrolled one-handed through work email.

The train banked hard and barreled around a turn, a metallic squeal of brakes echoing off the tunnel walls. Cara's briefcase swung, throwing her off balance and back into the guy.

"Sorry," Cara mumbled, without looking up, and adjusted her position with a widened stance that gave her more stability in the new stilettos. She'd debated wearing the red-soled Louboutins, but reasoned, if she had to spend her birthday at a miserable job, at least she'd do it in style. Too bad she'd forgotten her sneakers at the office, or she would've carried them in her bag.

After another hit of bad cologne, she took a glimpse at the man. Despite the fine suit, something about his hard black eyes, the V-shaped scar on his cheek, and the long, slicked-back hair made her skin crawl.

Cara contemplated her options. Rising on tiptoe, she scanned for an escape route through the crowd.

The only open space was at the far end of the train car, near a hulking guy with a dark-blond ponytail who looked like an extra in *The Matrix*. Six-foot-six and dressed head-to-toe in black, he was intimidating but handsome in a Chris-Hemsworth-as-Thor kind of way. Her gaze lingered while he examined his phone.

As if detecting her stare, he glanced up and froze. His crystal-blue gaze locked on hers and stole her breath.

Cara revised her opinion. He was hotter than Thor.

For a split second, she had an overwhelming sense of déjà vu. Her vision tunneled, and all she could see was him.

He dropped his lips into a dismissive frown, breaking the spell, and abruptly turned his back.

Really? The unexpected sting of rejection heated her cheeks, and whatever she'd just experienced evaporated. Why was she surprised? Guys like him never looked at her twice — or, in this case, even once. Besides, she had flawed judgment when it came to men, and a nonexistent love life to prove it. Then again, having a love life is difficult when the only man you've ever loved is married to someone else.

Sighing, Cara abandoned her escape plan. She'd take her chances with the guy drowning in sandalwood.

Returning to her email, she spotted a message from one of her best clients, opened it, and read a paragraph-long rant: "… incompetent… scheming… pulling my assets…unauthorized trade." She paled.

Trade? What trade? She hadn't made a trade for this client yesterday or even this week. Only one other person could've done that. *Rick.* Her bastard boss. She ground her teeth and fingered the diamond solitaire on a chain around her neck — her anchor in times of distress.

And then *it* happened. The thing she feared most — an unexpected panic attack. Her vision narrowed to pinpricks, and the train car shrank into a boxy, claustrophobic prison.

A tingling sensation in the center of Cara's chest turned into a thumping heartbeat and an impending sense of doom. Panic bloomed, and she gasped for air like a fish pulled from its tank. If she could at least make it to the next stop and get above ground, she'd be fine.

Tapping her foot in a nervous tattoo, she focused on calming her breath and de-escalating her body from adrenaline-fueled flight.

Time warped. Seconds felt like hours, and the feeling of suffocation went unabated. Desperate times call for desperate measures. Cara rummaged inside her handbag for the Xanax bottle in her emergency kit and clutched it like a security blanket.

Gaze clinging to the passing underground landscape, she bargained, *Just hang on for another minute.* Anything to quell the panic. Logic said she'd make it, but her psyche enjoyed taunting her. Had it really been five years since her last panic attack? It felt like yesterday.

"Heal me." The whispered demand cut through her anxious haze, ripping away the precious ground she'd gained in the last few seconds.

"Leave me alone," she snarled as the subway car screeched to a halt at Chambers Street. *Thank you, Sweet Baby Jesus.*

She shoved the man aside, clawing her way past a girl with blue-streaked hair and a guy in a Brooks Brothers suit, and flung her body through the open doors onto the crowded subway platform.

She inhaled a few relieved breaths before a hand seized her shoulder and spun her. The man with the V-shaped scar's black-eyed gaze bore into her. Pain seared the skin beneath his fingers through her coat, and soul-deep darkness washed over her, turning panic into terror. She tore from his grasp and ran blindly toward the stairs that led to the exit and into the light.

CHAMUEL

ON THE OTHER SIDE of the train, Chamuel grumbled at his cell phone's lack of service. Then, one cell bar lit, and he shot an urgent text to Isaac, the Tri-State Guardian House leader. *What's Achanelech doing in NYC, and why is he sniffing around my new charge?*

The question had spun on repeat since the Archdemon of Fire had stepped onto the train and planted himself beside Cara Collins.

Chamuel glanced up and cursed, noting the auburn-haired woman staring at him over the crush of people separating them. Under better circumstances, he might've relished gazing into her eyes, but not here, and not today.

He had no choice but to turn away so she wouldn't detect his fixation on the demon leering at her like she was a breakfast croissant he couldn't wait to eat. Fortunately, the archdemon had too much at stake to act on his baser instincts. Regardless, Chamuel would break cover and run Achanelech through with his blade if the archdemon attempted to snack.

Chamuel waited a few beats and turned back. Cara no longer stared in his direction, but a new sense of panic and revulsion rolled off her in waves. Had she known the true nature of the male beside her, he'd understand her reaction. But she couldn't possibly know that yet. No. Whatever frightened her had nothing to do with Achanelech.

The train screeched to a halt at Chambers Street.

Cara scrambled toward the door, and Chamuel followed, hanging back and exiting a few yards behind Cara and the archdemon.

Achanelech seized Cara's shoulder and spun her to face him. Chamuel growled low in his throat and reached for his weapon's hilt beneath his black duster. *So, help me, if that demonic bastard —*

Before Chamuel could move, a light flashed from the Archdemon's hand in a covert move to assess her power. Cara's face went white with terror. In a show of adrenaline-fueled strength, she wrenched free and bolted toward the exit like a woman on fire.

Chamuel lunged forward as Achanelech caught his gaze, gave a knowing sneer, and disappeared into the commuter horde. Swearing beneath his breath, Chamuel took off after Cara. He'd leave the archdemon for Isaac and his team.

People cleared the way as he took the stairs two at a time. When he reached street level, his new charge had made good ground, zigzagging through pedestrian traffic, her auburn hair swinging side-to-side. She was fast on her feet. He'd give her that. A skill that would serve her well in the future.

Chamuel caught up and remained at a safe distance until she entered a fast-food restaurant. He followed her inside.

She ran past the long lines of patrons ordering breakfast and down a narrow hallway, disappearing behind a door at the end.

Once inside the passageway and out of view, he summoned a cloak of invisibility, his energy flagging with the caloric demand. He should've eaten breakfast. A mistake that had him conserving energy earlier and paying the price. Now that Cara had seen him, cloaking was a necessity since he wasn't exactly inconspicuous in his Guardian attire, and his resemblance to a well-known NFL player with the same physical attributes didn't help.

Chamuel strolled noiselessly down the hall. Cara had gone into the Ladies' Room. He considered ducking inside, then wisely rejected the idea.

His stomach growled with the scent of eggs and bacon wafting in the air. He was tempted to grab a breakfast sandwich, but he'd never forgive himself if Cara slipped out while he was in line. Nope. He wasn't letting her out of his sight until she made it safely to work.

Crossing his arms, Chamuel leaned against the wall and waited. He replayed the scene on the subway. Warmth stirred in his chest at the memory of Cara's lovely gaze. *Not that it matters*, he reminded himself. He could never let this job get personal. But since his *job* as Cara's Trinity Guardian didn't officially start until tonight, he gave himself a pass for the innocent musing.

He couldn't claim Fate had led to this morning's early reconnaissance, more like boredom and curiosity, though some close to him would argue there were no coincidences. Regardless, his unexpected discovery would enable them to plan their next move.

The cell phone buzzed in his pocket. Slipping it out, he read Isaac's text. ***New charge? Damn it, Cham! Where are you? Call me. That's an order!***

Chapter 2

CARA

INHALE. HOLD. EXHALE. Cara repeated, wrestling her heart rate under control and convincing herself she wasn't about to die. She knew it was idiotic, but thoughts of death loomed large in the throes of panic. Especially after the creepy guy in the subway had scared the bejesus out of her.

Still, the last place Cara expected to be on her twenty-seventh birthday was crouched inside a graffiti-covered stall in a filthy bathroom. She stared at the blue oval pill lying in her palm, while her coat hem grazed the grimy floor, and she contemplated taking a drug she swore off years ago. Although her former therapist warned that attacks might return in times of extreme stress, Cara hadn't wanted to believe her.

God, she didn't want to be that person again. That meek, helpless shadow of herself, too afraid to leave the house. She'd come a long way since then, fighting her way out of anxiety's grip and becoming a tough-as-nails investment banker, a profession that skewed heavily male and wasn't for the faint of heart. Despite having to work for Rick, her dick-of-a boss, she was good at her job and proud of her accomplishments. She wouldn't let anxiety take them away. Not now. Not ever again.

Cara's body shook uncontrollably in the throes of flushing the remaining adrenaline from her bloodstream—a signal that she would be fine.

As her breath came more freely, she pressed her hands to her thighs and straightened. Residual tremors rippled through her quivering muscles, along with a giddy sense of relief. She'd live to see another day. *Yay, me.*

Cara returned the blue pill to the plastic container in her emergency kit, abandoned the stall, and beelined to the sink.

Balancing her briefcase awkwardly on one shoulder, she splashed cold water onto her cheeks, patted them dry, and reapplied some blush. Then, she stared at her image, her jaw hardening with determination and brow furrowing over wary, green eyes. *You can do this.*

A new text pinged in her bag—a welcome distraction. She retrieved her phone with a shaky hand and smiled at the message. ***Happy Birthday, Pumpkin! Mom will call you later. Have a great day! Love, Dad***

Tears unexpectedly welled in her eyes. Her father was a hopelessly unhip scientist who still signed his texts and owned a flip phone—and she loved him dearly. Despite the uplifting message, the text triggered a lonely ache in Cara's chest, reminding her how much anxiety created a barrier between her and the people she loved. Although Cara's parents tried to understand, the only person who truly understood was her best friend from high school, Sienna, a fellow anxiety sufferer.

Cara wished she could call her, but Sienna was somewhere over the Atlantic, returning from Paris Fashion Week. Fortunately, they had plans for later this evening. For now, anxiety be damned. She needed to get her butt to work and avert a client crisis. Judging from the time, she was already late, and Rick would be waiting to pounce.

CARA HUNG UP with the office assistant and cringed. OK, so maybe it wasn't an unavoidable emergency in the truest sense of the word, but that sounded better than, "I lost my shit in the subway."

Cara's mood lightened as she walked, though she couldn't say the same for her feet. If she could've foreseen walking the last leg of her commute, she would've worn flats. Sadly, tottering in heels was still faster than taking a taxi or waiting for an Uber in rush hour.

That said, she might overheat in her winter coat on the walk. Thank you, Global Warming, for sixty-eight degrees in March. She should've ditched the wool for something lighter. Live and learn. Relevant advice she continually failed to follow.

On the bright side, behind Saint Paul's black wrought iron fence, the churchyard garden had a fine array of daffodils and crocuses popping up beneath newly budding trees. Spring flowers were kinder to her allergies than most flowers, so she walked by with nary a sneeze.

Making the most of her time, Cara pulled out her phone and opened her trading app since getting to the bottom of her client's wrath, and her boss's shenanigans topped her priority list.

If she weren't worried about retaliation, she'd sue the pants off her employer for creating a hostile work environment. But Cabot Investments was privately held and had no issues with nepotism, lack of diversity, or the CEO having his *assoholic* son-in-law share his direct reporting line. That would've been a conflict of interest in a public company. No doubt her idiot boss, Rick, would've been fired for the stunts he pulled over the last year.

Cara missed Charlie, her old boss and mentor. This miserable last year would've never happened on his watch. To think she was a rising star until Charlie died suddenly of a massive heart attack. Since then, her work life has been a living hell. Rick still sent her on coffee runs and thought strip clubs were acceptable client entertainment. But what choice did she have? In this job market, making him an enemy wasn't an option if she planned to pay her mortgage.

Out of nowhere, a wizened homeless woman grabbed Cara's wrist and jerked her to a stop. Cara gasped, still jumpy from the train incident, and tried to free herself from the woman's iron grasp. She'd happily hand over a few dollars. Cara tugged harder, but the woman held tight.

Hairs rose on the back of Cara's neck. "Let go," Cara gritted.

The woman's black-eyed gaze locked on Cara. "Heal me," she said in a thin, reedy whisper.

Not again! The same question from two strangers on the same day couldn't be a coincidence, and why did they both have to smell so bad? The woman reeked of body odor, making her wish for the man's godawful cologne.

Back to mouth-breathing, Cara nervously glanced around, searching for the dark-haired man before returning to the unkempt crone. Wild gray hair framed her wrinkled, dirt-streaked face, but the woman's black eyes held a sharp intelligence that sent a shiver over Cara's skin that had nothing to do with the temperature.

Morbid curiosity and a blunted sense of self-preservation held Cara in place. "I don't understand what you want," Cara said, trying to reason with her as commuters passed, oblivious to her plight.

The woman's grip tightened on Cara's wrist. Her gaze traveled the perimeter of Cara's body, and she said, "The light of Heaven surrounds you." Then, the woman yanked Cara to eye-level, sending her swaying in her stilettos, and demanded more forcefully, "Heal me!"

Cara's confusion turned to ire, and she gritted, "I don't know what you're talking about." Twisting her wrist in the woman's grasp, Cara failed to break free.

The crone *tsked* and seized Cara's other hand. "Stupid child." She planted Cara's palms onto her grimy shoulders.

The impact was immediate. A force slammed into the top of Cara's head, rooting her in place. Warm, rushing energy coursed from her crown into her chest, coalescing at her heart, then shooting down her arms and exiting through her palms into the woman.

Cara stood agape as the light traveled through her and filled the crone until she glowed, rays of light escaping through the woman's pores and surrounding her body in radiance.

Cara gasped in disbelief. The lines on the crone's face disappeared like in a time-lapse movie, transforming her into a beautiful, raven-haired young woman.

"You're ready," the woman said with a knowing smile.

The woman released Cara and severed their connection. Cara stumbled backward, reeling, as the woman turned and ran.

"Wait! Ready for what?" Cara shouted, and for the second time, she sprinted in her stilettos and ignored the briefcase knocking her hip. She silently thanked her high school track coach and let loose. She wanted some damn answers.

Her advantage didn't last. The woman wove with incredible agility along the crowded sidewalk, widening the distance between them before turning left onto Barclay Street toward the Woolworth Building.

Cara rounded the corner a moment later, but the woman was gone.

With a defeated sigh, Cara stepped aside, chest heaving, and rested outside a bank. So far, her birthday has sucked. She wanted a refund. Maybe she should go home, crawl into bed, and ask for a "do-over."

Instead, she giggled. She couldn't help it. If she didn't laugh, she'd cry. You couldn't make this stuff up. Not one but two strangers had asked her to heal them, and then she channeled some Fountain of Youth from the heavens. Maybe her anxiety attack triggered a psychotic break, not that she felt particularly crazy. Still, something to contemplate later over a glass — no, make that a bottle — of Merlot.

In the meantime, she had a boss to deal with and a client to save.

Happy Birthday to me.

Chapter 3

CHAMUEL

CHAMUEL IGNORED ISAAC'S text, continuing his surveillance on Cara from a few yards behind until the crone grabbed her, putting him on high alert. Still cloaked, he closed in but halted when a shimmering column of light descended into the top of Cara's head and lit her body from within. Light seeped from her pores before erupting through her palms and shrouding both women in an orb of golden light unseen by passing humans.

"Holy Father," Chamuel muttered, stunned, watching the unawakened young woman wield the Flow before her official *Calling*. The display was raw and powerful, but it shouldn't have happened. Not yet, anyway.

Cara's unexpected light display must explain Achanelech's interest.

A shift in the air and unfamiliar Nephilim energy stole Chamuel's attention from the two women. His muscles tensed at the unexpected intrusion. Senses heightening, Chamuel's nose twitched, scenting the air. Nothing. Tilting his gaze skyward, he scanned the nearby rooflines.

Still nothing.

A wisp of energy brushed Chamuel's skin with a childlike curiosity. This time, closer and from behind a veil of invisibility, allowing the owner to move unseen and unheard, like Chamuel, though not unfelt.

Who was this? Chamuel knew everyone under Isaac's command, and this week's visitor roster was empty.

Chamuel swiped at a tickle on his cheek. The uninvited probing lacked manners but held no threat. Something was off. The behavior was more befitting of a teasing juvenile than a mature adult. Protocol dictated that a visiting Guardian should connect veils and exchange a courtesy greeting, especially as a guest in someone else's territory. That didn't happen. Instead, the energy abruptly disappeared, leaving Chamuel unsettled and wary.

Chamuel's gaze returned to Cara and the homeless woman. The light was gone. He blinked at the crone's beautiful, unlined face and swore under his breath. Damn it, he should've known.

Not an old woman in need of healing—a Sentinel.

So, Achanelech hadn't come to New York alone.

The woman ran, and Cara gave chase in those formidable red-soled shoes. No room for a proper takeoff, Chamuel pursued invisibly on foot. Cutting through the crowd, he left an unexplained breeze and confused stares in his wake. Overtaking a guy talking on his cell phone, Chamuel passed Cara and leaped over a mountain of garbage bags piled at the curb. The Sentinel picked up speed as he chased the fluttering hem of her skirt.

The female glanced over her shoulder and smirked. She knew he was there. An overhead wind buffeted Chamuel's hair, and the energy he sensed earlier sliced through the air above him. A moment later, the Sentinel vanished—scooped up and concealed beneath the Nephil's cloak.

What. The. Hell?

Chamuel stared at the empty sidewalk, his hands fisting in frustration. He should've investigated the unknown presence when he'd had the chance. But he never imagined or anticipated what he had just witnessed. An Angelorum Guardian working for Achanelech and the Dark Ones? How in Heaven's name had *that* happened?

The Dark Ones had no Nephilim Guardians.

A shiver traversed his spine at an incredulous thought. Could there be a traitor in the Guardianship? It had never occurred in their two-millennium history, but there was a first time for everything.

He stored the worry as Cara rounded the corner, weighed down by her belongings, her chest heaving, and her coat askew. Strands of auburn hair clung to a flushed, ivory cheek as she drew to a slumping stop. Her disheveled appearance had an endearing quality that warmed him. Then, she brushed the errant strands behind her ear and…giggled.

Chamuel stared, perplexed. There wasn't anything funny about what happened to her since he started surveillance. So far, her morning hit the scale between daunting and terrifying. As much as he would've liked to find out what had amused her, they wouldn't have direct contact until after her Calling. Until then, he would guard from a distance, unseen.

Cara's lips hinted at a smile as she straightened her coat and headed downtown. Chamuel hung back to follow. He was again thankful for jumping the gun on his assignment. The Dark Ones already knew about Cara. That didn't bode well, but forewarned was forearmed.

"WHAT TOOK YOU SO LONG?" Isaac snarled through the phone in a gruff, battle-hewn voice befitting a drill sergeant.

Chamuel pictured his closest friend and the leader of the Tri-State Guardian House with his blond brush cut, icy blue eyes, and pissed-off frown. Withstanding Isaac's ire was a fair exchange for first ensuring Cara's safe passage to work. Chamuel didn't regret delaying his call to Isaac, whose ire didn't disappoint.

His friend droned on about how Chamuel needed to get back on the proverbial horse and follow protocol in his new role. Blah-blah-blah. A role that held more honor and less rank than Chamuel was accustomed to. Yada-yada.

Chamuel listened graciously, leaning against the limestone exterior of Cabot Investments, one eye on the door and the other on a food truck at the curb. His stomach rumbled in the middle of Isaac's tirade.

If he didn't eat soon, his cloak would melt, and the last thing he needed was getting arrested for loitering.

So, he cut Isaac short. "I get it, *I*," he said, using the familiar to soften his bluntness. "No disrespect, but given what happened, I think you would've done the same." They had more pressing issues to discuss than quibbling over protocol. "Achanelech had a Sentinel grab her on the street to test her power, which means the Dark Ones are worried. But how did they know about her, and why is she so special?"

Isaac muttered a curse and growled. "Let's back up. Start at the beginning, and don't leave anything out."

Chamuel recounted his morning, including the Nephilim accomplice. When he finished, Isaac let out a troubled sigh and murmured, "Saints alive…At least she's safe." The weight of the situation hung between them.

"Yeah." Chamuel passed a hand over his face. The circumstances disturbed him more than he cared to admit. "So, what have you got?"

"Achanelech flew into Teterboro this morning. His flight plan has him returning to the West Coast in less than twenty minutes. In all honesty, I'm more worried about the Nephil's identity than how he found out about your charge." Isaac went quiet, his fingers drumming a steady beat in the background, and then he said, "Regardless, something is brewing. I got a call that the High Council is flying in one of their own to mentor Cara."

A sinking feeling twisted Chamuel's gut. "Why would they do that?"

"Dunno," Isaac said.

Chamuel mentally spun through the twelve faces on the angelic protectorate's secret governing body before landing on one. If he was right, that would explain a lot—like why he'd been assigned to a Trinity so quickly after taking a century-plus hiatus.

Pinching the bridge of his nose, he anticipated Isaac's response before asking, "Who are they sending?"

Isaac snorted. "When do they tell us anything in advance? You know that old conundrum—can't reveal the future because it interferes with free will. We'll get our information on a need-to-know basis, and right now, they don't think we need to know."

Of course not. Chamuel heaved an irritated sigh. The High Council was bound by two sacred rules: they couldn't use their knowledge to interfere with free will or directly involve themselves in human affairs. They could only watch and orchestrate.

Occasionally, they stretched the boundaries on the latter when it suited them, but for the most part, they relied on the Trinities to carry out their work. The rules made sense in theory, but in practice, they were aggravating.

Isaac gave a mirthless laugh. "We both know who they'll send."

Chamuel scowled and rubbed a hand along the back of his neck to relieve the tension. *Of course, it would be Constantina.* "But *why*? When was the last time a Council member mentored a Soul Seeker like Cara Collins?"

"Hasn't happened in my lifetime," Isaac replied.

"Right." So basically, *never.* Chamuel didn't like where this was headed. This new development made him second-guess his decision to reenter active duty. "Let me chew on that piece for a while…What about the traitor? The last thing we need is a security breach."

Isaac sighed. "Agreed. I'll transmit a global order to the Guardian Houses to account for their members. We should have a complete report within the next twelve hours."

Chamuel bobbed his head in silent agreement and asked, "Send me the report?"

"Of course. But only out of respect. You turned over the reins, remember?" Isaac chided.

True. Chamuel passed control of the Tri-State House to Isaac a week ago when he reentered Trinity rotation, leaving control of the region's security in his friend's capable hands. Now, he was assigned to a three-person team and a mission that could tip the scales between good and evil. Until their mission was revealed, his job was to keep his charge safe. But the Council's involvement in Cara's preparation had Chamuel suspecting the mission would be more important than a garden-variety "thwart a demon" assignment.

Pushing off the wall to pace, he said, "Be patient with me. I need to settle into the transition."

"Will do. Remember, to serve in a Trinity is our highest honor," Isaac said, spouting the party line with uncharacteristic reverence. Then he lowered his voice. "Cham, you're ready for this, aren't you?"

Chamuel stopped pacing. He had avoided discussing the tragedy with anyone for decades, especially Isaac. His friend's concern warmed him, but he still didn't want to discuss it. So, he cleared his throat and played it off, "I can't hide forever. Ready or not, here I come."

Isaac blew out a breath. "I want you to know…I'm here for you."

Chamuel swallowed. "I know. It means a lot."

Isaac took the hint and lightened the mood. "So, you rolled out of bed to spy on your new charge. Why?"

"Bored, maybe," he said, glad to move on.

Chamuel had left the Tri-State house in Connecticut two weeks ago to live full-time in his SoHo loft. He already missed wrestling control of the kitchen from their cook, Luigi. Although he routinely escaped to his Manhattan loft a few days a month, he had considered the Tri-State House his home. Giving up his place among his brethren left him disquieted as he acclimated to living alone with no end in sight.

"Well, good that you followed her," Isaac said.

A sudden, heated flush twinged in Chamuel's gut—a warning he was running on empty. He glanced at the food truck. He needed food. STAT. "Send me the report when you have it. Talk to you later." He ended the call and glanced at the glass door of Cara's building.

Staring back was a male with vivid, intimidating blue eyes, wearing the standard-issue, all-black Guardian duster, T-shirt, cargo pants, and steel-toed boots. So much for his cloak.

He ambled to the food truck and bought three egg sandwiches and an extra-large coffee. Not exactly gourmet, but it would do.

Unwilling to take chances with Cara's safety, he planted himself outside the building, devoured the food to recharge, and cloaked.

A smile touched his lips as he thought about catching another glimpse of his new charge. When he'd gotten a closer look, he saw Cara's eyes were a lovely shade of green. Then the thought fell away as quickly as it came.

The time drew near when thinking about her eyes would be absolutely against the rules.

Chapter 4

ACHANELECH

Teterboro Airport. New Jersey.

ACHANELECH SHIFTED HIS weight on the jewel-topped cane and paced the cabin of his private jet, impatient for his consort to return so they could take flight. He'd taken a look at the Collins girl for himself. *She* was the First of the Holy Twelve? Not a very impressive showing, in his opinion. The battle was over before it had begun if that girl was the best the Angelorum had to offer.

He hobbled to and fro, wincing with each step he took in the Armani leather shoes. All the milling around he'd done in the subway had come at a price. His feet had swollen in the shoes, forcing the claws at the ends of his toes to curl into tender flesh. Even after two millennia parading in human form, he hadn't mastered transforming his forked tongue or talon-tipped toes into their human equivalents. An ache in his thigh from an old battle injury compounded his misery, a constant reminder of a score he had yet to settle with his angelic nemesis. Though no amount of retribution would replace what and who he'd lost at his enemies' hands.

He had hoped the Collins girl could relieve his injury, but he doubted the girl could heal a toothache after his failed requests in the subway.

If the discomfort in his lower extremities wasn't enough, the incessant pulsating beneath the sigil on the back of his neck from his demon children demanding food compounded his misery. Until he satisfied their hunger, nothing would quiet the demonic whispers reverberating in his head.

He glanced impatiently at his watch. Where was his consort?

They had a timetable to keep and meals to deliver. The last thing he needed was a demon escaping for an unsanctioned feeding frenzy.

He'd already drawn the Angelorum's attention, which he had hoped to avoid by swooping in early. A complication, but no matter. He played nice. No rules broken. No laws violated. Nothing to trigger a fireside chat in Hell with his Master, Luc Morningstar.

As much as he abhorred humans, he preferred his station topside on this dusty little chunk of Purgatory to the frying pan down below. The only thing worse would be sharing a cell with Luc's former brethren, Semyaza, and his fornicating Watchers in one of Heaven's prisons as they awaited Judgment Day—a day that would never come if Luc played his hand right. With Achanelech's help, of course. Help that would solidify Achanelech's place as Luc's second and reap him unfathomable rewards.

The insistent whispers rose to a crescendo inside his skull. "Be patient, pets. Sustenance shall be forthcoming," he lied in Hellspeak, rubbing his sigil to settle his pulsating skin. Procuring fresh souls would have to wait.

The plane door opened, and his consort waltzed in under the guise of a homeless crone. One of the many personas she employed in testing investigations. A tall, blond male wearing loose, white slave garments accompanied her. The male hung back, eyes averted in a show of deference that had been beaten into him since birth.

Vile abomination, Achanelech thought, staring in disgust at the byproduct of angels consorting with humans. The simple garments could not hide the halfling's angelic beauty, a beauty that churned Achanelech's loathing. At least he finally found a use for his captive. A good thing since torturing the creature had long lost its appeal.

His consort had recommended employing the male for special assignments. So far, he'd proven reliable, but Achanelech still wondered if he could trust the beast after a century of oppression. Especially since the golden-haired Nephil was bred to protect the other side.

The Creator certainly had a taste for irony.

This new breed of Nephilim was unlike Semyaza's abominations of yore. Achanelech remembered well the Creator's wrathful act of scrubbing those evil creatures from the earth in a fit of pique before the Fall. These creatures were different. Blessed. Bred as protectors of the Angelorum and *His* creation *against* the Dark Ones. Damned humanity. The Angelorum's eternal weakness. To consider humans as more than what they were—a mere food source—was stupidity of the highest order.

"Mission accomplished," Emanelech said in a happy sing-song and snapped her fingers with a saucy hip jut, an incongruous gesture given her aged visage and ragged appearance. Then, the air shimmered, and she shifted into her preferred human form —a tall, raven-haired beauty wearing a slinky blue dress that matched the color of her eyes. Achanelech found this form most pleasing.

"*That* was fun," she said, a delighted gleam in her eye that he found irksome. "She's quite powerful, that young Soul Seeker."

Frowning, he waved her off. "There wasn't even a glimmer when I touched her."

His consort threw up her hands and huffed. "I told you to leave this to me…The anxiety attack blocked her power. Not so when I found her."

Achanelech's frown deepened. Emanelech was nothing if not canny. He admired her intelligence most days unless she used it to manipulate him, which was *most* days. He finally conceded, "Fine, but is she the *One*?"

She shrugged and studied a red, manicured nail. "Our source believes so. Based on my assessment, she's much more than a hearty meal."

"You sure we can't dispatch the girl? I was less than impressed," he said with a petulant flick of a wrist. She would make a nice appetizer for his hungry horde.

Em clicked her tongue. "Don't be hasty. She's unawakened. I think it would be wise to get our facts straight before we send word to Luc, don't you?" she said, a bit too smugly.

He growled and bit back a retort, despising that she had a point. Instead, he channeled his annoyance at the silent male, raking him with a glare. "What about this one? How did the halfling do?"

He had stolen the foul creature as an infant as retribution and raised it in his dungeons. Achanelech took pleasure in possessing something the Angelorum valued and let the abomination believe he had sired him. A revolting thought, but an effective means of control. Emanelech assured him the male was loyal to her and not very smart, but Achanelech had doubts.

She cast a glance in the halfling's direction. "No complaints."

"Mongrel, what say you?"

The male kept his head bowed. "The mission was a success, Father," he responded softly, but not softly enough to mask the rich, melodic tone.

Achanelech ground his teeth and hungered to whip fresh scars into the flesh beneath the abomination's clothes. He took delight in marring the Nephil's beauty with suitable instruments to ensure the marks remained. A malevolent smile touched his lips, and he raised a finger, intent on sending a sizzling reminder he was an affront to Achanelech's sensibilities.

Emanelech swatted Achanelech's hand away and glared. "Don't even think about it. He did well. Why must you be so petty?"

Achanelech gave her a wide-eyed stare. "What? I wasn't going to do anything," he lied.

She huffed dismissively to let him know she'd seen through his thinly disguised plea of innocence, then tapped a finger to her lower lip. "Acchie, I was thinking…."

Achanelech ground his teeth at her use of his pet name in front of the male. "Oh? That could be a dangerous proposition."

Her ice-blue eyes shifted to black. "I understand you need some souls to feed your demons. Unless you'd like to procure them yourself, I'd suggest you rethink your tone."

Brushing a hand over his face, he released a heavy sigh. *Females.* "Fine, *chérie.* What were you about to say?" If she were less powerful, he would've dispatched her long ago and saved himself a good century's worth of exasperation. But the benefits of her ice to his fire far outweighed the petty annoyances.

Her eyes returned to blue. She glanced at the male but spoke to him. "We should chat in private."

Achanelech snapped his fingers. "Outside, Mongrel."

The male left the plane, closing the door behind him.

Emanelech glanced at the exit. "He would be the perfect spy to confirm our suspicions about the girl."

Achanelech knew better than to question her sanity, regardless of how tempting. "Why him?"

She raised a perfectly arched brow and scowled as if he'd bungled an incantation.

"What?" he asked with an exaggerated shrug.

She shook her head and sighed. "The same reason he's been useful in the past. He can stay close without causing panic or drawing attention to himself. The worst thing that could happen is they mistake him for one of the Angelorum Guardians."

"What if he betrays us?"

She sniffed. "To whom? He's spent most of the last century in a dungeon away from his kind. He doesn't know who he is—you ensured that." Her lips falling into a sexy pout, she sauntered over and rested her arms on his shoulders. "Besides, he's loyal to me."

Frowning, he narrowed his eyes suspiciously. "You believe that?"

Her pout turned to a glower, and she rolled her eyes. "No, you idiot. You implanted him with an explosive tracking device, remember?"

He bristled at the insult but couldn't deny her point. Again. If the male went rogue, he could either hunt him down or detonate the explosive.

"I'll give it some thought," he ground out.

Emanelech's expression melted into a satisfied smile. Then she kicked off her heels and reclined on the leather bench seat. "Decide before we take off unless you want him to fly back under his own power. And for Lucifer's sake, give him some proper clothes."

A cold smile touched Achanelech's lips as he joined her. "Don't get too smart, Em, or someday I might just dispatch you."

"Ha! Give it your best shot, hot lips," she purred, grasping his collar in both hands and pulling him into a kiss.

Chapter 5

CONSTANTINA

Angelorum Sanctuary. France.

CONSTANTINA UNLOCKED THE wooden door to the High Council's inner sanctum with trepidation and exhilaration. Before departing for New York, she had to ensure Fate had not slipped her a card or taken one away.

Her cloak's velvet hem swept across the threshold into the upper level of the cavernous, circular chamber—the most sacred space within their hidden, underground city. The chamber housed the High Council meeting rooms and the Trinity Pool below her.

Sage and lavender-scented candles burned in iron sconces, flickering on the wall and lighting Constantina's path. She wound along the stone steps to the High Council's elevated dais, which faced semi-circular bench seating, layered like a wedding cake, to accommodate the Angelorum's Three Hundred during formal addresses.

She removed her velvet cloak, revealing a new gray suit, clothes that would allow her to blend in outside the Sanctuary. She draped the long, ocean-blue garment over the back of her designated chair, glad to be rid of its weight. From there, she proceeded on her descent toward the Trinity Pool's viewing deck in the center of a suspended catwalk.

A sea of glittering Trinity Stones, Heaven's three-tipped vessels of destiny, sat atop the vast, white sand expanse. Each stone hummed with angelic whispers and pulsed with light in three unbroken streams—each of which represented a soul in the triumvirate.

Millions of decisions and destinies twinkled below her for events happening now and in the future. The number of stones constantly changing within the Trinity Pool, absorbing destinies fulfilled or thwarted, and replenishing as free will requires.

Within those millions, only twelve souls would ultimately save humanity.

Those were the fates Constantina sought to examine.

Constantina crossed the catwalk, her steps reverberating on the metal bridge, toward an ornate wooden platform that held a viewing apparatus suspended from the high-domed ceiling. Taking a calming breath, she grasped the viewer's smooth wooden handle and prayed nothing had changed since her last visit.

Given the unpredictable nature of free will, one decision could ripple through a host of destinies, altering the direction of their mission.

Her pulse quickened with anticipation, and a tingling awareness rippled through her sword hand, along with the ethereal feel of her blazing weapon's grip in her palm. She had waited centuries, but today was the day the *First* of the Twelve came of age. It was time to fulfill the Prophecy and close the divine loophole. A chance to right the wrong that weighed heavily on her soul.

Constantina gazed through the viewer and searched the glittering stones until she found the four Trinity Stones clustered in a magnetic embrace — the twelve souls who would deliver their fate.

"Constantina?"

Her head snapped up to see Angelis crossing the catwalk to join her.

"You're up early, my friend," she said, smiling at the tall man with spectacles and short, dark gray-streaked hair. He wore a long white robe with an intricate purple and gold-threaded design, designating him as the High Council leader. In truth, he looked more like an accountant than the head of an angelic protectorate.

His smile creased the corners of his kind, brown eyes. "I couldn't let you go without a goodbye. Ready for your journey?"

Her smile faded, and she nodded. "I believe so." Despite the risks, her blood pulsed faster at the bittersweet knowledge of what lay ahead.

He glanced at the magnifier. "Any changes in the cluster?"

She beckoned him with a gentle wave. "I haven't looked yet. Care to join me?"

He sidled up beside her to peer through the viewer.

Constantina focused on the four attached Trinity Stones. She examined the pulsing lines of color running through the clustered stones and listened. Like a spinning roulette wheel, images and potential outcomes spun with uncertain fates, pieces locking into place as free will decisions collided with destiny and paths were chosen.

As of now, only Cara's fate was inevitable. There was no guarantee her currently assigned Guardian or Messenger would remain in place beyond Cara's initial mission or stake a claim among the Twelve. There were still challenges to face and choices to make. A singular decision could unwind it all, trading one soul — or an entire Trinity — for another.

Thankfully, nothing that grave had happened. *Yet.*

Though only Cara's fate was sealed, Constantina alone knew of four other candidates within the Twelve. None whose fates were sealed, but one who required special protection away from the High Council's prying eyes—protection Constantina had arranged *personally*.

But right now, Constantina's focus was drawn to the melodious song coming from Cara's Trinity Stone, the whispering threads unwinding into singular voices. One caught her attention. She paused to listen and gasped. "Did you hear that?" she asked Angelis, unsure if the stone had chosen to reveal its voice to him. His grave expression indicated it had.

"The Dark Ones already know the identity of the *First*," he said, his worried gaze meeting hers. "How much time do we have?"

She studied the stone. "A couple of weeks at most." Constantina peered back at Angelis. "Two weeks is barely enough time to prepare her, but I guess it will have to do." She returned her gaze to the humming cluster, and the crooning voices whispered another secret without revealing additional candidates. "Whoever these souls are, they will be a *passionate* bunch."

Angelis clucked his tongue and gave her a knowing smile. "Don't think your Guardian selection for the Collins Trinity went unnoticed. You do like to tempt fate, don't you?"

She said mildly, "Tempt? Not quite. Besides, you know as well as I that interference is against the rules. When have you ever known me to break the rules?"

He scoffed and lifted a brow. "It's not the breaking. It's the bending that you take such joy in."

She shrugged. "I do what I must with love in my heart." Her voice losing its playful edge, she said, "I'll admit, if this combination of souls stands, there will be some rule-bending, and we will all be tested before this is over." The traitor among the Council had already ensured that, but Constantina kept her suspicions to herself for Angelis's protection.

For now, she would use the knowledge to her advantage.

"I concur." Angelis pushed the magnifier away, giving her a puzzled frown. "The Collins Trinity Stone still baffles me. What do you make of the Soul Seeker's destiny thread?"

"It's quite…fascinating," she hedged, letting the question pass and retracting the viewing apparatus above their heads. Sharing her thoughts with Angelis would only place more lives in jeopardy. Two lives had already been lost protecting that answer.

Placing a gentle hand on Constantina's shoulder, Angelis heaved a breath. "You'll be vulnerable outside the Sanctuary without your amulet."

She lifted her gaze to his. "I'll be fine." One way or another. She'd given her amulet to her daughter's mate sixteen years ago to keep them safe on their mission. A mission tied to the secret of Cara's destiny thread. Constantina had no idea what had become of her amulet since Hope died, only that without it, she couldn't cloak her energy from her enemies beyond the Sanctuary walls.

Angelis lasered her with a look. "Is this why you renounced Council leadership? To take my place?"

Yes, her choice had been deliberate. She covered his hand with hers and nodded. Her angelic roots, tied to holy retribution, would serve them better than Angelis' scholarly angelic order. Besides, she had a personal stake that Angelis did not. For better or worse, she was the logical choice. Especially after the visage of her old nemesis, fiery arrogance and all, flashed across the Trinity Stones. The archdemon had much to answer for.

"I can still go...."

"No, Angelis. You can't," she whispered.

Agonizing guilt shone in his eyes. "You have enemies. You will be a target."

That ship has already sailed, she thought.

Angelis's voice softened, and he spoke the words she dreaded. "You've already sacrificed one of your children."

A lump rose in her throat, and grief squeezed her heart. Her failure to protect Hope stung, but she wouldn't make the same mistake twice. Tears shimmered in her eyes, and she whispered, "Hope sacrificed her life to save us all. How could I do any less?"

Angelis gave her shoulder a final squeeze and a resigned nod. "My deepest gratitude, Constantina. Journey forth in peace and love."

"And you," she replied, glancing at Angelis as he departed, his footsteps fading behind her.

Alone, she retrieved the viewer for one last look and let the flashing colors and soothing hum draw her back into their thrall. The hum became a whisper, the whisper, a voice. She swallowed hard and listened.

"Dearest Eae, behind one hides the other."

She blinked, not understanding, and then her mouth went husk dry, afraid to hope for the impossible. Angelis had been incorrect. She hadn't lost just one child, but two. A tear trickled down her cheek, and she voiced the only logical question, "He lives?"

She waited, but the stone remained silent, and the colors faded.

No explanation would be forthcoming.

Tucking away a glimmer of hope, she brushed a hand across her cheek and collected her cloak on the way to the exit. She'd find her answers another day. Right now, she had a job to do and little time to do it.

Chapter 6

CARA

Perry Street Apartment. New York City.

"MOM, SERIOUSLY?" Cara said, pacing in exasperation beside her living room coffee table. She didn't need her mother pointing out her lack of a social life. She already knew that. These days, her priority was financial security. Her job required sacrifice, and she was insanely good at what she did, enough to afford a West Village apartment. And it wasn't like she was alone. She had Chloe. Admittedly, her canine companion had a better social life than she did, thanks to doggie daycare and her dogwalker.

As if sensing Cara's thoughts, Chloe's head popped up from beneath a pink blanket where she lay nestled on the sofa. Ears up and brow furrowed, Chloe assessed Cara with interest.

A purebred Whippet, Chloe was half the size of a Greyhound with the same grace and narrow, expressive face ending with a black nose that begged for a *boop*. Chloe wasn't a barker, making her popular with the neighbors, but an epic failure as a watchdog. Despite her weakness in deterring break-ins and a strong diva streak, Chloe was smart, with a rich personality, and the most lovable dog Cara had ever owned. Not to mention, her closest friend.

Brushing past her loyal hound, Cara gave her a quick ear scratch.

Her mother's tone hardened. "Honey, all I'm saying is, if Rick makes you miserable, find another job. You shouldn't pour your heart and soul into a place that doesn't appreciate you. You need to get out and live."

"I *do* live." Cara pouted.

"Name one friend you've made since college and the last time you went on a date," her mother challenged.

"I...," Cara's jaw hinged like a ventriloquist's dummy before snapping shut. God, she hated it when her mother was right. "I have Sienna, Chloe, and Kai," she said with a hint of defiance. Then she added, "Plus Jessa and Irene," her two college girlfriends living in Northern California and

Washington, D.C. She had friends, damn it! They even texted birthday wishes with GIFs of girls gone wild and dancing men with chiseled abs.

Her mother sighed.

Cara also hated when her mother sighed, anticipating a lecture.

She wasn't wrong.

"Cara," her mother said sternly, "Kai is married. He has his own life, and—"

"And Chloe is a dog," Cara interrupted, rolling her eyes. "Yeah, yeah, I know."

"Sweetheart, I want you to be happy."

"I *am* happy," Cara lied, not wanting to admit how stuck she felt. She wasn't exactly saving the world by making rich people richer, but she didn't want to feel any worse about what turned into a very crappy—not to mention, weird and harrowing—day.

Who said she had to have all the answers at twenty-seven?

God, she felt old.

And boring.

And pathetic.

She glanced at her watch. "Mom, I've got to go. Sienna is coming with a birthday present."

"Happy Birthday, darling. I only want the best for you. You know that, right?" her mother said more softly.

"I do," she conceded.

"Give Sienna my love," her mother said, "Love you."

"Will do. Love you, too, Mom."

Cara hung up and dropped onto the sofa beside Chloe, feeling glummer.

For the thousandth time, she checked her phone for texts—still nothing from Kai. She scowled at the device like it was to blame for his silence and tossed it onto the coffee table. Kai never missed her birthday.

What the hell?

They broke up years ago, but he was still one of her closest friends. They still had an undeniable connection that no one, not even her, understood. Sadly, he set a high bar for anyone who came after, and only one person had—Tyler, her one epic mistake. Since then, her experience with dating apps led to awful results before she gave up completely.

Five years was a long time without so much as a kiss.

She sighed, picked up her wine glass, and stroked Chloe's silky head.

Swallowing her disappointment, Cara returned to obsessing over her strange morning. Her ability to compartmentalize saved her from buckling under the day's stress—a helpful trait she shared with her mother.

By 10 AM, she had unwound the unsanctioned trade and smoothed relations with her client. After which, she worked eleven hours before hauling her exhausted backside home with a bag of Indian takeout for two in preparation for Sienna's visit. Hypoglycemia made her friend prone to *hanger*, and no one wanted a *hangry* Sienna.

Cara relaxed on the sofa and replayed the woman aging in reverse, like Brad Pitt in *The Curious Case of Benjamin Button,* but faster. Cara still felt the loving warmth running beneath her skin and behind her eyelids. Its otherworldly golden threads had shimmered with *life* — like a collective consciousness of pure love. Words couldn't adequately describe what she had experienced, only that it felt like an encounter with the divine, which sounded crazy even to her.

Cara released a slow breath and sipped the remains of last night's red, letting the notes of plum and red raspberry linger on her tongue while she ruminated. The incidents didn't seem coincidental.

Had they targeted her? If so, why?

Cara wasn't religious, a revelation she kept from her devout Irish Catholic mother, who would be apoplectic if she discovered her daughter had stopped attending mass when she left for college. Ironic, as Georgetown University was the oldest Catholic Jesuit university in America.

The door buzzed — jerking Cara's butt an inch off the sofa and pulling her from her reverie.

Chloe leaped from the sofa with grace, landed with a muffled thud, and scampered, doggie toenails tapping, across the hardwood. Her thin, brindle body disappeared behind the armchair, which left only the white tip of her tail visible as she rooted in her basket for a suitable toy with which to greet their guest.

Cara released the apartment's outer door, letting in the force of nature that was Sienna. Despite the late hour and jet lag, her friend insisted on bringing Cara's gift before her birthday ended.

Cara unchained the door when the elevator dinged and glanced into the hallway. All she saw over a giant, red-paper-wrapped box was Sienna's silken black hair and sky-blue eyes peering at her. From beneath the box, a designer handbag dangled from her friend's arm as she tottered toward Cara in platform shoes.

Cara suppressed a giggle. "*Senny*, is that you? You look like a box with legs."

Muffled sarcasm echoed down the hall. "Very funny. Of course, it's me. Who were you expecting, Prince Charming?"

Sadly, no.

Cara opened the door wider to accommodate the oversized box. "Let me help you with that. You look like you might tip over."

Tail wagging, Chloe rushed to the door with a bone-shaped plush toy in her mouth and waited patiently at Cara's side.

Sienna gave Cara a peck on each cheek, European-style, and handed the package over to her waiting hands. "Happy Birthday, *Carissima*."

Cara flushed with delight. "Thanks, Senny," she said, hefting the package into her arms, the weight giving her a healthy respect for Sienna's strength and balance.

Released from her burden, Sienna closed the door for Cara and sashayed past with a smirk. "I would've brought you a cake with twenty-seven candles, but I didn't want to set the place on fire."

"Gee, thanks," Cara said dryly and retorted, "But you'll always be older than me." By only three months, but older was older.

Sienna batted her lashes. "Don't forget 'wiser.' *Muuuch* wiser."

Cara snorted a laugh. This, from a woman who freed thirty-five frogs from their cages in high school biology.

Chloe squeaked her toy, signaling her turn for Aunt Sienna's attention.

Sienna stooped. "Hello, princess!" she crooned affectionately and kissed the dog's head. "Aunt Senny has a prezzie for you, too." Rummaging inside her purse, Sienna pulled out a stuffed squirrel.

Chloe's soulful brown eyes lit with longing, the plush bone dropping from her mouth as she eyed the new toy.

Sienna straightened, squeaked the new toy, and pitched it across the living room. Chloe raced for her prize, catching the toy before it hit the ground. Clutching the squirrel between her teeth, she squeaked her triumph while doing a victory lap.

Cara rolled her eyes. "Okay, now *that's* going to be annoying."

Sienna tapped Cara playfully on the shoulder and tottered toward the overstuffed sofa. "Oh, lighten up! Smile, for flip's sake. It's your birthday."

Cara trailed behind her and placed the present on the coffee table. "I don't know how you walk in those things," she said, staring at her friend's shoes. Head of Ready-to-Wear for Italian designer Nicolas Alda, Sienna was the queen of bold fashion choices.

Sienna shot her a look. "Who walks? That's what Uber's for."

Cara shook her head and chuckled.

"Speaking of apparel," Sienna said, kicking off her platforms. "I made a reservation at seven o'clock on Saturday at Raphael's for your birthday dinner. Dress for a night of drunken debauchery, and no *shmattes*," she said, spinning a finger at Cara's oversized T-shirt and yoga pants before tucking her legs beneath her on the sofa.

Cara rolled her eyes. "I own nice clothes, you know." And none of them were rags as Sienna's Yiddishism implied. Not that it mattered. All eyes would be on Sienna rather than Cara, the quiet, pale sidekick who faded into the background next to her friend's dark hair, exotic looks, and larger-than-life personality. Especially during the summer, when Sienna tanned to an attractive bronze while Cara's pale skin freckled and turned the color of dappled shrimp. Not attractive—even for shrimp.

"Point taken," Sienna conceded.

Cara sat in a chair across from her and changed the subject. "So, how was Fashion Week? Amazing, or what?"

Sienna shrugged and released a long-suffering sigh. "*Or what.* Unless you call amazing running around like a lunatic with a roll of duct tape and a sewing kit."

Cara snorted a laugh. "I'm surprised you're still awake with your jet lag."

"That's what sheer will and three Starbucks Venti lattes will do for you," Sienna said and patted the cushion for Chloe, who stood patiently at the sofa's edge. Chloe accepted the invitation, leaping up and nestling her head on Sienna's thigh with a content sigh.

Cara rose. "I have wine and Indian take-out."

Sienna threw up a hand. "I'm awake, but I have my limits. Yes, to wine. Hard pass on the food." Glancing at the empty glass on the coffee table, she scrutinized Cara. "Looks like you had a head start. Everything OK?"

Far from it. "I'm fine," Cara lied. They'd shared most—if not all—of their secrets since they were sixteen. But Cara's day was too bizarre. She wouldn't know where to start and decided to stay silent until she gained some perspective. Although Sienna was surprisingly open-minded about all things spiritual, this strayed into off-the-charts territory, and Cara didn't have the energy.

Sienna frowned. "Lemme guess. Cara's Misery for five hundred dollars, the married loser, or Cara's Misery for one thousand dollars, the prick of a boss. Ding-ding-ding!" Sienna said, *Jeopardy*-style, reminding Cara of everything that had annoyed her before the strange encounters and wishing it were that simple.

"Red or white?" Cara said, releasing an exasperated sigh.

"Huh?"

"Wine. Red or white?"

"Come on, Carissima. Don't be that way." Sienna pouted.

Cara threw up her hands. "What do you want me to say? Kai forgot my birthday, or Rick sabotaged me...*Again*?"

"Screw the job!" Sienna said. "And Kai? You need to let go. Why are you still friends with him, anyway? He's been married for five years."

"That doesn't mean we can't be friends," Cara mumbled. Having him as a friend was enough, though she couldn't deny carrying an ember in her heart with his name. An ember, not a flame, she reminded herself. There was a difference.

Sienna rolled her eyes. "Whatever."

Cara scrubbed a hand down her face, trying to erase the grimace. "Senny, we're friends. That's all."

"So, you've said. But, honey, that relationship is unhealthy. You need to move on." Sienna batted her lush lashes and taunted, "No one deserves to get laid more than you."

"Thanks," Cara deadpanned as an image of the blond guy from the subway flashed through her mind. Ha! She wouldn't have a chance. "How about that glass of wine?" Cara headed toward the kitchen without waiting for Sienna's response. Sienna was right, but the thought of not having Kai in her life sucked the oxygen from her lungs.

"I'm not going to let this go," Sienna yelled from the living room.

Shocker. Cara didn't need her best friend berating her about her choices. It wasn't lost on Cara that she needed to get a handle on her life, but the last few months had beaten her down. She could handle her personal or professional life being out of whack, but not both at once, which might explain the panic attack. Or not.

Leaning against the kitchen sink, Cara took a cleansing breath and drew solace from her surroundings as one of her coping mechanisms. *Country Living*-inspired, her tiny kitchen had soothing, light blue-painted walls and antique touches that brightened her day—a 1920s light-green enamel canister set, vintage farm-themed prints, and a weathered old cupboard with chicken wire for linens and pantry goods. All items she purchased during summer pilgrimages with her mother to Brimfield, Massachusetts. She'd poured her heart and soul into making her apartment a space that made her happy, even when the rest of her life couldn't.

Cara grabbed a corkscrew from the bar tray, an unopened bottle of Cabernet, and two glasses, then returned to the living room.

"I'm sorry you had a crummy day," Sienna said with an apologetic smile and nudged the box. "Open your present."

"Yes, ma'am." Resting the wine and accompanying paraphernalia on the coffee table, she unwrapped and opened the box. Gasping, she slipped a red cashmere swing coat from between the tissue paper and put it on. "It's beautiful," Cara said breathlessly, running her fingertips along the feather-soft sleeve. Grinning and giddy, Cara twirled, sending the coat's hem rippling around her.

Sienna stood, crossed her arms, and smiled smugly. "Straight from the runways of Paris." Then, she tugged at Cara's sleeves and ran her hands over the shoulder seams, assessing the fit and nodding her approval. "Perfect."

Cara scooped Sienna into a hug, touched by the thoughtful gift. "Thank you, Senny. I love it." Sienna stood the same height as Cara at five-foot-seven, but her friend felt fragile in Cara's arms, reminding Cara that a soft heart beat beneath her friend's hardened shell.

Cara had loved Sienna like a sister ever since they'd met in the girls' bathroom during high school, both crouched beside a toilet in adjoining stalls, experiencing the same anguish, and afterward, forging a bond over their shared anxiety disorder. Even so, Cara decided not to share her earlier panic attack, fearing she'd sound like a recovering alcoholic admitting to having a drink.

Sienna hugged her harder and whispered, "Be happy."

"I'll try," Cara said.

The doorbell rang, startling them from the embrace.

Sienna glanced at her watch and frowned. "It's almost eleven. Are you expecting anyone?"

Cara stared blankly and shook her head. Chloe raced to the door and stood guard while Cara peered through the peephole. A guy wearing a bicycle helmet stood outside with a large envelope. "It's a courier." Cara left the chain intact and opened the door a few inches. "May I help you?"

Note to self: Raise security concerns at the next co-op meeting. Her neighbors had to stop letting people in without buzzing the units.

"Cara Collins?"

She eyed him warily. "Yes?"

He slipped a manila envelope vertically through the door, followed by a clipboard, and pointed. "Sign there."

Cara scribbled her signature, grabbed a ten-dollar bill from her purse, and passed the clipboard with the tip through the door.

" 'Night," he said with an appreciative nod and headed toward the elevator.

Cara closed the door and stared at the return address, dumbfounded. Watson & Haskins, New York.

She'd never heard of them. Panic rose in her chest. Had Rick done something to get her sued? The large envelope shook in her hands as she stared, afraid to open it.

Sienna cleared her throat and motioned toward the envelope. "It's not going to open itself."

"Give me a sec." Cara shimmied out of her new coat, hung it on a hook beside the door, and regrouped with Chloe and Sienna on the sofa. Then she ripped open the envelope to find a smaller one inside with a neatly written message on a sticky note. "It's an appointment reminder for tomorrow at ten a.m.," she said, puzzled.

Sienna's brows rose. "You didn't make the appointment, I take it?"

Cara shook her head and tore open the inner envelope. Her heart stuttered at the name on the personalized stationery: Hannah Brunt-Collins.

No way.

Sienna scrutinized her and registered Cara's alarm, "What's the matter? You look like you've seen a ghost."

Close enough. Ignoring Sienna, Cara silently read the handwritten letter.

"Well, don't keep me hanging," Sienna said impatiently.

Cara forced a breath and mumbled, "It — it's…from my grandmother."

"Huh?" Sienna blinked. "Aren't your grandmothers both dead?"

Affirmative. "It's from Grandma Hannah on my dad's side." Cara squinted at the date. "The letter was written twenty-three years ago."

Sienna pointed with growing excitement. "I'm not getting any younger. What does it say?"

Cara pressed the letter to her chest and composed herself. "Okay, okay…," she said and read the first paragraph aloud.

Dearest Cara,

Happy birthday, my dear. If you are reading this letter, it's your twenty-seventh birthday. I wish I could have been with you longer to share the many joys of your life as you grew into the amazing woman that I'm sure you are now. I'm sorry we didn't have more time together, but I will always be grateful for every moment we had.

Without missing a beat, Cara skipped to the last paragraph and read.

If all has gone according to plan, you have an appointment to meet with Watson & Haskins tomorrow. They will provide more details. I love you dearly, and my spirit will be with you always.

Love,
Grandma Hannah

Cara brushed a tear from her cheek. If she hadn't been convinced before. She was now. This morning's incidents were no coincidence. Whatever it was had to do with this letter — a letter she couldn't share with Sienna. Another addition to the growing list of things she couldn't share with her best friend.

Sienna raised her eyebrows. "That's it? Doesn't say much, does it?"

Cara shrugged, folding the letter and returning it to the envelope. "I guess I'll find out tomorrow." Setting the letter aside, Cara folded her legs and hugged them hard to hide her trembling hands.

Her grandmother had died when she was young, but Cara remembered her with love. One of her earliest and fondest memories was as a three-year-old child sitting on her grandmother's lap and receiving a round purse full of Easter candy. She couldn't quite remember her grandmother's face, but she remembered Grandma Hannah's snow-white braid, kind smile, and warm, blue eyes.

"Are you okay?" Sienna asked softly.

Cara swept her fingertips beneath her eyes. "Hearing from the dead is a little jarring."

"Do you think she left you money?"

Cara kept her expression neutral and shook her head. "My grandmother didn't have any." She eyed the unopened wine on the coffee table, looking for an escape. "How about that drink? Will you do the honors?"

Sienna stifled a yawn and glanced at her watch. "One glass, then I need to go home and crash." She reached for the wine bottle, and with the expertise of a sommelier, she trimmed the foil, twisted out the cork, and filled two glasses without losing a drop. Sienna handed Cara a glass and raised hers in a toast. "To finding a hot, *available* man, a better life, and hidden riches from your grandmother."

Cara sniffed a laugh. "I'll drink to that." She raised her glass and changed the subject to avoid more scrutiny. "So, I want to hear more about Fashion Week."

Sienna sighed. "Well, if I must...."

Cara silently thanked the universe when, ten minutes later, Sienna finished her story and rose to leave. On the way out, Sienna wagged a finger. "Remember, wear something nice on Saturday night. Translation: show some cleavage, OK?"

Cara scowled. "You sure you want the competition?"

Sienna glanced at her B-cups and snapped her fingers. "Bring it on! All you need is a perfect handful. Any more is a waste." Then, she winked. "Let me know what you find out about the letter."

"Will do." Cara hugged Sienna.

"Bye, Clow-Clow," Sienna called to the sleeping ball-o'-dog on the sofa.

Closing the door, Cara released a sigh of relief. She nestled beside Chloe, snatched the letter, and reread the entire missive, including what she hadn't read to Sienna.

Dearest Cara,

Happy birthday, my dear. If you are reading this letter, it's your twenty-seventh birthday. I wish I could have been with you longer to share the many joys of your life as you grew into the amazing woman that I'm sure you are now. I'm sorry we didn't have more time together, but I will always be grateful for every moment we had.

Cara, what I am about to write must stay secret. I can't emphasize this enough. Otherwise, people you love could die.

My dear, you were born with a gift. From the moment I saw you until now, as I write this letter, you have always signaled that you are one of us. You can't imagine how thrilled I was to make that discovery.

A new world awaits, along with an inheritance that carries great responsibility. What you will inherit is determined by who you are and your ultimate mission. Half will be yours while you act as custodian for the rest. You will pass it on to the next generation when the time is right — just as your sponsor did for you. I'm merely the Messenger in this transaction. As I am no longer able to answer your questions, someone will be sent to explain in the coming days. Since a considerable amount of time will pass between the writing of this letter and its delivery, I am unable to tell you who that will be.

If all has gone according to plan, you have an appointment to meet with Watson & Haskins tomorrow. They will provide more details. I love you dearly, and my spirit will be with you always.

Love,
Grandma Hannah

The letter trembled in Cara's hand. This morning, she woke up ordinary. Boring, even. Now, she wasn't so sure. She grasped her head and rocked, trying to ground herself in a reality turning to quicksand.

Chloe awoke with the movement and touched her wet nose to Cara's elbow. Cara stared into her girl's expressive eyes, petting her with an unsteady hand and grateful for her warmth and company.

One thing was sure. Cara had questions. Lots of questions. She kissed Chloe's head and whispered, "Watson & Haskins better have some damn good answers."

Chapter 7

CARA

Perry Street Apartment. New York City.

HE'S SO PERFECT. To her, anyway. Cara savored a few guilty seconds of unguarded observation, drinking in Kai across the gallery, where he stood, his gaze transfixed on a painting. Blond and blue-eyed, Kai wore all white — linen pants and a collared linen shirt rolled to the elbows, revealing sun-bronzed skin — an unconventional choice for a man who usually wore khakis and a golf shirt. Cara had to admit he cut a jaw-dropping figure against the luminescent white walls. Breathing deeply to calm the butterflies fluttering in her stomach, Cara began her approach, glancing around the unfamiliar surroundings.

Where are we?

The answer — *Sanctuary* — whispered through her mind as Kai turned, his intense blue gaze finding hers. He gave a dimpled smile and opened his arms. Cara rushed into Kai's waiting embrace, relaxing against his lean, six-foot frame as he enclosed her in a tight hug.

Pure joy raced through Cara's veins with a vague awareness that this wasn't real. They were in one of her lucid, premonitory dreams. She'd had several of Kai over the years, all heralding some pivotal moment in his life. But this one was different. Cara had never been a participant before, only an observer. She wondered what it meant, but for now, she sank into Kai's blissful closeness in a place that existed somewhere in their future.

Cara surrendered to the feel of Kai's arms wrapped around her, his hands clasped at the small of her back. God, how she'd missed him. She tucked her face into Kai's neck and inhaled, relishing his skin's heady scent while desire warred with logic in her prefrontal cortex. The warm press of his body was sweet torture.

Straightening, Cara found Kai's gaze fixed on hers, his lips dangerously close. "It's so good to see you," he whispered and cradled her face in his palms.

Then, Kai pressed his lips to hers, squelching her surprised gasp. Guilt rushed through her traitorous body as it responded to his touch. The taste of his mouth and sweep of his tongue was everything she remembered. In waking life, this would've never happened. Kai took his marriage vows seriously, and she respected that, making the moment painful in its cruelty.

When Cara thought her knees would buckle along with her nerves, Kai released her. Stepping back, he tilted his head. "I want to show you something." Taking her hand, he twined his fingers through hers. The familiar silver ring he wore—a gift from his father—lay cool against her skin, inviting more memories and another pang of misplaced longing.

Cara strolled alongside Kai, frantically trying to make sense of the dream's metaphorical meaning. Would Kai's marriage end? Would she have another chance with Kai? But that couldn't happen unless....

Would Kai finally believe her about the incident that had ripped them apart in college? The incident involving someone else's lie that weakened Kai's trust in her and sowed enough self-doubt to change the course of their relationship? The incident that stole a future that should've been hers, yet bestowed a consolation prize of a friendship riddled with unresolved feelings?

Even though Kai was beyond her reach, all Cara had wanted since they reconciled was for him to say he believed her—*and mean it.*

They stopped in front of a painting with angels, and Kai's expression turned regretful. "Cara, I...."

She held her breath. Could this be it? Would he finally set her free?

Kai brushed his knuckles gently along her cheek, her breath hitching in anticipation. "I—" The gallery shifted, disintegrating into shimmery waves.

"Kai!" Cara lunged towards his wavering image, but he was gone, and the message along with him. All that remained was the feel of cool silver against her finger.

A DELICATE, WARM TONGUE licked Cara's cheek, ripping her from the dream. Grunting in frustration, Cara opened an eye to find her loyal hound bathing her in kisses.

"*Ugh.* I love you, too." Cara cradled Chloe's narrow head to make her stop, kissed her crinkled brow, and, unable to stay mad at a face that cute, tapped a finger to her dog's wet nose. "*Boop.*"

Taking the hint, Chloe burrowed beneath the covers and snuggled against Cara's leg. Grimacing, Cara brushed away slobber with fingers still tingling from where they rested beside Kai's.

Damn her dreamscape. Even if she wanted to ignore it, she couldn't. Thanks to Chloe's "dreamus interruptus," Cara wasn't sure what message she was supposed to receive. When it came to Kai, her dreams invariably came true, like the job offer in California, the birth of his daughter, and even the circumstances that led to their breakup back in college. Only one, about a year ago, had scared the shit out of her. It ended in Kai's death.

In the dream, Cara powerlessly watched from the shadows as someone slit Kai's throat. The vision of his lifeless body and glazed stare, surrounded in a halo of blood, still haunted her.

She had warned Kai about the dream, and he altered his work schedule. His colleague, Dr. Tom Peyton, was murdered the same day in the employee parking lot. The memory sent a shiver down her spine, and the karmic burden weighed heavily on her psyche. Had she saved Kai only to sacrifice Dr. Peyton? She had endlessly racked her brain on what she could've done to save them both.

Cara and Kai rarely spoke of the dream or the events that followed, but her sixth sense still tingled.

What if she hadn't stopped Kai's death, only delayed it?

At least this dream had been *a positive one.*

She combed her fingers through her bedhead and sighed. Could her dreams be the gift Grandma Hannah mentioned in the letter? If so, why were they tied almost exclusively to Kai?

Which reminded her…she grabbed her cell phone from the nightstand and checked for messages—nothing. It didn't make any sense. Screw waiting around. She'd call Kai when she got to the office. They needed to talk about more than missing her birthday, which, coincidentally, fell on a Wednesday this year, the same day as their weekly 11:00 AM conference call. Not to mention, the man had a legit photographic memory. How had he forgotten to call her?

The memory of their kiss rushed back, and Cara flushed. Would Kai someday be free? A voice whispered through Cara's mind, just as it had in the dream: *"He is not meant for you."*

Cara startled. *What the hell?*

Hearing voices in a dream was one thing. Hearing them while awake was quite another. Cara's pulse spiked, and she frantically scanned the bedroom.

Was she losing her mind?

After yesterday, she wouldn't rule it out.

Chapter 8

KAI

Solomon Residence. San Francisco.

"IT'S SO GOOD to see you," he whispered, feeling the euphoria of their kiss on his lips. His arms lingered around Cara before inviting her to walk the gallery in comfortable silence. He'd asked her here for a reason, and he had to tell her why.

He stopped and gazed into her eyes. "Cara, I...." Her name hung in the air as he gathered the words, his heart pounding. And then Cara disintegrated with the dream.

Kai awoke with a start to find his four-year-old daughter, Sara, creeping up between him and Melanie on the queen-sized bed. His wife, a heavy sleeper, snored softly beside him, undisturbed. Not surprisingly, Kai's tendency to wake easily made him the "go-to" parent for late-night emergencies and the agreed-upon choice for predawn feedings when Sara was a baby, which he hadn't minded. In the quiet, early morning, feeding his daughter had strengthened their bond, making the lack of sleep worthwhile.

"What's the matter, sweetie?" he whispered, staying nestled in the pillow and desperately wanting to jump back into the dream where he'd left off. He shoved down the guilt over the kiss. *What was I thinking?* But guilt wasn't enough for his sleep-addled brain to abandon the dream. He had plenty of time for self-recrimination later. He needed to know what he planned to tell Cara, sensing a vitally important message he couldn't remember while conscious.

"Daddy, I'm scared. I dreamt about monsters. They were trying to get me," Sara whispered, burrowing her way beneath the covers. "Can I stay here for a little while?" As a rule, their bedroom was off-limits except for extreme emergencies, but how could he refuse? In Sara's young mind, scary dreams and monsters constituted an emergency.

"For a minute, then you have to go back to your big-girl bed," he said, scooping her tiny body into his arms and snuggling her to his chest, her hair tickling his bare arm. His daughter was the perfect mix of him and Melanie, with her mother's silky blonde hair and his blue eyes. He loved her with an intensity he hadn't thought possible, always fearful that something unexpected could take her away. Since having Sara, Kai found it incomprehensible that a father could abandon a child…like his father had done to him.

"The monsters said they were going to kill you, Daddy. I didn't know what to do," Sara said in a shaky whisper.

"*Shh*," Kai soothed. "The monsters won't get me, I promise." Though his daughter's creativity and imagination continually impressed him, he made a mental note to check the television's parental controls.

"Luke said he'd protect us, but I'm still scared."

Huh? "Who's Luke?" Kai asked, hoping like hell Luke was an imaginary friend.

"Our Guardian Angel," she said, settling into him while Melanie turned in her sleep and gave them her back. "He came at the end of the dream."

Kai relaxed, assured Luke wasn't real, and stroked Sara's hair. "Everything will be okay."

Speaking of dreams, Kai's thoughts returned to Cara and the strange gallery. The dream reminded him of how things used to be with Cara before Melanie. But that was a long time ago, and he'd never cheat on his wife. Thankfully, Melanie and Cara had a warm relationship, making it possible for him to continue his friendship with Cara.

That said, Kai had regrets when it came to Cara.

Kai still lamented letting an irrational seed of distrust ruin their romantic relationship. Even when he suspected he'd been lied to, the damage had been done. The incident rocked him to his core, and he'd been too afraid to let her get that close again. So, he opted for friendship, which felt safer. Especially since Cara had three more years at Georgetown after he left for MIT to earn his Master's and Ph.D. Not to say he didn't visit Cara during grad school or let temptation get the better of them. But anything physical ended when he married Melanie.

Even now, there was a lot left unsaid between them—and that was on him. The truth? He would always love Cara. An unexplainable connection existed between them that he couldn't deny. He expected people to come and go in his life, but he believed Cara would always be there for him, even if he didn't deserve her.

Cara didn't know the real reason he married Melanie. That she'd been pregnant. Right or wrong, he never told Cara that Melanie had slipped into the future meant for her—the future Kai had finally realized he wanted to give her.

But Kai had to do the right thing for Melanie and his unborn child. He couldn't be like his father. He couldn't abandon them. Sadly, Melanie miscarried only weeks after the wedding. Sara was born a year later, and his daughter was the one precious thing he'd never change. Ever.

He hugged his little girl tighter and kissed the top of her head as she snored softly in his arms. He pulled her closer and squeezed his eyes shut, trying to fall asleep. But his lids refused to stay closed. Self-loathing swirled inside him as he stared at the ceiling. He couldn't escape the truth that he loved two women—something he would never acknowledge aloud.

The glowing numbers on the alarm clock indicated he had ninety minutes before it chimed.

Screw it. Kai carefully untangled himself from Sara and slipped from bed.

Padding to his office, he clicked on a small desk lamp and fired up his computer to check the nightly lab reports, anxious to see the results of his most recent experiment. He'd made a bold move and tried something different using CRISPR gene-splicing technology. He was curious to see if his latest gene splices had yielded any changes. Full results wouldn't be available until later this morning, but he could determine the viability of the samples—information he needed before the next implantation.

If this had been fifteen years ago, lengthy experimentation cycle times would've crippled his efforts. Now, with CRISPR technology and the latest genomic sequencing equipment, he had access to better and faster results.

Kai reached for his messenger bag and slipped out two laboratory notebooks marked FIREFLY, the project code name, and the volume number. He set them on the desk, and his pulse sped up as he opened the earlier of the two hard-bound books and stared at the numbered pages filled with copious handwritten notes.

A Forrester Research Labs employee for nearly 4 years, Kai had spent the last 12 months working on Project Firefly, a top-secret genetics project for a sponsor known as The Foundation. Forrester, one of the leading privately funded research facilities globally, is best known for its medical research on cancer and degenerative diseases. However, over the last two decades, it has expanded into longevity research.

Kai had jumped at the chance to continue the work his former colleague, Dr. Tom Peyton, had started when the division president asked him to take over the project as Senior Scientist. When Kai stepped in, he expected to quickly pick up the work, but that didn't happen.

Many aspects of the project remained shrouded in secrecy by the sponsoring client, handicapping Kai even on a good day. Over the past year, he hit one roadblock after another, along with added pressure from The

Foundation. They were losing patience with his progress, and the situation was growing tenser by the day.

Kai had almost stepped down and left the project until he found these two scientific notebooks that the late Dr. Tom Peyton had left behind. One notebook Kai had received when he started the project a year ago, and the other he'd stumbled across a few days ago in a locked file cabinet while rummaging through his old files in pursuit of new ideas.

He couldn't believe his eyes when he found the missing notebook among his files, not knowing how it had gotten there. This one preceded the one he received initially.

Two nights earlier, Kai smuggled both notebooks from the lab and examined them side by side. He noticed odd inconsistencies in the notations, raising Kai's suspicion that a section of the documentation had been replaced or, more accurately, fabricated.

Kai flipped to the notebook page he wanted, again seeing what didn't make sense. Upon inspection, the books didn't appear to have been tampered with, yet the scientific notations didn't match the page sequence.

Ordinarily, scientific lab notebooks have special bindings with numbered pages, used to prove a chain of custody, making it impossible to hide missing pages, since ripping out one page causes the adjoining page to fall out.

That wasn't the case here. Kai wondered if it was purposeful and possibly a clue. He suspected another set of notes might be floating around somewhere.

When Kai started the project, the director told him they were investigating genetic modification for a rare degenerative disease that caused accelerated organ failure. Kai suspected that wasn't the entire truth based on recent discoveries, so he started a new set of experiments.

Kai logged in to the Forrester system, accessing the lab equipment and the last two sample sets he'd prepared: one before reading the new notebook and one after.

He opened each file and arranged them side by side until he looked at ten magnified thumbnail images, each labeled with the date and protocol, distinguishing one sample from the next.

Fat healthy cells. That's what Kai wanted to see.

Kai scanned the five older samples. None showed allele modifications indicative of gene mutations. He reviewed the latest five, and his pulse quickened. One of his samples had the modification he hoped to see.

"Yes!" He punched the air. The cell, repaired at the breaks, seemed to function without the deleted protein. He jotted the requisite notations in the latest notebook.

At least one sample would move to the next stage. Now, Kai would try to replicate his success with some new combinations.

Kai's gaze caught a series of calendar reminders in the lower right-hand corner from yesterday that he'd ignored. Reminders he didn't usually need. He started deleting them one by one and froze.

He did a double-take. *Shit!* He'd missed Cara's birthday. He'd been so wrapped up in yesterday's discovery that he'd forgotten what day it was. Is that why he dreamt of her?

Glancing at the time, he added three hours, determined it was a reasonable hour, and reached for his cell.

Chapter 9

CARA

Perry Street Apartment. New York City.

CARA HIT THE off switch on her blow-dryer just in time to hear Kai's ringtone, the chorus from Journey's *"Don't Stop Believin'."* Her heart leaped, and she ran for the living room, where her phone was charging. Her towel loosened and fell to the floor. She stumbled over the wet terry cloth mound and cursed. Naked, she lunged for her cell phone.

"Hey, I'm a terrible friend. I can't believe I missed your birthday," Kai said.

She smiled at the sound of his voice, and her shoulders drooped with relief as she scooped the towel from the floor. "You suck. How could you forget my birthday?"

"I know. I feel like crap. Forgive me?"

"Depends. I'm open to flowers," Cara joked, securing the towel tightly around her chest.

"You hate flowers. Besides, you're allergic to them."

True, but she'd appreciate the gesture. Then again, Kai could send her a sack of potatoes, and she'd be happy.

"At least you remembered that." Understatement. Having a photographic memory, Kai remembered *everything* except, clearly, her birthday.

His voice softened. "I remember a lot of things."

Her breath caught, and she pressed her eyes shut, a flash of memory sizzling behind her eyelids and stabbing her heart. A look of yearning in his blue eyes as he ran his fingers through her hair, cupping her face, their bodies entwined the last time they were together, the night she'd thought they'd finally left the Friend Zone. She'd been wrong. Less than a week later, he announced that he and Melanie were back together and planning to get married.

She opened her eyes, glanced at her watch, and swallowed. It was only 5 AM in California. "At least you get points for calling so early. I still can't believe you forgot. Don't you ever look at your calendar?"

He chuckled. "Don't usually need to. Fine, expect a fruit basket."

She laughed. "You're sending me fruit? Seriously?" The more she thought about it, the funnier it seemed, and the more she laughed.

"What?" His laughter mingled with hers until they sank into an uncontrolled laughing fit. The first time this happened was during their art class together in college over something equally as innocuous. The teacher threw them out for disruption. "I thought you liked," he gasped between breaths, "Pears," and erupted into another laughing fit.

Chest heaving and side aching, Cara struggled to catch her breath as mirthful tears rolled down her cheeks. Then she thought of the dreams and sobered. She cleared her throat and swiped her fingers beneath her eyes. "Hey, I planned to call you later anyway. I had a dream last night."

His laughter died, and she heard him draw in a few breaths before he said, "Yeah…I had one, too."

Cara blinked. What? "You did? What was it about?"

He hesitated. "No death, if that's what you're worried about."

Her mouth went dry. "Were we in an art gallery?" she asked, bracing herself for the answer.

"Yeah!" he said, a beat passing, then added in a hesitant whisper, "I kissed you."

Gah. Cara slapped a hand to her forehead and cringed. That never happened before. They'd never shared the same dream. Then again, she'd never been a participant before either. "Do you remember anything else, like why you were there?" she asked, holding her breath.

"No. Sara crawled into bed and woke me. I was about to tell you something important, but I have no idea what."

She deflated and hedged, "I'm not sure what the dream means." Other than giving her a bruising reminder of what she'd lost.

He snorted. "That makes two of us. To be honest, the dream was so real it was eerie."

"Yeah, well, welcome to my world," Cara said. "Actually, I wanted to talk about last year's dream. You know, the one where you *died*?"

Kai went silent, then asked warily, "I still have no clue what Le Feu means or who it could be," he said, referring to the warning the dream version of Kai yelled to her before he was killed—*Le Feu! Cara, run!*

"Me neither, but that's not it." She took a deep breath and added, "I think you're still in danger."

Apprehension crept into his voice. "What makes you say that?"

"All my dreams have come true except for that one."

Silence.

"You still there?" she asked.

"But it did. Didn't it? Tom died…," he whispered.

She winced and pressed her eyes shut. "True, but in the past, everything that happened in my dreamscapes came true, which means you could still be in jeopardy." As soon as the words passed through her lips, her sixth sense tingled its concurrence, and she added, "Watch out for Melanie, too. OK? If that kiss happens in the future…." She cleared her throat. "I can't imagine you'd do that if she were in the picture."

"It wasn't real, Cara," he said without a hint of defensiveness. "But I promise I will." He sighed. "Hey, I have to get ready for work, and I probably made you late."

She considered telling him about the letter, but the words died in her throat as she remembered the warning. People she loved could die. The thought of anything happening to Kai terrified her. She needed to research Le Feu and see if anything had surfaced since last year. She wondered again if her dreams were connected to the letter and if Kai was in danger.

"Wait! How's everything going with your project?" she asked. He'd been stressed about it last week when they'd spoken.

"Ha! I don't want to give my favorite investment banker an insider trading tip, but things are progressing," he said with forced levity that didn't ring true after the weight of the conversation.

She huffed. "Orange isn't my color. It clashes with my hair. Stay safe, and I'll watch for that fruit basket."

He laughed. "How about a digital gift card from Amazon, and we call it even?"

"Deal."

"I'll call you in a few days to catch up, if not sooner." He added softly, "Happy birthday, *Car*."

Warmth filled her chest as she disconnected the call. She liked it when Kai called her Car. Holding the towel closed, she headed toward the bedroom.

He is not meant for you.

She stopped cold as the second unwelcome reminder rang inside her head.

Shivering at the intrusion, she hoped to find answers at Watson & Haskins. In the meantime, anger welled in her chest. She didn't need a disembodied voice confirming what she already knew.

Cara flipped the universe a middle finger. *Got it! He'll never be mine.*

Then she stomped to the bedroom to get dressed and face whatever came next.

Chapter 10

CHAMUEL

Perry Street Apartment. New York City.

WHAT THE HELL is he doing up here? Chamuel towered over the young, dark-haired Guardian sleeping on the roof of Cara's apartment building. Zeke lay flat on his back, legs crossed at the ankles, arms folded across his broad chest. Still dressed from club-hopping the night before, the Nephilim male wore form-fitting slacks and a tight, short-sleeved knit shirt that revealed his tattooed forearms.

In repose, Zeke looked no more than fifteen. Nevertheless, his boyish face regularly forced him to prove he was old enough to drink. His driver's license listed his age as 22, which was much more believable than the truth. Sixty-three in Nephilim years made Zeke almost the human equivalent of the age printed on the license. On some days, Chamuel swore Zeke's psychological age hovered closer to a fledgling of twelve.

Chamuel shook his head, feeling slightly guilty for dashing the young Guardian's plans for a night of female companionship.

God, I'm getting old, Chamuel thought and nudged Zeke with a steel-toed boot. "Wake up."

Zeke opened an eye and groaned, "I'm hatin' on you right now, Cham. Next time, call me before I have a few drinks." He pushed onto an elbow, raised a hand, and wiggled his fingers at the paper coffee cup clutched in Chamuel's palm. "Gimme."

Frowning, Chamuel dangled the cup out of reach from Zeke's waiting hand.

Zeke rolled his eyes. "Please?"

"It's not coffee. It's a double espresso," Chamuel mumbled and gave Zeke the cup.

"Whatever. Right now, I'd drink mud if it had caffeine."

Chamuel gave him a disapproving look. "Show some respect to your elders. What're you doing up here uncloaked, anyway? I told you to wait on the fire escape."

Zeke chugged the espresso and swiped a hand across his mouth. "Chill. I've only been here a few minutes. I didn't have enough energy to stay cloaked after I saw your charge naked," he said, wearing a cocky grin. "That was too much for me to handle."

Chamuel's brows shot to his hairline along with his blood pressure. He growled low in his throat with his hands clenched at his sides. "I'm sorry, what did you say?"

"Don't get your panties in a bunch. I wasn't doing a Peeping Tom on her." The young Guardian rose to his feet and brushed asphalt pebbles from his pants with a free hand.

"Then how did you see her naked?" Chamuel gritted. The thought of anyone seeing her naked made him irate and more than a little jealous.

Zeke released an exasperated sigh. "Stop, will ya? She ran to answer her cell, and the towel dropped when she lunged for the darn thing. I caught an eyeful from the fire escape through the kitchen doorway."

The explanation did nothing to dampen Chamuel's desire to wipe the smug smirk from Zeke's baby face *with his fist.*

He and Isaac had taken Zeke under their wings as a small child, but there were times when Chamuel wanted to give Zeke a swift kick. The young Nephil knew how to push his hot buttons, but beneath the kid's smart-ass demeanor was a reliable, trustworthy, and good-hearted male.

"So, you came up here?" Chamuel asked, crossing his arms and ratcheting his temper down a notch.

"Yeah, after my eyes nearly popped out of my head," Zeke mumbled, dropping the one-liner like a live grenade, unaware of how it landed. He gulped his espresso, and his eyes sprang wider. "That's some good stuff."

Another growl rumbled low in Chamuel's throat.

Zeke's gaze snapped to his, and he clapped Chamuel on the shoulder. A look of sincerity replaced the taunting smirk. "Cham, don't worry. I'm just jerking your chain. Your charge is safe with me. You have my oath."

Chamuel nodded, a little embarrassed at his instinctive possessiveness. She was his charge, not his mate, and she never would be. Keeping her safe and alive were the limits of his assignment. At least they should be. "Fine, but don't get any ideas."

"You know I don't mix business with pleasure. Cara is pretty hot, though." Zeke winked.

Chamuel answered with a menacing glare. He didn't need a reminder, nor did he need the thought of her naked body tormenting him all day.

Zeke threw his hands up and chuckled. "I promise. Not going there."

Chamuel removed himself from Zeke's baited hook and changed subjects. "Those couple of hours of sleep did me good, not to mention the shower. I owe you one."

"Hell, yes, you owe me one!" Zeke removed a slip of paper from his pocket and squinted to read it. "And her name is Sophia."

Chamuel snorted. "You're unbelievable."

"In more ways than I can count." Zeke grinned, but his smile faded as he cupped a hand to his ear and looked at his watch. "You'd better get moving. I just heard the lock click on her apartment door. She's heading toward the elevator." Zeke drained the remaining espresso from the cup and returned it to Chamuel. "Peace out, brother!"

Zeke took a running leap. Majestic white-feathered wings burst through slits in the back of his shirt and unfurled a moment before he cloaked and disappeared over the edge of the roof.

Chamuel peeked at the ground below and spotted Cara's bouncing, auburn hair and red coat as she crossed the street.

His face flushed with heat at the thought of her naked. He swallowed hard. He had a bad feeling about this assignment.

Chapter 11

CARA

Watson & Haskins. New York City.

CARA STIFLED A yawn and stepped out of the elevator into a warm hall lit by a large, antique crystal chandelier. She felt marginally better after speaking with Kai. Other than her early-morning dream, Cara barely slept. The pot of coffee she consumed, coupled with adrenaline, barely made up for the deficit.

Mozart played quietly in the background, and CRAP!

She stared in horror at the enormous spring bouquet with arcing floral plumes in what looked like a Ming Dynasty vase on the marble-topped entry table. One whiff of the perfumed air and the sweet scent of lilies sent her headlong into an unrelenting sneezing fit that had her scrambling for the tissues inside her purse.

Oh, God. Eyes watering, she blew her nose and caught her reflection in an antique gilt mirror a few feet away from the offending blooms.

Her watery green eyes glimmered like a deer-in-headlights as she dabbed her reddened nose and said a silent 'thank you' for waterproof mascara. She looked like an allergic mess. At least her hair looked nice, cascading over the shoulders of her new swing coat. Sienna's gift was like a security blanket anchoring her to reality.

Ah-choo! She caught her sneeze in another tissue.

"Miss Collins? Are you all right?" A Chanel-clad woman with a sleek, smooth bob came from behind and lightly tapped her shoulder.

Cara blushed. "Hi, yes. Sorry." She sniffled and pointed to the riotous blooms. "Allergic."

Concern creased the woman's brow as she glanced at the offending flowers. "Oh, my! Let's get you away from these. Follow me."

Cara pointed to the Ladies' Room door and excused herself to take an allergy pill and compose herself. Of all the possible allergies, why did it have to be to something so pretty?

The woman stood waiting when she emerged. "All better?"

Cara nodded.

"Wonderful. Mr. Gladstone will see you now. If you need anything, my name is Claudette," she said, her smile pleasant and genuine. The woman appeared to be in her late thirties, and everything about her, from her impeccable appearance to her demeanor, implied a sense of efficiency.

Claudette led Cara down the hall to a set of ornate cherry doors, through which they entered a lush, wood-paneled hallway covered in plush Oriental rugs. The wide, windowless passageway stretched out in front of them. Soft music gave the office the tranquility of a spa, but the lack of outside light made it feel like a vault.

No surprise. Beautiful oil paintings, illuminated with picture lights, lined the walls between offices. As an art history minor in college, Cara was passionate about period paintings, and this place had no shortage.

Cara's heart almost stopped as she paused to examine the signature of an early 17th-century Dutch master. Was that a *Vermeer*? Who were these people?

As she caught up with Claudette deeper in the maze of hallways, she stopped again to admire a magnificent nineteenth-century Hudson River school canvas painted by Thomas Cole. A few steps later, an early-twentieth-century New York street scene during a snowfall by a personal favorite, Guy Wiggins.

What she'd give for more time to appreciate the law firm's acquisitions, which rivaled a trip to the Met. So lost in the artwork, Cara almost slammed into Claudette, who had stopped in front of two polished, wooden doors.

Claudette knocked softly before pushing one of the doors open and ushering Cara inside. "Mr. Gladstone, this is Cara Collins. Please call if you need anything."

Cara nodded her thanks and stepped into the office, still marveling at the magnificent gallery outside. The office resembled a beautiful library, with paneled walls and built-in bookshelves. A massive partner's desk sat directly ahead. Behind it on the wall…

Cara's mouth dropped open. *Was that a Bruegel? The Fall of the Rebel Angels* from the 1500s? She could've sworn that hung in Belgium's Royal Museums of Fine Arts.

Smiling jovially, a tall man in his late sixties with a cherubic face and a shock of white hair circled the desk to greet her. "Hello, Miss Collins. May I take your coat?"

Cara's gaze was still glued to the painting. "Is that real?" she asked, mindlessly handing her coat to Mr. Gladstone, who hung it next to his on an antique coat tree.

"Why, yes, it is." He gestured for her to sit in one of the guest chairs as he returned to his seat.

"But…but, I thought that painting hung in Belgium."

He smiled. "Yes, but we borrow it back from time to time."

All right, then.

She clutched her purse and shook her head to clear it. She most definitely needed a field trip back here to examine the art.

Gladstone's eyes were kind and intelligent. "Please, Miss Collins, take a seat. If there's time later and you desire, we can retreat to the fire." His manner immediately put her at ease. She glanced at the two leather Chesterfield-style chairs and antique tea table in front of the fire glowing in the hearth. The pleasant scents of leather and pine, mixed with the smell of burning wood, lingered in the air.

"This is fine." She sat and rested her purse next to the chair.

"Should I call you Miss Collins, or may I call you Cara?"

She cleared her throat. "Cara, please."

"A lovely name," he said, smiling, his response sincere. He pulled his chair closer to the desk. "I'm sure you have questions."

You have no idea.

He clasped his hands and rested them on the neatly organized desk. "As a quick introduction, my father handled your sponsor's affairs, and that responsibility passed to me when he retired. The purpose of today's discussion is the transfer of certain holdings, along with a description of the process and parameters to access those holdings. My instructions are precise, so let's see how far that gets us, shall we?"

"Who is my sponsor?" Cara asked.

"That, my dear, I cannot reveal," he said with genuine regret. "May we proceed?"

Unsurprised, Cara took a deep breath and nodded. She'd dig deeper when the person her grandmother promised came calling.

"Very well." Mr. Gladstone put on his reading glasses and pulled a leather pouch sealed with a round, gold metal clasp from a desk drawer. He pressed the center of the lock, which opened with a soft click. The lawyer slid out several sheets of creamy-white paper. "Let's start with the real estate holdings."

Her brows rose. "I'm sorry, what?"

He gave her a kind smile. "As a part of the trust, you've inherited two real estate properties: a penthouse apartment on Fifth Avenue and a farmhouse outside Greenwich, Connecticut."

Cara's lips parted in surprise, and she swayed in the chair. She hadn't expected property.

He stared over his lowered glasses with a look of concern. "Are you all right, dear? Would you like me to call Claudette for a glass of water or perhaps some hot tea?"

She blinked and grabbed a chair arm to steady herself. "No, please continue." This all felt incredibly surreal.

"Also, two garaged vehicles are parked beneath the Fifth Avenue property." *Okayyy*, she already had a car, a luxury for a Manhattanite. Three cars were just plain overkill.

He adjusted his glasses. "There are two accounts with equal sums. You are the trustee on one; the other is in your name. The initial $25 million investment—"

Cara threw up a hand and almost choked, regretting her decision to decline the glass of water. "Excuse me?" she croaked. "Did you say $25 million?" Holy Hell. She wasn't sure what she expected, but this wasn't it.

Gladstone smiled politely. "Yes, my dear. I will provide you with a copy of the investment plans for each account. We can schedule a follow-up meeting to discuss any necessary changes to the portfolio. Our goal is twofold: to drive growth and generate income. Your accounts have grown without any withdrawals of funds for over 25 years, resulting in substantial appreciation. The original $50 million split between the accounts has tripled in value within that time and is now worth more than $150 million. I hope you are pleased nonetheless."

Cara swayed in her seat. *This can't be real.*

The lawyer's expression registered alarm, and he pressed a button on his phone. "Claudette, please bring a pot of tea."

"I'm fine," Cara said, waving a hand.

"I understand. It's a lot to take in. May I proceed?"

She nodded, feeling eight kinds of foolish.

He squinted and passed a finger down the page. "The funds will be distributed in increments of five hundred thousand dollars annually and adjusted for inflation yearly. Let's call that your pin money. The upkeep of the properties and cars will be paid directly by us from a maintenance fund. Submit those expenses, and we'll send you a quarterly statement."

She blinked rapidly, trying to steady her breathing and process the staggering wealth she had just inherited. Wow. Just wow. "I need a minute," she said and took some calming breaths, then asked, "My grandmother's letter said this all needs to stay confidential. Why?" She held back the part about people dying.

Lips pursed, he shook his head. "I'm sorry. I cannot say."

Frustration bubbled up inside her. "What *can* you tell me?"

He tapped his fingertips together. "Well, you will designate the portion of money you're keeping as trustee at some future point. The parameters of this will be explained in due course. If something happened to you before that time, that portion would merge with your holdings, and the assets would revert to the trustees. You own these resources for life, but they will revert to the trust when you die, except for the original twenty-five million dollars, which will go to your heirs."

"My future husband and children?" Cara asked, twining her fingers together.

He nodded. "In the meantime, you can spend your annual stipend as you see fit, along with the original twenty-five million. Just contact us with a disbursement request."

Cara gulped and wrung her hands. "I think I understand." Her thoughts wandered to the Park Avenue penthouse. "I have a dog," she blurted. "Are pets allowed?" A somewhat silly question, considering she could afford to replace any ruined rugs and then some.

He smiled. "Animals are more than welcome."

Claudette entered the room with a tray bearing a silver teapot and all the accouterments.

"Thank you, Claudette," Gladstone said as she set down the tea service.

He handed Cara a small stack of papers. "Please sign wherever you see a little sticky note." He poured the tea as she reviewed the paperwork. "Milk and sugar?"

"Black, please." Cara sighed and looked at him earnestly, the pen hovering over the first signature line. "What do I tell people? How do I explain this inheritance?"

He slid the tea and saucer across the desk. "No one needs to know the contents of your bank accounts. For everything else, it's always wise not to stray far from the truth. Since these assets are in your care, perhaps I may suggest that a lucrative property management role has become available through the firm of Watson & Haskins?" His mirth-filled eyes crinkled at the corners, and he winked. "It wouldn't require you to quit your current position."

Her mood lightened. She liked the unconventional suggestion. "I thought you were going to suggest an inheritance from a dead relative," she replied, poised to sign.

"Ah. The shortcoming in that excuse would become immediately apparent within your own family."

A lump formed in her throat, and she shivered. Her whole life was about to change, and worst of all, she'd have to lie to her friends and family. A hollow feeling of loneliness echoed in her chest.

Resigned, she nodded and lowered the pen.

Nothing in the contract had given her pause, so she proceeded.

While she signed, Gladstone removed an orange Hermès leather pouch from a desk drawer and slid it across the desk to her. Whoever these people were, they had taste.

Gladstone said, "Inside, you'll find marked keys to the properties and cars. In addition, you'll find the property addresses, license plate numbers, and descriptions of the cars, your ATM card, a checkbook, and my business card. We have already deposited this year's disbursement into your account. Today will be the anniversary of your annual disbursements. Finally, please see Claudette on the way out. We have a warehouse in Brooklyn where we store furniture. You're free to swap pieces to your liking in either residence. Furnishings are part of the arrangement. We're also happy to dispose of or store any of your current possessions. Claudette will provide you with the address and all the necessary details. The Manhattan residence comes furnished and fully stocked with food. The Connecticut residence also comes furnished and will be provisioned with a phone call when you decide to visit."

When the man finished his presentation, Cara's head was spinning. She nibbled her lower lip, overwhelmed.

Gladstone's gaze softened. "Cara, dear, this is a lot to absorb, and please don't be alarmed, but there's a car waiting downstairs to take you directly to the Manhattan apartment."

She froze. "Why?"

"I promise you will learn more shortly. In the meantime, I hope you don't mind, but we moved your precious Chloe and some of your belongings to the Park Avenue penthouse. You'll have the opportunity to return to your old residence over the next week and decide what else to move, dispose of, or put into storage. Again, contact Claudette."

Cara's heart quickened, alarm pricking her senses. "Why would you do that? Why would you move Chloe and my things?"

Gladstone tented his hands, his expression turning grave. "We don't believe you'll be safe in your current residence, and we need to take every precaution to ensure your safety. The trustees agreed this would be the best course of action. I'm so sorry that I don't know more." He leaned closer. "And please don't leave the apartment until someone makes contact."

Cara sucked in a breath, apprehension prickling her skin. His warning was the first she'd heard that *her* safety was at risk. Her encounter with the man in the subway and the homeless woman had unsettled her, but neither had been overtly threatening.

"Wait," Cara said, asking the question weighing most heavily on her mind. "The letter said that people I love could be in jeopardy, or even die. What does that mean?"

He shrugged. "As long as you don't share what you've learned here, you're not likely to put anyone in immediate danger. Try not to worry."

Easy for him to say. Cara swallowed, her nerves strung tight as piano wire.

Gladstone came around the desk to clasp her hand in a warm handshake between his palms. "It was lovely meeting you, Cara. If I can be of further assistance, you have my card. We'll send all correspondence to the Park Avenue address. Let us know if anything changes."

Cara wished someone would pinch her awake from this surreal dream. Leaving the tea untouched, she slipped the pouch into her purse and retrieved her swing coat from the coat stand.

Gladstone opened the door. Almost on cue, a perfectly coiffed Claudette stood waiting on the other side.

"Best of luck to you, Cara," said Gladstone, his gaze holding an empathetic glow, and left her with Claudette.

So flustered from their encounter, Cara barely registered the incredible artwork as she left. But she noted the floral arrangement was gone when they reached the lobby, and the entry table stood bare.

Claudette handed her a white envelope. "This is the name of our contact, your account number, and the location of the Brooklyn warehouse. They'll take good care of you."

"Thank you," Cara said, grateful, and added the envelope to her overstuffed purse.

"Let me take you downstairs. The driver's waiting."

Stepping into the elevator, Claudette pushed a button located behind the keypad. They descended to an underground parking garage, where a Bentley limousine with tinted windows waited, its back door open.

Cara shook her head, amazed at yet another staggering display of wealth.

She slipped into the plush backseat.

"Best of luck, Miss Collins," Claudette said, giving her a reassuring smile, and shut the car door.

Sighing, Cara allowed a host of unresolved questions to surface. How much of her old life would she have to leave behind? Who wanted to hurt her? What was so special about her? Were her dreams of Kai somehow related to her gift? And the kicker — what the heck was her gift?

Cara promised herself she'd do her part to ensure no one died today. She'd stay put, even if that meant locking herself in an opulent Park Avenue apartment and binge-watching Netflix while devouring chocolate cookie dough ice cream.

First-world problems.

She thought of something else and smiled. There was *one* bright spot that went along with this windfall. Tomorrow, she'd quit her miserable job. A small win, but she'd take it.

Cara's brow was knit in confusion when the car emerged from the garage. They were several blocks from the Watson & Haskins offices. That was intriguing. She felt like a spy without any of the skills.

Her cell phone pinged with a new text message. She fished her phone out of her purse. The text was from Sienna.

What happened with the letter? Did you inherit some money? XOXO

Cara sighed. *Yes, but at what price?* As someone who needed control over her life, Cara felt powerless. Even the decision to quit her job couldn't compensate for the lies she was about to tell.

Cara hesitated for what felt like an eternity before replying, *Nothing big. Boring family stuff. Fill you in Sat nite. Love ya!*

Except for "Love ya," nothing Cara wrote was true. Her whole body slumped. Would her future be filled with an endless stream of half-truths and lies?

Sienna replied, *Really? That's weird. See you Sat! XOXO*

Cara smiled despite the lump in her throat and wiped away a tear.

After ten minutes in traffic, the car entered an underground lot. She checked her inbox and groaned at the 245 work emails. She powered off her phone, unable to deal with reality.

The car stopped in front of an elevator. She jumped when the driver, hidden behind a dark panel, spoke through the intercom. His voice had a soothing, unearthly quality.

"Miss Collins, you can exit here. Your apartment key will get you to the top floor. Insert it into the lock next to the elevator button."

"Thanks." Cara fingered the key, gathered her things, and exited. She tried to glimpse the driver, who wore a black suit and a chauffeur's cap, but the smoky windshield obscured his face. All she could make out was a strong jaw and lips. Nice ones.

Then she turned away, and like a swimmer about to step off a diving board, she took a deep breath and swan-dived into her new life.

Chapter 12

KAI

Forrester Research. San Francisco.

KAI PULLED HIS black Audi A6 into the Forrester Research facility parking lot. The facility, tucked away in a private, one-hundred-acre, tree-filled campus, was located just north of San Francisco. After the fog burned away, the day promised to be unseasonably warm and sunny.

Taking a deep inhale of crisp air, Kai strolled down the landscaped pathway to his lab, housed in an ultramodern building that was designed to blend seamlessly into the landscape. Between the promise of additional discoveries and his removal from Cara's shit list, Kai felt invigorated and hopeful about his research for the first time in months.

He would tackle his next batch of samples this morning. Full results would take a couple of days, but he could wait now that he had a decent shot at isolating the correct protein.

The lab notebook anomaly tickled him like an unwanted itch. Why had that second notebook been separated from the other? The more he thought about it, the more convinced he became that the erratic notations were a clue.

He could be wrong, but what if he wasn't?

Kai slid his badge into the card reader and entered the secured area.

The lobby café buzzed with activity, and the scent of freshly brewed coffee wafted his way. Kai craved a cup. According to the Titanium fitness ring he wore, waking up at 4 a.m. hadn't done his sleep scores any favors. During the pandemic some years ago, Kai had swapped his wedding band for a Finnish device to track his activity and kick his butt into exercising and managing his health. It kept him honest—honest enough to recognize that he needed more sleep and a better handle on work stress.

His doctoral intern, Kristi, already in a lab coat, walked straight toward him, ponytail swishing behind her. Freckles sprinkled across the bridge of her nose made her look about fourteen.

I must be getting old, he thought.

"Mornin', Dr. Solomon! I got your email and started to prepare the materials you requested," she said with a perky Alabama accent. The University of California student worked for him three mornings a week.

He stopped and met her broad smile with one of his own. "Thanks, Kristi."

Giving him a conspiratorial smirk, she leaned close enough to whisper, "Triple W called in sick today."

Kai's smile broadened. The Wicked Witch of the West was their code name for Emily, the Foundation's project manager. He knew he shouldn't encourage Kristi, but sometimes he couldn't resist. They both shared a strong distaste for Emily.

"You just made my day." He winked. "I'll see you in the lab in fifteen."

"See you then!" she said, flouncing off in the opposite direction.

The lure of coffee set him on a course for the café.

Free of Emily's prying eyes for the day, maybe he could make some calls and investigate his notebook hypothesis. A raven-haired beauty in her early thirties, Emily had piercing blue eyes that could simultaneously size you up and cut you down with a glance. She presented a pleasant demeanor on the surface, but Kai glimpsed cold calculation behind her attractive façade. Something about her made his flesh crawl.

Emily had shown up shortly before his colleague's murder. She was assigned to oversee the project and represent The Foundation's interests. That's how Kai's boss positioned it, anyway. But Kai struggled to figure out what she contributed beyond delivering genetic donor material to the lab and making his life a living hell since information only flowed in one direction. Hers.

Despite her impressive credentials, she offered no scientific knowledge or skills to the project and stayed holed up in her office doing God knows what. Yet, she had an uncanny knack for showing up in the lab at critical moments, demanding updates and detailed explanations of the findings.

The highly unusual nature of this arrangement bugged him.

All he could figure was that Forrester must anticipate a lucrative revenue stream at the end of this to accommodate the fifty shades of crazy partnership.

Kai settled behind his desk and pulled up his former colleague's contact info on his cell.

A good two decades older than Kai, Dr. Frank Garrett had mentored Kai when he had started at Forrester. Kai had a lot of respect for the man and a healthy dose of gratitude. A competitor had lured Frank away, but they still met several times a year at conferences and local Meetups.

Kai fielded frequent job inquiries himself. His last published research paper on a rare blood cancer attracted attention and made him a hot recruitment ticket. Initially developed for a strain of liver cancer, the protocol had shown unexpected results in an experimental trial for Leiomyosarcoma, a rare disease that didn't get much funding. Kai's protocol had arrested all instances of the disease, resulting in the test patients living cancer-free. Not much profit for Forrester, but he felt good about saving some lives.

Ah, well. Though Emily annoyed him, he wasn't fed up enough to leave. Yet.

He dialed Frank, hoping to catch him before he disappeared into the lab for the morning. Frank signed a nondisclosure agreement while working on Firefly, but asking some discreet questions couldn't hurt. Anything that might help Kai unravel what was going on here.

Kai got him on the second ring.

"BioLife, Dr. Garrett."

"Hey, Frank. It's Kai. How's it going?"

"Kai! Good to hear from you. What's up?"

Kai leaned back in his chair. "Besides meeting for drinks soon?"

"That may be sooner than you think. The next Biotech MeetUp is in two weeks downtown at the Fairmont Hotel. Better venue than last time. I think the last hotel had day rates. Are you going?"

Kai chuckled. "I forgot about that. Yeah. It'll be great to catch up. In the meantime, do you have a few minutes to talk shop?"

"Sure. What can I do for you?"

Kai hesitated. "Remember the project I couldn't talk about? The one I'm working on?" He rubbed his chin. "It's Project Firefly."

Dead air filled the line.

"Frank? You still there?" Kai wondered if he'd lost the connection until Frank let out a breath.

"Yeah. I'm here. Tragic what happened to Tom. How's it going? The project, I mean." He lowered his voice. "Is the Ice Queen still there?"

Kai snorted. "Yup, she still haunts our halls." Phrasing his next question carefully to avoid directly discussing the project, Kai asked, "How closely did you work with Tom while you were here?"

"Not too close. I only pitched in during my last few months there." Frank took the phone off speaker and said in a low voice, "Listen, I'm not giving away any trade secrets here if I tell you that Firefly was one bizarre project."

Kai gripped the phone tighter. "Bizarre, how?"

"Well, the Ice Queen, for one, and it bothered me that we used a series of undisclosed proteins as donor cells for the splice. I like to know what I'm working with to anticipate potential mutation drivers, but we didn't have that luxury. Funny, I'm calling something a luxury that's a given on any other project. The project made me uneasy. I can't explain it beyond a feeling in my gut."

Everything Frank said resonated with Kai, justifying his conclusions.

Kai rested an elbow on the desk. "Interesting. We're using advanced mammalian cell lines patented by The Foundation as a fixed variable within the testing. I figure the secrecy must be about The Foundation wanting to go to market under their own brand, and maybe throwing us a bone on production, considering the boatload of cash they're paying us. Otherwise, none of this makes sense."

"I don't know. I wish I could tell you more."

Kai tried another angle. "I found something strange in Tom's lab notes. A couple of sections are missing based on the notations. Specifically, a gap in the last three to four weeks before his death." Kai decided to leave out his suspicions that the notes were fabricated.

"*Hmm*...I'm not sure it's related, but something happened."

Kai sat up straighter, and his senses ignited. "What do you mean?"

"Rumor had it that Tom had been working closely with Stanford University on a few projects. According to my sources, his wife's cousin was a respected scientist and prodigy in their Genetics Research program. Longevity, if I'm not mistaken."

"Was? Where are they now?"

"She's dead. Her name was Dr. Sandra Wilson. From what I understand, three weeks before Tom died, her car broke down, and someone murdered her in a dicey section of San Francisco."

Gooseflesh rose on Kai's arms. He remembered the news story. "What makes you suspect a connection?"

"Her death hit him hard. He took a week off after she died. That could explain a partial time gap in the notes."

"How sure are you that they were working together and it wasn't just a coincidence?" Kai asked.

Frank lowered his voice again. "A couple of months before Dr. Wilson's murder, we received a fresh shipment of the cell samples. They were different, but I'm not sure why. Tom ran full genome sequencing on a few of them. When the results came back, something agitated him. Within ten minutes, he headed to the door. I saw him swipe some samples and pack them in a backpack. He stopped at my station and asked me to cover for him with Emily. When I asked, he said he'd found something and wanted to get his consultant at Stanford to take a look. I didn't think anything more about it at the time. Given the nondisclosure agreement, I didn't expect he would tell me anything more. Just throwing it out there. Maybe there's a connection."

Kai's gooseflesh did nothing to recede. Not one, but two people murdered within a few weeks? If they were working together... He shivered. That was no coincidence. "Maybe...Thanks, Frank. I appreciate it," he said, thinking about his next move.

"No problem. Good luck, Kai. I mean it. See you at the Fairmont in a couple of weeks?"

"Sounds good." Kai ended the call and grabbed his portable keyboard to search for Dr. Sandra Wilson. The first result returned a newspaper story on her murder in the *San Francisco Chronicle*. Kai clicked on the link.

The esteemed Dr. Sandra Wilson, thirty-five years old, was murdered on Saturday morning in the Lower Haight district of San Francisco, not far from her home in Haight-Ashbury. Her time of death was around 1:45 a.m. All indications show that her attacker killed her while she attempted to flee.

The attack did not appear to involve rape or robbery. However, the police are not releasing information about the weapon used in the attack. The autopsy revealed the cause of death as massive internal hemorrhaging sustained from her injuries. Colleagues, friends, and family are perplexed about the motive.

The funeral will be held this Tuesday at 9:00 a.m. at St. Agnes in Haight-Ashbury.

Kai reviewed the following few pages of search results. She had several published articles written about her work. Considered a prodigy, Dr. Wilson graduated from Stanford with a Ph.D. at twenty-three years old. At thirty-one, she had already published a few impressive papers on genomics regarding aging and longevity.

Kai texted Kristi in the lab and let her know about the change of plans. Kai freed his calendar of meetings until early afternoon. He planned to take a field trip to Stanford and conduct a little research of his own.

But before Kai left, he had to send Cara the card he promised, or he'd be back in the doghouse.

She loved to read, so he pulled up Amazon and chose a $25 animated gift card with a spinning birthday cake and lit candles. He typed in a note: "Hey, sorry I missed your birthday. Enjoy a few good reads on me." He signed it, "Love, Kai," and hit Send.

As he prepared to shut down his laptop, he debated whether to give Cara a heads-up on what he had learned from Frank. What Frank told him could be connected to the dream Cara had that saved his life.

The weight of Tom's death still rode hard on his shoulders. He would've done more if he had thought someone else would've gotten hurt in his place. Much more.

Releasing a deep sigh, he decided not to tell Cara until he knew more. He was freaked out enough for both of them. He didn't need to take her down with him.

Chapter 13

KAI

Stanford University. Palo Alto.

KAI PARKED NEAR Stanford University's School of Medicine, which contained more than one genetics lab. Dr. Sandra Wilson's biography listed her most recent position as Head of Anti-Aging and Longevity Research, giving Kai a start. According to the online directory, Dr. Philipp Granger had taken over after her death. Even if Dr. Granger wasn't in his office, a lab manager or assistant should be on duty.

Kai followed signs to the Alway Building, moving with the flow of students and faculty. He blended in without his Forrester lab coat, looking more like a student than faculty in his jeans, polo shirt, and sneakers. He tipped his head toward the sun and let the rays warm his face. Being on campus had him yearning for his MIT graduate days when life was less complicated and ripe with possibilities that included Cara.

He thought of the kiss. So right, yet so wrong. He couldn't be with Cara, yet he couldn't let her go. Agnostic by choice, he didn't believe in destiny or the divine. He believed in science. Yet he had no words for the unexplainable, invisible thread that bound them together in a connection that snapped back like an elastic band when stretched to its limits, drawing them together and filling the ache in his chest when she wandered too far.

The weekly phone calls kept her on the comfortable fringes of his life without interfering with his marriage. But that kiss? It crossed the line, and he knew it.

Whatever he planned to say to Cara in the dream eluded him, but he sensed its vital importance. It made him crazy that he couldn't remember, a phenomenon he had never experienced while awake.

His photographic memory allowed him to recall everything he had ever experienced in the finest detail, including every word he read. This rare skill has served him well in most areas of his life. Except for the memories he wished he could forget. Unlike most people, his memories never lost focus or their torturous details, no matter how much time passed.

Every gift exacted a price. His gift subjected him to reliving bad memories with excruciating clarity, hindering him from moving on — like the night in college when his roommate Jordy, wearing a smug, almost gleeful sneer, told him Cara had cheated on him.

Every moment of that conversation etched into Kai's memory: the scent of Jordy's beer breath, the upturned collar of his royal blue Ralph Lauren polo shirt, an erratic drip from the kitchen faucet, an open copy of Harper's Illustrated Biochemistry textbook on the desk, and every cruel microexpression on Jordy's fucking face as he swore he'd seen Cara kissing some guy at an Alpha Delta Sigma frat party and then follow him upstairs. The feeling of choking on acid at Cara's betrayal and having his heart ripped to shreds rushed back with every recall, along with everything that happened afterward.

Of course, Cara denied it. Deep in his soul, he believed her, even then, but he'd let Jordy's claim cast doubt in his mind and shatter his trust in her. Maybe because he thought he never deserved her in the first place, or she'd leave him like his father.

He glanced at the silver ring on his right hand, the only solid proof that he even had a father. It gave him hope that the man cared about him at least a little. Cara had always liked the ring; sometimes, he associated it more with her than the man who had supposedly left it for him.

The part of him that believed Cara hadn't betrayed him made their friendship possible. Before he got married, when he could quiet his mind, he had let desire and the love he had for her slip through. But Jordy's words always resurged…until, one day, they didn't.

During Kai's last trip to see Cara, they'd spent the weekend in bed. Afterwards, he finally put his doubts to rest and decided to join Cara in New York after he graduated. But before he could share the news, Melanie, with whom he'd recently broken up, announced she was pregnant, ending his chances for a life with Cara.

In exchange, he had a happy enough marriage with a woman he cared about and a precious child he loved more than life itself. He wouldn't change having Sara for anything, even Cara. As much as it pained him, he accepted that a future with Cara was off the table, which made that unforgettable kiss even more unsettling.

Kai took a deep breath and pushed open a glass door into the building. He wasn't sure what he hoped to find beyond a linkage between Dr. Sandra Wilson, Tom, and Project Firefly.

He rode the elevator up to the Longevity lab. An attractive girl with brown hair drawn into a ponytail sat behind the desk, absorbed in a large textbook and typing notes on a tablet.

"Hi," Kai said, leaning an elbow casually on the counter.

The girl's gaze flashed up, and she let out a startled gasp. A hand flew to her chest, and she removed an earbud. "Oh, my God," she laughed nervously, "I didn't see you standing there."

He raised his hands in a non-threatening manner and smiled warmly. "Sorry, I didn't mean to scare you. I'm looking for Dr. Granger. Is he in?"

She glanced at the wall clock behind her. "Dr. Grainger is teaching a class, but he should be back at eleven."

Kai had no desire to wait another hour. He leaned in. "Is there anyone here who worked with Dr. Sandra Wilson?"

Surprise flickered in her eyes. "Yeah...," she drew the word out, tapping her lip, "Calvin. He used to work with her. Let me check if he's available." She set down the tablet and paused as she reached the door. "Who should I say wants to speak with him?"

"Dr. Kai Solomon."

She nodded and disappeared into the lab.

A few minutes later, she reappeared with a tall, lanky guy wearing a white lab coat and funky black glasses that complemented his spiky, black hair.

"Dr. Solomon? Calvin Wright," he said, extending a hand as he approached. "Wendy mentioned you had questions about Dr. Wilson." He inclined his head toward the lab door. "We can talk in my office."

"Thanks," Kai said, following Calvin to a small office inside the lab. Stacks of paper and volumes of scientific books filled the shelves and littered the floor.

"Sorry for the mess. Have a seat." Calvin swept a hand toward a guest chair and sat behind the desk. Kai noted the Chinese characters tattooed on Calvin's neck, peeking up from his collar, and a sleeve of colorful waves that reached his wrist from his coat. "What can I do for you, Dr. Solomon?"

Kai tented his fingertips. "This may be a long shot, but I'm working on a genetics project for Forrester Research Labs. I believe Dr. Wilson consulted on the project for my predecessor, Dr. Tom Peyton."

Calvin sat up straighter, and the color drained from his already pale face. His gaze froze on Kai for a few beats, and he stared blankly, his eyes unfocused, as if he were in a trance.

Kai frowned and suppressed the urge to snap his fingers.

Then Calvin's expression changed, and he regained focus. "Oh! You work at Forrester. We've partnered with them on projects, but all before my time. Sorry, I'm not sure I can help." The rigidity of Calvin's posture and his flat tone sent a shiver along Kai's spine.

Kai shifted in his seat and backpedaled. "Hey, I didn't mean to barge in asking uncomfortable questions. I'm trying to understand some of the findings, and I believe Dr. Wilson may have been involved in the project. Any chance you ever met Dr. Peyton?"

Calvin rolled his shoulders and caught Kai's gaze. "Nope. Never met him." His stare intensified, and he drew his gaze slowly to the ceiling. Kai looked up at the white tiles, but saw only air conditioning ducts.

Unless…Holy shit, was the room bugged?

Kai returned Calvin's stare, who gave Kai an almost imperceptible head shake as he wrote on the back of a business card and said, "Sorry, I wasn't able to help."

Calvin stood and shook Kai's hand, pressing the card into Kai's palm. Kai surreptitiously slid it into his pocket and came to an unwanted conclusion—someone was watching, or at the very least, listening.

Kai played along. "Thanks, anyway. Is there anyone else that I can talk to? Did Dr. Wilson have any other lab assistants? Maybe Dr. Granger would know?"

Calvin caught Kai's eye and winked, acknowledging Kai following his lead. "Not possible. If there were a Forrester project, I would've known about it. Everyone who worked here would have. We post our projects online, with all findings shared on a weekly basis. We never had a project with Forrester during my tenure."

"Dead end, I guess. Sorry to bother you."

"No problem. Let me walk you out."

Kai followed Calvin in silence.

"Good luck, Dr. Solomon." Calvin shook Kai's hand and returned to the lab without looking back.

Once safely inside his car, Kai extracted the business card from his pocket and flipped it over.

Califon Café. Tomorrow, 6 p.m.

Kai's pulse quickened. Maybe he was right after all. He shifted into reverse. Pain hit like a sledgehammer to the skull, raising the hairs on the back of Kai's neck. He jammed his foot on the brake, clutching his head between both palms. *Holy Hell.*

He rubbed a temple and caught sight of an amorphous black haze in his rearview mirror, roughly the size and shape of—he blinked, not believing his eyes—a seven-foot creature with horns?

Seconds later, the pain and the inky black haze vanished, leaving gooseflesh in their wake.

Kai shuddered. *What in the hell was that?*

Chapter 14

CARA

Fifth Avenue Penthouse. New York City.

HOURS INTO AN HGTV marathon with Chloe, Cara had learned how to renovate a bathroom and design a garden, but still hadn't discovered why she was trapped inside a multimillion-dollar piece of real estate. She let out her umpteenth sigh and glanced at her canine companion, who slept beside her with Sienna's stuffed squirrel clamped beneath her neck.

Cara had explored every inch of the opulent Park Avenue penthouse with her inquisitive canine before collapsing onto the hard-as-a-rock midcentury modern leather couch (which had to go, thank you very much!) to immerse herself in DIY renovations. None of which she'd ever need.

HGTV couldn't hold a candle to this place.

Although the prewar penthouse shared the top floor with another apartment, there was still enough space to accommodate a foyer, four bedrooms, three bathrooms, and a library, in addition to a living room, kitchen, dining room, and a terrace. Renovated with modern amenities, the apartment mixed old-world charm with current touches. Cara tipped her hat to the decorator who used the fireplaces, twelve-foot ceilings, plaster crown moldings, crystal chandeliers, and artwork to their best advantage, creating fresh and appealing décor without it feeling heavy or dated.

The place was nothing short of stunning. Though Cara loved the kitchen best.

She had salivated like one of Pavlov's dogs while soaking in the massive space, filled with cherry wood floors, white maple cabinets, sleek granite countertops, a center island with seating for six, and, hello, an enormous Viking range and a built-in Sub-Zero fridge. Not to mention, a beverage bar with a wine refrigerator, a fancy Italian espresso maker, and a feeding station for Chloe. Who needed renovation tips when you had a kitchen from *Architectural Digest*?

Although Cara despised cooking, she lusted after kitchens like Sienna lusted after hot men. The only thing better than her new kitchen would be a hot chef to make good use of her oven. *Pun intended.*

Cara considered living in the kitchen until she found her and Chloe's things in the main bedroom's walk-in closet. *Holy cannoli.* Sienna would weep. The dedicated wardrobe space was larger than Sienna's West Village bedroom, filled with lit racks, built-in cabinets, and an entire wall of shoe cubbies.

But the icing on this real estate cake was the terrace, separated by a wall of floor-to-ceiling doors, that spanned the length of the building and overlooked Central Park. Waist-level potted boxwoods lined the transparent Plexiglas, giving enough privacy when sitting on the lounge chairs while providing an unobscured view when standing. Over the treetops, Cara could see the Conservatory Water and the Angel of the Waters atop Bethesda Fountain farther west.

Cara had to pinch herself a few times throughout the day, feeling like a trespasser in someone else's home.

Now, after hours of waiting, Cara fidgeted in front of the television, about to reach the end of her tether when the doorbell chimed.

Jolting off the sofa with Chloe, Cara wondered why the doorman hadn't given her a heads-up. Standard protocol required ringing the residents before sending guests. At least according to the notes Cara found in a pink folder on the foyer table beside a three-foot *faux* floral arrangement and an apology card from Claudette.

Cara's bare feet whispered across the marble floor, along with Chloe's nails tapping a nimble trot beside her. Cara peered through the peephole and did a double-take through the fish-eye lens.

Holy Moly.

Staring at the door was a guy in his twenties who looked like he had taken a wrong turn on his way to a *GQ* photo shoot. He was tall with expertly tousled black hair, a heart-shaped face, high cheekbones, and a sexy cleft chin. Clean-cut yet hip, he wore a white collared shirt open at the neck, a brown leather jacket, and jeans. The stranger reminded her of a male version of Sienna with the same glossy polish.

Was *this* who they sent?

Glancing at her T-shirt and yoga pants, she regretted her lack of forethought. There wasn't much she could do except slip the elastic from her ponytail and let her hair cascade around her shoulders, hoping she didn't look like a *shlub*, to use one of Sienna's favorite Yiddishisms.

Erring on the side of caution, she cracked open the door and peeked through. "May I help you?"

"Cara Collins?" he asked, flashing an easy smile.

"Yes?"

"I'm Michael Swift." When she continued to stare, making no move to invite him in, he cocked a brow and added, "Your grandmother's letter…that's why I'm here."

Her shoulders relaxed, though she had expected someone older, like Mr. Gladstone.

Wearing a sheepish grin, he pointed past her. "May I come in?"

Cara blinked and shook herself. "Of course," She opened the door wider and stepped aside. "Sorry, I didn't expect someone…my age."

An amused look crossed his face. "Hope you're not disappointed."

She chuckled nervously. "No. You're fine. It's just been a long day."

"I'm sure it has," Michael said and extended a hand. He met her gaze with intense, royal-blue eyes flecked with steel gray. "It's nice to meet you, Cara. This must be a little overwhelming." *Understatement.* He gave a reassuring smile, revealing a small dimple. "I'm here to help."

Cara's brows furrowed as she shook his hand. Something about his smile was vaguely familiar, but she couldn't place why.

Chloe interrupted with a whine. Impatient for her turn, she greeted Michael with a flying face lick and wagged her tail so vigorously her entire backside moved.

"Who's this?" Michael cooed, bending down to pet Chloe, who wasn't done dispensing kisses. Her tongue darted over Michael's lips, which he wisely pressed shut. Her dog's exuberance surprised Cara. Chloe usually saved her five-star greetings for her favorite people, like Cara's dad and her aunt Senny, though Sienna had a strict no-face-licking policy.

Cara winced when the glow from the crystal chandelier revealed dog slobber sheening Michael's face. She grabbed her overzealous hound's collar, prying her from their guest. "Chloe, off!" Then said to Michael, "I'm so sorry, but she'd give you an entire bath if you let her."

Michael gave Chloe a final scratch and rose. "No worries. She's really sweet." He chuckled and wiped his lips with the back of a hand.

"More like a flirty teenager in a dog suit, but seriously, she knows better." Cara threw a stink-eye at Chloe, who sat daintily, one paw in the air, and stared at Cara with a "what did I do?" look of innocence.

Michael chuckled and slipped off his jacket. "It's all good."

Cara pointed to the foyer closet, still in awe of having a dedicated space for outerwear. "May I hang that for you?" He handed her the buttery brown leather. She detected a hint of spicy cologne as she hung the jacket.

Closing the door, Cara said, "Let's chat in the living room," and led the way as Chloe darted ahead.

Michael rolled his shirt sleeves as they walked, revealing muscled forearms and biceps that strained against the taut white fabric. Without the jacket, Cara noticed his shoulders were broader than she expected, tapering to a lean waist. He was in excellent shape, but it was the sight of a Patek Philippe on his wrist that drew her attention. The watch cost as much as a car, which she knew only because of Sienna. She wondered if Michael had also inherited money, though now wasn't the time to ask.

When they reached the living room, Cara asked, "May I get you something — water, soda, a glass of wine?" *A dose of sanity?*

"I'll take water, thanks." He sat on one of the facing leather sofas, a low glass-and-chrome coffee table separating them.

"And a towel?" she offered.

He stared at her blankly.

She circled a finger. "For your face."

He smiled and passed the back of a wrist over a cheek. "That would be great."

Chloe jumped onto the sofa with the grace of a gazelle and settled beside Michael, nuzzling her head into his lap. Michael didn't seem to mind. He stretched an arm along the back of the sofa and petted Chloe with his free hand. His movements were relaxed and graceful, like Chloe's.

Cara smiled wryly. "She likes you. It means you're a good soul. She knows."

Michael glanced at Chloe. They locked gazes, and a look of surprise sparked in his eyes. "She's a good soul, too," he whispered, stroking her neck. Chloe licked his forearm and stared at him with adoration.

Cara sniffed a laugh. "I think you made a friend for life," she said, and headed to her dreamy kitchen, returning a few minutes later with a tray that held a bottle of water, a glass, and a hot washcloth rolled and placed on a small plate, just like in Japanese restaurants. She put the tray on the coffee table and sat on the sofa opposite Michael, tucking her legs beneath her on the stiff leather. Cara had already booked the Brooklyn warehouse to swap the midcentury monstrosities for her comfy sofa and two chairs downtown. She couldn't wait.

Michael grabbed the washcloth with a grateful glance, wiped his face and hands, and discarded the cloth onto the plate.

Cara got down to business. "You mentioned my grandmother, but weren't you still a toddler when she died? You can't be more than...." Waving a hand, she lifted a brow, encouraging him to fill in the blank.

Huffing a laugh. "Twenty-six." *Huh.* She was older. Michael continued, "Your grandmother didn't choose me by name. Only that they would send a Messenger, like me," he said, sipping his water directly from the bottle.

Well, that didn't tell her much. Cara crossed her arms. "OK. Now that you're here, can you explain the most bizarre thirty-six hours of my life?"

Michael's gaze softened, though he held a wary reserve. "Some. Yes."

Better than none. Cara fanned an arm like Vanna White on *Wheel of Fortune*. "Why am I in this gilded prison?"

The side of his mouth quirked with mild amusement. "Before we unpack this party box, can I give the short answer? Then we can get to the more complicated one."

"Fine. Since you asked so nicely," Cara conceded begrudgingly.

"You're safer here," he said simply.

Gladstone had already said as much. She sighed. "Safer from what?"

He shifted forward, leaning his elbows on his thighs. "To set expectations, this conversation will probably take a few hours. There's a lot you need to know…to prepare. Tonight is only an appetizer on a three-course menu."

Her heartbeat quickened. "Prepare for what?" What did she have to *do* beyond keeping the inheritance a secret? She should've known there was a catch.

Dark eyebrows furrowing, Michael's stare intensified. "I know this must seem incredibly surreal, and I apologize," he said, his voice soft and soothing, "But I can't stress the magnitude of what's coming."

A chill traversed her spine. "You're scaring me."

Michael relaxed his expression, an easy smile tugging at his lips. "Sorry, my dad says I need to lighten up. I don't want to scare you." He rubbed his chin contemplatively and abruptly shifted topics. "How do you feel about pizza?"

"*Feel?* I have a very positive relationship with pizza. I especially like to eat it," she joked to diffuse her unease.

"My treat," he volunteered. "I didn't have a chance to eat after work, and this promises to be a long discussion. I'd rather not do it on an empty stomach."

She shrugged. Fine. She could roll with that. "Pizza it is. Since I'm new to this *posh* part of town," she said with a highbrow accent. "I'll have to ask the doorman for a recommendation."

He laughed softly, stretched, and laced his fingers behind his head. "Sounds good."

Now comes the true test, Cara thought. "What do you like on your pie? We can do half-and-half if you're a meat-lover's heart-attack-on-a-plate type." Cara asked, suspecting he wasn't.

"How's mushroom?" he asked, naming her favorite with an amused twist of his lips like he'd scored the answer key to a final exam.

Cara narrowed her eyes. "I like you already."

She headed to the kitchen intercom. Not only did the doorman have a bead on good brick-oven pizza, but he also informed her that she had a line of credit for takeout deliveries.

She returned to the living room. "Pizza in thirty minutes. It looks like I'll be treating you. I have a *house account* for ordering in." Snorting a disbelieving laugh, she returned to the sofa.

His lips quirked into another amused smile. "Enjoy the perks."

She shook her head, glancing around. "What do you know about this place and my inheritance?"

He followed her gaze around the living room, pursed his lips, and shook his head. "Not much. As for the inheritance, only that you'll need it someday."

Wow. Way to be vague.

Losing patience, Cara blew out a breath and said sternly, "Listen, Michael, you're obviously here to fill me in. Let's start with why someone could *die* if I tell them about the inheritance."

At the word *die*, Chloe's head popped up. Then, she rested her chin on Michael's leg and directed her soulful gaze to Cara as if joining the conversation.

Michael hesitated and studied his hands.

Cara suppressed an eye roll, folded her arms, and waited. They'd be here *all freaking night* at this rate. She studied Michael's strikingly handsome face as he mulled over an answer. High cheekbones were his next best feature, after his eyes, in a face with no bad features. He even had Sienna's skin tone. They would make an incredibly attractive couple.

They would make healthy babies.

Cara almost fell out of her chair when the voice whispered through her mind. Michael's gaze lifted to hers.

"Did you hear that?" she asked, startled by both the phrasing and delivery. *Healthy* babies? Cara would've chosen *adorable*.

Though Michael gave her a questioning stare, his cheeks brightened. "Sorry, hear what?"

Cara squinted. If he hadn't heard the voice, why was he blushing? Regardless, she had more pressing issues than hearing voices. "Never mind." Cara repeated her question, "Why could someone die?"

Michael passed a hand through his tousled hair and heaved a sigh. "I can't tell you specifically *why* someone could die. But after what you'll learn in the next few days, you'll have the answer to your question."

That didn't bode well. Cara chewed the inside of her cheek and moved on to her next question. "Earlier, you said you're a Messenger. It sounded specific, like a job title rather than someone delivering a message."

Michael leaned toward her and steepled his hands. "If I promise to answer your questions, will you let me unpack this story in a digestible way?" Something about the rich timbre of his voice made her feel safe.

Cara desperately wanted to trust him. She needed to trust *someone,* didn't she? Hoping she wouldn't regret her decision, she bit her lip and nodded.

The tension in the room eased, and they both relaxed into their respective sofas. "I promise to make this as simple as I can," Michael said, petting Chloe in long strokes, her eyes dipping shut at the start of every stroke. "Let me start with a question: Have you ever met someone and had an instant connection? Like you'd known them forever?"

Kai. Of course. "Yes. Why?"

"Many people get that feeling, but it means something more powerful for you. It means you have a meaningful connection that tethers you at the soul level."

Her gaze dipped to her manicure. "If you believe in that stuff."

"Do *you* believe in that stuff, Cara?" he asked, sounding a bit judgmental for the first time.

Her gaze snapped up; the question and his tone hit a deep-seated hot button around faith and religion, a button her mother loved to push. She tried not to sound defensive, and really hoped he wasn't from some crazy religious cult. "I do. I believe in God, the power of love, and that the soul survives after death, but I'm not *religious,*" she said with air quotes. "My faith doesn't need someplace to go on Sundays."

As for instant connections, besides Kai, Tyler was the one other person with whom she felt an immediate connection. He had been her rebound relationship the year Kai married Melanie. But she severed their bond and banished him when he betrayed her. So, yeah, she'd experienced that known-you-forever feeling twice. She almost felt it now with Michael, but in a brotherly way.

Michael's voice softened. "You've had that connection twice in the past, right?"

She reared back as a tingling sensation traversed her scalp. "How did you know that?" she snapped, unnerved, feeling like his gaze could pierce flesh and bone to her soul.

He shook his head. "Not important. Tell me about them?"

Not important? Was he kidding? She regretted promising that she'd let him go at his own pace. She let out a frustrated sigh. "One is my friend Kai. We met in college. The other, Tyler, was after," she hesitated, his name bitter on her tongue, "We lost touch, and I plan to keep it that way." The last thing she wanted to do was discuss Tyler with him or anyone. She hated to think they had a soul connection.

Michael didn't press. Instead, he gave her a brief, empathic nod. "Any strange occurrences involving either of those two relationships?"

Cara's brow furrowed, and she threw it out there. "I have dreams...You know, the premonitory kind."

Michael tapped his fingertips together. "Makes sense. Your full abilities are like an iceberg. Only the tip is visible above the surface of your consciousness. Everyone can use intuition, but some people, like you, were given more. During training, you'll unlock the full potential of your gifts, including the ability to heal others."

"Heal others?" Her mouth went dry, and she blurted, "An old woman...she stopped me on the street yesterday. I touched her and made her *younger*."

Michael swiped a hand over his chin and mumbled, "That was unexpected."

Cara's brows shot to her hairline. "*You knew?*"

He nodded. Worry lines etched between his eyes. "We've been following you since early yesterday morning." Elbows resting on thighs, Michael leaned closer. "You're safe for now. But that's the reason we took extra precautions and moved you here."

Cara wanted to snarl in frustration at the nameless, faceless entity. "Who the hell is 'we'?" She wrapped her arms around her drawn-up legs to ground herself.

"I'm one of those people. The first person of several who will enter your life...If you'll have us," Michael said softly.

Cara squinted. "What do you mean, *if* I'll have you?"

"These gifts, both your abilities and the inheritance, come with responsibilities and obligations. But you can still turn it all down."

She studied him warily. "You mean I can say no and give it all back?"

He shrugged and tented his hands. "Ideally, you could live your life as it was before. But given what's already happened, it might be too late."

Hairs rose on her arms. "Too late for what? Will someone die if I refuse?"

Michael dipped his head, averting his gaze. "Hasn't someone died already?"

Cara's stomach lurched. "What do you mean?"

When Michael looked up, his expression was pained. "You saved one but sacrificed another. Didn't you?"

The breath left Cara's lungs at the accusation. The dream. He knew about Dr. Peyton. But how? Tears sprang to her eyes. "I didn't know that man would die in Kai's place." *Next time, it could be Kai,* she thought with horror.

Michael moved around the table to sit beside her. He took her hands in his. They were warm and strong as he held her tightly. His voice softened. "All I'm saying is that both paths are perilous. I'm here to help."

"Do I have to choose right this second?" she asked, gently pulling from his grasp and brushing away a tear. What choice did she really have if both paths put her and those she loved in danger?

He gave her space but stayed close. "You have time. You'll receive a formal Calling. That's when you'll make your final decision."

She had so many questions. "You said there are others. Who else will I meet?" she asked, grabbing the square pillow beside her and clutching it to her stomach.

Michael said, "Two more in the immediate future. One is your mentor. She'll be responsible for your training and explaining exactly what all of this means. The other, Chamuel, is your assigned Guardian. His job is to protect you."

Another bolt of fear shot through her. "Protect me from what?"

Michael sighed. "This will sound cheesy and cliché, but dark forces are interested in thwarting your success."

Her eyebrows drew together. "Success? What kind of success? Making a 10% return on my client portfolio?" She tossed aside the pillow. "You realize that's my only marketable skill, right? I'm a freaking investment banker!"

Michael took a patient breath and shook his head. "You're much more than that." He pointed to the center of his chest. "In here."

She liked it better when he sat across the room. Either way, she needed distance. She chewed a nail and stood to pace. "Keep going."

"Chamuel and I have been assigned to you. Together, the three of us make up what's called a Trinity, which is formed to fulfill a covenant."

Growing up, she paid enough attention to Sunday school to understand that a covenant is an agreement with contractual strength. "Whose covenant?" she fired back.

"Yours."

She stopped dead and glared at him. "What?"

Michael said, "Those connections we talked about earlier? They were to illustrate a point. Before your birth, you tied yourself to another soul through a promise. Now, you're both attached to an event that could tip the balance between good and evil. You're the connection point to the person at the mission's core—the Center Stone—and the event. You're a Soul Seeker, and I'm your assigned Messenger. My job is to provide the communication bridge between our Trinity and those guiding us."

Cara's skin tingled, and a wave of dizziness crashed over her, along with an odd yet familiar sweetness on her tongue. She leaned on the back of the couch across from Michael to steady herself. "Are Kai and Tyler involved? Are they a part of this?"

Michael shrugged. "I honestly don't know."

"Can I tell Kai?"

Michael shook his head vigorously, his tone brokering no dissent. "No. Not unless we find out later that he's a part of this. You'll only jeopardize his safety if you tell him."

Still clutching the sofa, she let the sick feeling in her stomach settle and the dizziness pass. "That's a lot to take in," she whispered.

He rose, rounded the living room to reach her, and settled a hand on her shoulder. "I'm sorry. I know."

"I need some air." She slipped away, headed to the glass doors leading to the terrace, and slid one open. She had no coat, but the bracing night air felt good.

She walked to the edge of the terrace between two potted boxwoods, rested her elbows on the Plexiglas barrier, and inhaled deeply. Michael sidled up beside her. Their elbows lightly touched, reminding her she wasn't alone.

Whoever was at the heart of this had sent the right person to deliver this message. Michael's prescience was unnerving, but his demeanor and physical presence were unnaturally soothing. She easily imagined the "don't shoot the messenger" aphorism playing out poorly if "they" made the wrong choice.

She gazed out at the city's twinkling lights and Central Park. "When is this mission coming? Do we know what the event is? Or if I've already met the person tied to me?"

"The only thing we know is that the event *is* coming. Your Center Stone will be revealed after you accept your Calling. In the meantime, we must prepare you with training that awakens your abilities to maximize our success."

Cara nodded, her forehead crinkling. "When will I meet my Guardian, Chamuel?" That she needed a bodyguard was unsettling, but having someone watch over her was comforting.

What a difference a couple of days made.

He shrugged. "That depends on when you are Called. Guardians prefer to stay out of sight for security purposes until after the Calling is accepted. You may not see him, but that doesn't mean he isn't there."

"Okay." She relaxed a little. "Is this your first Messenger assignment?"

"Yup. I was contacted a little over a month ago. It's only been a couple of weeks since I finished training, so I guess I'm new to this, too." He gave her a bashful grin, lit in the shadows by the Penthouse's interior glow.

She was relieved she wasn't the only newbie. Since they'd be spending more time together, she might as well get to know him. "What do you do in real life, Michael?"

He instantly brightened, which made him look younger than he had all evening. "I own a martial arts studio in Brooklyn."

A real job like a normal person, which also explained why he was in good shape and moved with such grace. At least he could defend himself.

"So, you're an investment banker?"

She cocked an eyebrow and snorted. "But you already knew that, didn't you?" she said, suspecting he knew a lot more than that.

He answered with a cryptic smile and a noncommittal shrug, then reached down to pet Chloe, who appeared at his side.

Cara eyed them together. "She *really* likes you."

He chuckled softly and said almost sadly, "Sometimes I think I'm better with animals than people." His unexpected vulnerability caught her off guard and snuck past Cara's defenses. Then, she stupidly remembered this wasn't all about her. She wasn't alone in this. Michael's involvement wasn't without personal risk.

"Were you given a choice?" she whispered.

His gaze twinkled in the darkness, reflecting the city lights. "Yes, but there's no way I would've refused," he said.

Cara's curiosity flared. "Did you get a letter from a dead grandparent, too?"

He swallowed hard and hesitated as if weighing his words before he spoke, "Not exactly... My father asked me."

"You're lucky," Cara said, her gaze snagging on the lit Angel of the Waters Fountain over the trees. The statue's extended wings, set off against a midnight-blue sky, gave an otherworldly glow that invited refuge. "It would've saved a lot of angst if my grandmother had been alive to tell me in person."

"Cara" — Michael clasped her arm gently, pulling her gaze to his — "my father died six months ago."

Cara gasped. *Holy crap, he can see dead people.*

Chapter 15

CARA

Cabot Investments. New York City.

CARA ROLLED INTO Cabot Investments with a letter of resignation tucked inside her purse. The office was already alive and buzzing with activity. As tempting as it had been to call in sick for a second day in a row, that would only delay the inevitable.

One unexpected benefit of her trip to see Gladstone, it cured her addiction to answering work messages 24/7 and reset her priorities. Talk about seeing life through a whole new lens.

But before she made a grand exit from Cabot Investments, she needed a coffee refill to clear the cobwebs. Michael hadn't left until one in the morning. Kudos to him for handling her gazillion questions and sharing what he could. Then again, as a Messenger, wasn't delivering news part of his job description? Admittedly, the whole Trinity, fate, good and evil thing still boggled her mind.

Over pizza, she'd discovered Michael couldn't see *all* dead people, just his father, and he'd only seen him once. Other than that, Michael wasn't forthcoming about his gifts. But he opened up about his life. She discovered Michael grew up in Chicago, where his mom and sister still live. He studied martial arts from a young age and, with his father's help, fulfilled his dream of opening a dojo. They had been very close, and Michael still grieved his death. Her heart ached for Michael's loss. Cara couldn't imagine losing her warm, jovial dad.

By the end of the evening, she saw much more than a pretty face and a potential match for Sienna. Michael was smart, had a genuine warmth and maturity, and possessed a self-deprecating wit. She really liked him, not in a romantic way, but like a dear friend. He was solid and exactly what she needed at the moment. Cara hoped she could return the favor.

Cara dropped her briefcase beside her desk and spotted a sticky note from Rick on her computer monitor.

Meet me in my office when you arrive. Rick.

So much for that coffee refill.

Cara hung her red swing coat on the back of the door and headed down the hall to Rick's office. He waved through the glass, motioning her inside.

She closed the door behind her and took a seat as dread and distaste roiled in her gut.

Only a few years older, Rick was a condescending prick who apparently never got the memo on sexual harassment or hostile workplace environments. He was an active member of Cabot's good-old-boy network filled with wealthy, entitled Ivy League fraternity brothers who treated women as potential conquests. But not her. She'd made that clear, making him more passive-aggressive and condescending. If Bob hadn't died last year, she wouldn't be sitting in front of this horse's ass (no disrespect to horses).

Rick wore his insincerity like a fashion accessory, pursing his lips with mock concern. "Poor baby, so sorry you were sick. How are you feeling?"

"Fine," she replied tightly and gripped the chair arms in place of his neck. "What's on your mind?"

He clasped his hands and wore his patronizing face, a sure sign he planned to mansplain something. "As you know," he started slowly, "We've been up against some hard economic times, and we need to make some cuts across the *junior* leadership team. I'm sorry, Cara darling, but we're eliminating your role." He did his sad face with pouty lips, and, as if doing her a favor, he tacked on, "Of course, given your tenure, you're entitled to a severance package and a prorated bonus."

Had he delivered this news on Tuesday, she would've been upset. That said, she still wanted to throat-punch him, though she had something better in store that wouldn't end in an assault charge.

She cocked her head with a jaunty tilt. "That's *fascinating*, Rick. Was anyone else eliminated? Any *men*? Given my performance record, I'm surprised you chose me. Care to elaborate?" She pasted on a smile, giving him an innocent green-eyed stare. For fun, she batted her eyelashes.

Twice.

Rick's head jerked, and he dared to look affronted. "Uh, I don't believe that should be part of this discussion," he said, fingering the folder in front of him. Beneath the shiny exterior, Cara recognized Rick for what he was — a total coward.

Her brows knit in contemplation. "You know what's really interesting, Rick?" she asked and shook a finger. "Including me, you've single-handedly eliminated every woman and person of color at the leadership level within this firm. I'm not a lawyer, but I'm sure an employment attorney would love to chew on that for a while, given the last five people downsized. Smells like a class-action suit to me. Just sayin'..." *You misogynistic, racist prick.*

His gaze held disdain. "Good luck proving that was more than a coincidence," he said with an oily smile.

Rick had openly joked about his culpability in firing her former colleagues at the office Christmas party and stupidly never thought he'd be called out—or that Cara had the opportunity or cojones to record him on her phone. *Legally*, thanks to New York's "one-party consent" law.

Idiot.

Cara saved the recording in her personal cloud account in case she ever needed it. A self-satisfied smile crossed her lips. "Well, lucky I have evidence proving the moves were unwarranted and intentional." She leaned closer. "You really shouldn't drink so much at office parties, Rick. It loosens your tongue."

He straightened in his chair and paled. His voice shook and rose an octave when he spoke, "What do you want?"

Rick may be related to the CEO and part of the Cabot Boys' Club, but the firm wouldn't survive any negative press or legal action, especially after last year's scandal that cost almost one-third of its clients.

She leaned an elbow on his desk and winked. "I'd have documents on my desk to sign within the hour that include benefits for one year, vesting and payment of all options upon my exit, a *full* bonus, and acknowledgment of today as my last day as part of a paid sixty-day notice period. Are we on the same page?" She finished with a saccharine smile that didn't reach her eyes and then leaned back in her chair and waited.

Her mercenary move wouldn't cost her a moment's sleep, the proceeds of which she would split between Whippet Rescue and the Humane Society. God knows, after yesterday, the animals needed the money more than her.

Rick shuffled the paper on his desk and stammered, "W-well, can you give me until eleven?"

She examined her nails and pursed her lips, Rick-style. "You got it, Rick," she said, lingering on the k and mimicking the usual swagger in his tone. *See you never, douche nozzle.*

Severance package in hand, Cara left the building, closing the chapter on Cabot Investments with sadness and relief. She would ensure that copies of the recording reached all five former employees who had been unjustly terminated, with a promise to testify if they decided to pursue a lawsuit.

So, free for the remainder of the day, she decided to take a quick trip to her West Village apartment. As much as she liked the penthouse, it didn't feel like home. She arranged for the Watson & Haskins movers to pick up more of her things. All she had to do was tag them with the stickers they left behind after fetching her sofa and chairs.

She contemplated calling her driver, whom she'd been instructed to use for all her transportation, but, frankly, it gave her that same bird-in-a-gilded-cage feeling as the penthouse. Besides, it would take him over thirty minutes to arrive in traffic. The subway was a better option. He could meet her at the apartment when she was done.

Cara hopped off the number one train at Sheridan Square and Christopher Street and walked the remaining four blocks up and over to her Perry Street apartment. She loved the intimate feel of this section of the city with its narrow, tree-lined streets, some of which were still cobblestone. Tight buds tipped the tree branches in anticipation of warm spring days, and the time of year Cara consumed allergy pills like candy.

As she entered her brownstone, it felt longer than twenty-four hours since she'd been there. She couldn't shake the feeling that her world had shifted, widening the gap between past and present.

As she stepped from the elevator, a prickling sensation hit the back of her neck, along with a mild headache. She touched her forehead with the back of a hand, testing for a fever and finding none.

She entered the still air of her apartment and closed the door. The living room was as she'd left it—inviting, organized, minus a sofa and chairs. Marie Kondo would be proud.

Setting her purse and briefcase on the floor, she kicked off her heels and slipped out of her jacket, placing it on a hook by the door. She picked up a sheet of stickers left by the warehouse manager on the entry table and dropped her keys in their place. She started for the kitchen, mentally inventorying what she wanted to take with her.

Ten minutes later, she'd affixed blue and white moving stickers to her antique cupboard, canisters, and about half the remaining contents of the kitchen. Cara stood reevaluating her choices when she heard a soft snick of a door. Hairs rose on the back of her neck, and a thumping pain hit behind her temples.

Gladstone's warning flashed to mind, triggering the lizard part of her brain to fire. Sensing danger, adrenaline surged through her bloodstream, mobilizing her limbs. Gooseflesh rose on her skin, and she reached for a butcher's knife from the wooden block.

She crept to the kitchen doorway and peeked into the living room. The front door stood wide open and menacing.

Glancing at the kitchen counter, she remembered her cell was inside her purse by the front door—the only exit beside the fire escape.

Crap! Hadn't Gladstone said she could pick up a few things? And where was that Guardian of hers?

Fear sweat trickled down her spine as she peered around the doorjamb, using the wall for cover. Something was out there. She felt it in her bones.

She shivered. The apartment temperature had plummeted, and she could see wisps of breath. Energy lurked in the air, dark and threatening. Her heart hammered in time with her throbbing head. She glanced at the seven-inch blade in her hand, calculating the distance to the door, and prepared to make a run for it.

Tightening her grip on the knife's handle, she eased toward the door in stocking feet. She counted to three and ran.

Halfway there, the door slammed shut, revealing an inky, black haze that grew larger before her. A solid shape emerged.

Cara's senses screamed, and she slid to a stop, transfixed, her brain working overtime to process what she saw. Terror mixed with the taste of tar coating her tongue.

A beast that looked like something that escaped from Hell filled the room and nearly hit the ceiling. The body, scaly with blackened, red skin, resembled a satyr: human-looking on top with clawed fingers and a goat-like bottom, complete with cloven hooves. Horns grew in curved points out of its forehead, and strings of drool dripped from a mouth of razor-sharp teeth.

The beast's glowing eyes locked on her. It roared inside her head while excruciating pain stabbed her temples.

She backpedaled and ran hell for leather toward the fire escape in the kitchen. But hot, claw-tipped digits wrapped around her neck, jerking her to a stop, and squeezed.

The creature lifted her from the ground.

Cara frantically kicked at empty air, struggling for breath as hot, fetid breath landed in burning puffs on the back of her head.

Knife in hand, she took an arcing swing backward and made contact with spongy flesh. Hot spray seared her back, and the demon shrieked. The demon batted the blade from her hand without loosening its grip.

She choked, starving for air. Eyes bulging, she clawed with panic and despair at the scaly skin crushing her throat. White pinpricks of light filled her vision as the burn in her lungs grew unbearable.

No! She didn't want to die, not like this.

And then, everything went black.

Chapter 16

CHAMUEL

Perry Street Apartment. New York City.

CARA'S CHOKING AND panicked struggle filled the air. Chamuel held his breath and rammed the Hunter demon through with his blazing angelic blade. An ear-splitting shriek filled the air, and the demon disintegrated into a column of black ash.

Cara dropped to the floor in a heap.

The blade vanished in a shower of sparkling dust that never hit the carpet. Sidestepping the demon's ash pile, Chamuel clipped the empty hilt to his belt with a shaking hand. He dropped to his knees beside Cara. Turning her over, he pressed two fingers to her jugular.

Finding a steady pulse, Chamuel's shoulders slumped in relief. *Thank you, Heavenly Father.* He scanned Cara for injuries, finding none besides the bruises blooming on her neck.

That was close. Too close.

He stood and examined the orderly room, seeing few signs of a struggle. For their hellish size and demeanor, demonic Hunters were notoriously nimble. But who sent this monster?

All signs pointed to Achanelech, which didn't make sense. If he'd planned to break the rules, he could've killed Cara in the subway. No, that couldn't be it, but that didn't mean others weren't gunning for her.

Chamuel suspected something significant about this Trinity mission. Cara had already attracted highly unusual attention from the Demon King of Fire and the High Council. The stakes seemed higher for a reason unknown to him.

He frowned at the ash pile, offended that the demon remains had defiled Cara's space. Chamuel made a mental note to clean up before leaving. The demon had conveniently collapsed downward, leaving Cara relatively unscathed. Even the black, bloody spray from her valiant knife jab had turned to dust. Chamuel hadn't escaped so easily. He'd taken a hit through the blade's exit wound.

Eyeing Cara on the floor, Chamuel removed his ash-covered duster, turned it inside out, and draped it over the nearest piece of furniture — a side table. Fortunately, his black T-shirt and cargo pants had been spared. Chamuel scooped Cara into his arms and looked for someplace comfortable to set her down. He frowned at the bare living room and empty space where a sofa and some chairs should've been.

Before Chamuel could open a telepathic link to update his Messenger, Michael's voice rushed over their Trinity connection. *"I'm on my way! I tried to reach you. Why didn't you answer?"*

"A little busy saving Cara's life." Chamuel bristled with irritation. *"Did you know about the demon?"* Michael should've received a warning through the Flow and contacted Chamuel before he discovered Cara's predicament, which obviously didn't happen. Hopefully, this wasn't an indication of how things would go, or they were in trouble.

Agitation rippled through Michael's reply, *"No! I ran from class when the vision hit me and tried to contact you. Why wasn't she at work?"*

Chamuel's jaw tightened in frustration. *"I don't know."* She should've been at the office, and this should not have happened.

Michael sighed, and weariness crept into his voice. *"I'm in a cab. I'll be there in twenty minutes. Oh, and Constantina arrived."* Chamuel sensed Michael's flagging energy over their bond, the vision exacting its toll.

"I know. She called me earlier," Chamuel responded in the same weary tone, thinking about the familiar voice that sounded like tinkling crystal bells. He'd asked her point-blank why he'd been chosen for this mission, and as expected, she refused to answer.

"Take care of Cara, please?" Michael's request sounded like a plea.

Chamuel frowned. Did Michael actually think he wouldn't? True, they had not yet achieved a working rhythm, but still. *"Of course, and do me a favor? I don't want her to see me when she wakes. I plan to cloak."*

"No problem. I won't give you away."

Chamuel closed their telepathic link and looked at the unconscious and very beautiful woman he held to his chest. Her long auburn hair draped over one arm, her stocking feet poking from a pair of brown slacks that matched her sweater draped over the other. A diamond solitaire pendant remained intact around her neck, the stone's shape imprinted in the angry bruises forming at her throat.

His cheeks burned with self-recrimination, livid that he'd misjudged the situation. Had he known Cara planned to leave work early or avoid her driver, he would have stuck to her like glue. She would've been safe in his presence, since demons couldn't transform in front of anyone but prey. Cara was most protected when in the company of other humans or in a safe house, such as the Penthouse. Alone, she was an easy target.

Had Fate not intervened and called Chamuel to investigate her apartment for threats, the demon would've had its snack. Though the nasty bruises circling her neck were a reminder that he hadn't arrived soon enough.

Chamuel questioned if he was up to the task. In less than twenty-four hours, he'd almost lost her, and the near-miss stung. He couldn't let history repeat itself.

His weapons jangled on his waist as he carried Cara's limp form into the bedroom. Rather than setting her on the bed, he sat on the mattress, unable to relinquish her. She rested against his chest. The feel of her small, fragile body felt strangely at home. There was barely any weight to her, nowhere near the solid weight of a Nephilim female.

Holding her gave him an unexpected sense of peace, something he hadn't had in over a century. Granted, he hadn't held a woman in that long either.

Did that explain the pull of her energy on him?

As she lay in the crook of his arm, he studied her with fascination, drinking in her creamy pale skin and the long lashes that brushed her cheeks as she slept. His gaze lingered on her mouth. Her lips, soft and lush, begged to be kissed. What would they feel like on his? How would they taste?

Chamuel leaned closer and inhaled the sweet scent of her shampoo. Aromatic vanilla and sage filled his senses, drawing him like a bee to a flower and casting a spell over him. Soft strands of hair the color of autumn leaves whispered over his skin, setting off a tingle of awareness. He felt like a virginal teenager. Embracing the feeling, both foreign and heady, he wondered if his debt had yet been paid, his atonement complete.

A strand lay over her face. Instinctively, he raised a hand to brush the hair away and froze.

Was he out of his ever-loving mind?

Forbidden. That's what she was, at least to him. The rules were clear; she could never be his. His lips could never touch hers.

My God. How could a single touch elicit such a response? How was it possible? He didn't know which surprised him more: his unexplainable desire or wanting to break his celibacy.

Pressing his eyes shut, he took a deep breath. Forcing himself to his feet, he gently set Cara on the bed and broke contact. He sat on the floor beside the bed in deep contemplation until Michael buzzed.

Chamuel slipped into his duster as he walked and let Michael in. "She's in the bedroom," Chamuel said, pointing the way.

Without sparing a glance, the Messenger raced by in a *gi* and martial arts shoes.

Chamuel joined Michael at Cara's bedside. "She sleeps," Chamuel said flatly, hovering beside Michael. "Her energy is strong, but I think she needs some help to wake."

Michael ran a hand through his hair. "Let's check if she has anything containing ammonia. It's the next best thing to old-fashioned smelling salts." Michael looked around and pointed. "You take the bathroom. I'll check the kitchen."

Chamuel checked the bathroom cabinet beneath the sink—nothing.

"Found it," Michael yelled from the kitchen and rejoined him. "If you don't want Cara to see you, I suggest cloaking now," Michael said, holding up a bottle of window cleaner.

Chamuel planted his hands on his hips and squinted at the bottle. "You sure you want to use that?" he asked, concerned the fumes could harm her.

Michael glared at him, raising a questioning brow. "You have a better idea?"

He gritted his teeth. "No." The faster they delivered her to Constantina, the better, since Constantina's skills far exceeded any hospital.

Michael pressed his lips together, gave Chamuel a dismissive look, and twisted off the cap. Chamuel grumbled, backed away from the pungent ammonia fumes, and cloaked.

"Cara," Michael whispered, wafting the bottle near her nose. "Can you hear me?"

Cara's eyes flew open. She gasped and sputtered with a choking, raspy cough. Michael moved the bottle away, and she pushed upright with an elbow.

She sucked air into her lungs in greedy breaths. Closing her eyes, she moaned, her hands cradling her head before they moved to her battered neck. Her moans turned into soft sobs, and tears streamed down her cheeks. She looked at Michael, at first unseeing, then focusing on his face.

She choked out in a hoarse voice, "Demon tried...kill me. Hurts. Everything hurts."

Chamuel cringed at the broken blood vessels in her green eyes and the pain she must feel. Once she accepted her Calling, they would detect each other's pain and strong emotions through their Trinity bond, unless they willfully blocked them. But for now, only he and Michael were connected.

Michael looked at Cara with kindness in his eyes. He stroked her hair and said softly, "I'm sorry. This shouldn't have happened."

His words hit Chamuel like a gut punch.

Michael took her hand in his. "We're safe now. Chamuel took care of the demon. Just rest for a minute until the driver arrives. He'll take us to the penthouse. There's someone there who wants to meet you."

More tears fell from Cara's eyes. "I thought I was dead."

Michael squeezed her hand. "We won't let this happen ever again. I promise."

Chamuel's chest ached with longing at how she clutched Michael's hand, wishing it were his hand offering her strength. Then, he angrily dismissed the thought. *Forbidden, remember?*

"Guardian?" she croaked. "Where…was my Guardian?"

Chamuel pressed his eyes shut. Her words stabbed him like a knife to the heart. She thought he failed her.

Michael dipped his head. "I'm sorry. We didn't know you'd leave work early… and I didn't get the message soon enough to warn you. I promise this *won't* happen again."

Chamuel read the challenge in Michael's words but respected the Messenger for owning his part.

Michael helped Cara gather her things and led her from the apartment as Chamuel watched them go, feeling a jumble of emotions that unnerved him. He cleaned up the demon ash and avoided the phone call he dreaded making. Constantina's words couldn't sting more than the guilt he already carried.

When Chamuel exited the building ten minutes later, his head jerked to the side. A wisp of Nephilim energy. The same energy signature as the one who helped the Sentinel escape. Anger pinched his brow. Had the Nephil led the demon to Cara? Had he been wrong? Was this Achanelech's doing?

Chamuel growled low in his throat and fanned his senses, searching for the cloaked Nephil, prepared to flush him out. But the traitor disappeared as quickly as he came.

A nagging feeling pressed on Chamuel. If the rogue had been present during the attack, Chamuel would have sensed him. He hadn't, though that didn't mean he wasn't involved.

Not only did Isaac still owe him that report, but he also promised patrols. They needed to find this Nephil and bring him down.

Chapter 17

CARA

Fifth Avenue Penthouse. New York City.

DURING THE RIDE to the penthouse, Cara had stayed wrapped in Michael's embrace, her head tucked beneath his chin. His strong arms secured her as she rested a cheek against his warm chest, listening to the steady thump of his heart through his karate *gi*. They didn't talk, but she found Michael's presence calming and welcomed his hand, soothing a path up and down her back. His gesture held no romantic intent, only a sincere willingness to comfort her, which she appreciated.

Her affection for him grew directly with her disappointment in her so-called Guardian. Despite Michael's explanation that it wasn't Chamuel's fault, she blamed him anyway. So far, he wasn't much of a protector.

Cara touched the tender skin around her neck as they entered the penthouse. Her injured throat, raw inside and out, made it difficult to swallow or speak. The injuries would heal. She survived, and that's what mattered. It could've been worse. Her experience answered at least one question—how someone could die.

Cara quirked a brow at her hound's absence as they entered the foyer. Always one for an exuberant greeting, Chloe was nowhere in sight. Before Cara could voice her concern, Michael passed a hand down her arm and said softly, "Follow me."

A woman stood in the middle of Cara's living room. A full head shorter than Cara, she wore an ocean-blue, hooded velvet cloak the same shade as her eyes. Possibly in her mid-thirties, she was absolutely stunning, with long, silky blonde hair and aristocratic features that reminded Cara of old photographs of Grace Kelly she'd seen in Monaco during her junior year abroad. The woman's carriage held a combination of silent strength and gentle grace.

Chloe sat sentry at the woman's side, which Cara found odd. Cara frowned at her dog, who cocked her head but didn't budge.

A radiant smile lit the petite woman's face as they approached.

Michael offered an introduction: "Constantina, this is Cara," he said, giving Cara a reassuring squeeze on the shoulder.

Cara pasted on a welcoming smile and croaked, "Hello."

Constantina's sparkling ocean gaze fell on Cara, and she took Cara's hands in hers. "It's such a pleasure to finally meet you, Cara," she said with a slight French accent. As the woman held Cara's hands, a faint glow grew around Constantina, and Cara's muscles relaxed. "As Michael said, I am Constantina. I will be your mentor." Her speech pattern reminded Cara of delicate wind chimes, calming Cara like lapping waves on a sandy beach.

Warmth flowed into her from Constantina's palms. "Pleased to meet you," Cara said. The rasp in her voice eased as her body aches and general discomfort subsided.

Had this tiny woman done that?

Constantina gave Cara's hands a final squeeze, and the glow around her dimmed. Then, she rose on tiptoe to kiss Michael once on each cheek. "Ah, dear one, it's so good to see you again."

Michael smiled and graciously returned the greeting.

The petite woman sobered, her gaze traveling between Cara and Michael. "Chamuel briefed me on the *incident*. I'm so sorry. We didn't expect the Dark Ones to make such a bold move so soon, which gives us less time to train."

Gooseflesh rose on Cara's arms. "Who are the Dark Ones?" Were they the dark forces Michael meant?

Constantina sighed gravely. "I will explain as part of our first lesson."

Eager for answers, Cara croaked, "When can we start?"

Constantina gave a sweet, melodious chuckle. "That's the spirit! We shall start today." She said to Michael. "You may take your leave, dear one. I shall take it from here."

Michael bowed his head and crossed his hands at the waist. "Call if you need me." Constantina mirrored his gestures and replied, "Please join us in the morning for tomorrow's lessons."

"Of course." Michael squatted to ruffle Chloe's ears and winked at her. Cara blinked. Had Michael winked at her *dog*? Michael rose, glanced between her and Constantina, and tipped an imaginary hat. "Have a good evening, ladies." Then, he left the room.

Anxiety gripped Cara. "Please excuse me," she said to Constantina and rushed after Michael, stopping him at the front door.

"Will this be okay?" she asked nervously, needing his reassurance. "I wish you were staying."

He draped an arm over her shoulder and pulled her into a hug, her cheek resting against stiff cotton. "It's more than okay. Constantina's amazing, you'll see. You're safe now," he whispered.

"I felt calm when she held my hands," she said into his shoulder, her vocal cords better but still raw.

He chuckled softly and released her. "She did an energy push to soothe you. You'll learn how to do it, too." He tipped her chin to meet his gaze. "It's all good, I promise."

Cara wrung her hands. "Why is Chloe stuck to her side? She didn't even greet us." If Cara was honest, everyone seemed to be hiding something—including Chloe.

A flicker of hesitation interrupted his smile. "Constantina is like an animal whisperer. Seriously, don't worry. You're in good hands."

Cara really wanted to trust Michael, so she nodded. "All right…Thank you for before. It meant a lot to me," she said, already missing his protective warmth.

His gaze softened. "Hey, I'm sorry I didn't get there sooner. I'm not your Guardian, but know that I'd protect you with my life," he said earnestly, tapping a fist to his heart.

Cara didn't have anyone else to turn to about this, so that meant something. A lump formed in her throat, and she launched herself back into his arms. "Thank you."

He gave her a parting squeeze. "See you tomorrow."

When Cara returned to the living room, she channeled her mother's hostess skills. "May I get you anything before we begin?"

"Not presently, but thank you for the offer," Constantina said, tipping her head. "I hope you don't think me too presumptuous, but I've put my travel case in the guest room at the end of the hall. I've always been fond of that room."

Cara's brows rose, only understanding now that she had an overnight houseguest. In truth, she had plenty of space and would enjoy the company.

"Sounds good. I can keep Chloe in my room at night so she doesn't bother you."

Constantina waved a hand. "Not necessary. She's a dear companion."

So, I've noticed, Cara thought, glancing at Constantina's new Whippet protector, who cocked an ear and blinked at Cara.

Slipping on a comfortable smile, Constantina clasped her hands. "How much time do you need to prepare?"

Cara looked at her clothes. She needed more than a moment to clean off the demon attack and gather her thoughts. A shower could only improve her day. "Forty-five minutes?"

"Done! Wear something more comfortable, and we'll meet in the library when you're ready."

Ready? That would be *never,* but she'd give it her best shot.

WHEN CARA ARRIVED in the library, Chloe was curled on the tufted Chesterfield sofa, and Constantina was leafing through a leather-bound book. The room was as clichéd as its Downton Abbey-like masculine beauty, with rows of bookcases, a polished mahogany desk, and leather club chairs, the works. The only thing missing was a humidor filled with cigars, which she'd probably find if she looked hard enough.

Constantina's honey-blonde hair was gathered at her nape. Unlike Cara's yoga pants and T-shirt, Constantina wore loose-fitting pants and a tailored, flowing blue silk tunic.

Constantina's gaze found Cara and warmed. She replaced the book and did the bowing thing she and Michael had done earlier. "I've been looking forward to this since your grandmother, Hannah, told me of you."

Cara's breath caught, fingers flying to her lips. "You knew my grandmother?"

She nodded, smiling softly. "I did."

Only four when her grandmother died, Cara didn't need to be a math genius to realize she'd misjudged Constantina's age. She must be closer to fifty. Cara swallowed past a rising lump. "Will you tell me about her?"

"I shall do that and unlock your gifts—as I promised her. But first, let me share this room's secret," she said, motioning toward the floor-to-ceiling bookcases.

Constantina removed a book, uncovering a hidden lever. Glancing over her shoulder, she smiled and pulled. The bookcase on the right swung forward, revealing a staircase.

Of course. Cara rolled her eyes. "Seriously? A hidden staircase?"

A tinkling laugh came in reply. "It's fun, isn't it? I feel like Agatha Christie every time I open it," she said in a conspiratorial whisper, ushering Cara ahead. "I can promise that mysteries await us." Cara expected those mysteries to be a far cry from Mrs. Peacock killing the butler in the library with a candlestick.

Chloe whined, reminding them of her presence, and trotted to Cara's side as she stepped into the hidden stairwell. Cara pointed to the sofa and commanded, "Chloe, stay."

"Allow me," Constantina said and knelt. She stroked Cara's insistent hound and whispered a few words Cara didn't catch. Then, without protest, Chloe trotted away, leaped onto the couch, and curled into a ball.

"Whatever you did, you need to teach me," Cara mumbled.

Constantina hit the release, and the bookcase closed as they ascended the stairway into a large cavernous room with a barrel-shaped ceiling made of heavy plaster and decorated with elaborate murals similar to those Michelangelo painted on the ceiling of the Sistine Chapel.

The ceiling's bright color palette reflected off the white walls, giving the room a warm glow with square footage easily encompassing both penthouse apartments below. A blue padded mat, made of interlocking tiles, similar to those found in a gym, covered the expanse. At the room's far end, a high table sat with an elevated golden orb surrounded by colorful candles. A much smaller table sat beside it. The room's beauty lay in its bare simplicity.

Cara swore one of the murals was a replica of The Last Judgement. "Wow. What is this place?" Cara whispered, looking around. The warm space reminded her of a meditation room, yet it had the sacred feel of a church. Cara pointed at the high table. "Is that an altar?"

"It is. The penthouse is one of our safe houses, and this room is a meeting place." She gave Cara a wry smile and winked. "Though it doubles as a ballroom for special events." Not a surprise. Cara imagined it could easily accommodate three hundred people.

Constantina tugged on Cara's hand. "Come." Cara let Constantina tow her to the altar, a simpler version of the one inside Cara's Catholic Church, while growing up. White cloth covered the surface and overhung the sides. Tall wire stands of varying heights cradled different colored candles, half of which flickered.

As they approached, Constantina explained, "The orb hides our energy from detection and makes this a safe dwelling. The altar, in turn, makes the penthouse hallowed ground and protects us from demonic forces."

Wait, what? "Hide what energy from whom?" Cara's heart rate accelerated. "Are there more demons hunting me?"

Constantina sighed and shook her head. "That's a complicated question, which I hope to answer for both of us. For now, I believe the answer is no."

For now? Cara pressed on. "So, I inherited the penthouse and the Connecticut farmhouse for protection?"

"Yes, and no. Both are safe houses and have been in our possession for over a century, but that's not why you inherited them. Many factors go into our bequests. Not everyone is as richly gifted. Actually, very few are gifted this handsomely, and some are not gifted at all. Trust that, over time, you will discover the underlying purpose. My only advice is to caution you against frivolity regarding this gift. In the future, you likely will need it. Until then, your wealth affords many things, including privacy and security, to ensure your safety and freedom."

Cara nodded her understanding. Spending the inheritance was the last thing on her mind.

When they reached the small table beside the altar, Constantina withdrew a match from a long box beside a candle snuffer.

The altar's height exceeded Constantina's five-foot-one inches. Taking the match, she circled the altar and ascended a set of stairs hidden from view. She knelt on top and lit the remaining candles. "I had hoped to finish before we met in the library."

"What are the candles for?"

"Ah, each candle represents an Angelic Order," she said, igniting the remaining wicks.

Cara counted twelve candles, so twelve orders. She sighed. "Angels and Demons. What's next? Vampires?" After this morning, she'd believe it.

"Thankfully, not." Constantina chuckled, descended the stairs, and rejoined her. "You've been patient and rightly inquisitive. Come and sit. I will explain." Taking Cara's hand, she led her to the middle of the room and motioned to the floor. They sank to the mat facing each other. "We'll start with a short prayer and take it from there, okay?"

Cara shifted uncomfortably, having flashbacks to her discussion with Michael the other night. Not that Cara was a skeptic, but many people sold crazy under the guise of faith and religion.

God, she hoped again this wasn't some off-the-wall cult.

"Don't worry." The small woman joined their hands. "I will lead. Your job is to close your eyes and focus on good things."

Cara warily did as she was told.

"Our Father, we gather in the name of peace and love, and we ask all the Angels to lend their celestial support in goodness, love, wisdom, power, and light, that they may watch and banish any whose intentions are less than pure. We embrace your gifts with an open heart and journey forth in peace and love. Amen."

That wasn't so bad, Cara conceded. Still, she decided now might be the time to share her feelings about religion, as she had with Michael, in case that changed anything. Taking a breath, she nervously fingered the hem of her T-shirt and blurted, "I'm not religious…I'm sorry. Organized religion suffocates me. I believe in God but not the patriarchy that uses fear to scare people into having faith and obeying rules that don't make sense." Cara wrinkled her nose. "Does that make me a heathen?"

A smile grew on Constantina's lips. "Not at all. I cannot disagree. The purity of the Scriptures has long been tainted by man or the patriarchy, as you call it," she said, surprising Cara with her answer. "Many choices, additions, and deletions were made over the centuries, motivated by politics and control. What saddens me most is that what you know as today's modern Bible and the Word of God will always be incomplete. Some omissions you've heard of in other contexts. But there is one particular book known to only a rare few. It speaks of us. Who and what we are."

Cara smirked. "Entering *The Da Vinci Code* territory, are we?" she asked, referencing one of her favorite thrillers.

An amused chuckle came in reply. "That's a work of fiction, dear one, but grains of truth are woven into such stories. Mary Magdalene was most definitely *not* a prostitute. She was, in fact, an apostle. But that's a different story for a different day." Constantina winked. "And a stark example of the patriarchal interference you mentioned."

A thrill and a sense of vindication sparked inside Cara's chest. Channeling her inner Sophie Neveu, Cara asked, "So, the world *has* been duped for thousands of years?"

"Not duped, exactly. Much truth remains in the modern Bible, but much has been lost and misinterpreted. Please don't get me wrong," she said, throwing up a hand. "Religion has an indisputable purpose for humanity in driving faith, which promotes our collective spiritual well-being. But make no mistake, good and evil are real. As does faith, the duality of good and evil transcends all religions, and many crimes against humanity have been committed in the name of God, as have many great acts through faith in God and love. But it's love that remains and transcends all."

Cara's lips curved into a smile. No one had ever articulated what she believed so perfectly. "What's the missing Book you mentioned?" she asked, the croak returning.

Constantina's brow drew into a frown. "My apologies. I should have done this earlier. Let me fix that rasp and fully heal your injuries."

Her mentor closed her eyes, clasped her hands at her chest, and spoke words in a language Cara didn't recognize. A column of golden light poured from the ceiling into Constantina's crown.

Cara swallowed, awestruck at the familiar light display.

Constantina gently separated her hands and knelt. Bright, golden light radiated from her palms as she placed them on Cara's throat. Soothing heat penetrated Cara's skin, pulsing and massaging until the pain disappeared.

Constantina's hands fell away. "Feel better?"

Not trusting her senses, Cara touched her neck and stared at the woman. "That was amazing! What did you do?" she asked, voice refreshed.

She grinned and shrugged. "I channeled the healing energy surrounding the earth—what we call the *Flow*—into your throat to raise your cells' molecular vibrations to accelerate healing. Simple."

"Simple?" Cara squeaked. Nothing about that seemed simple.

Constantina waved a hand. "You have the same ability and will learn to call upon it in training. I did something similar when we met earlier. Did you feel it?"

Cara nodded. "I saw a glow, but nothing like this."

"Ah!" Constantina clapped her hands, her expression lighting with understanding. "In the living room, I didn't use the Flow. I shared my own energy."

Oddly, things started falling into place, and Cara's pulse quickened. Had she channeled the Flow for the homeless woman? "Did Michael tell you about the woman on the street?"

"Yes, the Sentinel." Constantina's good humor dampened.

"Did I channel the Flow?"

Constantina frowned. "Not exactly. She used you as a conduit…like a tire pressure gauge."

"Okayyy…" Cara struggled to make a connection.

Constantina said patiently, "A tire gauge measures the pressure in a tire, yes? Similarly, the Sentinel acted as the gauge to draw the Flow and measure your power. The more healing energy is drawn, the younger the Sentinel becomes. It was a test. And you did quite well, dear one."

"Good to know." She snapped her fingers and said, "The guy in the subway—"

Constantina interrupted, "Achanelech. Yes, I know." Distaste twisted her lovely features into a fierce grimace so out of character with the loving warmth she exuded that Cara blinked.

The moment passed, and Constantina's demeanor softened. "My apologies. Talk of Achanelech brings out the absolute worst in me." She shook her head, gaze growing unfocused and distant. "He and I…we have a history. He had no intention of harming you, only sending a message that he could."

Cara's eyes widened. "Did he send the demon?"

Constantina nibbled her bottom lip. "He wouldn't be that stupid."

"Who is he?"

Constantina sighed. "I will tell you more during our lessons. Will that do?"

"Sure." She could live with that. This man clearly upset Constantina, and Cara didn't want to upset her further.

"Thank you," Constantina said, her relief and gratitude palpable. Brightening, she shifted topics, pointing to the ceiling halfway across the room. "Let's begin there."

Cara's muscles, cramped from sitting cross-legged on the flat surface, protested as they rose. Chairs would've been nice. She massaged her quads and followed her petite mentor until they reached their starting point. Craning her neck, Cara looked at the ceiling. Lights along the walls illuminated the murals from every angle. Most of the painted vignettes featured winged angels and mortals.

Constantina pointed. "See the man writing the book?"

Cara located the vignette Constantina referenced of a man scribing inside a cave, with a body of water in the background as another man looked on.

"The same priest who penned the Dead Sea Scrolls, including the Books of Enoch, wrote it over two millennia ago. The world knows of Enoch's first four books. Ours is the fifth—the last scroll. It's known as The Book of Human Angels, translated from Latin, *Libre Homo Angelorum.*"

Constantina's finger shifted to the left. "The man standing next to the priest is his brother. They are from the first Messenger family. Since the completion of its penning, Enoch 5 has been passed between Messenger families to keep it safe and hidden."

Cara's gaze shifted to Constantina. "Why does it need to stay hidden?"

She sighed. "Our scripture contains more than our story; it contains crucial information, a blueprint for our future success. It's imperative that the book not fall into the wrong hands."

Cara chewed her lip. "Where is it now?"

"Hidden, as it will stay until it is needed." Her words were soft but resolute. "Let's move on."

Cara trailed her the ten feet to the next location. Constantina sank down, lay flat on the mat, and smiled playfully. "I don't know about you, but my neck can take only a few minutes of staring at the ceiling, and this part of the story may take a while." Cara grinned at the admission, suspecting Constantina was doing her best to set Cara at ease with the weight of all this knowledge, and joined her on the floor.

Constantina rolled her head toward Cara. "You mentioned you're not an avid follower of religion, but have you heard of the Great War in Heaven in the Book of Revelations? And Lucifer, what about him?" she teased.

Cara gave a wry smile. "Just because I'm a recovering Catholic doesn't mean I didn't listen in church during my formative years." Then she lobbed. "And I've watched every season of *Lucifer* on Amazon Prime."

Constantina chuckled warmly. "Ha! Brilliant show. Now, focus on the center vignette."

Cara homed in on the largest and most violent of the images. More angels than she could count battled demons amid a bright cloudscape.

"See the dark-haired angel to the left?"

"Yes," Cara said, locating the massive angel.

"That is the real Lucifer, named after the Morning Star. He was the Cherubim leader and one of God's most beautiful and beloved angels. One of the reasons we are in this room today is because of him and the Great War."

"I remember the story. Didn't Lucifer start the Great War because he was jealous of humanity?"

Constantina smiled. "Yes, that's partially correct. There were two incidents, really. The first occurrence took place after the Resurrection, when God called the Son home. God loved Jesus and humanity so much that He expected the angels to bow down to Jesus. Lucifer believed he was better than the Son and refused to bow to what he considered an inferior being. The second incident involved Lucifer's aspirations. Believing himself superior to God, he convinced a faction of the angelic host to follow him in an attempt to overthrow God as the Ruler of Heaven. And so started the Great War."

Cara silently congratulated the painter who had captured the arrogant defiance in Lucifer's eyes. "Ballsy move."

"Yes, it was." Constantina pointed to another figure, a gorgeous yet fierce-looking angel wielding a sword of brilliant light. "That is the Archangel Michael, who led the angelic army as they waged war and defeated Lucifer and his minions. In the end, Lucifer and his followers fell from grace. Stripped of their wings, they were cast from Heaven. Some reside here on Earth, but most reside lower in Hell or the corridor in between. Today, we refer to Lucifer and his fallen angels as the Dark Ones."

"*Ahh,*" Cara nodded slowly. So that's what they meant. She glanced at Lucifer. "Why wasn't he painted as a demon?"

A frown cut her mentor's delicate brow, and she smiled sadly. "To remind all of us that he was once loved and sometimes evil comes in beautiful packages." Constantina continued, "God loved his angels enough to give them free will as he did mankind. But with free will comes the ability to sin. So, in essence, Lucifer was undone by his sins of pride and envy. What happens next is where we come in." Constantina lifted herself off the mat and crooked her finger. "Follow me."

Cara and Constantina moved to another sizeable angelic mural and lay prone, staring at the next vignette. Cara was grateful for the mat as they examined a peaceable crowd of angels facing a brilliant light. The angels wore different forms of dress and carried various implements. Some held swords. Some books. Others had farming implements or other objects.

"Many angels didn't understand or agree with Lucifer's decisions. A faction of angels representing all twelve angelic Orders worried about Mankind's fate with Lucifer and his minions living among them. Since God had gifted His children free will, He couldn't interfere with their paths or decisions."

"His," Cara understood but disliked the patriarchal reference and wondered aloud, "Is God really a He?"

A beat passed, and Constantina whispered, "God is neither masculine nor feminine, male nor female. Those constructs do not apply. God is All and Every, making *They* more appropriate. But old habits are often hard to break."

Cara smiled, not really expecting Constantina to answer. "Thank you. Mind if I try?"

Constantina rubbed her arm. "I'd welcome it."

Relief filtered through Cara. "If *They* can't interfere, what happens when They hear our prayers?" She'd been raised to pray to God for help and guidance, and it didn't sit well with her that those prayers may have been in vain. Despite her earlier discomfort with other aspects of religion, she still believed in the power of prayer.

Constantina smiled. "Just because *They* cannot interfere doesn't mean They don't listen or send help. But what you ask for may not be what you need. Their love for humanity is why the Book of Human Angels exists, and it is why I am here. After the Great War, three hundred angels representing each angelic Order approached God and made an unusual request: to form a new angelic protectorate. These angels would descend from Heaven to live among humans, protecting humanity while maintaining the balance of good and evil on earth. In their proposal, they agreed not to directly interfere with free will and only provide guidance when needed, using Trinities to carry out their work."

Cara swallowed hard. "Angels live among us?"

Constantina met her gaze and nodded solemnly.

Everything coalesced in Cara's head simultaneously: the title of Enoch 5, the light Constantina channeled, her mentor's demeanor, and her strange way of speaking. She blinked. "Are you an angel?"

Constantina smiled warmly. "I'm human like you. Yet…different."

A shiver slipped over Cara's skin. "What do you mean?"

"The agreement with God specified that angels couldn't descend in angelic form but must be born to live among humanity, with one difference between a descended angel and an ordinary human soul. Descended angels are born 'awakened.'"

Cara frowned. "Awakened?"

Constantina lifted her arm, pointing at the ceiling. "According to the Kabala, the Night Angel Layela accompanies a soul on its journey to earth. As the soul enters an unborn fetus, she places a finger against the lips to erase memories of Heaven and past lives." Constantina touched her finger vertically to her upper lip. "The Night Angel's finger lies here—leaving a vertical indentation over the upper lip." Then she turned her head toward Cara and removed her finger, revealing smooth skin. "Layela does not accompany us."

Chapter 18

CARA

Penthouse Meeting Room. New York City.

CARA SPRANG TO a sitting position, a hand flying to her mouth. She should've seen that one coming. "You're one of the three hundred descended angels. Does that mean you're immortal?"

"Not in the way you think." Constantina rose alongside her. "I'm just like you with a human body and an immortal soul. The biggest difference between us is my ability to retain memories of past lives and of Heaven. I've lived many lifetimes over the last two millennia, and I remember them all, witnessing humanity shift and advance throughout the ages."

Cara shook her head slowly. "I have *so* many questions." *Understatement.*

"I'm sure you do," Constantina said with a patient smile and patted Cara's knee. "I shall regale you with as many stories as you would like when we have time, but for now, I will only say that remembering is a blessing and a curse. But all this time, I've had but one purpose."

"Which is?" Cara asked.

"To protect the balance for humanity and to reach this day," Constantina said warmly.

The weight of Constantina's expectations pressed on Cara. She felt like an imposter in her own life—a life that, until today, consisted of treading water in a firm she hated and having an emotional tie to someone she could never have. Not much purpose there. "I'm not sure I have one," Cara lamented.

"Cara, look at me." Constantina reached for her arm. "Not possible. All souls have a divine purpose. Some span multiple lifetimes. You are destined to know yours."

A luminous glow returned to Constantina's skin, and Cara got that warm feeling again beneath her touch. Soothing energy leached into her, and Cara realized she wanted to know her purpose and was desperate to confirm that death wasn't the end. "So, my soul will go to Heaven when I die?"

Constantina nodded and pulled away. "Of course, dear one."

Relieved, Cara asked, "What's Heaven like?"

A dreamy smile touched Constantina's lips. "Ah, that's hard to describe with words. In its simplest form, Heaven contains all that is good—love, light, beauty, peace, and happiness. There's no real comparison here on earth. The only thing close is the euphoria of falling in love. You'll know both that and Heaven's glory one day."

Cara wanted to believe her. "Do you miss it? Heaven?"

Constantina sighed. "Heaven and Earth are nothing alike, but I love them both. They both serve a purpose. Only when we live among you can we truly empathize and understand you, and as a creature of Heaven, we understand the importance of the Light and threat of darkness for God's creations."

"Like the demon who attacked me?" Cara asked.

Constantina's brows knit in contemplation. "Although frightening, that variety of demon lacks any real intelligence. Prey drive motivates them, not purpose. To them, you are merely a source of food."

Cara's stomach lurched. "It wanted to *eat* me?"

Constantina's soft chuckle held no mirth. "Not exactly. Your body is only biodegradable packaging. The Hunter wanted something far more precious," Constantina said, tapping her chest. "He wanted what's in here."

"My heart?" Cara asked, confused.

Constantina shook her head. "No, dear one. Your *soul*. But this type of demon can only reap a soul from the dying, and if it had succeeded, you would have been trapped in a corridor of Hell, unable to return to Heaven."

A chill rippled down Cara's spine as she hugged herself.

Constantina's voice softened. "Worry not. That demon was never destined to have you. You are meant for far greater things."

Cara mulled that over. "As part of a Trinity? Michael explained the basics but didn't give details."

A twinkle returned to Constantina's blue gaze. "That's what you would call a 'good segue.' I already mentioned the conditions placed upon the accord we struck with God, and that we rely on the Trinities to carry out our work. Since we of the Angelorum are born awakened, we have knowledge and access to information that's forbidden to share for fear of changing an individual's destiny without allowing them the ability to choose their own path. That's why you exist. Your destiny—shaped by a choice you made before birth—is tied to an event and a person who could tip the balance of good and evil. A balance the Angelorum has been tasked to protect."

A soul promise, as Michael had said. "Is every Seeker a healer?" Cara asked.

Constantina shook her head. "Not all. A person's gifts can differ to fit the circumstances for which they were chosen as part of a Trinity. Sometimes, we act under the guise of Fate without the necessity of a dedicated Trinity. For example, ensuring two people bump into each other on the street, resulting in a meeting that has significance two generations later. Our primary focus is on using Trinities around the world to combat the Dark Ones.

"Some assignments take days, months, or years. All these collective acts sit on the scales of good and evil, counterbalancing wrongs with rights. But just as we work for good, demons work for the opposite. They will hunt us if we try to get in the way. That is why Guardians are part of a Trinity—to protect us and even the odds."

"Was my grandmother a Soul Seeker like me?" Cara asked.

"No, she was like Michael, a Messenger. Your grandmother, Hannah, sensed your destiny from the moment of your birth. Her gift was to see souls who held the most important missions. It's only when her health started failing that she sought me out and wrote your letter."

The mention of her grandmother tugged at her heart. "Are Messengers human angels, too?"

Constantina shook her head. "Not angels, no. Messengers and Messenger families are human, just like you. Their role and gift allow them to communicate between their Trinity and the Angelorum protectorate. Although I channeled the Flow's healing energy earlier, Messengers use the Flow for communication, like a telepathic phone, to maintain a safe distance between us and the Trinity for our mutual protection. You see, an awakened angelic soul acts as a beacon to the Dark Ones without a protective amulet."

Cara searched Constantina—expecting an amulet dangling from a necklace—and found none. "Where is yours?"

Constantina shut her eyes, lashes brushing her cheeks, and shook her head. When her eyes reopened, her gaze held unfathomable sadness, and she whispered, "It is…*lost*."

What? No amulet? Alarmed, Cara asked, "But if the Messengers are meant to keep us separated, why are you here? Are you in danger without an amulet? Can you get another one?" Cara hated bombarding her with questions, but she felt a growing kinship with her new mentor and was concerned for her safety.

Constantina covered Cara's hand with hers and squeezed. "Worry not, dear one. I'm in no immediate danger. Even without my amulet, I'm safe here, protected by the orb. As long as I travel with a Guardian, their energy will cloak mine."

Cara held up a finger. "Wait. How can a Guardian hide your energy?" For the first time, she wondered about Chamuel and the gifts he may possess. Until now, she had imagined some mysterious Navy SEAL-type guy surveilling her every move from a discreet distance.

Placing a hand on her stomach, Constantina sighed. "Would you mind if we had a bite to eat? I fear that is a tale best told on a full stomach."

"Of course." Cara glanced at her watch and blanched. It was nearly eight p.m. "Chloe!" Not only was she a terrible hostess, but a horrible dog mom. Luckily, she had scheduled the dog walker to come while Cara and Constantina were upstairs. When they emerged into the library, they found a sullen Chloe begging for food.

Chapter 19

ACHANELECH

Lucifer's Dungeon. Hell.

"IMBECILE," LUCIFER HISSED through his fangs in Hellspeak, looming large in his true demonic form of scales and scarlet skin. Only when going topside could Achanelech's Master take on the attractive human guise of Luc Morningstar.

Achanelech's own human skin had melted away upon entering the gates of Hell. Now, in demonic form, Achanelech knelt before Lucifer on a bed of hot coals, his scaly flesh bubbling and popping from the heat as pain permeated every nerve ending. He wanted to cry out, but knew better. His carelessness had landed him down below for a fireside chat.

Achanelech's demon had slipped away without his permission. He suspected his discussion on the jet with Emanelech about the Collins girl making a hearty meal was too much for his child to resist. Though the Hunter had been reduced to a bucket of black ash for its poor judgment, the price was too paltry for the trouble Achanelech's child wrought. So, Lucifer was exacting a higher payment from Achanelech's demon flesh.

"She's mine and mine alone," Lucifer snarled. "I told you to capture Cara Collins, not to kill her." With a nod, Lucifer signaled the demon behind Achanelech. A whip cracked on Achanelech's bubbled flesh, ripping a chunk free. Pain shot through him like he'd been attacked by a mountain of scorpions.

"Yes, Massster," Achanelech replied, his serpent tongue straining to speak through the panting.

"Bending the rules is permissible, but forfeiture is not an option if you plan to continue eating, which I most certainly do."

The whip came down once more for good measure, toppling Achanelech where he knelt.

Lucifer gnashed his teeth. "Be gone, and keep your demons properly fed and under control."

Achanelech pried open his eyes to find he was topside on the bedroom rug in his mansion. The low hiss of burned flesh sizzled in his ears. Agony engulfed his flayed body. If he had tear ducts, he would've cried. Much sustenance would be required to heal his injuries.

Emanelech ran to his side and crouched. "Acchie, what's been done to you?" she whispered, a hand hovering but not touching.

Despite her penchant for cruel and amoral behavior, she was always compassionate after his rare visits to Hell. The last time had been almost a century ago, but this, by far, was the worst visit in a millennium.

"I've prepared a nice meal for you, my darling," she purred sympathetically.

If only he could get up and eat...His skin was fused to the Persian wool, and to move would prove excruciating.

"Who is on the menu for today?" he croaked. He hoped for at least one nubile young thing to speed up his healing, or else it would take a long line of hardened souls to do the job.

"No one who'll be missed. Additions for our reserve army," she said in a sing-song voice. "Let me make you a little more presentable for our...guests."

Her icy coldness swept over him, soothing the burning within and around his body. Emanelech gave new meaning to the phrase "When Hell freezes over." Fire and Ice, that's who they were. The Archdemon of Fire and the Archdemoness of Ice. Two halves of a whole. That's what she liked to tell him anyway. *I'm a sentimental idiot*, he thought, knowing this was as close as he'd ever come to love.

His charred flesh no longer painful, he let her help him to a chair next to their bed.

"Wait here." She disappeared through the bedroom door, returning a few moments later, escorting a large human male. Eyes glazed under Emanelech's spell, he walked trancelike to Achanelech. Hunger rose inside him, consuming him from the inside out. He resisted the urge to drool.

"Do you willingly give yoursssself?" Achanelech asked in a breathless hiss, awaiting permission to strike. *Another asinine ground rule in the battle between good and evil*, he thought, thoroughly aggravated.

"Yes." The man said, unaware of what was to come.

Achanelech struck with lightning speed, wrapping the man in a vise-like embrace. The demon's mouth hovered over his prey's parted lips, then his hand turned to mist, and he reached into the human's chest. His demonic fingers searched for the ethereal silver cord tethering the soul to the body, snipped it free with two clawed fingers, and sucked the man's soul through his open mouth. The human's life force worked to repair the damage and take the edge off his hunger. The skin on his hand turned from crispy black to reddish pink as the human turned into dead weight in his arms.

"Darling, please help," Achanelech croaked.

"Got him." Emanelech whisked the man from his arms with little effort. "I'll be back with another after I dump this one in Recovery." She winked and closed the door.

Recovery. He snorted. A nice word for *dungeon.* Recycling humans to serve in his soulless army was the ultimate in "being green." Although it took a week or two of "training" to get them used to their new state, it was better than the old days when they murdered their victims and left their carcasses to rot.

Achanelech relaxed in his chair and waited for his next course. After dinner, he would have a "Come to Lucifer" discussion with his demons. They'd been quiet since his return, suspecting trouble. They were right to be afraid. Any more unsanctioned assassination attempts, and he would turn the lot of them into black ash and call it a day.

He sighed. They needed that vaccine.

That would change everything.

Chapter 20

KAI

Califon Café. Palo Alto.

KAI ENTERED THE restaurant a few minutes before six. He had a clear view of the open kitchen and restaurant floor. A hip, pulsing beat played in the background, and he spotted Calvin hunkered down behind a menu at one of the tables along the wall.

Besides getting answers, Kai hoped for a decent meal so he didn't have to forage in the kitchen later. Melanie and Sara had left earlier, heading south toward Los Angeles to see Melanie's mother for the weekend. He would've accompanied them if he weren't playing in a golf tournament early the following day. Honestly, the timing couldn't have been better. It gave him time to focus on his investigation without having to explain his whereabouts to Melanie.

Kai had received the results of Wednesday's experiment, which looked promising. Things finally seemed to be moving in the right direction. If he could just get his hands on those lost lab notes, maybe he'd learn something to accelerate his success.

A hostess with jet-black hair and a sleeve of tattoos glanced up and greeted Kai. Smiling, he pointed to his party and proceeded past a long communal table to where Calvin sat.

Kai slid into the chair across from the lab assistant. "Hey, thanks for this. I appreciate it. Your note caught me by surprise."

Calvin shrugged and glanced at Kai sheepishly. "Sorry about that. You weren't the first person to ask questions."

Kai's shoulders tensed. "W-what do you mean?" he stammered, taken aback.

A gum-chewing waitress dressed in black jeans and combat boots appeared with a pad. "Can I take your order, hon?"

Unsure of whom she addressed, Kai tapped the menu. "Give us a few minutes?"

"Sure." She retreated, bubble popping.

Calvin intensely scrutinized the menu with a pinched brow.

Remembering his cash-strapped grad days, Kai hoped his dinner companion's scrutiny didn't involve weighing the cost of each entree. "This is on me. Go wild," Kai said, nodding at the menu.

Relief flooded Calvin's expression, which validated Kai's suspicions. "Thanks, Dr. Solomon. If I knew this place was so pricey after happy hour, I would've chosen someplace else." Calvin let out a chuckle. "But I hear the chef makes a mean short rib."

Kai chuckled softly. "Call me Kai." Hell, they couldn't be more than a few years apart in age.

"Will do," Calvin replied with a lopsided grin.

Kai lowered his menu, leaned in, and asked the one question driving him to distraction. "Are we meeting here because your office is bugged?"

Calvin's good humor dimmed, and he shifted uncomfortably in his seat. His gaze darted nervously around them before returning to Kai, then he lowered his voice. "I'm not sure, but I suspect it was at some point. With Sandra and Tom dead, I'm not taking any chances."

Kai frowned. "You're sure their deaths are related to this project?"

Calvin's gaze intensified. "This was the only project we kept under the radar. The two people who worked on it were killed within three weeks of each other. Call me crazy, but once I tell you what I know, I calculate the probability of a connection at 99.9999 percent."

Kai's pulse quickened. "Gotcha."

Calvin discarded his menu and leaned forward. "Dr. Wilson—Sandra—ran an amazing lab. She was brilliant. What I told you in the office was true. There were no projects for Forrester Research on our docket, but I know she consulted off-book for Dr. Peyton."

When the waitress returned, Kai and Calvin said in unison, "Short ribs."

Her brows rose. "All righty, then. Short ribs, it is." She scribbled the rest of their order on her pad and left.

When she was out of earshot, Kai asked, "Who else asked questions?"

Calvin fingered his napkin. "A few days after Sandra died, this woman, Emily, came poking around. Long, dark hair, frosty exterior—know her?"

Kai scowled. "Unfortunately." So, Emily knew about the connection. Why was he not surprised?

"She said she represented The Foundation, the project sponsor, and wanted to access any work from Sandra's research with Dr. Peyton. She said there was a nondisclosure violation, and they owned all discoveries. But I didn't tell her anything more than I told you yesterday." The side of Calvin's mouth lifted in a mischievous grin. "She went ballistic. Threatened all sorts of legal action and took the matter to the department head. Since the project wasn't official, there wasn't any paperwork. Anyway, I was waiting for you."

Kai's brows rose. "Me?"

Calvin scanned the restaurant, leaned closer to Kai, and whispered, "*You.* Sandra told me *you* would come. I just didn't remember until you showed up. Don't get creeped out, but when Wendy said your name yesterday, it was like a curtain lifted. A message and the compelling need to tell you popped into my head. Freaked me the hell out. Believe me when I say this is as weird for me as it is for you."

Gooseflesh covered Kai's arms as he recalled the odd look that crossed Calvin's face during their meeting. "You are blowing my mind. How did she know I'd come?" Kai hadn't known Dr. Wilson or anything about the project until after her death. But he knew Tom.

Then it dawned on Kai, and he threw out his idea. "Random question, but did Dr. Wilson ever hypnotize you?"

"Affirmative," Calvin smirked, crossing his arms over his chest. "Hypnosis was her party trick of choice. She said I was one of the easiest people to hypnotize she'd ever met." He sobered and shook his head. "God, I miss her."

"I'm sorry for your loss," Kai said.

Calvin sighed. "Thanks…And I don't know why she suspected you'd come. Obviously, she didn't want me to know anything consciously."

Fear rippled down Kai's spine as the puzzle pieces snapped together. Tom and Sandra must have chosen him as their backup plan—because they knew they might die. Had Tom and his partner banked on him discovering the discrepancy in the notebook notations and pursuing a connection with Stanford?

Calvin's brown eyes locked on Kai from behind his funky black glasses. "Are you okay? You look a little pale."

Kai swallowed. "I'm fine. Tell me what you remembered."

Calvin leaned in. "Everything started when Dr. Peyton came barreling into the lab late one morning last January. That was the first time I'd ever met him. He introduced himself and asked to see Sandra, but she was still in class. So, I left him in her office and went about my business. She came back while I was restocking supplies in the room next door. I don't think Dr. Peyton knew the walls were paper-thin, or that I could hear through the vent."

Calvin paused as the waitress dropped off their drinks, then tracked her with his eyes until she was out of earshot before continuing, "Dr. Peyton had found something unexpected in one of the samples from The Foundation. His research had been restricted to gene samples. He thought he had finally isolated some of the single nucleotide polymorphisms, or SNPs, that were driving some genetic changes affecting the traits associated with longevity. He had success in some test and control mice. He also suspected that multiple labs were involved beyond Forrester—basically, The Foundation was piecing out the work on Firefly.

"But the samples he received that day were clearly not meant for Forrester. They contained samples of the full cell nucleus. Peyton had wanted to get his hands on those samples for some time, but he had been denied access. So, from what I overheard, he submitted three samples for full-genome sequencing. They contained the same markers as the samples he'd been working with, so he knew they'd come from the same source of genetic material that he'd been testing. But something about the genome didn't make sense."

"What did he find?" Kai asked.

"Let me first ask you a question. The donor cells. Where were you told they came from?"

Kai's eyes narrowed a bit. "What do you mean?"

"Simple question—animal, mineral, insect?"

"Human donors, why? Are you telling me they're something else?"

"I can only tell you what they're *not*...After Dr. Peyton compared the results to the HapMap, he realized that they weren't exactly human. He said they were 'beyond human.'"

The hairs on Kai's arms stood for a twenty-one-gun salute. The genome didn't appear on the HapMap's catalog of common genetic variants? How was this even possible?

The waitress arrived with their short ribs. Kai's appetite had fled, though Calvin's clearly hadn't. He launched a full-frontal attack on his short ribs. "These are amazing. Dig in," he said, mouth full.

Kai's head spun. The implications of what Calvin told him presented a world of possibilities. He couldn't begin to fathom the impact of the situation or what it meant. However, it shed some light on the dead ends that Kai continued to encounter in the current research. He needed to find those hidden pages from Tom's work. STAT.

"So, what happened after that?" Kai asked, hoping to speed this up.

Calvin rested his fork on the side of his plate. "Sandra took me into her confidence. She asked me to help conceal the connection between the lab and Forrester. Dr. Peyton started appearing more frequently to work with Sandra, but only on my shift until they moved the work off campus."

Hope sparked inside Kai. "Can you take me there?"

Calvin shook his head. "It's gone. I returned the day after Tom died, and the place was wiped clean. Transformed into raw warehouse space like it had never been there."

Kai shivered. "Do you have any idea where Tom left his research?"

"I can tell you where it *wasn't*. On the night Tom was killed, Sandra's lab and office were ransacked. The university kept it out of the papers."

"Ransacked? You sure they didn't find anything?"

Calvin shot him a wicked smile. "It was never there."

"Where was it?" Kai asked slowly, brow knitted.

"Before Sandra died, when she did the hocus-pocus on my head, she instructed me to tell this story only once…and only to you. She also gave me the most critical piece."

Kai's heart pounded. "Critical piece?"

"She told me to give you this." Calvin pulled a business card from his pocket and handed it to Kai. On the card, an address for Watson & Haskins in downtown San Francisco.

"The code word is *Ishmael*."

Chapter 21

CARA

Penthouse Meeting Room. New York City.

"TO UNDERSTAND THE Guardianship, we must visit the Old Testament for the conclusion of our story," Constantina said as they lay beneath a mural after sharing Thai take-out. Cara stared up at a massive, winged angel standing on a mountaintop, facing a man wearing leather sandals and a homespun garment tied with a rope belt.

"This painting depicts Enoch's meeting with the leader of the Watchers, Semyaza, on Mount Hebron. Here, Enoch warns Semyaza that his angels, the Watchers, have violated their covenants with God. Not only did they share knowledge of the stars, weapons, and sorcery, but they also indulged in physical relations with human women, resulting in the birth of Nephilim. These half-angel beings were a selfish and evil scourge on humanity. Rather than repent and stop what was happening, Semyaza, prideful as ever, ignored Enoch's warning of God's wrath."

Cara nodded, remembering the Old Testament reading from Sunday mass during her childhood. The story stuck in her memory since it was the first time she'd heard angels depicted as anything but *heavenly*.

"Do you know what happened next?" Constantina asked.

Chewing her lip, Cara shook her head, unsure. Biblical chronology wasn't her strong suit.

"All right, then," Constantina said, pulling Cara to her feet. "Let's move to a story I'm sure you are quite familiar with." They settled under another mural fifteen feet away.

Cara pointed to the ceiling. "Is that Noah's Ark?" Cara asked, staring at a beautiful desert valley with a large boat nestled in its base and pairs of animals queued in a line that stretched into the horizon.

"The one and only," Constantina replied. "It took a while for the sins of Semyaza and the Watchers to catch up with them. Unhappy with the direction of things, God decided on a cosmic reset and used The Great Flood to mete out his punishment."

Constantina pointed to the inset vignette of a brilliant, winged figure near a campfire speaking to a man of much smaller stature. "After Semyaza and his two hundred Watchers were captured and imprisoned for their disobedience—where they will remain locked in darkness until final Judgment—the Archangel Uriel visited Noah, Enoch's great-grandson and a descendent of the original Messenger family line. Here, Uriel carries the message from God for Noah to hide and save pairs of all manner of beasts so that *They* may cleanse the earth of man and the Nephilim abominations."

Cara tried piecing together a timeline. "When did that all happen?"

"Before the Great War. Depending on the religion, timelines and circumstances may vary within the scriptures and texts. My representation to you is that of our reality."

Interesting, but... "What does this have to do with the Trinity Guardians?" Cara asked.

Constantina's lips quirked to the side. "Given the history I shared, would it surprise you to learn that our Guardians are of angelic origin? That they are Nephilim?"

Cara's eyes widened, a chill tickling her spine. The Bible's portrayal of the Nephilim made them barely less fearsome than the demon who attacked her. "But—"

Constantina put up a finger. "Fear not, I will explain."

Cara relaxed and listened.

"The Angelorum knew our humanity made us vulnerable, so we requested protectors. We believed we could create a better Nephilim with the necessary adjustments, unlike Semyaza's past abominations."

Sounded like a tall order.

"What kind of adjustments?"

Rolling onto her elbow, Constantina squinted at the ceiling and pointed farther left. "See that warrior angel?"

"The angel holding a sword next to a golden chariot?" Cara asked to verify.

"Yes. That's Archangel Uriel, Messenger to Noah. He was a Watcher and leader of the incorruptible Powers, the ninth Order of Angels. Since neither Uriel nor any in his Order broke trust with God, we enlisted him as our sponsor when we presented our case. As part of the agreed-upon concessions to sanction these births, Uriel's Order agreed to father these children, but only with women of the Angelorum, since we also possess angelic essence. We would raise and bear these children with love. Since we are limited in number, so are they—we give birth to only enough Guardians to meet our protection needs and the needs of the Trinities. God agreed as long as we added an additional fail-safe."

"What was that?"

"They would be unable to procreate."

That seemed fair. Cara asked the next logical question. "Are they *good*?"

Constantina smiled. "Our Nephilim are the best of us. But like you and I, they were given free will. Though part angelic, like us, our Guardians are also human and blend in, just as we do."

Fascination consumed Cara. "How are they...." She squinted, her face flushing with embarrassment, "You know, conceived? Do the angels of the Powers take human form?"

Constantina leaned in and whispered, "We offer a visitation prayer in the angelic language. Once granted, the visitation occurs with a merging of energy that creates an immaculate conception of a Nephil child born of the womb."

Cara's eyes grew wider. "Really? Like the Virgin Mary?"

Constantina's lips twisted with amusement. "Similar but with different paternity. Each woman bears many Nephilim children during her human lifetimes."

Based on Constantina's earlier explanation and a subsequent clarification that not all the Three Hundred were female or of child-bearing years, she wondered about the number of Guardians. "How can you create enough Guardians having a limited number of children per lifetime?"

"Ah, good question. While I, and the rest of the Three Hundred, have typical human lifespans, the angelic characteristics and Nephilim genetics grant them almost five hundred years of longevity with aging that slows dramatically after age twenty-one."

"Do they have wings?" Cara asked, awestruck that this secret world operated almost in plain sight.

"They do, but mostly, they stay hidden," Constantina said, smiling patiently, and continued, "Our Guardianship is exclusively Nephilim, who have the battle resolve of their fathers, the angelic Order of the Powers, which makes them the perfect warriors. When Nephilim children reach sixteen, they graduate from the Angelorum Sanctuary and enter the Guardianship to begin warrior training, which lasts until they're twenty-one. After which, they're officially Called and Marked."

Cara squinted. "What does that mean? Michael mentioned Calling, but not Marking."

"Excellent question." Constantina sprang from the mat, pulled Cara to her feet with surprising strength, and led her to another vignette. "Let's save the Calling for later since it's more complex and also pertains to your role. Let's start with what it means to be Marked."

Constantina pointed to a group of twelve angels, only one of which was female. Each bore an intricate red tattoo on the pectoral nearest their heart.

"Are those Guardians?" Cara asked.

"They are, and the number has significance. Only one in twelve Nephilim is born female."

"That's all?" Cara asked.

Constantina nodded. "Yes, and they are treasured as mates—if they choose to have one. Like their male brethren, they are Marked in red ink over their hearts when they take an oath to serve the Guardianship. The Guardian Mark includes a sigil representing their angelic name, along with their maternal lineage, over a Guardianship crest. Messengers follow a similar process, except their crest represents their paternal lineage."

Cara narrowed her eyes. "Will I have a tattoo?" She didn't mind tattoos on others, but she didn't relish having one herself.

Constantina shook her head. "As a Soul Seeker, your connection to us is solely spiritual, so no Mark is required. Guardians and the Messengers are Marked because their connection to us is through blood and familial lines." Constantina winked. "But that's a complex story for another time."

Relieved a tattoo needle wasn't in her future and already close to overload, Cara was fine with that. "So, the Guardians... You mentioned they can live up to five hundred years. How old is my Guardian, Chamuel?"

Constantina wore a playful grin. "Maybe you should ask him yourself when you meet."

"Fair enough." Cara tried another angle. "How old would he *look* if I saw him on the street?"

"*Hmm.*" Constantina tapped a pursed lip, thinking. "I'm dreadful at judging age, but I believe he looks only a few biological years older than you." Her mentor sobered and raised a warning brow. "But there's something you must know about Chamuel."

"What's that?" Cara asked, taken aback by her mentor's shift in tone.

"You are both forbidden from engaging in a romantic relationship while the Trinity exists. It is the law. The penalty is severe for a Guardian who crosses that line."

Cara's eyebrows flew up. "I thought you said they couldn't procreate?" She'd pictured the Guardians lacking genitalia like her father's 1970s Led Zeppelin poster with the winged Icarus hanging in their basement.

Constantina let out a melodic chuckle. "I'm sorry, I wasn't clear. They may not be able to father or bear children, but they're fully equipped to, *umm....*" Constantina cleared her throat, a mischievous sparkle in her gaze. "Conduct a physical relationship."

Cara's cheeks warmed. "My bad. Has this ever happened? A Soul Seeker getting involved with a Guardian?" She had enough baggage and couldn't imagine adding a relationship with a mythical creature who lived for hundreds of years.

"It's happened enough over the centuries for the necessity of the rule."

Cara arched a brow. "Good to know. You said, 'while the Trinity exists,' what does that mean?"

"By design, Guardians outlive the Messenger and the Seeker, becoming a part of multiple Trinities. Messengers can also enter new Trinities. Though some missions are lifelong, most Trinities end with a mission's successful conclusion or death."

Cara wasn't loving the death clause. "Are all Guardians off-limits or just mine?" Best to be precise.

"Just yours," Constantina replied with a tight smile. "Though Nephilim tend to pursue relationships within the confines of the Angelorum. Either with their own kind or from Messenger families."

Cara nodded thoughtfully. "You mentioned multiple Trinity assignments for Messengers and Guardians. What about Soul Seekers?"

"Sometimes. Soul Seekers are a spiritual bridge between us and the soul or souls connected to a mission. Once the mission ends, they may never be called into another — yet they remain a part of us with the freedom to live their lives." Constantina clasped her hands. "Your story will be slightly different, which is why *I* am here."

A chill passed over Cara. "What do you mean?" she whispered.

"There's one last piece to our story. When God granted our request, *They* attached a prophecy of a battle led by twelve souls called the Holy Twelve. I believe you, my dear, are the first of the Twelve. My visit transcends your Trinity assignment, which will be the first step in gathering the others."

Cara started to hyperventilate. *Battle, what battle?* "What? Like an angel/demon throw down?"

"A wrestling match would be quite amusing and far less destructive, but I doubt we will have that option," Constantina said.

"Wait...." Cara pinched the bridge of her nose. "Are you talking about some End Times battle?"

"Not exactly." Constantina gave a bitter chuckle. "I dare say that our earthly timeline will fall very short of End Times if we lose this battle. Revelations will be rewritten, and Heaven as we know it will be no more. We are not trying to stop Judgment Day. We are trying to preserve it — along with mankind."

Cara blinked rapidly and gulped. "Excuse me?" she whispered. "Why *wouldn't* we want to stop the Apocalypse?"

"Let's not get ahead of ourselves." Constantina patted her leg. "First, we must ensure souls have a place to return if the Apocalypse ever happens. But we will trigger what we want to avoid if we don't close the loophole that allows Lucifer and the Dark Ones to evade Judgment Day. Everything the Son died upon the cross for will be undone, and Hell will overtake the earth."

The enormity of Constantina's words ignited panic in Cara's chest. "But why me? I'm a *banker*, for Pete's sake. I've never even touched a weapon!"

Constantina sighed. "Life is rarely as obvious or convenient as in books and movies. Real life is messy, Cara. Nothing comes wrapped with a neat bow. You need to understand that entwined within your humanity is a spark of the divine. That spark will lead you and the others into battle." She leaned forward. "I know this is hard to believe, but you wouldn't be here if you couldn't do this."

Cara tried to rein in her panic. "You said there are twelve. Who are the others?"

"I cannot yet say. Many free-will decisions still need to be made. It's best if we prepare for your Calling first. I ask that you trust me and refrain from sharing this knowledge with anyone in the interim. Not even Michael. It would only put you all in more danger."

Cara pressed fingers to her throbbing temples and nodded reluctantly.

Constantina patted her shoulder. "I promise you'll understand more soon. But this is why I am here to train you personally. This Trinity is extra special because of you. I will do my best to ensure you do not fail."

A flush of warmth filled Cara, though her mind felt like an exploding head emoji. Despite opening Pandora's Box of what lay ahead, Cara was grateful for her time with Constantina. Though she might never get out of bed again if she thought about this too deeply.

Constantina stifled a yawn with the back of a hand. "Now, let's take our leave and continue in the morning when Michael arrives, shall we?"

Cara glanced at her watch. It was almost midnight. "Of course." She hadn't realized the depth of her exhaustion until she stood on legs filled with pins and needles after their closing prayer. Although counterintuitive, Cara felt... good. A little scared, but good. Despite the overwhelming knowledge she gained, Constantina had given her something she didn't have this morning—a way to make a meaningful difference.

She had so much to process, and tomorrow was a new day. Here's hoping it's demon-free.

Chapter 22

CARA

Fifth Avenue Penthouse. New York City.

CARA RACED TO the kitchen counter and scooped up her vibrating cell phone. A text from Sienna lit the screen: ***Raphael's 7 PM. Wear something nice!*** Dress, shoe, and lipstick emojis ***XOXO***. "Crap," Cara blurted at the stark reminder that today was Saturday and life existed outside the Penthouse. Not to mention, the world had either tipped on its axis, or Sienna was still jetlagged to be awake before ten o'clock.

Michael and Constantina fell silent, their eyes fixed on her from where they sat at the island. "What is it, dear one?" Constantina asked, sipping her café au lait. An empty plate sat in front of her with a few flakes of croissant from a French bakery around the corner.

Cara sighed and dropped her phone on the island. In all the saving-the-world excitement, Cara had forgotten about her plans. "I'm supposed to meet my best friend, Sienna, tonight for a belated birthday celebration."

Constantina traded a glance with Michael, who closed his eyes, his face a mask of peaceful contemplation.

Cara eyed Constantina and whispered, "What's he doing?"

Her mentor placed a finger to her lips. Cara closed her mouth and crossed her arms, watching Michael do whatever he was doing. *Meditating, perhaps?*

Opening his eyes, Michael smiled reassuringly at Constantina. "She'll be fine. I'll check for updates during the evening."

Cara wagged a finger between them. "What was that?"

Michael cocked a brow at Constantina, who set down her cup, and replied with utmost patience, "In yesterday's lesson, I mentioned the Flow carries messages along with healing energy." She motioned to Michael and said, "That's how Messengers communicate with the Angelorum. While your ties to us are spiritual, Messenger genes run in families, giving them latent psychic abilities. A sacred attunement ceremony unleashes their gifts when they accept their Calling, allowing them to communicate through the Flow."

Cara propped a hip on the island and unleashed her curiosity. "How does that work?"

Constantina shrugged. "Simple. Messengers are like radio receivers tuned to a specific station. Each has a unique frequency, like a telepathic phone number, which allows them to communicate with the Irin—the keepers of the Flow—who act as psychic telephone operators."

Michael tapped his head. "I created a mental key during my attunement. I focus on a sound and an object to open a line, identifying myself. My job is to keep our Trinity connected to the Angelorum for news and direction."

Cara snorted softly and shook her head. *Of course.* She should've suspected as much. "Daniel Bernoulli would've given his eyeteeth to have been part of this conversion," she mused, thanking her high school physics teacher for introducing her to the eighteenth-century Swiss mathematician and physicist and his theory on string vibration and infinite harmonics.

Constantina's laughter tinkled in the air. "I'm sure you're right. So, go and enjoy yourself this evening. We'll make contact if anything changes." Then, she glanced at the clock, slipped from her stool, and clapped cheerfully. "Let's get to work, dear ones. You will be glad to know energy manipulation is on today's agenda."

Chloe, fast asleep in her dog bed minutes ago, whined and scampered around the kitchen. Michael volunteered to take his four-legged fan club for a quick walk before they started, while Cara and Constantina made haste with the dishes and headed to the meeting room.

An angel's warm painted gaze welcomed Cara from the ceiling when she entered the room's embracing glow with Constantina. By Cara's estimation, they had barely covered a tenth of the ceiling vignettes and stories the night before. At this rate, they could lie on the floor, staring at the ceiling, for a month and still not get through all the paintings. That worried her less than leaving the Penthouse and having her two worlds collide.

Dread pooled in her stomach, anticipating the barrage of questions sure to accompany her night out with Sienna.

Cara gently tugged Constantina to a stop as they reached the center of the room. "With everything that's happened, what should I tell my friends and family without blatantly lying? Mr. Gladstone suggested I tell them I'm housesitting as part of a new property management job for Watson & Haskins."

"Which is true." Innocence sparkled in Constantina's ocean-blue eyes. "You're caring for these properties and assets, are you not? No one needs to know of your stake in them." She smiled. "If all goes well, you may consider a future role with the Watson & Haskins investment team. The Gladstone family is a well-respected and prominent Messenger line in our employ. I'm sure they would gladly take you on."

Cara blinked. She loved investment banking. It was her boss she had hated. "Thank you. That's a great idea." Her spirits lightened.

Michael came up the stairs two at a time. "Chloe is resting comfortably under her Princess blanket on the library sofa," he said, rubbing his hands together and looking pleased with the accomplishment.

Why did her stubborn Whippet obey everyone but her?

Cara begrudgingly smiled her thanks. They sat in the center of the room while Constantina lit the candles on the altar. Cara squeezed Michael's hand and whispered, "I'm glad you're here."

He winked. "Glad to be here."

Having Michael close made this easier, but her conversation with Constantina yesterday nagged at her. Abiding by her promise not to share the prophecy with Michael created another uncomfortable secret that placed a barrier between her and someone she cared about. She hated that. Even if it was for their benefit.

Constantina joined them, said an opening prayer to the Angels to protect and guide them in their training, and began, "Today, I'll share a series of energy-related exercises. We'll start with something simple and a bit fun—how to use energy and our sense of taste to detect the truth."

A small thrill fluttered through Cara. That did sound fun—and useful. She traded a side glance with Michael, who nodded with a look of excitement equal to hers.

"First, let me do a quick attunement to unlock your abilities." Constantina clasped her hands and bowed her head in prayer.

The pillar of light that Cara had seen yesterday poured from the ceiling into Constantina's crown. Golden threads of energy pulsed inside the glow as it cascaded into Constantina. Cara swallowed, finding the shimmering sight as awe-inspiring as the day before.

When Constantina opened her eyes, the pillar's glow surrounded her petite frame in a full-body halo, and her unnaturally bright, blue gaze fell on Cara. "To taste the truth, you must be within three feet of a person to absorb their aura's energy," Constantina said, tracing the air around Michael as she spoke. "When I ask Michael to speak a truth, I want you to breathe in his energy. Not through your nose, but like this...."

Moving to Cara, she knelt before her and touched glowing fingers to the chakra between Cara's eyes. Then, she ran her fingertips downward along Cara's cheekbones, warming and sending tingles over Cara's skin.

"Focus on absorbing right here. Then wait and notice the flavor on your tongue."

Constantina moved to Michael, running her fingertips over his face using the same path. Then she sat back, closed her hands, and murmured a closing prayer. The light retracted through the ceiling, taking the glow surrounding Constantina with it.

"You first, Cara. Are you ready?"

Cara nodded, unsure how the mechanics were possible, but it was no crazier than a pillar of light spilling from the ceiling. She'd give it a go.

"Face Michael, and try it."

Cara scooted around and sat cross-legged, settling her hands on her knees. She wondered how to suppress the instinct to use her nose and met Michael's gaze, a teasing glint in his royal blues. "Is this really going to work?" she whisper-hissed.

An enigmatic smile accompanied his bemused stare. "I think you already know the answer."

She narrowed her eyes. He was doing it again, reading her. She wanted to shoulder-knock the smile from his face. Instead, she silently accepted his challenge and readied herself.

"Michael, share a truth with Cara," Constantina prompted.

Pausing, he cleared all expression from his face. "I graduated from Yale with a degree in English."

Cara concentrated on the chakra between her eyes and let his words wash down her cheeks. Closing her eyes, she rolled her tongue skeptically around her mouth, tasting.

At the first hint of honey sweetness, Cara's eyelids flew open. She gave a thumbs-up, mildly astounded that it worked, and impressed to discover Michael's Ivy League pedigree. Sure, he was super smart, but he lacked the oversized ego of the Ivy League jerks who worked at Cabot. If anything, he had more humility than anyone she'd ever met.

"Now, tell her something false," Constantina told Michael.

"I'm a fantastic cook."

Cara repeated the process, and this time, the bitter taste of radicchio assaulted her taste buds. Relieved to find a chink in his perfect armor, she made a mental note to be wary of dinner invitations that didn't include take-out.

"Did you taste a difference?" Constantina asked.

"Truth tasted sweet like honey, and lies, bitter like radicchio."

Her mentor beamed like a proud parent. "Excellent!"

Michael had been right. Damn him! Then something clicked. This wasn't the first time an unexpected taste echoed on her tongue. She snapped her fingers. "During the demon attack, I tasted…tar."

Constantina nodded, squinting. "Interesting. That's exactly how evil tastes to me, too."

Cara glanced expectantly at Michael, who shrugged. "Nope. I haven't met any demons yet."

"Count your blessings, dear one," Constantina quipped. "Now switch."

They spent the next hour testing each other's taste buds.

Cara's amazement grew along with her bank of trivia on Michael: he can't sing, he volunteers at a local animal shelter once a month, he's a Star Trek fan, and he won his first karate competition at the age of ten.

When the lesson ended, Constantina said, "The tastes will get stronger with practice and develop richness and nuance beyond truth and lies to include a full range of emotions."

Cara idly circled a finger on the mat. "How does it help us?"

"No gift is ever wasted, and all of them have a purpose."

"But—" Cara caught herself before spilling her secret and asking how this would help defeat Lucifer and the Dark Ones. "Never mind."

Constantina winked, catching her meaning, and moved on. "Next in the queue—energy healing. A handy gift. Cara, dear one, you experienced this when I healed your throat yesterday and attuned you earlier. This time, I'll explain as I demonstrate. But first, a quiz. What was the first thing I did each time?"

Cara raised a hand and received a nod from Constantina. "You opened with a prayer."

"Correct! We start with a prayer of protection for healing, spoken silently or aloud. You must invite loving energy and ban forces that harm. Using the angelic language is best, but any language will do. It's the intent that matters. This time, I will use the angelic language." Constantina spoke a few melodic sounds that resonated inside Cara's chest and were unlike anything she'd ever heard.

"Next, I will reconnect to the Flow. To do this, imagine reaching up with the top of your head and then breathing down the energy, welcoming it inside you."

Closing her eyes, Constantina heaved her chest in an exaggerated movement to demonstrate. The pillar reappeared with pulsing threads of energy, spilling from the ceiling into the top of Constantina's head.

When Constantina opened her eyes, the light remained, but the glow around her had not yet appeared. "The third step is coalescence." She took Cara's hand and placed it over her heart. Tingling warmth radiated from her mentor into Cara's palm. "In simple terms, I take the energy swirling around my heart, and through my intent, I add love." Constantina removed

Cara's hand and looked at Michael. "Do you have the blade I requested, dear one?"

Alarm bristled the hairs on the back of Cara's neck. *Blade, what blade?*

Michael scooted closer to Constantina and removed a small dagger from the pocket of his hoodie. He unsheathed the knife and handed it to her, handle first.

Cara's heart thumped against her rib cage. "What are you doing?"

Michael gave her knee a reassuring squeeze. "It's okay," he said softly, pushing up a sleeve and extending a rippled forearm. "I've done this before."

And that's supposed to make it okay? Cara thought.

The pillar of light funneling from above surrounded Constantina in a radiant glow. She took the blade and passed it over Michael's arm. He winced as bright-red blood flowed from the gash, droplets splashing onto the light blue mat.

Cara held her breath and prayed that this would work.

Constantina placed her hands on Michael's shoulders. Bright light engulfed them, swallowing them whole. Seconds later, the light receded, and they reappeared.

Michael's lips kicked to the side as he held up an unblemished arm. "Told you."

Cara's jaw hung open. Even the blood that had dripped into the mat was gone. "I can do that?"

"You can," Constantina said brightly. "Now, it's your turn."

Cara's pulse spiked. She shook her head and scuttled backward like a frantic crab, widening the distance between them. "What if I can't do it?"

Michael crawled to her. Clasping her shoulders gently, he met her gaze. "Hey, trust us. Okay?"

She hesitantly returned to where Constantina sat, yoga-style, her hands resting on her knees. "Get comfortable like me. There is nothing to fear," Constantina said.

Taking a tentative breath, Cara reluctantly followed suit.

Constantina talked her through each step.

Energy slammed into Cara's crown, and her eyes flew open. She swayed with the force as it blazed a path to her chest, and the pathway connecting her crown to her heart tingled with vibration as the force swam inside her chest like a living thing, awaiting its next instruction. Had she really done that?

She stared wide-eyed at Constantina and Michael. They were smiling.

"Well done," said Constantina. "Now, fill the energy with love and let it swirl."

Intuitively, Cara knew what to do, visualizing her feelings for Kai, Sienna, her parents, siblings, and anyone else she could think of, including the two people in the room. Exhilaration filled her senses.

"Ready?" Constantina held the dagger.

"Yes," Cara whispered.

Instead of scoring her arm, Constantina plunged the dagger into her own chest. Cara gasped in horror and screamed.

Lunging for Constantina, Cara latched onto the woman's small shoulders and dug her fingers into flesh. The living energy swirling inside her found an outlet through her palms, engulfing them in bright light that threatened to burn her retinas. The Flow traveled through Cara, entering Constantina through one hand and returning through the other in a continuous cycle.

Sweat beaded on the top of Cara's upper lip as she held onto Constantina for dear life and poured a steady stream of love into the light until the returning energy grew stronger and equaled the energy leaving.

"You may let go," Constantina said calmly from within the light. "Healing is complete when the energy is in balance."

Cara's trembling hands fell from Constantina's shoulders, and the light disappeared.

Injuries gone, Constantina clapped, beaming with pride. "Brilliantly done."

No, just no. Angry tears welled in Cara's eyes, and she roughly brushed them away, shaken. "What the actual hell?! What if I failed? What if you *died*?" she yelled at Constantina, who smiled serenely, and she shook her head.

"You couldn't fail, dear one. The Sentinel's test told me as much."

Cara swallowed. She wasn't ready for this. Why had she been chosen? Surely, there was someone more worthy. Trembling, she jumped to her feet and paced, cradling her tear-streaked face in her palms. Insecurity replaced any confidence she had gained the night before. "I don't know if I can do this."

Constantina *tsked*, then stood and pulled Cara gently to a stop. "You can, and you did. I have faith in you. But you must have faith in yourself. Come back and sit. We must close the exercise."

Cara wiped at her eyes and morosely followed her mentor to where Michael waited, giving her a supportive smile. She dropped down beside him and examined her cuticles. She didn't appreciate the baptism-by-fire approach. Getting out tonight would do her good. She needed a break to regain some perspective. She planned on having a glass of wine — or three.

Michael threw an arm around her. "It's all right," he whispered.

She leaned into him and smiled despite herself.

"To close, you must complete the final step. Say a silent prayer of thanks to the Creator."

Gladly. Because a higher power had healed Constantina, not her. She was nothing but a vessel in that exchange. *Thank you, God,* she thought, and let out a defeated sigh, then mumbled, "That was pretty cool until you stabbed yourself."

Constantina chuckled softly. Kneeling before her, she took Cara's hands as Michael's arm fell away. "The power to heal has always been inside you, dear one. I only showed you how to unlock it."

"Promise you'll give me a warning next time?" Cara asked, feeling like an imposter, despite the miraculous feat she performed.

Constantina gave Cara's hands a final squeeze. "I promise, and later, I'll show you how to temper the energy for smaller remedies and to conceal the light."

Cara blew out a breath and nodded, then turned to Michael. "Your turn, buddy."

Michael shrugged. "Nope. Not a healer."

"You and Michael both have special gifts, but they are not the same," Constantina said, trading a glance with Michael and clapping briskly. "Enough chatter, dear ones. Let's finish our lessons so Cara can leave us and enjoy her evening."

Cara caught the glance, wondering about Michael's other abilities. She also wondered what secrets Constantina asked him to keep.

Chapter 23

CARA

Raphael's. New York City.

CARA STEPPED OUT of a taxi in front of Raphael's in SoHo, feeling like a convict out on parole. She welcomed a reprieve after the last couple of emotionally taxing and exhausting days and silently thanked the angels, more specifically, the Irin, for making it all possible.

The balance of good and evil could survive a night without her. The most difficult part of the evening would be sidestepping Sienna's curiosity. They'd shared all their secrets since they were sixteen until now. Cara hated lying even by omission, but in a stroke of brilliance, she'd come up with an acceptable half-truth while browsing the bookshelves in the library.

Cara couldn't believe her eyes when she found a treasure trove of first-edition eighteenth and nineteenth-century classics: Charles Dickens, the Brontë sisters, and Jane Austen, to name a few of her favorites. She'd tell Sienna her grandmother left her a rare book collection—accurate on a technicality and enough to satisfy her friend.

The rest could wait.

Cara caught her reflection as she approached the restaurant's glass door. She wore her red-soled stilettos, which had survived the sprint through Lower Manhattan no worse for wear, and followed Sienna's emoji instructions to the letter, hoping to get her seal of approval.

Cara entered the small restaurant's semi-dark interior and approached the hostess, a pencil-thin young woman in her early twenties with closely cropped hair and Edith Piaf eyebrows. She looked up and smiled as Cara came over. "May I help you?"

"Seven o'clock reservation for Sienna Sargent?"

The hostess perked up at the mention of Sienna's name. "Ah, yes! She hasn't arrived yet. Would you like me to seat you, or would you like to wait at the bar?"

"I'll wait at the bar, thanks." Cara traded her red swing coat for a coat-check ticket.

It was still early for dinner by Manhattan standards. Half the barstools sat empty, with a party of four having drinks and a male couple chatting quietly over champagne glasses.

Cara decided to seize the opportunity for a pit stop before taking a seat. She eyed the twisty spiral staircase beside the bar. Housed in a turn-of-the-century building, the restaurant retained its original tin ceiling, cozy charm, and this deathtrap of a staircase to the upstairs bathrooms. An addition that would never comply with today's building codes.

She sighed and carefully navigated the narrow, pie-sliced metal stairs to the second floor.

The ladies' room was small and tight, but the mirror was well-lit. Cara used the facilities and then gave herself another once-over. Her auburn hair cascaded below her shoulders in a full-bodied wave, and her foundation did an excellent job of covering the dark smudges beneath her eyes from a few nights of crappy sleep. Other than that, she kept her look understated. She wore her favorite red lipstick, a coat of mascara, and smoky eyeliner to emphasize her green eyes.

The new Dolce & Gabbana sleeveless black dress hugged her waist and hips while tastefully emphasizing her chest with a hint of cleavage. Turning to the side, she ensured the dress didn't cling too tightly to her butt. She gave a satisfied nod. Her judgy best friend should be pleased.

Cara gripped the pole tightly on the perilous journey down the winding stairs, watching her feet so her heels didn't snag on the metal grates.

She rounded the last turn, looked up, and froze.

No, it couldn't be.

A Viking-gorgeous man headed for the bar. His dark-blond hair framed his chiseled face and touched his shoulders. The duster was gone. He wore a black V-neck sweater that stretched across a broad, muscled torso and faded jeans that hugged powerful thighs. Standing a full head taller than the cluster of people ahead of him, he followed at a polite distance.

Recognition raised the hairs on Cara's arms, and she continued her descent. *Oh my God, the guy from the subway.*

He glanced up. His vivid, crystal-blue gaze locked on hers, stealing her breath.

Cara's heel clipped the edge of a metal tread, and she lost her footing. Panic gripped her as she sailed through the air.

Strong arms caught her before she hit the ground. Her heart thundered as her fingers grazed the warmth of a massive bicep beneath black cashmere. A clean, citrusy scent mixed with something deliciously male filled her senses.

"I've got you," he whispered, his breath a warm caress on her cheek as he set her on her feet, a hand remaining on her arm to steady her. The color of his eyes was even more startling up close. "Are you okay?" His inquiry, soft and intimate, caught her off guard.

A flush hit Cara's cheeks, and she stared awestruck at one of the most beautiful men she'd ever seen. His gaze held none of the cool avoidance she observed on the subway but warmth and a spark of mischief.

Her skin tingled under his large palm, lightly clasping her bare skin. She cleared her throat. "Thank you. Stupid shoes," she mumbled. Then she did the only safe thing she could imagine. "Sorry, I need to go." She slipped from his grasp and sprinted.

Sienna made her entrance as Cara reached the hostess desk, muttering to herself, "Good job, Collins. Way to make a total ass out of yourself."

Sienna ran toward Cara in yet another pair of platform heels. "Hi, sweetie! Happy birthday!" A huge Prada handbag dangled from her arm, and she wore one of her runway creations, a dress shaped like an asymmetrical orange box. Anyone else would look ridiculous, but Sienna pulled it off with panache. Chopsticks—at least they looked like chopsticks—secured Sienna's hair into a chignon atop her head with tendrils hanging loose around her face. Between that and her eyelash extensions, her sky-blue eyes looked huge.

Sienna threw her arms around Cara, kissed her once on each cheek European-style, and stepped back to assess Cara's outfit. "Love the dress, Carissima." Sienna's gaze traveled to Cara's chest. "Nice job packaging the wares."

Cara silently high-fived herself for passing muster and smiled. "Thanks...I think."

Sienna gushed to the hostess, "Gabrielle, *darling*, it's so lovely to see you! Did you get us my favorite table?"

"Of course!" Gabrielle said with equal enthusiasm. "Anything for you. The chef prepared a special appetizer this evening. He'll be out later to greet you personally." Grabbing two menus, she held them up. "In case you need them. Follow me."

Sienna whispered to Cara, "Gabrielle is one of my fit models," before sinking into a business conversation with the hostess.

That explains a lot, Cara thought, trailing behind the chatting women.

Cara spotted her Viking savior on a barstool, conversing quietly with the bartender as she passed the bar. His profile was to die for, with a strong jaw, straight nose, and full, sensuous lips. God, those lips. Something tightened low in her belly, taking her by surprise. It had been ages since her body reacted to anyone that way.

Heart pounding, she tried sneaking past unnoticed, but he leaned back, caught her eye, and smiled. His gaze warmed with sincere male appreciation. "Have a nice dinner," he said, his voice rich and deep.

Trapped in a spell woven by those eyes, she returned his smile, turning her head just in time to avoid running into a man getting up from his chair.

What is wrong with me? At least he couldn't see her face flush with embarrassment.

She slipped into the booth opposite Sienna.

Sienna eyed her. "What's wrong? You look like you're having a hot flash."

Cara unfolded her napkin, dabbed at her brow, then placed it over her lap. "I can barely manage my own two feet. Before you arrived, I tripped coming down the spiral staircase."

Sienna's face registered alarm, and she reached for Cara's arm. "Are you hurt?"

Cara sighed. "I'm fine. A very tall, very gorgeous man caught me before I hit the floor."

Sienna's eyes went wide. "Really? Where is he?" she asked, readying to gawk.

"He's at the bar." Cara peeked around the booth and glanced at where he'd been sitting. The seat was empty. "Correction. He *was* at the bar."

Sienna dug into her purse, pulled out a pen, and handed it to her. "Give him your number. No offense, honey, but you could use a date."

"Thanks, but no," Cara smirked, pushing aside the proffered pen.

A sommelier arrived, setting down two glasses and presenting them with a bottle of Cabernet. She looked at Cara and smiled. "A gentleman at the bar sent this bottle with his compliments...In celebration of your birthday."

Cara traded a stunned glance with Sienna as the sommelier removed the cork from the bottle and handed it to Cara.

Cara gave it a sniff and nodded, too shocked to speak. It could've been sewer water for all she knew.

Sienna glanced at the label and examined the menu. Her mouth dropped open. "That's the second most expensive bottle of wine on the menu," she whisper-hissed across the table.

Oh, God. She needed to thank him. "Is he still here?" Cara asked the sommelier, hoping he hadn't left. At least until she knew his name.

"I believe so," the sommelier said as she poured.

Remembering most of what she'd learned from wine-tasting classes during her year abroad in France, Cara observed the legs, sniffed, rolled a sip on her tongue, and accepted with a nod. Much better than sewer water.

The sommelier filled their glasses and said, "Let me check with the bartender to see if he settled his check," and left them to their wine.

Sienna grinned. "Carissima, classy move. I like him already. He dropped serious coin on this Cabernet. Don't let him leave without a number." Her smile dampened. "Wait, he wasn't wearing a wedding ring, was he?"

Cara's brow wrinkled in annoyance. "I wasn't looking at his fingers during my death-defying midair acrobatics. Not that it matters. Men like him don't normally like me." Admittedly, he'd been friendlier here than in the subway.

Sienna snorted and slapped the table. "Yes, they do. You've always been too oblivious to see it. You need to stop looking at the ground and look at people." Sienna swung forked fingers between their eyes.

Cara huffed. "That's why I almost face-planted. I wasn't looking at the ground."

Sienna puffed her chest, smiled smugly, and pointed at the wine. "Case in point. Look who you met." She leaned across the table. "Maybe the birthday wish I made for you will come true, and you can finally dump Kai, the married loser."

Cara ground her teeth and gave Sienna a side-eye. "He's my friend, not my lover, and you don't dump friends."

"Some friend," she shot back. "He didn't even call you on your birthday."

Sienna's dart hit home. Cara straightened her spine. "He called the next morning and sent a gift card." But rather than falling on her sword over Kai, she changed the subject. "Speaking of doomed romances, how's Oliver?"

"Not fair." Sienna pouted. "He's my Hamptons hook-up. But..." She held up a finger and brightened. "I did meet a hot model in Paris, who, wait for it, is straight and lives in New York."

"That sounds like another hook-up," Cara sniffed.

Sienna gave her a hurt look and swatted a hand. "Hey, I'm not ready for anything serious. Mark crushed my heart. I need some fun for a while."

Ugh, Mark. What a dick. If Cara could wring his neck with her bare hands, she would. He made Kai look like a Boy Scout.

After dating Sienna for four years and giving her signals he planned to propose, he dumped her last summer for some gold digger with silicone boobs he'd met in the Hamptons. Mark was a walking stereotype of an arrogant Wall Street jerk, making the guys Cara worked with at Cabot seem like choirboys. To his credit, he'd always been generous with Sienna, but he'd let her down in the end. Secretly, Cara was glad their relationship ended, suspecting he was a serial cheater. Cara wanted more for her friend—someone who could make her happy and treasure her for who she was.

Someone like *Michael*.

Cara tucked the thought away as the sommelier returned and said, "I'm sorry. He left. But he asked to give you this." She handed Cara a small, neatly folded piece of paper. Cara accepted it and thanked the woman.

Sienna squealed with excitement as the sommelier departed.

Cara stared at the paper and hesitated, a thrill coursing through her. When she made no move to open the note, Sienna snapped her fingers with impatience. "What're you waiting for? Your next birthday?"

Cara cut Sienna a glare and worked up her nerve. "Give me a second."

Sienna threw up her hands, her lips dropping into a sullen pout, "Fine."

Cara unfolded the paper and read the neat, looping script. *"I'd be honored if you would meet me here on Tuesday evening at eight o'clock for dinner."* No signature.

"Nice!" Sienna waggled her perfectly arched brows.

Cara stared at the note. *"Hmm."* Then she got up from the table. "I'll be back in a sec."

"Wait—" Sienna called after her.

But Cara ignored Sienna and walked to the bar. "Excuse me?" Cara leaned over the polished mahogany and waved at the bartender. "Do you remember the tall guy with long, blond hair who sat here earlier?"

The bartender approached, buffing a highball glass with a bar towel. "Sure. He comes in for dinner every so often and eats at the bar."

"Do you know his name?"

The bartender paused to think, then shook his head. "Sorry. Never mentioned it. Pays in cash. For what it's worth, he's always pleasant. Low-key. Generous tipper."

She braced herself and danced into dangerous territory. "Does he always come alone?"

He shrugged, picking up another glass. "Yeah. Has always minded his own business until tonight. Usually has a meal and leaves." Cara thanked him and returned to her table.

She slipped back into the booth across from Sienna. "The bartender doesn't know his name."

Sienna's eyes widened like an anime character. "So, you're going to meet him, right?"

Cara blew out a breath. "I have a couple of days to decide...." Given her change in circumstances, dating didn't seem like a wise idea.

"Decide what? You'd better go! Otherwise, I'll show up and meet him," Sienna said, dead serious. "Not to get all princess-y on you, but this is what fairytales are made of. Don't overthink it; just do it."

"Okay, Mother Goose, let's order," Cara replied. She'd had her fair share of fairytale moments this week, and not all of them good.

Sienna looked at Cara over the menu. "So, tell me more about your visit to that law firm."

Cara sighed. *Let the games begin.*

Chapter 24

CHAMUEL
Prince Street. New York City.

CHAMUEL CLOAKED AS he exited Raphael's, slipping past a couple entering. Having no desire to explain why he was out of uniform, Chamuel sped unseen down the street past Zeke and Noah without greeting them. He'd apologize later for the snub, using Isaac as an excuse.

His food had just arrived when his cell vibrated with a new text. He'd groaned, sensing trouble, and took a bite of perfectly cooked steak and some crispy *frites* before checking the caller.

He wasn't wrong.

It was Isaac. *We have a situation. Sent relief. I'll call in 15.*

He'd still be at the bar fulfilling Constantina's protection request if it weren't for that damned text. Instead, he was avoiding his relief crew and taking his dinner to go. Though Constantina's call had taken him by surprise. Chamuel hadn't expected to resume surveillance for at least two days until she finished Cara's preliminary training.

He'd been using the downtime to finish a landscape painting. Inhaling two days' worth of paint and turpentine must've messed with his head. Why else had he dressed in street clothes and watched his charge from inside the restaurant instead of from a safe distance on a rooftop?

Cara had spotted him three minutes after entering the restaurant, a few seconds before tripping on the stairs.

Before he knew it, she was in his arms. If he'd thought she was enticing while unconscious, awake, her enticement multiplied one hundred-fold. When their gazes locked, he couldn't deny a heady moment of connection. He saw the glimmer of recognition when it entered her lovely green eyes. She remembered him from the subway.

Luckily, she didn't know his true identity and could blame the meeting on a coincidence. After all, this was his neighborhood, and he was a regular patron of the restaurant. What were the chances that Cara would choose *Raphael's* of all the eateries in New York City?

That said, he could only blame himself for the dangerous and stupid game he decided to play. He couldn't deny that while he held her a second time, her energy sang to his in a melody that awakened something unexplainable. Stronger than after the demon attack.

He'd survived over a century of celibacy without female companionship. Why was Cara, forbidden among all females, the one tempting him?

Breaking his celibacy would pale in comparison to what would befall him if he pursued her and the High Council found out. The law left no room for misinterpretation. Trinity Guardians were forbidden from engaging in romantic relationships with members of their Trinity. Punishment was swift and severe for crossing the line, starting with a mandatory 100-year prison sentence. That alone should've taken Cara off the menu.

Period. End of story.

Yet, he felt like a moth to a flame.

He really needed his head examined for sending that bottle of wine. Still, he could've walked away with no strings after that. But, no! He doubled down, idiotically, and issued a dinner invitation.

Chamuel passed a hand over his face. Not only had he put himself at significant personal risk, but meeting Cara under false pretenses was unforgivable. He wouldn't be able to maintain the ruse forever. Once she accepted her Calling, she would know the truth.

Nothing about this decision was logical, but that didn't quell his desire to give her a chance to know him as a male.

My God, she's human. What am I thinking?

Plodding home, he pulled up short on the sidewalk with a sudden thought. Could the feeling Cara triggered be a form of *soul recognition*? Could they have known each other *before* birth? He'd learned of this rare phenomenon during his schooling as an adolescent. He knew very few who had experienced it, but what else explained his recklessness?

Shaking his head, he huffed a mirthless laugh. That would be a cruel joke—finding a soul mate who is untouchable. Maybe that was the ultimate penance Fate had in mind.

His mind wandered back to Cara's lips. Would the feel of them be worth a century of imprisonment?

Absorbed in thought, he nearly passed his Greene Street loft, which he'd purchased under a shell corporation in the 1970s when SoHo properties were still industrial and dirt cheap. Formerly only a pied-à-terre, his fifth-floor unit was now his full-time residence. As much as he loved the loft, he missed the daily camaraderie of the Tri-State House.

Chamuel checked his watch. Five minutes until Isaac called.

He strode to the elevator, twisted his key in the control pad, and ascended to the top floor.

The generously sized, three-bedroom loft also housed his painting studio, the reason Chamuel purchased the property. A patron and lover of the arts, he was an artist in his own right, a talent he honed for over a century. Many of his works hung on the walls, blending well with a tasteful mix of antiques and modern pieces, creating a comfortable, eclectic vibe. But Chamuel's genuine pride and joy lay claim to the center of his loft, where he'd poured a small fortune into installing a chef's kitchen.

He found as much solace in cooking as in painting, having studied at the now-defunct Le Cordon Bleu in Paris while on a hiatus from the Guardianship in the 1990s. For years afterward, Chamuel commandeered the Tri-State Guardian House kitchen on Sundays—Luigi's one day off—where he flexed his culinary skills and prepared five-course tasting menus with wine pairings for his appreciative brethren.

Chamuel set the oven to 300 degrees to keep his meal warm and sat at the kitchen island, waiting for Isaac's call.

It's only dinner, he thought, revisiting his rash invitation. He drummed his fingers on the granite and froze. *What if she doesn't show up?* Disappointment flared at the thought, and he calculated the probability of being stood up.

His cell phone rang, and he glanced at the caller ID. "I, what's so important?"

"Our Seeker in Boston was attacked, and her Guardian was abducted. He's off the grid. The timing couldn't be worse."

Chamuel straightened. "Xavier? The Senator's assignment? What happened?" That made at least a dozen missing Guardians over the last fourteen months, all disappearing without a trace.

"Not sure. Will you go to Boston to check it out?" Isaac asked. "Given the sensitivity, I don't want to alarm the team. Other than Zeke and Noah, everyone just left for the spring induction at the Guardian Academy. I've spoken to Constantina. She gave approval."

Chamuel swiped a hand down his face. He could do that and still keep his doomed Tuesday night date. "I'll drive up tonight and meet with the Boston Seeker in the morning. Any news on the rogue?"

Isaac's report confirmed no one from the Guardianship had been in Cara's proximity during the Sentinel encounter or the demon attack, except for him and Zeke. Energy footprints don't lie and can't be replicated. Perplexing, to say the least.

"None. The House leaders are triple-checking. I can't figure out how the Nephil eluded our technology. As implausible as it sounds, I believe the rogue exists outside the Angelorum records, which puts us at a disadvantage. Regardless, we should've found a footprint besides yours—registered or unregistered. Constantina and I are meeting tomorrow to discuss the Guardian attacks and rogue Nephil."

Chamuel scowled, missing his former privileges as a Guardian House leader.

"Cham, be careful. I'm not sure if the rogue incident and the abductions are related. We're mobilizing a task force to investigate. If you weren't part of a Trinity, I'd ask for more than this."

A fleeting spark of hope ignited in Chamuel's chest. "Can we assign someone else to Cara?" That would solve his latest dilemma.

Isaac *tsked*. "Never happen. Constantina wants you, and there's no dissuading her."

Chamuel deflated like a popped balloon. "Don't I know it," he muttered. "Give me twenty-four hours for the Boston situation."

"Fair enough. I'll text you the details. Thanks, brother." Chamuel hung up and ran his fingers through his hair, deeply disturbed over the events of the evening.

He finished his steak without tasting it and headed to his private rooftop retreat that featured a garden he'd filled with small fruit trees he cultivated from seed and an elaborate system of built-in containers featuring perennials, herbs, and vegetables that bordered a full-sized deck with statuary and fountains. A pergola covered a dining area in the center, featuring a bar, grill, table, and ample seating to host a sizable party. Too bad it hadn't seen guests in some time. For a moment, Chamuel imagined a romantic dinner with Cara.

Yeah, not happening.

He needed to stretch his wings and forget about tonight for a while.

Stripping to his boxers, he laid the folded black cashmere sweater and jeans on the nearest lounge chair. The bracing night air skated over his pectorals and the single, red tattoo over his heart, branding him as an Angelorum Guardian.

Thanks to his DNA, which allowed him to self-regulate his body temperature, he relished the breeze coursing over his skin. A familiar tingle started in the center of his back as he scanned the horizon and chose a southerly path toward the ocean and the full moon. Chamuel invoked his wings with a silent prayer, transforming the tingle into a V-shaped burn transversing his shoulder blades.

Radiant, snow-white plumage emerged through his skin and unfurled, breathtaking and powerful, into a wingspan triple his height. Iridescent feathers covered an intricate expanse of muscle, tissue, and nerves, sending awareness through his entire body.

An integral part of him, his wings unleashed his spirit.

Flexing his shoulders, Chamuel rustled his wings, readying for flight, and crouched. With a mighty leap and a few powerful flaps, Chamuel soared into the night sky, hoping to find a solution to his dilemma that wouldn't land him in chains.

Chapter 25

CARA

Fifth Avenue Penthouse. New York City.

I MUST BE DYING, Cara thought, head throbbing with the mother of all hangovers. A fitting punishment for her crimes. After dinner, she and Sienna met some of Sienna's friends at a club in the Meatpacking District. Cara couldn't remember when or how she had gotten home, only that she should've refused that last tequila shot.

Her nose twitched at the tantalizing aroma of coffee. Ungluing an eye with the back of a hand, she stared through a half-cracked lid, and a figure came into focus. Michael wore a crooked grin and waved a mug, sending rich, nutty goodness wafting her way.

"Is that what I think it is, or am I dreaming?" Cara mumbled, her face half-buried in the pillow.

"Tough night?" Michael whispered.

She grunted. He had no idea. "What time is it?"

Michael set the mug on the nightstand. "Two o'clock."

Her eye opened wider, the only movement she could muster without her cranium exploding. "In the afternoon?" It felt more like two in the morning, but she'd gone to bed later than that, so…. "Did you bring aspirin with that coffee?"

He picked up the bottle on the nightstand and shook it, the pills slamming against plastic and assaulting her eardrums.

"*Ahh*, stop," she wailed, covering her exposed ear.

He cupped his palm and tipped the bottle. "Two?"

"Please." Cara's cortex fired, and she realized it was Sunday. "What're you doing here? Isn't this a day of rest or something?"

"Constantina hoped for another session today. Don't worry. She had a change of plans and left a while ago for St. John the Divine." He placed the pills beside the mug.

"Constantina went to *church*?" Cara deadpanned. Seemed kind of pointless for an angel. If anything, she could take the pulpit.

Michael huffed. "It's an Angelorum affiliate. She's meeting Isaac, head of the Tri-State Guardians, on urgent business."

Cara eyed him warily from her horizontal vantage point. "If she canceled the lesson, why are you here?"

Michael's blue eyes danced with mischief. He glanced at his watch and poked her. "We're going for a run in Central Park. You have ten minutes to change," he said and strode to the door.

"Wait! What?" Cara lifted her head in alarm. Big mistake. Pain stabbed behind her eyes.

He was gone before she could lodge a protest.

Ten minutes later, Cara grumbled and slunk on unsteady legs into the kitchen, wearing running clothes with her hair in a ponytail. She sat on a counter stool, propped an elbow on the granite, and held her chin to keep her head upright. Michael slid a glass of green juice toward her.

Cara glanced at it, horrified. "What's that?"

"Celery juice to restore your battered liver and make you good as new." Michael snapped his fingers like a magician about to pull a rabbit from a hat, which would've been easier than banishing her headache.

The aspirin barely made a dent. Cara doubted the juice would fare much better. Groaning, Cara pressed her palms to her temples and whined, "Do I have to?"

Michael assessed her with mild amusement. "What did you drink last night, anyway?"

"It's easier to tell you what I didn't drink. Mixing alcohol? Bad idea," she mumbled.

"A good run will help you detox."

Cara wanted to cry at the thought of moving, let alone exerting herself. "You're doing this to torture me, aren't you?"

Hand to heart, Michael widened his eyes with mock innocence. "Would I do that?"

She glowered. "In a heartbeat. I thought you were my friend."

"If I weren't, I would've let you wallow in bed all day. And I definitely wouldn't have made you my world-famous juice." He smirked and pointed at the glass. "Drink up, Buttercup."

Scowling, Cara grabbed the juice and glanced at Michael. He looked like he stepped out of a Nike catalog with a white T-shirt, navy tracksuit with sleeves pushed to the elbows, and carefully mussed hair. His impeccable grooming made her feel like she was with Sienna, but today, she really did look like hell. "You sure I won't embarrass you?"

His lips quirked to the side. "Never. Come on, it's a beautiful day. Besides, you owe me for waiting around. You're not the only one who had to get out of bed."

"*Grr.*" She conceded and slugged the celery juice, hoping for the promised relief.

Michael glanced at Chloe, who glanced back from her dog bed, her head cocked and ear extended, awaiting his command. "Hey, girl! Want to go for a walk?" She jumped to her feet and wagged her tail furiously.

Cara snorted. "That's like asking a child if she wants candy."

Michael grabbed the leash off the hook in the kitchen, and Chloe bolted ahead of them to the front door. Cara followed, snatching her sunglasses to protect her eyes.

They took the secret underground passageway, one of her security perks, to exit from an adjoining building and crossed the street to Central Park.

Sunny and in the low sixties, it was the perfect day for a run if one was hangover-free. Too bad the chirping birds sounded like screaming pterodactyls.

"Is Chamuel hiding behind a tree somewhere to keep us safe?" Cara sniped as they strolled toward the running path. Her Guardian had yet to redeem himself after the demon debacle.

Michael raised a brow but let it pass. "Chamuel left town on urgent Guardian business. Isaac sent someone else."

"So, Guardians are interchangeable?" she muttered.

"They're not, but this matter is highly sensitive."

She didn't want to dwell on the attack but had to ask. "Any chance we'll run into more demons?"

Michael's shoulders tensed, and he averted his eyes. "No," he said, his discomfort palpable.

Cara probed, treading carefully. "Constantina said there is more than one type of Hunter."

Michael pulled her to a stop. "There are, but you need to understand something. Usually, the Dark Ones dispatch Hunters from their soulless human army to eliminate threats. They're expendable, fly more easily under the radar, and don't shift the balance. Demons like the one in your apartment…" Michael paused, shaking his head gravely. "That shouldn't have happened."

Cara shivered. "Why?"

"There's a cost. Like the Angelorum's Three Hundred, only three hundred higher-order demons can take human form and live topside at once—that's part of the balance. The Guardianship monitors that number closely. When lower demons—like the Hunter who attacked you—are released, the balance shifts, and the Guardians hunt. Outside of Trinities, that's what Guardians do—hunt demons. For the Dark Ones to dispatch that demon, you must be a pretty big threat."

A chill prickled Cara's skin, and her taste buds captured the citrusy lime of Michael's concern. "You're afraid for me."

"I am, but I don't expect another demon attack," he said, his gaze guarded.

Cara frowned as they resumed their walk to the running path, Chloe trotting beside them. "I could use a Demons 101 primer. Do you mind?"

Michael shrugged. "Sure. Ask away."

Cara took a deep breath and launched into her list of questions. "So, if the demon wanted to kill me and eat my soul, how are soulless created without dying?"

"Good one," Michael said, nodding his approval. "The Dark Ones need a steady diet of souls to stay in human form and keep lower-order demons fed. But there are rules. Human souls must be given with consent, and souls given without consent or containing angelic essence are off-limits unless the demon wants to flame out of existence — permanently."

Cara squinted behind her sunglasses. "So…Are there still three hundred demons on Earth?"

Michael sniffed. "Two hundred ninety-five by the last official count. We've also lost one on our side."

"How did *that* happen?" Cara asked, hoping it had nothing to do with eating souls.

"Someone switched sides and *Fell*," Michael said. "Free will and all that."

Cara shook her head. They could unpack that one later. For now, "Why would anyone sane give up their soul?"

He shrugged. "Same reason people vote for crazy politicians or believe in conspiracy theories. Free will doesn't make people smart. The Dark Ones profit from bad life choices in a two-for-one deal that provides them with a soulless army. When the soulless die, they rejoin their soul in Hell, where souls land after *digestion*."

"Sounds disgusting." Cara grimaced, happy to skip the mechanics. "What about souls taken without consent?"

Michael shrugged. "Same. They end up in Hell, but it takes a demon off the chessboard. In the case of a higher-order demon, it decreases their topside number by one."

"Who keeps track?"

"The Irin. They communicate the violation to the Guardianship."

Makes sense. "How would I tell a soulless person from someone normal?"

"They have black auras, like the haze preceding a demon manifestation."

A chill rose on Cara's arms. Constantina covered aura reading in their last lesson, and she remembered the black haze from the demon attack all too well.

After a few steps, Michael stopped again. "There's one big difference between soulless and Hunter demons."

"What's that?"

He worried his lip, his gaze anxious. "Anyone can kill a soulless, but only a Guardian can wield an angelic weapon to kill a demon."

Great. Cara resumed walking. "Then Chamuel better step it up."

Michael strode beside her, his brow furrowing. "Listen, I get that you're still pissed at him, but I'm as much to blame as Chamuel. That attack took us both by surprise." Maybe, but he'd been the one to comfort her afterward.

"Why are you throwing yourself under the bus? You just said only a Guardian can kill a demon."

Guilt filled his gaze. "Because I should've seen it coming."

Cara pardoned him with a nod as they walked silently past the Alice in Wonderland installation and the Conservatory Water, where a mini-regatta of model boats was underway.

When they reached the jogging path, Michael let Cara set the pace and adjusted his stride so they could run together while Chloe eagerly galloped beside them on her lead.

On a positive note, the sobering conversation dulled the pain in Cara's head. She stole a glance at Michael's striking profile as they jogged. Right or wrong, she forgave him more easily than Chamuel for the demon attack. Maybe once she met Chamuel and knew him better…whatever.

In the meantime, she enjoyed having Michael as a new friend. Her mother would be proud. As much as Cara hated admitting it, she hadn't realized how much she needed more meaningful relationships to boost her mental health and fill her emotional well. It didn't hurt that Michael was a font of knowledge. Cara still had a million questions. "Do you ever pinch yourself and wonder if this is all real?"

He flashed her an empathetic look. *"Every damn day."* His words echoed inside her head.

She stumbled and froze.

Michael pulled Chloe to a stop a few yards ahead and glanced over his shoulder. He raised a quizzical brow. *"What's the matter? You saw me speak to the Irin through the Flow."* Then, he said aloud, "Didn't Constantina mention Trinity members can speak telepathically?"

"Not exactly!" Cara stammered, "I—I thought I had to accept my Calling first."

Amusement filled Michael's gaze as he and Chloe jogged back to where Cara stood. Michael grabbed her hand. "Don't look so shocked. She told you I have different gifts. One is enhanced telepathy. I'm a Universal Sender, so I can initiate conversations on any Angelorum vibrational frequency. That includes Guardians and other Trinities—not just ours. Whether you accept your Calling or not, you vibrate within our spectrum, so I can speak to you." He pulled her forward until they were running again. "If I were a Universal Receiver, I could pick up nearby telepathic conversations and respond. I'm not, so I can only pick up our Trinity conversations unless I initiate the communication. Make sense?"

"Kind of." Cara narrowed her eyes, thinking about how he seemed to know things about her. "Can a Universal Sender read my mind?"

He snort-chuckled. "That's a different gift."

She tasted honey—the truth—and kept grilling him. "So, I can talk to you with my mind?"

"Yes. It's based on intent, so just think a sentence at me."

She shot him a look and tested it. *"Do you have a girlfriend?"*

A blush rose on his neck, and his head swiveled to glare at her. *"That's a little personal, don't you think?"* Even telepathically, his tone had a bite.

Cara bristled at the unexpected rebuke. Maybe the question was personal, but not overly so, given everything they'd been through this last week. Lowering her sunglasses, Cara assessed Michael's uncharacteristically grim expression and apologized aloud, "I'm sorry. I didn't mean to hit a nerve. I only wondered if spending time with me kept you from a girlfriend or boyfriend." Her proclamation was true enough to pass a sensory test, though her motivation was partially for Sienna's benefit. If Michael were unavailable, she would drop any plans to fix them up.

Michael ground to a halt with Chloe. Cara looked back as other runners passed. A muscle jumped in Michael's cheek. "Not that it's anyone's business, but I prefer women," he said tightly as if she needed an explanation. "And I'm a strong LGBTQ+ ally...My sister is part of the community."

Michael's out-of-proportion reaction disturbed her. So did the rush of painful emotions wrapped in a trauma-filled package. She didn't need sensory training or the taste of cinnamon to feel Michael's shame and understand something terrible had happened to him. Something that impacted his romantic relationships.

Cara knew only one person with baggage to rival Michael's. That was *Sienna*. Cara couldn't shake the feeling, now more than ever, that they were meant to connect.

"I didn't mean to upset you," she said gently, wanting to diffuse the tension and dispel the sudden rift between them.

Michael shook his head, his shoulders slumping. "I didn't mean to snap..." His voice trailed off, and he averted his gaze. "Just some old baggage. Sorry about that." He looked up, his royal-blue gaze regretful. "People make assumptions about me sometimes..." He paused and shook his head. "To answer your question, I don't have time for a girlfriend right now, between the dojo and Trinity business."

Cara gave his arm a reassuring squeeze. "You don't need to explain. I'm here if you ever want to talk."

Michael nodded awkwardly, but Cara knew he wouldn't. Then, he pulled her into a side hug and whispered, "You didn't deserve that. I'm sorry...I appreciate you. Forgive me?"

"Of course."

They resumed a slow, silent jog. Clearing the tree canopy, the sun warmed Cara's hair as they ran, and she let the mood settle.

When the tension left Michael's shoulders, Cara asked, "When did you meet Constantina?"

Michael threw her a smile, back to his affable self. "My induction ceremony. I know this situation has been weird for you, but being part of a Trinity makes me feel closer to my dad. Constantina was a close friend of my father's, and I discovered he had this whole secret life." He caressed the Patek Phillipe on his wrist as he spoke.

Then, it clicked. "Is that your father's watch?" Cara asked gently.

He glanced at her and swallowed, grief filling his gaze. "Yeah."

So, Michael had inherited the old-fashioned way. But the math hit Cara's gut. "Your dad died young?"

Michael gave a slow nod. "Fifty-three. Heart attack. It was...a shock." He paused. "It's been tough."

Michael's pain washed over her through their new connection. She brushed his arm as they ran. "I'm so sorry for your loss, Michael. I'm sure he was very proud of you."

His fingers found her hand and squeezed. "Thanks."

She had wanted to get to know Michael better. Mission accomplished. But the last thing she expected was a wounded soul beneath Michael's picture-perfect exterior. She should've known from Sienna that appearances can be deceiving.

Michael switched topics. "Before I forget, Constantina asked me to get you up to speed this week on basic self-defense."

She quirked a smile. Michael didn't know everything about her either. "Awesome. Will my *kickboxing* experience come in handy?" She'd taken lessons with Sienna during high school to "kick anxiety's ass." Cara resumed practicing after college when she moved to Manhattan, using kickboxing and running to manage work stress and stay in shape.

Michael's head swiveled. "You kickbox?" he asked, admiration shining in his eyes. "Impressive. That will definitely help."

She shoulder-checked him. "Don't look so surprised."

Chloe jerked Michael to a sudden stop, straining against the leash toward the grass. He had no choice but to follow. Nose to the ground, Chloe sniffed out the perfect spot to do her business.

Cara welcomed the break. The pain in her head had eased, or maybe she'd just gone numb. Either way, she felt marginally better. Then, her gaze snagged on Chloe, and she frowned. Her dog was licking…nothing? And rubbing against…no one?

Cara elbowed Michael to get his attention, tipped her chin at Chloe, and went telepathic. *"Is it just me, or has Chloe been acting strange lately?"*

Michael eyed Cara and cleared his throat. *"Chloe's greeting our…substitute Guardian, Zeke."*

Cara blinked rapidly, watching her enthusiastic hound prance beside open air. "Huh?"

"We can't see him, but Chloe can…and I can speak to him." Michael paused, holding up a finger. "He says 'hi' and not to worry about demons. He has our back…and don't be too hard on Chamuel. He's a good guy."

Her jaw dropped open. No one bothered to tell her Guardians could be invisible. "How do I know you're not just making this up?" Cara mumbled, staring at her dog and the tree beyond.

Before Michael could answer, the disembodied head of an attractive teenage guy with black hair appeared above Chloe, making him about six-four — if he had a body.

Cara gasped, clasping a hand to her chest. "Holy shit."

Zeke chuckled, smiling. "Michael speaks true, girlfriend."

Cara blinked rapidly. "You're just a head?"

The head tipped back and laughed. "I only partially uncloaked to prove I'm real. Cham would have my *head* — pun intended — if he knew I showed you even this much. But, hey, sounded like you needed some convincing." He glanced at Chloe, who gazed at him, wagging her tail. "Cute dog, by the way. You good, now?"

Cara fumbled for speech. "I'm good," she squeaked, nodding furiously.

"Cool." His invisible fingers snapped. "Peace out." And he disappeared.

What the actual hell? She glared at Michael, who shrugged, wearing a self-satisfied grin, and said, "Told you."

"He looks barely old enough to drive," she mumbled.

"I heard that!" said a disembodied voice.

"Has he heard everything we've said?" Cara asked Michael with alarm.

Michael replied, *"They're duty-bound not to eavesdrop or divulge anything they overhear on assignment — like a priest."*

That didn't make Cara feel any better. Nope, not one bit.

But Constantina was right.

Guardians seemed like anyone else, which would make them hard to pick out in a crowd — as long as they had a body.

Chapter 26

KAI

Solomon Residence. San Francisco.

ON MONDAY MORNING, Kai sat in his kitchen ruminating over coffee and killing time before the Watson & Haskins appointment. His curiosity had been in overdrive since his dinner with Calvin. With Melanie and Sara in L.A. over the weekend, Kai had Saturday and Sunday to obsessively dissect Calvin's revelations. Fortunately, a two-day golf tournament with a fifth-place finish offered some distraction.

In between, Kai exhaustively researched the word *Ishmael*, finding only Moby Dick and biblical references. He had a gut feeling that whatever awaited him at Watson & Haskins was the missing link to his research.

What else justified Dr. Wilson's extreme caution and decision to hide her message in Calvin's subconscious? A prescient decision given her and Peyton's murders. It also wasn't a big leap to assume Emily's visit to the Stanford lab pointed to The Foundation's involvement, which put Kai and his family at risk and gave Cara's premonitory dreams more credence.

He contemplated calling Cara several times over the weekend but abandoned the idea out of fear she'd be on the next plane to San Francisco — the last thing he needed if this broke bad.

Sara wandered into the kitchen, wearing pajamas and rubbing the sleep from her eyes with balled fists. She spotted Kai seated at the counter and propelled herself in his direction. He prepared for impact, using her momentum to scoop her onto his lap.

"Hey, sleepyhead. How was Grandma's?" He kissed her crown as she snuggled close.

"Good," she said, her voice muffled against his shirt.

"Did you miss me?" he asked quietly. She nodded *yes* against his chest. "Where's Mommy?"

"Shower."

"Do you need help getting ready for *school*?" he said, applying the term to Sara's preschool to help acclimate her to the idea before kindergarten started next year.

She shook her head *no* as Melanie walked into the kitchen, still in her bathrobe, her hair wrapped in a towel.

Melanie kissed Sara on the head and Kai warmly on the lips. "Good morning," she purred. "Mind pouring me a cup of coffee while I get the milk?" Dark circles beneath her eyes signaled she needed the caffeine.

"Tired?" he asked, carrying Sara to the coffee maker. His four-year-old daughter was getting heavy to haul around, but he enjoyed the warmth of his only child. Having Sara cost Melanie her uterus due to complications in childbirth. He'd nearly lost them both, making Sara all the more precious.

Kai opened the cabinet and extracted a mug with his free hand.

Melanie said, "Sorry, we got home so late. I wanted to leave earlier, but Sara was having fun with Maggie next door. So, we stayed for dinner." She fetched her daughter from Kai's arms and grabbed the coffee mug.

He was glad they were back. The house seemed empty without them. "I missed you both."

Melanie smiled. Leaning against the counter, she cradled Sara close. "We missed you, too. Got your text. Fifth place. That's a nice finish compared to last year. Are you happy with it?"

Kai shrugged. "Happy enough, I guess." He'd been too distracted to savor his result, but the memory brought a smile to his lips. "Sorry, I was asleep when you got home. I was exhausted." He hesitated, deciding what to share with his wife about what he learned, and said tentatively, "I may be on to something at work."

"Really?" Melanie asked, surprised. "Like what?"

"I'm not sure. But I think I found a clue to turn these experiments around—" Melanie's cry cut him off. Her mug slammed onto the countertop, coffee spewing over the rim.

"Mel!" Rounding the island, Kai bolted to his wife's side.

Melanie wobbled and lowered Sara to the ground. Steadying herself against the counter, her face a mask of pain, she rubbed her temple. "I'm OK," she panted, her voice quaking.

Kai pulled Melanie into his arms. "Is it another headache?" Sara clung to his leg, and the three of them stood huddled together.

"The headaches have gotten worse this week."

Kai frowned. "Are you taking the meds I picked up for you?"

"Yeah, but they make me groggy. I'm not sure I can take the pills during my trip. I leave tomorrow."

"I remember." He didn't need a reminder, though Melanie always felt compelled to give one, not confident his gift wouldn't let him down.

Though he wished she weren't required to make quarterly trips to China to meet her company's retail distributors, especially given world politics.

"Maybe you should postpone the trip," he offered. "It's time to get that MRI we've talked about." Melanie had put off setting the appointment for more than a month.

She pulled away. "I can't postpone the trip, Kai," she said impatiently, but conceded, "I'll schedule an MRI for when I get back." Her claim lacked conviction.

Refusing to be mollified, Kai planted his hands on his hips and stood his ground. "For the record, I'm not comfortable with this. We need to get these headaches diagnosed. They could indicate any number of things. Promise me you'll set up an appointment with the neurologist for an MRI before you leave?"

Meeting his gaze, she said quietly, "I promise," then added, "In the meantime, can you change the meds?" Kai couldn't personally, but he had a few physician friends who trusted him enough to write a script as a professional courtesy.

He nodded reluctantly and decided to schedule the neurology appointment himself.

"Good luck today. Let me know how it turns out," Melanie said and glanced at Sara. "Someone needs to get ready for school."

"Do you need my help?" Kai asked, but Melanie shook her head. Kai gathered them into a collective hug. Resting his cheek on Melanie's hair, he said softly, "Hey, I love you. I'm just worried about you."

"I know. I love you, too," she whispered.

He leaned in and kissed her tenderly on the lips. "Go, get Sara ready. I'll check in later and pick up a new prescription on my way home."

She gave a grateful smile. "Thanks."

Kai watched as she padded from the kitchen, holding their daughter's hand. He checked the time on his phone. Time to go. He finished his coffee on the way to the sink and left with the business card for Watson & Haskins tucked safely in his wallet, hoping it would be the passport to some answers.

WATSON & HASKINS was in San Francisco's Financial District on Montgomery, across from Sutter. Kai smiled when he saw the charming little Art Deco building — with King Tut-themed relief carvings flanking an arched entrance — tucked between two tall modern buildings.

Kai rode the elevator to the fifth floor and stepped out into décor that reflected the building's historic 1930s flavor, with original marble floors and architectural details. An elegantly dressed receptionist sat behind a large wooden desk, facing a massive set of double doors that led into the offices.

"May I help you?" she asked.

He showed her the business card. "The password is *Ishmael*," he said, feeling ridiculous.

She accepted the card, her pleasant expression unchanged. "I understand. Please have a seat," she said and disappeared behind one of the doors.

Kai sank into a plush leather chair in the reception area and waited.

Less than five minutes later, she returned. "Mr. Gladstone will see you shortly," she announced quietly and settled into her chair.

Kai let his head fall back and listened to the classical background music, his nerves quieting.

When the phone buzzed softly, the receptionist exchanged a few muted words, hung up, and stood. "Mr. Gladstone will see you now. Please, come this way."

Kai followed her inside, where a tall, stocky man in his mid-sixties with white hair and a good-natured twinkle in his blue eyes awaited him.

"Ah, Dr. Solomon!" Gladstone said with genuine joviality. "We've been anticipating your arrival. I'm so very pleased to make your acquaintance." The man took Kai's hand inside both of his and shook vigorously.

The unexpected greeting took Kai by surprise. Gladstone was expecting him? Kai followed the older man to his office through a maze-like hallway filled with beautiful artwork and wood paneling.

Gladstone led him into a spacious room decorated in a navy, green, and burgundy palette with plaid and leather accents. Built-in bookshelves lined the walls, surrounding a large desk with guest chairs and a seating area that faced a fireplace. The space looked more like a clubby, personal library better suited for smoking jackets and Meerschaum pipes than a law office.

"Please sit." Gladstone motioned to a guest chair. His attire, an expensive gray flannel suit and bowtie, reflected the taste of their surroundings.

Kai took a seat, feeling woefully underdressed in a polo shirt, khakis, and Merrell shoes. "Thanks for seeing me on such short notice."

Gladstone waved a hand. "Think nothing of it." He retrieved an ornate leather folder from his drawer, set it on the desk, and depressed the round, gold clasp. The lock snapped open, and Gladstone upended the folder. A key clattered onto the desk.

"I'm afraid this is all there is...," Gladstone said, sliding the nondescript key to Kai.

Kai deflated like a leaky balloon. "That's it?"

"I'm afraid so."

Kai picked up the key. "What does it open?"

The lawyer shrugged. "I hoped you would know."

"Do you know what *Ishmael* means or why Dr. Wilson chose that password?" Kai probed, hoping for more.

"Why, it's a name, of course," Gladstone said jovially, his gaze twinkling and reminding Kai of a thinner, beardless Santa Claus.

Kai failed to appreciate the lawyer's attempt at levity and hid his impatience behind a tight smile. "Do you know *whose* name it is?"

"That, you must discover on your own. All I can tell you is 'Ishmael is the key, and the key is Ishmael.'"

Disappointed, Kai examined the engraved number on the key — 550056-94306 — and blew out a frustrated breath. "This could mean anything."

Gladstone held up a finger. "That's where you're wrong, Dr. Solomon. It can only mean one thing, and that's the thing you must find."

"Is there anything else you can tell me?" Kai asked, desperate for another clue.

Gladstone leaned forward and tented his hands. "I know it doesn't seem like much, but small things often lead to big discoveries." Then, Gladstone rose from his chair and pointed to the key in Kai's palm. "Everything you need is in your hand." He smiled sadly. "Sandra and Tom believed in you, Dr. Solomon. Now, you must believe in yourself."

Kai swallowed, the weight of two dead scientists' expectations settling on his shoulders. The frustration drained out of him. If they believed in him, then they chose a puzzle he could solve.

Gladstone held the office door open.

"Thank you. I won't let them down," Kai said on his way out.

Contemplating the key, Kai left the building and headed across the street to the parking garage.

Pain assaulted his skull and bristled the hairs on the back of his neck. He stumbled to a halt on the sidewalk, pressing his fingers to his temples. It was the same stabbing pain that hit him as he left Stanford. For the first time, he wondered if he might be a connection to Melanie.

Could they both be sick?

His vision blurred, and the taste of new pavement coated his tongue. Heart hammering, Kai was unsure if he could even get to the car, let alone drive. Panicking, he took a few more steps, and then the sensation fled as quickly as it had come. Like it did the last time.

A shiver raced along Kai's spine. Maybe Melanie wasn't the only one who needed an MRI.

Chapter 27

CARA

Fifth Avenue Penthouse. New York City.

"I DECIDED TO meet my mystery man for dinner," Cara announced to Constantina under the protective watch of the Angelorum's painted vignettes during their afternoon training session. Over dinner at the penthouse on Sunday night, Cara had told Constantina and Michael about the hot guy catching her in his arms at the restaurant and his note. She omitted the part about recognizing him from the subway. That day had been too triggering, and she didn't want to spoil the good vibe.

Cara had studied the note's looping script no less than a hundred times over the past few days. She wanted to go, but given the circumstances, she questioned the wisdom of her decision. Still, she couldn't forget the Viking god's startling blue eyes or the electricity between them. She hadn't felt anything like that since Kai. If nothing else, she needed to convince her heart to give someone else a chance, even for one night.

"Oh?" Constantina's brows shot up in mock surprise.

Cara's shoulders drooped. "Am I that obvious?"

Constantina replied with a melodic chuckle, amusement dancing in her eyes. "No, dear," she said, a hand drifting to her heart. "But Michael and I *may* have made a little wager. I bet against him to make it interesting, hoping to make him five dollars richer. I'll alert Chamuel of your plans."

Cara groaned, her excitement dampening. "I'm not sure which is more egregious: only betting five dollars or sending Chamuel as my chaperone." Honestly, Cara hadn't considered a security detail, which triggered cringy high school memories of her father driving her and her tenth-grade boyfriend, John Carmichael, to the movies and sitting two rows back.

Constantina patted Cara's arm and gave her a sympathetic smile. "I respect that you have a life, but danger is close, and we can't be too cautious. You won't even know he's there." The rigid set of her mentor's petite shoulders said the topic was closed for discussion.

"Sounds more like a stalker than a protector," Cara mumbled, wondering how close her Guardian would follow and hoping she wouldn't need a table for three. Especially after discovering Guardians could pull a Harry Potter behind a veil of invisibility. Zeke had gotten close enough to pet her dog. His disembodied head still gave her the creeps. It would've been better if he hadn't shown himself at all.

Constantina snickered and waved away her concern. "Think of him as your Guardian Angel—someone to help when needed, not to spy...or *stalk* you."

Cara sighed, relenting. Fine. If Chamuel hovered close enough, maybe he could make himself useful and pour them wine with dinner. She wouldn't recognize him if he did, and perhaps that was a good thing.

"At least I've met Michael. He's been amazing, so far." Cara didn't know what she'd do without him. Besides apologizing twice more, Michael had gone out of his way to be kind and engaging since his meltdown on Sunday.

Constantina nodded, looking pleased. "I can see the rapport between you. He's a very kind and caring young man. We're lucky to have someone so special in our lives. But I assure you, Chamuel is equally special." Her mentor wagged a finger in the Guardian's defense. "There's no one I trust more to be your Guardian. Promise to give Chamuel a chance when you meet him?"

Cara folded her arms and sighed. "Fine."

Truthfully, trust wasn't her issue; privacy was. That, and the small matter of Chamuel's near miss on the demon attack.

Constantina's gaze softened, and she squeezed Cara's arm. "Nothing about this situation is easy, dear one. It's strange, I know, to be the center of something that requires you to abandon the life you've led. Your Calling will come soon, and you can still reject what's been offered. What we're doing here is preparing your mind and body for the mission your soul chose before birth. But as a conscious being, you still retain free will and a choice."

Cara sighed. "I know." And if she didn't accept, the Dark Ones would swoop in and grab her, people could die, blah blah. She got it. Besides that, Michael and Constantina already meant a lot to her, and she didn't want to lose them. Their presence filled a void she hadn't realized existed, and she begrudgingly admitted this new fate excited her.

At six-thirty, Constantina clapped her hands, signaling the end of their training. "Enough for today." Her serious demeanor turned effervescent, and she took Cara's hands. A gleam akin to maternal pride shone in Constantina's eyes when she said, "Shall we get you ready for your date?"

Cara swallowed hard, her mentor's kind offer hitting an unexpected nerve. Cara had never been more keenly aware of the warmth and affection missing from her relationship with her own mother. Her mom had never helped Cara get ready for anything, even her high school prom. She loved her mom, but her mother's reserve and critical eye usually put them at odds.

A tear cut a path down Cara's cheek as her heart swelled with gratitude.

Constantina gasped, alarm lighting her gaze. "Oh, my! Is everything all right, dear? Did I overstep…"

Cara brushed away the teardrop and hugged the petite woman, catching her unaware. "Thank you. I'd like that very much," she said, giving Constantina's small frame a final squeeze and releasing her. Cara fanned her face to dry her eyes. "I'm fine. My mom…" she trailed off, abandoning her explanation for fear of appearing disloyal. "Never mind."

Ocean-blue eyes softening, Constantina squeezed Cara's hand, reading her as if staring through a pane of glass. "Oh, sweetheart, we all love in our own way. Your mother loves you very much."

Cara's throat tightened, and she nodded. Constantina's understanding struck a chord with Cara's tender vulnerabilities. "I know," Cara squeaked.

"*Shh.*" Constantina smiled and brushed new tears from Cara's cheeks with her thumbs. Then she took Cara's hands in hers, and a wave of cleansing energy surged up Cara's arms to her chest. "Just breathe."

Cara inhaled deeply. The lapping waves cleansed her emotions—a parlor trick that continued to amaze.

"Feel better?" Constantina said, dropping her hands.

Cara nodded, the tightness in her throat gone.

"Good." Constantina brightened. "Let's focus on the fun stuff. May I arrange your hair?" Her choice of words and girlish enthusiasm made Cara smile.

Cara swallowed. "I would be honored."

Giggling with delight, Constantina took her hand and pulled her toward the stairs.

An hour later, Cara sat at the bathroom vanity. Her diamond pendant sparkled at her throat, and a simple black dress clung tastefully to her curves. Black Dior heels and an alpaca shawl for her shoulders would complete the outfit.

Cara relinquished control of her hair to Constantina, who styled it with body and fullness, so it fell in waves and pooled around her shoulders. Being grateful putty in her mentor's hands gave Cara time to think and work up the nerve to ask some questions. Despite their growing closeness and all Cara had learned in the last few days, she knew nothing about the woman's life outside the penthouse. She didn't want to be nosy, but given Constantina's excitement over her date, Cara was curious. So, as her mentor squinted with concentration, putting the finishing touches on Cara's cheeks with a soft brush, Cara asked, "Do you have someone special?"

The brush on Cara's cheek slowed. Constantina hesitated, then sighed. "Not in this lifetime."

"I'm sorry." A sad ache hit Cara's chest, and she regretted the question.

Constantina smiled kindly. "No need for apology."

"But love is allowed...for you?" Cara asked, checking her understanding.

"Of course! We all need love." Gaze wistful, Constantina said, "But it is not my fate this time. He is not here...on earth." Then, she rubbed Cara's arm. "Do not be sad for me, dear one. I know love, and I will see my soulmate again, but let's not speak of me. Tonight is your night."

Learning Constantina had a mate relieved Cara's angst, but raised more questions. "Does everyone have a soulmate?" Cara asked.

"Yes, but sometimes it takes more than one lifetime to find them. Hold still." Constantina applied lipstick to Cara's top lip. "Go like this." She rubbed her lips together to demonstrate. Then, Constantina studied her handiwork with a critical eye and nodded in approval. Satisfied, she motioned for Cara to spin and face the mirror.

Cara turned, and a hand flew to her mouth. She barely recognized herself. Constantina had made Cara look beautiful in a way she couldn't accomplish on her own. Rising, Cara embraced Constantina and whispered, "Thank you."

"Well, don't stand here all night with me." Constantina chuckled softly. "The driver is downstairs. If you plan to meet your gentleman by eight, you'd better go." She slipped from Cara's hug, held her at arm's length, and gave Cara a final glance. "You look breathtaking. He shall be pleased."

CARA'S DRIVER DROPPED her in front of the restaurant at a minute before eight. Exiting the car, Cara inhaled the crisp night air, drawing in a few calming breaths, and approached the restaurant.

A large hand reached past her to grab the door handle. "Allow me," said a deep, rich male voice. She glanced over her shoulder and sucked in a breath.

It was *him*, and he was even hotter than she'd remembered. Like Prince Charming stepping from the pages of a fairytale, the night already had an air of too-good-to-true magic.

He'd bound his dark-blond hair neatly at his nape, as it had been on the subway, which exposed an impeccably chiseled bone structure. Gone were the jeans and casual sweater. In their place, dark tailored pants, a wool jacket, and a white-collared shirt, open at the neck.

God, he was tall. Even in her stilettos, Cara had to tilt her chin skyward to meet his warm blue gaze. She smiled, catching a hint of his citrusy, spicy cologne. Cara breathed in the heady scent, glad she accepted his invitation.

"After you," he said, lips quirking to the side, and opened the door. She entered the restaurant to a rush of warmth, awareness of him tingling at her back.

The hostess, not Gabrielle, brightened when she spotted Cara's date. "So good to see you again!" she gushed, grabbing two menus and a wine list. "Follow me. We have a nice, quiet table in the back." Cara caught an envious glint in the woman's gaze, but couldn't hold it against her.

Gentle fingertips touched the small of Cara's back, guiding her as they followed the hostess. Her skin sizzled beneath the light pressure of her date's fingers, his size making Cara feel as petite as Constantina. Cara found the gesture *gentlemanly* but unassuming. Then again, maybe he feared she'd trip on the way to the table, given how they met. If so, she couldn't blame him, but she was determined to end the evening with her dignity intact.

They passed the metal deathtrap, and she winked her thanks. Credit where credit was due. Without her near faceplant, she wouldn't be here.

"Here we go," the hostess said when they arrived at a back corner table covered in white linen. "Have a good evening," she said, her gaze lingering on Cara's date, who didn't seem to notice.

Points for the handsome Viking.

Cara headed to the chair facing the room, but her date gently redirected her and pulled out her chair. He waited until she was seated before rounding the table and taking his own. Cara appreciated the effort but hoped he wasn't anti-feminist.

Leaning forward, he smiled and broke the silence. "I hope you don't mind, but I prefer to face the door."

Cara noticed his voice held a subtle and sexy French accent. How had she missed that? Not that it mattered. He could've announced the restaurant was on fire, and she still would've melted like butter.

Though his comment piqued Cara's curiosity, which she'd pursue after procuring a more pressing piece of information. "Would it be too forward to ask your name?" she asked, demurely fluttering her lashes.

Brows creased, he blinked, and understanding sparked in his gaze. With a self-deprecating chuckle, he passed a hand over his eyes. "I forgot to sign the note, didn't I?"

Cara bit her lip and nodded, charmed by his manner — so at odds with his demeanor in the subway.

Crystal blue eyes caught her stare, and his lips tilted into a sheepish side smile. "My apologies. Thank you for accepting my invitation despite the *faux pas*. I wasn't thinking straight." He extended a large hand. "Simon Young."

She took that as a compliment. "Nice to meet you, Simon…Cara Collins." Her hand disappeared inside his, electricity dancing across her fingers. Her father always said she could learn a lot about a person from their handshake. He'd be pleased with Simon's firm, confident grip.

Simon's hand lingered a few extra seconds, and his smile lit his eyes. "It's truly my pleasure."

Dazzled, she wished they'd met under less embarrassing circumstances. "Thank you for the wine…and for catching me. Those stairs are deadly."

He laughed softly. "Yes, they are. I'm glad to be of service. It's been a while since I've caught a beautiful woman in my arms."

Cara raised a brow and unwound the alpaca shawl from her shoulders. "Somehow, I have trouble believing that."

His gaze lit with respectful appreciation as she draped the wool wrap over her chair. "Why is that?"

Cara leaned forward and whispered. "Half the women in this restaurant are staring at you."

A blush rose along his neck, and he cleared his throat. "Would it shock you to learn that this is the first date I have had in…," he paused, angling his squinting gaze at the tin ceiling, then laughed. "Actually, I don't want to answer that. It's too embarrassing. Let's just say, it's been too long."

She cocked her head and parroted, "Why's that?"

"My career doesn't allow much time for a social life," he said matter-of-factly.

Testing her new skills, Cara found no deception in his energy, only curiosity and excitement, which gave her a little thrill. Wow. He was serious.

"What do you do that's so consuming?" she asked, hoping he wasn't a professional athlete, a possibility given his size and fitness. She'd gone down that road with Tyler, a professional soccer player, and had no desire to travel that heartbreaking path again.

His throat bobbed in a moment of hesitation. "I'm in the private security business," he said, fingering his napkin and placing it on his lap. "The hours are undesirable, to say the least, and most of my colleagues are male, which makes dating a challenge," he said, smiling tightly.

Again, Cara sensed the truth, and a career in private security explained his choice of seating. It was marginally better than chasing balls down a field. But given their respective schedules, she had no idea if or when she'd have an opportunity to see him again, even if the night went well.

"Is that what you were doing on the subway? Working?"

His eyes flashed to hers and shuttered. Then, he slowly nodded. "I was preparing for a new assignment…Sorry, I…didn't mean to be rude."

She flushed, remembering him giving her his back. "I didn't mean to stare, but you're hard to miss. How do you manage covert surveillance?"

He huffed a laugh. "Usually, I'm more circumspect. It was a last-minute scouting mission," he said, his French enunciation more pronounced.

"Where are you from — originally, I mean?" she asked. His accent was mild, as if he had been living here a while. She wouldn't have placed it so quickly had she not spent a year in France during college.

His brow twitched in surprise. "I grew up in Europe as a child, near Paris. Why do you ask?"

"Your accent," she said. "It's nice."

He cleared his throat and adjusted the napkin across his lap. "I didn't realize I had an accent, but thank you," he said, almost shyly.

"Most people with accents say that," she teased.

"Is that so?" he asked, his gaze sparking with interest. "What about you? Where did you grow up?"

She brushed an errant lock of hair behind her ear. "Summit, New Jersey. My family still lives there, but I moved to Manhattan after graduating from college. Does your family live here, or are they still in Europe?"

A muscle ticked in his cheek, and he answered calmly, "My parents are both *gone*."

His answer held the honey sweetness of truth but was tinged with something odd. Simon couldn't be much older than her, and Cara's parents were still in their early fifties, which is what shocked her about Michael's father's passing at fifty-three. "I'm sorry. It's not often someone our age loses both parents."

He cocked his head, brow wrinkled, looking puzzled.

Cara cringed, wondering if that was too personal. "Sorry, was that the wrong thing to say?" God, she was out of practice. At this rate, they'd never make it to dessert.

His shoulders loosened. Giving a reassuring smile, he leaned closer. "You didn't say anything wrong. They've been gone a long time, that's all. And…" He flashed a teasing grin. "I might be slightly older than you think," he said, holding his thumb and forefinger slightly apart.

"Oh?"

Leaning back, he relaxed his grin and shrugged. "Does it matter?"

Not really. She shrugged and changed the subject. "So, the bartender had some nice things to say about you."

He straightened, his lips kicking to the side. "You asked the bartender about me?" he asked, his gaze teasing.

Inching forward, she kept her voice low. "I did, but he didn't know your name either."

Simon chuckled softly. "I'll properly introduce myself next time I tire of my cooking and come for a meal."

Cara's interest sparked. "You cook?" She could barely boil water, as Constantina quickly found out.

"I do." He folded his hands on the table, amusement glinting in his eyes. "I studied in Paris while on a career break."

Cara's eyes widened. He didn't cook. He *cooked.* "Impressive." Imagining him wearing an apron and holding a whisk made her smile.

His gaze turned hopeful. "May I cook for you sometime?" He quickly added, "If you'd like to see me again after tonight, that is."

In her experience, men offered things they had no intention of delivering as a ploy to seduce her. She felt none of that from Simon. Unless he sprouted a second head before dessert, his chances were good.

She swallowed. "I'd love that."

He glanced at the waitress. "Speaking of food, are you hungry? I've held off the server since I didn't want her to interrupt. Would you have a glass of wine if I ordered a bottle?"

"Yes, and yes." Cara's cheeks ached from all the smiling. She couldn't believe the charming, engaging man in front of her was the same intimidating guy she'd spotted on the subway.

He signaled the server and asked Cara, "Do you trust me?"

Cara gave a nod. "With my culinary choices? Absolutely."

Simon smiled at the server. "Tell the chef we're a *go* and please bring a bottle of this." He pointed to the wine list, then surrendered the menu.

As the server left, Simon said, "I've arranged a special five-course tasting with the chef. I promise it'll be fantastic."

Five courses? She'd need a forklift to get her out of the chair. Cara chuckled nervously and smoothed the napkin over her lap. "That's a lot of food."

"No need to clean your plate—just taste." Simon leaned forward and said in a conspiratorial whisper, "Let's hope the chef isn't in the mood for tripe."

Cara grimaced, making Simon grin like a naughty schoolboy. "Just kidding. I asked for no organ meats."

She snorted. "That was mean."

Amusement danced in his eyes. "You strike me as someone who can hold her own." True, six years in investment banking surrounded by chest-thumping men without a politically correct bone in their bodies gave her tough skin. But she found Simon's brand of teasing sweet. She accepted the compliment with a smile. "That I can."

Simon reached across the table, palm up, beckoning. The gesture took her by surprise. She placed her hand in his and met his gaze.

"So, I don't forget," he said, his throat bobbing in a swallow as he wrapped her fingers in warmth. "I want you to know that it hasn't gone unnoticed or unappreciated how lovely you look tonight."

Heat flamed in Cara's cheeks. "Thank you. That's very kind."

He leaned closer. "Kindness has nothing to do with it. It's true."

Her pulse quickened, and her gaze soaked in his symmetrical features, cheekbones that could cut granite, and full, kissable lips. His face had raw masculine beauty that should be illegal in all fifty states. But the soul behind his eyes had a greater appeal. Her lips fell open with an overwhelming urge to bridge the gap between them.

A throat cleared, breaking the spell. "Monsieur?" A sommelier stood beside the table, holding a bottle of white wine and a corkscrew.

Cara flushed with disappointment at the interruption as Simon relinquished her hand and straightened in his chair. His gaze clung to her, then drifted to the glass the sommelier filled for a small tasting. Cara was sure of one thing. Before the night ended, she wanted to kiss the man across from her.

Simon picked up the glass by the stem, studied the color, swirled the pale-colored wine, observed the legs as they meandered down the side of the glass, took a sniff, and finally rolled a sip over his tongue. He nodded his acceptance, and the sommelier filled their glasses, then nestled the bottle into an ice bucket beside the table.

Simon held up his wine. "A fine vintage Sauvignon Blanc from a family of renown French vintners. It should pair nicely with our first course."

Cara quirked a brow. "So, you know wines, too?"

He gave a small chuckle. "Don't be too impressed. It was one of the chef's recommendations. A toast?" She nodded, raising her glass. "To unexpected encounters and getting to know you." He gently tapped their glasses.

"Don't you mean getting to know *each other*?" she asked with a tilt of her head and sipped.

"Of course," he whispered with a flirtatious twitch of his lip.

"So," Cara said. "Tell me something about you."

Simon shifted back in his chair, discomfort interrupting his lighthearted ease. "I'm afraid I'm not good at talking about myself."

Cara blinked. *That's a switch.* Most men couldn't *stop* talking about themselves. Then again, Simon already broke the mold of "most men." Cara changed tacks, tapping into an icebreaker exercise she'd used at work during new hire orientation to coax people into revealing personal information. "OK…Let's try this instead. What's the most beautiful place you've ever visited?"

His gaze lit with interest, and the tension eased from his shoulders. "I like that question. That's easy. The Grand Canyon."

"What made you choose it?" she asked, her interest piquing. She'd never been there herself, but it was on her bucket list.

His gaze took on a faraway look before returning to her. "Because it's like seeing part of Heaven…What about you? What's the most beautiful place you've ever visited, and why?"

Cara sighed, remembering. "I love the South of France, but Monaco was the most beautiful place I've ever been. The views left me breathless. I've never been to the Grand Canyon, so I don't know how it compares." She hadn't traveled since college due to her demanding job.

He nodded. "A lovely choice. They're both beautiful in different ways. Someday, you must see the Grand Canyon. It will steal your breath."

"Do you travel much?"

"Only for work," he said, averting his gaze, "but there's no place like New York City."

She couldn't disagree and asked another icebreaker. "What's your favorite book?" Cara believed a person's bookshelf said a lot about them.

"Ah, great question. I believe my favorite is the twentieth-century novel *Siddhartha* by Herman Hesse."

Pleasantly surprised by his choice, Cara smiled and sipped her wine. "I love that book. Why is it your favorite?"

Simon pursed his lips and thought. "Although a person's life may not be perfect, there's hope that they can still learn and find the meaning they seek." His words held a personal resonance, and his bright gaze drew her in. "And what's yours, Cara?"

Her tastes varied from the classics to thrillers, but she had one book that stood above all the others. "Don't laugh." She ducked her head and hid a shy smile. "*Le Petit Prince* by Antoine de Saint-Exupéry. I read it in French class during my last year of high school."

"Ah, yes." Simon's face lit up.

Pleased, she said, "Then you know the story?"

"Of course." With thoughtful reverence, Simon quoted her favorite line in French describing the gift the fox bestowed on the Little Prince. Her heart quickened to hear Simon speak the words aloud. When he finished, he said softly, "Why do you love this book so?"

Her eyes unexpectedly welled. "In the end, the Little Prince was willing to face death to return to the Rose," she said, knuckling a tear. "I'm sorry. I don't normally get so emotional."

Simon smiled softly and took her hands in his. "No need to be embarrassed. There's nothing more powerful than love. Fair play to the Little Prince for knowing his heart and making his sacrifice."

She hadn't expected the icebreakers to backfire on her. Something about Simon made her want to share. She wondered if he was the kind of person who would sacrifice everything to be with the one he loved.

For the love of Pete, pull it together, she chided herself as the server came to her rescue with the first course, setting down two bowls of chilled spring pea soup with pancetta and a small swirl of crème fraîche and refilling their wine glasses before departing.

Simon lifted his spoon. "Bon appétit."

The soup was amazing, and so was the wine. Cara said a silent prayer of gratitude. So far, Simon had vastly exceeded her meager expectations. As they ate, Cara realized he was the first man who made her forget about Kai, even momentarily, in a very long time. The last time ended in disaster. Hopefully, history wouldn't repeat itself.

Dinner passed quickly, and the chef stopped at their table during the fourth course to check on them. By the time dessert had arrived, it was almost eleven, and Cara was stuffed.

Cara couldn't remember the last time she had such a good time. "The night just flew."

"That's the sign of a good date, yes? What are my chances for a second?" Simon's gaze held a glimmer of hope.

Playfully tapping her lip and gazing into her nearly empty teacup, she said, "*Hmm.* The tea leaves say your chances are good."

"Do you like art?"

Her eyes widened. *Did a cat drink milk?* "I minored in art history — so, yes."

"My schedule has some flexibility this week," he said slowly. "Would you like to go to the Met tomorrow?" His lemon-tanged nervousness vibrated on her tongue, and she noticed his unconscious hand wringing.

Had she given him a reason to doubt her acceptance?

She'd be there, even if she had to fight an army of demons with her bare hands. Hopefully, that wouldn't be necessary. Kudos to Chamuel for keeping them safe tonight and lurking undetected. Maybe she could arrange the same for tomorrow.

"I'd love to," she said, tempering her enthusiasm so she didn't appear overeager, "I have a commitment in the morning, but let me see if I can rearrange my afternoon schedule. Will that work?" She couldn't believe he liked art. He was too good to be true.

His tension eased. "Absolutely."

She beamed with pleasure. "I'll text you in the morning." She dug her cell phone from her purse, unlocked it, and handed it to him. "Program your number into my contacts?"

Simon nodded, did as she asked, and then texted himself. His phone vibrated inside his jacket pocket. "All set," he said.

As Simon took care of the bill, Cara's heart sank. She wasn't ready for the date to end. Almost as if reading her mind, Simon looked at her expectantly and asked, "Would you like to take a walk? Some fresh air would be nice after such a long meal."

Cara's heart leaped, and she wiggled her toes in her high heels. "I think I can manage a couple of blocks."

Simon's smile widened. He rounded the table, pulling out her chair. Cara wrapped her shawl around her shoulders, and Simon escorted her through the restaurant. She enjoyed the contact, his hand again resting on the small of her back. She hadn't realized how much she appreciated a man with manners. It was refreshing not to spend half the night wondering if her date would offer to pay his half of the bill, much less hold out her seat or compliment her outfit.

She could get used to this.

A shiver rolled down Cara's spine when they exited. The temperature had dropped significantly from when they'd arrived.

Simon moved to slip his jacket off. "Let me give you this."

Cara shook her head, determined to tough it out, and pulled her shawl tighter around her shoulders. "I'm fine. Which way?"

He tipped his chin east and extended his elbow. "May I?"

"Of course." She smiled and hooked her arm through his. His ease and grace were something out of the Victorian era.

"There's a lounge around the corner. Would you like to go for a quick nightcap?" he suggested. "Then I promise to get you home safely."

Her heart galloped. "I'd be happy to, kind sir. One condition—my treat for the nightcaps."

He stopped her on the sidewalk. "Please don't think I'm a dinosaur, but my mother raised me to believe a male of worth takes responsibility for the first date."

Cara narrowed her eyes. "Cheap shot, using your mother like that…."

He shrugged. "But it's true."

She huffed a laugh. "Okay—this time. But if you always insist on paying, I'll think you have something against independent women."

His lips parted in surprise, and not for the first time that night, he looked taken aback. "I adore independent women, but there's nothing wrong with showing respect and honoring your relationships."

She sighed. "I surrender, but I plan to bring it up again." If she were honest, it wasn't only his manners that seemed old-fashioned, but his vocabulary. English as a second language, maybe? He struck her as an old soul.

Before they rounded the corner, Simon froze, his fear hitting her in a bitter lime wave.

Chapter 28

CHAMUEL

Prince Street. New York City.

CARA HAD DAZZLED him from the moment he'd arrived on their date, and the temptation to kiss her grew every second they were together. Inviting her to the lounge was downright masochistic. He should've ended the date at the door, but he couldn't let her go knowing tomorrow's date may never come. Tonight may be their only chance, and he didn't want to waste it.

Free will: 1, Chamuel: 0.

The moment Chamuel sensed the other Nephil's energy coming within range, he panicked and ground to a halt. He'd almost wished it was the rogue. It wasn't. It was Zeke, and he knew Chamuel was on protection duty for Cara.

If Zeke spotted Chamuel out of uniform escorting his Soul Seeker, it wouldn't take an advanced degree in rocket science to guess what was going on. Not to mention what would happen if Cara found out she was a hair's breadth away from violating Angelorum law.

Cara clutched his biceps, alarm shining in her pretty green eyes. "Is everything okay?"

He patted his breast pocket and blew out a breath. "Sorry. For a moment, I thought I'd left my wallet inside," he said, trotting out one of his practiced responses like he had during dinner so she wouldn't taste his bluff.

Michael mentioned that he and Cara completed truth training with Constantina, which made dinner a minefield of well-constructed answers composed of facts to pass muster over her taste buds.

Even with his preparations, he'd stumbled a few times. Cara assumed his parents were dead when he said they were gone. In truth, his angelic father never inhabited Earth, and his Angelorum birth mother's human form had long since turned to dust before her current incarnation. Not lies, just a bending of the truth. But Cara's assumption about his parents' death wasn't what threw him. It was her assumption about his *age*.

He hadn't considered that. Then again, he'd never dated a human.

Cara relaxed her hold on his arm as the cell phone in his jacket vibrated. He slipped it from his pocket and glanced at the screen. Zeke. *Shit.* "Sorry, it's work. Give me a sec to send off a text?" he asked.

Cara smiled. "Of course."

Chamuel sent a quick note. ***Working. What's up?***

She still on her date? In the hood on patrol. Getting a burger at my fav place. Want one?

Chamuel held his breath and typed, ***Date-yes. Burger-no.***

K. See ya. Zeke's energy disappeared a few seconds later.

Relief washed through him. Just to be safe, Chamuel said a silent cloaking prayer, disappearing them from sight and masking Cara's energy. She would never be the wiser. Nothing would change from her vantage point. They could still see and hear each other, as well as everyone around them. He just needed to steer them carefully so they didn't collide with anyone who didn't see *them*.

As they turned the corner onto the street where the lounge was located, Chamuel relaxed and uncloaked. When they reached the door, Chamuel nodded to the bouncer, and they walked past.

A warm rush of air hit him as he followed Cara inside.

A jazz musician played on a small stage in front of the crowd. Red and purple velvet drapes lined the walls, and clusters of small seating areas created an intimate atmosphere. Already densely packed, he managed to find them an open banquette with a pair of round cocktail tables tucked in the back of the room.

The waitress arrived a few moments after they sat down, ready to take their order.

He dipped his head close to Cara so she could hear him over the music. "What would you like?"

She gazed up at him. The sparkle in her green eyes warmed him. "What're you having?"

"A glass of port. May I tempt you into joining me?"

"I believe you can," she said, her eyelashes lowering.

His neck heated when her eyes settled on his lips. *Heavenly Father, help me.* Chamuel turned to the waitress and ordered two glasses of twenty-year-old tawny port. As the server left, his phone vibrated with a new text. This time, he was relieved. "My apologies," he said with a regretful glance and slipped out his phone. "It's work again."

She smiled and nodded.

Chamuel escaped to the hallway in front of the men's room and checked Zeke's text, thankful he didn't sense the young Guardian's energy in range.

Yo, you should've taken me up on that burger. How's it feel to be the third wheel on a date? What's the guy like? Is he a putz? Do tell.

Chamuel snorted a laugh. Zeke gossiped worse than an old washwoman. *Don't you have better things to do? Thought you were on patrol.*

Three dots appeared, and Chamuel shifted on his feet, hoping he didn't need to fend off Zeke's company a second time.

Slow night. Knocking off early. Going barhopping. Can I crash at your place later?

He sighed, relieved Zeke hadn't wanted more. He was like an annoying younger brother, but Chamuel loved the kid. *You know where I keep the key. Be safe.*

Chamuel returned to the lounge, where Cara sat as alluring as ever. He made his way back to the banquette like a drunken bee attracted to a pollen-laden flower. When he sat beside her, all it took was a second for her energy to curl around his and reel him in.

"Everything okay?" she asked expectantly, staring up with wide eyes. He gave her a quick smile and nodded. "Nothing important. A coworker asked to crash at my place later." He couldn't refrain from asking Cara, "Are you having a good time?"

She beamed at him and brushed her fingers down his coat sleeve. "I am."

A tingle traveled along his arm, and he suppressed a groan. Sitting beside Cara without touching her was torture. Chamuel wanted to jump out of his skin. To keep his wits, he glued his gaze on the stage and tried distracting himself with the bluesy saxophone music, but couldn't help noticing the other couples in the room. He yearned for a normal, romantic relationship with Cara. Even a small taste of her company and attention this evening had taken him down a path of no return and shattered his resolve. After tonight, remaining in a state of lonely self-depravation would gut him.

He should leave now. Find a willing female companion to break his celibacy and unleash his carnal side. Anything to reduce the sexual tension building between him and this alluring woman. But that would never suffice, and he knew it. He would never throw his sacrifice away on anything meaningless. No, only Cara would satisfy his desire. No one else. Just the one woman forbidden to him.

I am so screwed.

Cara nestled closer, so their shoulders touched. Awareness infused every cell in his body. He said a silent prayer of thanks when the waitress returned with two port glasses filled with ruby liquid and the check.

Bracing himself, he handed a glass to Cara. "This should warm you for the ride home."

Cara accepted the port with an appreciative smile and held up the glass. "*À votre santé*," she said, toasting in French. She leaned into him, her thigh making contact with his and sending electricity sizzling over his skin. The scent of her perfume wafted closer, and Chamuel had an overwhelming urge to press his nose to her neck and inhale deeply.

Oh, sweet son of man. He resisted throwing his drink back in one swallow and considered sitting on his hands, but his resistance faltered. He slipped an arm around Cara and reveled in the feel of her body pressed to his side.

She leaned into him and rested her head on his shoulder. He touched an auburn wave and inhaled sharply, pressing his eyes shut and luxuriating in the silken strands of her hair against his fingertips.

By the time the musician finished his set, their drinks were gone. A cue to end the evening before he broke the law. As he dipped his head to say as much, she turned hers. Her green eyes held an invitation, as her wildflower-scented desire hit his hypersensitive olfactory nerve. Memories of holding her after the attack slammed into him.

He gazed at her full red lips, and the ache to kiss her nearly cracked him open. His heart pounded as her breath quickened, and her gaze shifted to his mouth. She brushed a finger lightly across his lower lip.

Oh, Heavenly Father. Chamuel sank into her feather-like touch and swallowed with a ragged breath. He would've broken into a sweat if he were human.

He cupped her petal-soft cheek. She closed her eyes and turned to kiss his palm. He groaned low in his throat, his Nephilim physiology taking over. In the dark, Cara wouldn't notice his eyes dilate until the blue rim was almost gone, overpowered by the black center, or the extra blood pumping to his skin and his sex, and—if they'd been visible—his wings to heighten their sensitivity. He sure hoped she hadn't noticed the rock-hard ridge inside his pants, straining the fabric. His body burned to mate.

If I do this, there's no going back, he thought. His lips moved in silent protest. No reprieve. No forgiveness.

She took his hand from her cheek and touched her lips to each of his fingertips.

Like a pane of glass battered by hurricane-force winds, Chamuel's control shattered into a million pieces. He bent down and kissed her, touching her velvet lips with his. Soft and full, the sensation of their joined mouths was better than he imagined.

Warm energy engulfed him, stealing his tension. He sank his fingers deep into Cara's auburn waves and lost himself in the taste of her. His tongue gently sought entry and found the port's sweetness. He deepened the kiss until their tongues met in a divine dance of exploration. His senses exploded, and he wanted to take her right there in the booth.

One transgression at a time, he chided himself sternly and kissed her until he spent all the oxygen inside his lungs.

Breathless and panting, they broke apart. But before Chamuel could pull away, she trapped his face between her palms, and with a half-lidded gaze, she captured his bottom lip in a gentle kiss. He moaned as she kissed the corners of his mouth, then traveled in a sensuous trail over his jaw and along the sensitive skin of his neck.

Another release of long-forgotten hormones surged through him, and he prayed he wouldn't have to stand anytime soon. Between the weakness in his knees and a disproportionate amount of blood pulsing in his sex, he couldn't get up even if he wanted to.

He mustered every shred of restraint and pulled away. "Thank you for the most wonderful evening," he said in a deep, husky voice and tucked her head beneath his chin.

He held her, giving himself a couple of minutes to recover while he memorized every inch of how she felt pressed against him, knowing these memories would be the only thing sustaining him when he got caught. He almost laughed, wanting to do it all again. Instead, he sighed. "We need to get you home." Forcing himself to his feet, he buttoned his jacket to hide the waning evidence of his desire before helping her up and propelling her gently toward the door.

He prayed the night air would slap some sense into him.

Cara turned. "Simon?"

"Yes?"

She stepped into him, rose on tiptoe, and dropped a kiss onto his lips. "Thank you for a lovely evening."

He was already screwed, so what the hell?

He pulled her into him and lowered his lips to hers, inhaling her scent, wild bluebells dancing in the breeze, and impressing the memory on his senses. "Until tomorrow?"

"Yes, until then," she said with a dizzying smile that filled him with longing and almost broke his heart.

He considered an Uber but rejected the idea. It would take too long, and he needed to end this torturous temptation. Instead, he held up two fingers, and a cab stopped at the curb. He ushered her inside and pushed a wad of cash through a slot in the Plexiglas partition. "Here's the lady's fare."

Cara's kiss lingered on Chamuel's lips as he watched the taxi pull away. He cloaked, invoked a prayer of swiftness, and tracked the cab on foot, reflecting on the evening.

He'd gravely miscalculated his ability to resist her. It had only taken a night to cross the line in the proverbial sand. *Nice job, you self-deluded idiot.* Now it would take imprisonment to keep him away.

He released a long breath and passed a hand over his face. At least the High Council only knew his given name. Constantina would never make the connection between him and Simon Young.

A smile grew on his lips. He'd forgotten how good it felt to have a woman look at him with interest and desire. Better yet, when those feelings were mutual. Good thing, since that's all he'd have in the lonely cell with his name on it. Next on his agenda for self-destruction, he planned to see her again tomorrow.

His smile widened. He couldn't wait.

The taxi dropped Cara off on Park Avenue. Once she disappeared inside the decoy building, Chamuel texted Constantina a bland incident report and notified her that Cara would arrive momentarily. Then, he smiled to himself and added his approval of the gentleman who'd taken Cara to dinner.

Despite the levity of his mood, he'd noticed something odd as he followed Cara through the city. Not one demon blipped on his personal radar the entire trip. Zeke had mentioned it was a slow night. Chamuel hadn't given the comment a second thought with Isaac's team back from the Guardian induction ceremony. But even a Tuesday night in New York City kept a team busy.

A void in demonic activity was more disturbing than stumbling across a demon horde snacking on joggers in Central Park. The last time demons disappeared was before a major offensive.

Was it connected to the spate of Guardian disappearances? Although most had occurred on the West Coast, Boston was the second incident on the East Coast. His investigation into Xavier's disappearance uncovered nothing useful. The Guardian's energy signature was on the grid one moment and off the next. Same as the rest. The abduction happened in a city camera blind spot, leaving them without leads.

But even in Boston, Chamuel detected a steady demonic sizzle, which didn't explain why New York City flatlined.

A chill traversed his spine, and he texted Isaac.

Where are all the demons?

Chapter 29

KAI

Forrester Research. San Francisco.

KAI RACED INTO his office, late after dropping Sara at preschool, and hung his messenger bag on the back of the door while attempting not to capsize his coffee. Taking care of Sara renewed his respect for his wife. He wished she'd take the headaches more seriously. At least he won that battle. Melanie scheduled an MRI appointment after her trip to China.

Since leaving Watson & Haskins two days ago, Kai had wracked his unyielding eidetic brain to find the key's origin.

He still had no clue. Maybe he'd break down and ask Cara's opinion. He'd made it to his desk in time for their weekly call and dialed her cell.

"Hey! The Hoyas kicked butt last night," Cara said with a nod to their alma mater for their win against Florida in the NCAA's March Madness tournament.

He smiled, appreciating that her love of basketball equaled his. "I caught the highlights—it was fantastic! The win put me ahead in our basketball pool." He'd dreamed of playing hoops for Georgetown, but soccer had been a better fit for his time and talent.

"So, what's up? Figure anything out about the dream?" she asked.

He paused for a second and decided not to tell her about the key. "Nothing yet." He winced, pinching the bridge of his nose. It wasn't *exactly* a lie. "So, how's the boss from hell?"

"Yeah, that...," she said slowly and clicked her tongue. "I was laid off a couple of days after my birthday."

Taken aback, Kai bristled. "Why didn't you text me or something?" It wasn't like Cara to keep something this big to herself for almost a week.

She snorted. "Why? There's nothing you could do about it. Besides, I found another job," she said as if it were no big deal.

His eyebrows flew up. "That was fast." And weird. His senses buzzed. Something felt *off*.

She chuckled. "Kai, you sound like my dad."

"Yeah...well, he's a smart guy," he stammered, hating her dad comparisons, almost as much as when she accused him of sounding like a big brother. He pressed, "Don't keep me hanging. What's this other job?"

"Are you okay? You sound tense."

He blew out an exasperated breath. Maybe it was him who was off. God, this woman knew him better than his own wife. He reconsidered his decision to tell her about the key and rejected it again. She was prone to overreaction. Flying out to babysit him wouldn't be off the table. He'd love to see her, but if this went south, he'd have his hands full protecting his family. If something happened to them or Cara, he'd never forgive himself.

"Kai, are you still there?"

He deflected. "Yeah, sorry. Melanie left for China, so I'm Mom and Dad this week. I'm already a hot mess."

She chuckled. "Stick to Melanie's shopping list and the microwave. You'll be fine," she said, giving her usual reassurances.

He ran an agitated hand through his hair as he paced in front of his desk, sensing he wasn't the only one deflecting. "So...this new job?"

He heard a long-suffering sigh on the other end. "It's...it's a high-end property management job."

What the hell? He stopped pacing. "Doing what?"

She hesitated and huffed a nervous laugh. "Well, *Dad*, I'm managing a portfolio of assets that includes a couple of properties and a book of investments for a...private organization."

His brows knit, not liking the sound of that. An odd feeling surfaced again. "Organization? What organization? The Mob?"

"No!" She laughed, but it sounded forced. "Why would you say something like that? A charitable organization."

"What are they called?" he pressed, leaning a hip against the desk.

"Can't say. I'm under NDA," she chided.

He frowned. That was his line. "Seriously?" he joked.

"Seriously," she said soberly.

He blinked in surprise. *Damnnn...* Now he knew how Cara felt, and he didn't like being on the receiving end. Fine, he'd try again next time. "How's Sienna?"

Cara groaned. "As wild as ever. We celebrated my birthday on Saturday night. My hangover lasted two days."

Kai chuckled. His intern, Kristi, poked her head in and signaled she needed him, then ducked out. "Hey, sorry to cut this short. Kristi needs my help."

"Wait! Be careful, OK? I haven't shaken the feeling about that dream."

Guilt twinged in his gut. He opened his mouth, but words failed to materialize, so he blew out a breath. "I promise to call if anything surfaces involving the mysterious Le Feu."

Uneasiness hummed inside him after their conversation.

He grabbed a pile of mail on his desk, ready to toss it in the trash on his way to meet Kristi. A laboratory supply company brochure caught his eye—specifically, the postal address.

He froze.

Dropping the mail on his desk, he retrieved his wallet from his messenger bag. His hands shook as he removed the key from the leather pocket behind his driver's license and looked at the last five digits on the key—94306. He glanced at the zip code on the brochure. 94301. The company was located in Palo Alto, California.

Kai's heart thumped. He used his cell to search for post office locations in Palo Alto. There were two. One was located on Hamilton Avenue in postal district 94301, and a second was on Cambridge, close to El Camino Real, in postal district 94306. He searched the post box numbers in zip code 94306. They all came up with six digits.

Holy shit. The key belonged to a post office box in Palo Alto, spitting distance from the Stanford Campus.

Kai punched the air in victory.

Since Emily was in the office today, he needed to take evasive action. He checked his online calendar and compared it to Emily's to find the best time to slip away. Then he dialed his intern. "Hey, Kristi."

"Hey, Dr. S., sorry to bug you while you were on a call. Did you check the samples I ran to see if they were viable?"

Kai cringed. He hadn't checked them yet. "Give me an hour, and I'll let you know. In the meantime, can you do me a favor?"

"You betcha!" Kristi said with her usual pep and enthusiasm.

"Set up the next set of gene splices while I review your samples? Also, I have to run over to Building Seven around ten forty-five for the rest of the day. If anyone asks, just tell them I'm there."

"Not a problem!"

Kai slipped the key into his front pocket, wanting to keep it close. His heart beat faster. He was one step closer to "Ishmael."

ACHANELECH

"OUR LITTLE SCIENTIST is on the move." Emanelech's voice purred through the speakerphone on Achanelech's desk. He'd been working all morning, and his leg ached from hours of sitting. The downside of topside living was that a demon needed to make a healthy living to blend in and hide their activities. After all the years he'd spent on earth, you'd think he could retire and live off the interest on his investments. If the Master stopped tithing him to death, maybe one day he could do just that.

Ironic, the Angelorum did the opposite, *bestowing* wealth on their most valuable Soul Seekers. Which wasn't all bad, he supposed. Sudden wealth made them more conspicuous and easier to hunt.

Achanelech scowled at Em's news. "It took him long enough. Hopefully, he'll lead us to the prize this time."

"Dr. Solomon's not the only game in the casino, you know," Em said.

He rolled his eyes at her modern turn of phrase and hissed, "*Sssss…*Em, we're not playing roulette here. The Forrester research is the most promising, but we're running out of time. Like it or not, our decision to solve two problems at once will be construed by the Angelorum as us throwing down the gauntlet. Expect the Master to flay us both if we fail."

"We won't fail." Her icy tone froze the air on his side of the phone. "We'll get our vaccine and capture her for Lucifer," she said, adding gleefully, "The plan's brilliant if I do say so myself. Then again, I did think of it."

"I admire your confidence, *ma chérie*. I wish I shared it," he said dryly. "Just be prepared to act fast."

She sniffed. "Aren't I always? My bigger problem is keeping your demon fed, so it doesn't swallow our prize. Having the scientist as a snack won't get us any closer to a vaccine and will surely get us disemboweled."

Achanelech gritted his teeth. He'd chosen the best behaved of his demon children to accompany her, and she best be up to the task of managing the beast. "If that happens, I will flay you myself."

An icicle popped through the phone and struck him in the forehead. "Promises, promises. I'd like to see you try. Later, Gator." She hung up on him.

Bitch, he seethed, turning the ice to a boiling puddle on his desk. He rubbed the tender skin over his eyes. Some days, he envied humans their ignorance. Today was one of them.

KAI

KAI ARRIVED AT the post office on Cambridge near the Stanford campus at eleven forty-five. The lot was peppered with cars when Kai pulled in. He breathed a sigh of relief, convinced he hadn't been followed.

He grabbed his messenger bag and headed to the entrance, but he couldn't shake the uneasy feeling of being watched.

Once inside, Kai's head was on a swivel, assessing the scene. A few people stood in a line in front of the counter, but the place was relatively quiet. Kai headed to the section with post office boxes and studied the numbers. It didn't take him long to find the one matching key 550056.

Kai glanced around, assessing, recording, and storing everything he observed. Another patron walked in and opened a post office box a few feet away.

A bead of sweat formed on Kai's upper lip, and he waited until the mustached man with a receding hairline took his mail and left. Kai slipped the key into the lock and did something an Agnostic ordinarily wouldn't do—he prayed.

Holding his breath, Kai turned the key, opening the small door. The cubby was jammed. He grabbed the mail with both hands and tugged, pulling out a jumble of generic flyers and legit-looking envelopes. Kai relocked the box, slipped the key into his pocket, and headed to a table beside a recycle bin.

After discarding the junk mail, Kai flipped through envelopes in varying sizes, and his mouth went dry.

All the mail was addressed to him.

He stuffed the envelopes into his bag with shaky hands and scanned the room. Picking up nothing unusual, he approached a shuttered window designated for mail assistance and rang the bell.

The gray slats rose, revealing a postal worker with a round face wearing a bored expression. "May I help you?"

Kai pasted on a polite smile. "I don't remember when the contract for my mailbox runs out. Can you check for me?" Kai asked and supplied him with the box number.

"Sure. Be right back." The postal worker reappeared a few minutes later, shaking his head. "Well, you don't have to worry. It's paid through January 2030."

Stunned, Kai thanked the man and headed outside. Obviously, Tom had made preparations in case Kai took longer than expected to make his discovery.

Kai slipped into the driver's seat and searched his cell phone for a place private enough to review what Tom had left him. He found a Starbucks a half mile from campus. Perfect. Cara always said he looked more like a college student than a scientist. It was time to test her theory.

Goosebumps rose on Kai's skin as he shifted into Reverse. His head throbbed with the beginnings of another weird migraine. Grimacing at the unpleasant taste of tar, he put the car in Park and searched the immediate area for a road repair crew. Just like when he left Watson & Haskins—there was none.

THE STARBUCKS WAS buzzing with activity. Kai ordered a decaf coffee and retreated to a back table with enough privacy to suit his needs. Cautiously, he removed the stack of envelopes from his bag and ordered them chronologically by the postmark date. He opened the oldest one first—it contained a letter from Dr. Tom Peyton.

Dear Kai,

If you're reading this letter, it's because I'm no longer alive. As scientists, our intellectual curiosity is unparalleled, and at times we're fortunate enough to discover something both earth-shattering and life-altering. I've made one of those discoveries, which I will pass on to you. By now, you've likely realized that the last part of the research I conducted is missing from Forrester and has been replaced with fabricated notes. Since we were both taught by Noble, I placed a bet that the notations would provide enough of a clue for you. I'm not sure how complete my research will be before you read this letter. However, you must keep it safe and hidden.

Project Firefly isn't what it appears to be...it never was. With Dr. Sandra Wilson's help, I was able to piece together the project's true intent. As I write this, Sandra has been dead for less than twenty-four hours, but she made some provisions for me before she died to ensure that, eventually, you would find these documents. As you read, I beg you in advance to set aside your preconceived notions of what is scientifically probable and possible and willingly suspend your disbelief—it will bring you closer to the truth. Kai, you must complete the work, but not at Forrester. The Foundation is a front for a ruthless and nefarious group of people who will do anything to get their hands on this discovery, including killing you and your family. It's why both Sandra and I are now dead, regardless of how our deaths were staged. Sandra convinced me that you're the only one who can help. Something about your destiny, if you believe in that sort of thing. I'm so sorry that you're now involved in this...

Sandra has assured me that there will be an opportunity to get this into the right hands, and it will come through someone you know, trust, and love. When you're sure you're safe, you must find Ishmael and the others. The DNA fueling the project hasn't been coming from where you think. You've been working with DNA belonging to Ishmael and others like him in the lab. At this point, I'll ask you to suspend your disbelief—Ishmael is not 100% human.

> *Stay safe and watch your back.*
>
> *Sincerely,*
>
> *Tom*

Kai's heart pounded, the stationery trembling in his hands. He swallowed hard and put the letter back in the envelope.

A chill passed through him, and his gaze darted around in a fit of paranoia. Spotting nothing out of the ordinary, he pressed the heels of his hands to his eye sockets and took several deep breaths to calm his racing heart.

What the hell did this all mean?

He grabbed his cell and started punching in Cara's number. Mid-dial, he threw it down. He couldn't drag Cara into this. Not now.

Instead, he pulled out the next envelope, swept a hand over his face, and opened it. He unfolded the pages and stared at the first section of real lab notes following the Noble annotations. The contents started at a brand-new point, not part of his current research.

Kai swallowed, and his scientific curiosity kicked into overdrive. The research instantly absorbed him and seemed closer to science fiction than scientific fact. He couldn't consume it fast enough, wanting to retain every detail.

The genome sequenced by Tom and Sandra held 99.99 percent human genes with a few distinct differences. The senescence displayed in the cells was almost nonexistent, indicating the owner's longevity was closer to half a millennium. In addition, they could rapidly replace cells, greatly accelerating healing beyond standard human capabilities. Finally, one gene had been edited out, with a note explaining that it should not be reintroduced into the genetically engineered product under any circumstances. The final notes focused on developing a DNA-based vaccine to deliver the material to a host. Fortunately, Kai had experience in vaccine development as part of his prior research.

Kai flipped through the pages again. The research notes appeared to be complete. Tom must have had just enough time to finish the work once he knew what he was looking for. But Tom never again mentioned the reason for the genetic abnormalities found in Ishmael or why he believed Ishmael wasn't human.

He felt like Mulder in a classic *episode of The X-Files.*

As Kai reread the notes, things clicked into place as to why he'd made so little progress over the last year. The more he read, the more he suspected it wasn't safe to keep any of this material on his person or in an easily accessible location.

Needing a plan, he nervously drummed his fingers on the table as he formulated one. He had to be prepared to reproduce the results without the luxury of these notes. Putting his photographic memory to work, he memorized the critical passages and took some cryptic notes on the notepad he had with him.

Having lost track of time, he glanced at his watch and panicked—it was almost five o'clock. He'd never make it back to San Jose on time to pick up Sara. Gathering all his documents, he stuffed them into his bag and returned to the post office.

He made a beeline for the man behind the counter when he arrived. Tom's letter mentioned getting the notes into the hands of someone Kai knew and trusted. Kai bought a large padded envelope and then dashed out a quick note: "Keep this safe. Kai."

Slipping the key and all the documents inside the envelope, he addressed it to one of the only people he trusted with his life. He printed Cara's West Village address on the envelope with no return address and handed it to the postal worker.

"Eleven dollars ninety-five cents," the man said after affixing a metered stamp.

Kai handed him a twenty and left without waiting for change.

Chapter 30

CARA

Fifth Avenue. New York City.

CARA PICTURED CHAMUEL hot on her trail under a cloak of invisibility as she made the five-minute walk to the Metropolitan Museum of Art on Fifth Avenue at Eighty-Second Street. She hoped to arrive a few minutes before two o'clock, the time she arranged with Simon.

Cara had expected resistance from Constantina and Michael when she requested a short reprieve to meet Simon at the Met. Instead, they yielded with raised eyebrows and a pair of knowing smiles. Grateful she didn't have to fight her way out of the penthouse, Cara joyfully selected her outfit—jeans, a black cashmere scoop-neck sweater, a long silver necklace, and black boots with a sexy medium heel, high enough to be flattering yet comfortable enough to walk around the museum.

As Cara prepared to leave, Constantina had surprised her when she said, "*Chamuel texted me when you arrived home last night. He approves of your date.*" Cara's cheeks had warmed, and she reconsidered her grievances against her unseen Guardian, promising herself she'd give him a chance when they met. It made tailing her a little less intrusive now.

Her call with Kai came back to gnaw at her. She couldn't pinpoint whether it was his distraction or her deception that accounted for her feelings of unease. At face value, the conversation went better than expected, though Kai hadn't missed a beat grilling her about her new *job*. She hated lying to him about everything, including Simon. Not that Kai should care if she had a date, but that hadn't stopped Kai's overprotective scrutiny of Tyler way back when. If she told Kai about Simon, she wouldn't put it past him to do a background check or something equally as foolish.

On the upside, she noticed the absence of longing, which usually followed their calls. Maybe meeting Simon had loosened Kai's stranglehold on her heart. For that, she was grateful.

On the downside, she had a nagging feeling she wasn't the only one hiding something.

Passing a street vendor, Cara caught the scent of spicy roasted nuts on her approach to the magnificent Beaux-Arts structure.

Four pairs of giant columns flanked three sets of doors, each covered by an arched triptych of windows. People sat or stood, alone or in clusters, along the grand three-tiered cut concrete stairs leading to the main entrance. Some used the stairs as a meeting place, as Cara did now, while others relaxed in the sun with no intention of entering.

Cara stood at the base and scanned the steps for Simon. Her heart sank when she didn't see him.

She swept her gaze over the crowd a second time and blinked.

Simon sat midway to the top, impossible to miss. It's like he appeared out of thin air. He wore his hair secured in a ponytail, a black leather jacket, jeans, a white button-down shirt open at the neck, and some serious shit-kicking boots. His gaze found hers, and a smile spread across his face that lit his eyes.

Gah! She waved, a flutter in her chest, and returned his smile.

Simon rose, towering over the people around him. His sheer size and astounding male beauty mesmerized her as he approached, but it was his aura of unfiltered delight when he looked at her that stole her breath.

He pulled her into an embrace. Cara tilted her head. Their gazes locked, and he lowered his lips to hers. His clean, citrusy scent enveloped her while his tongue met hers in a sweet, warm rush. A delicate shiver raced over her skin, and her whole body melted into him, uncaring who watched their public display of affection.

Pressing his forehead to hers, he whispered, "I had a great time last night."

"Ditto," she said breathlessly, pretty sure he had no idea that he awakened sensations in her that she'd long forgotten.

He released her slowly. "Shall we enjoy some art?"

"Wait." Cara held up a finger and rummaged inside her purse to retrieve her membership card. "I'm a member...."

She looked up to find him grinning shyly and holding a card indicating he was a Leadership Circle patron. Her jaw dropped. The guy donated $25,000 a year to the Met? "Holy—wow. You're a true patron of the arts." Her pricey Ambassador membership wasn't even in the same league.

"You could say that." He winked, slipped the card into his pocket, and took her hand. Tipping his head toward the doors, he said, "Shall we?"

They entered the main hall, where he flashed his card in return for two tags, which they affixed to their clothing. Cara stopped to check her coat before they entered the gate.

Pausing at the bottom of the large central staircase, Simon asked, "Where would you like to start?"

Cara thought for a second. "My favorite places are the American Wing, European Paintings, and the Sculpture Garden, but I'm open to anything. My first love is American landscape painters of the Hudson River School, but I also love the Impressionists, especially Renoir. What about you?"

He smiled. "I'm biased toward European Paintings, but I love all your favorites. Did you know that thirty-eight of John Kensett's paintings were donated to the museum when he died in 1872?" Simon asked, referencing a prominent Hudson River painter.

Cara tilted her head, impressed with his knowledge. "I knew some of his paintings were here, but no, I hadn't realized there had been such a large bequest."

"How about starting on the first floor and the American Wing? Then we can move on to the European Paintings."

Butterflies fluttered in Cara's chest as he took her hand. She liked the warm, gentle pressure and the ease with which he showed the world they were together. "Excellent idea," she said.

They set out for the Charles Engelhard Court, a large, open structure anchored on the north side by the multistory, neoclassical façade of the Branch Bank of the United States, originally located on Wall Street. The café buzzed with activity near the first-floor windows.

Cara enjoyed their easy connection as they meandered through the court, hands joined, looking at Tiffany glass. "You mentioned you paint. What's your favorite subject?"

"*Hmm.*" Simon paused to think. "I find landscapes inspiring, but I also paint still lifes and other subjects…including the occasional full-body portrait." He glanced at her with a mischievous glint in his eye. "I would love to have you as my model someday."

She cleared her throat. "You're talking about nudes, right?"

"Of course." He shrugged and asked innocently, "How else would you paint them?"

"I'm flattered." She choked out a laugh. "But only if you return the favor. I'm pretty good with a piece of charcoal," she taunted, expecting him to rethink his position.

His brows rose in surprise, then he swallowed and called her bluff. "It's a deal," he whispered, wearing a sly smile on his lips. "Tonight, at my place?"

Her smile fled. "What?" she croaked. True, she wouldn't mind a muscular eyeful, but not if it meant baring her skin.

Blue eyes sparkling, he threw his head back and laughed. "I'm kidding. I think we should wait until we know each other better, yes?"

Relaxing, she chuckled, beaten at her own game, and nudged him with an elbow. "Yes."

He leaned in and whispered, "You should've seen your face. Your expression was priceless." Slipping his hand from hers, he hooked an arm around her and kissed the top of her head. "Let's go upstairs."

As they exited onto the second level of the American Wing, Cara asked, "Do you collect?"

"Not really. Everything I own, I've painted myself. You?"

Her brow rose. "I'm no artist myself, but I have a few paintings and sketches. Nothing close to a collection."

They chatted quietly as they enjoyed the surrounding artwork.

In the European Paintings section, they paused in front of one of the largest paintings in a gallery filled with Rubens and several of his contemporaries.

Simon pulled her against his warm, muscled chest, encircling her waist from behind and gently resting his chin atop her head while they admired the work. As much as Cara enjoyed the art, she enjoyed Simon's embrace more.

"I'd like to see your paintings sometime," she whispered.

He kissed her crown. "That could be arranged," he said, his breath warming her hair.

Simon's cell phone vibrated in his jacket pocket, and his arms tensed around her. "Please, excuse me," he said and stepped away. Pulling out his phone, he glanced at the number. "It's work. I have to take it. Wait here?"

She nodded, and Simon headed for the stairway. He hadn't exaggerated about his job. If this was an example of the interruptions during his time off, she couldn't imagine what it was like while he was working. Then again, her job hadn't been much better.

Cara's phone chimed quietly inside her purse. It was a text from Constantina: *Returning to the Sanctuary on unexpected business. I've asked Michael to stay at the penthouse and Chamuel to stay on guard. Enjoy your date! Be in touch soon. Love, Constantina.*

Warm hands clasped Cara's shoulders from behind. "Everything all right?" Simon whispered near her ear.

"Good news. My appointment was canceled for tonight," Cara said softly, dropping her phone back into her bag.

"Well, that *is* excellent news. May I tempt you with a dinner invitation?"

Her pulse quickened, and she smiled. There was nothing she wanted more. "I might be persuaded."

"Would it sweeten the deal if I told you I was the chef?"

"Perhaps…as long as you don't throw in a cheesy line about showing me your etchings." She turned towards him to get closer to his lips.

"No chance of that." He snugged her into his hard warmth. "I don't have etchings. But I'd love to show you my paintings."

"And I'd love to see them…but no nude modeling, OK?"

His lips turned up in a sexy smile. "Deal. I promise to be a gentleman."

They spent another hour and a half exploring the European Paintings galleries, where Simon continued to impress her with his extensive knowledge. She couldn't believe she'd found a man who loved art as much as she did.

To think, two days ago she hadn't even known him, and now she didn't want to be without him. Hopefully, she wasn't barreling pell-mell towards disappointment. Then again, she could end up being the one doing the disappointing.

Chapter 31

CARA

Broome Street. New York City.

THE TAXI DROPPED Cara and Simon off at Gourmet Garage, a specialty food store on Broome Street in SoHo. Cara despised food shopping, but with Simon, taking out the garbage would be fun.

Cara contentedly strolled beside Simon and listened, attention rapt, as he consulted with the fishmonger, whom he obviously knew. They decided on halibut with Cara's input, and Simon added the fresh fish to the small basket he carried, already filled with artisanal cheeses and a fresh baguette, salad greens, and a few other items needed to prepare the meal.

As they stood in the checkout line, Cara still couldn't believe she'd met a man who loved art *and* knew his way around a kitchen. She was fairly certain she wouldn't find boxed macaroni and cheese in his pantry.

"You're much better at adulting than me," she whispered as he paid for their purchases.

He chuckled and peeled off bills from his money clip to pay the cashier. "I have a few years on you."

She let his age comment go at Raphael's but eyed him now with squinty appraisal. "*Hmm*, so you've said. My guess…thirty-two?"

He gave her a sexy wink. "You flatter me."

She sighed. "You're not going to tell me, are you?"

"Nope," he teased.

They walked in companionable silence the short distance to Simon's Greene Street loft in the falling darkness. He stopped in front of one of the historic cast-iron fronted row houses and fished out his keys.

Cara raised a brow. Private security obviously paid well, as if Simon's Met patronage wasn't a dead giveaway. A loft in one of these buildings must cost anywhere from four to seven million dollars, depending on its size. Though for an avid painter like Simon, it was a perfect choice.

Cara loved this part of SoHo, which had one of the largest collections of cast-iron architecture in the world. The nineteenth-century buildings and cobblestone streets, which served industrial purposes in the mid-1800s, were repurposed in the 1950s and 1960s as artist lofts before being converted into luxury retail and living spaces.

Simon held the door for Cara, and she entered the foyer, a sparsely decorated space with framed vintage black-and-white photographs and metal furniture. "Interesting décor."

He smiled warmly and took her hand. "It's not really my taste, but the co-op committee wanted to honor the building's history."

They took the refurbished caged elevator to the fifth floor, which required a key and access code. Shiny elevator doors opened directly into the loft space.

"You have the whole floor?" Cara asked when they stepped into the apartment.

"Yup," he said casually.

Okay, closer to $6 million.

She stared straight ahead into the entrance of a magnificent gourmet kitchen, bracketed by partition walls on both sides. A narrow hallway to their left led to the back of the loft, while a large dining area with windows facing the street lay to the right of the kitchen.

The ceiling was easily fourteen feet high, painted black to hide the ductwork and draw the eye downward. From where Cara stood, she could see that the walls were no higher than eight feet, leaving a six-foot gap to the ceiling. The kitchen's back wall bisected the loft, which meant rooms on the other side.

The place was huge by New York City standards.

"It's not as big as it looks at first blush," said Simon, as if reading her mind. He set down the bag momentarily to hang their coats on hooks beside the elevator, then took their food into the kitchen. "I'll take you to see the best part later," he said, flashing a grin as he unloaded their purchases onto the center island.

She trusted he wasn't referring to the bedroom. "You promised to show me your artwork, remember?"

"And I always keep my promises," he said, his lips quirking into a mischievous smile. He pointed to the kitchen wall. "My studio is on the other side, beside the living room."

Cara took a seat on one of the island stools.

The bag emptied, Simon rubbed his hands together. "Would you like to be my sous-chef this evening?"

"Does it involve sharp objects?" Cara asked warily.

Simon frowned, worry passing through his blue gaze. "Are you afraid of knives?"

She laughed it off and wondered why that concerned him. "No. More like a disaster in the kitchen."

His tension eased. "You're in good hands. I'll teach you proper knife handling."

Michael had already taken her through the full gamut of blades at his dojo, but she could feign ignorance for an evening. At this point, her chances of setting the place on fire were higher than slicing off a finger.

Simon washed the fish, set it on a plate, and rinsed his hands. "I'd like to change into something better suited for cooking, and then I'll give you the tour. How does that sound?" he asked, excitement returning to his gaze.

She couldn't help but smile. "Great."

As his footsteps echoed down the hall, Cara glanced around the spotless kitchen. The counters were free of clutter, except for an espresso maker, a knife block, and a basket of fresh fruit.

No frat boy kitchen here. A truly magnificent space, the kitchen had been designed to be functional yet sophisticated. The focal point was a heavy-duty stainless steel industrial stove with a hood and exhaust that disappeared into the black painted ceiling. The cabinets were sleek, a modern European style with dark granite countertops. Simon's kitchen rivaled hers at the penthouse.

As Cara drummed her nails on the granite, soaking in Simon's space, her gaze landed on a series of four 16 x 20 oil paintings on canvas with identical frames hung on the partition wall behind her. Three pictures were food-themed still lifes — fruit, vegetables, and fresh seafood — executed in the style of Severin Roesen, an American mid-nineteenth-century painter. Cara was impressed. Simon was clearly talented, given that he could create such awesome reproductions.

The fourth painting, a portrait of a young woman framed in the same nineteenth-century style, stole Cara's breath. The look in the sitter's eyes captured her love for the painter. Cara hopped off her stool to take a closer look. Ignoring a twinge of guilt for snooping, she lifted the painting off the hook to check if Simon had labeled the work on the back.

Cara frowned, confused. As an art history student, she learned to date unrestored paintings from the underside of the canvas. Cara hadn't expected the deep coffee patina, dust, and dirt. Cara examined the brushstrokes on the front more closely, then flipped it back. Simon told her he'd painted all the artwork displayed in his loft. Was this from someone else?

One thing was certain — this painting hadn't been executed in her lifetime or even in this *century*. She was sure of it.

As Simon's footsteps approached, she carefully rehung the frame on the wall and sat.

Simon walked in wearing faded blue jeans and a black V-neck T-shirt, which hugged his torso. The short-sleeved shirt accentuated his broad shoulders and showcased his bulging biceps and corded forearms.

Cara blinked. Wow. *It should be illegal to look that good.* She shook her head to clear it and pointed behind her. "Did you paint these?"

"Yup," he said without a glance.

Now, Cara was thoroughly confused. "Even the portrait?"

Simon glimpsed the painting. Cara detected a millisecond of alarm flicker through his gaze before he furrowed his brow and casually asked, "Yes. Why?"

Cara eyed the piece, confident in her assessment. "Sorry. The art historian in me wanted to take a closer look. The canvas...," Cara hesitated, hoping she hadn't misplaced her trust. But why would Simon lie? She sighed. "I dated the piece as late nineteenth century."

Unease danced across Simon's features, and then he brightened. "Ah! I purchased all the frames together, and they are indeed from the nineteenth century. Sometimes I also recycle old canvases." He nodded to the portrait. "I like the way they hold the pigment." He chuckled. "Sorry for the confusion."

Cara tasted the sweet truth and glanced at the portrait, reassured. "Did you know her, or was she a model?"

Simon hesitated, and a sea of emotions welled behind his eyes, dampening his good humor. When he spoke, his voice was suddenly hoarse. "Her name was Calliope... She was my first love."

His words landed like a kick to Cara's solar plexus. "Where is she now?"

Simon swallowed and averted his gaze. "She died."

Cara's hand flew to her mouth. Whoa, not the answer she expected. "Oh, my God. I'm so sorry. I didn't mean to pry," she whispered.

Simon shook his head and sighed. "You didn't. It was a long time ago. I don't talk about it, because there's never been anyone...I wanted to tell." Turning away, he leaned his palms on the counter and hung his head. "*Merde,*" he muttered softly in French.

Cara slid off the stool and went to him. Looking up the rippled mountain of his back, she glided her fingertips over the soft, black cotton. He drew in a sharp breath. She channeled healing energy through her palms as Constantina taught her. Simon's tension eased beneath her touch, and he leaned into her.

She encircled him with her arms and pressed an ear to the warm hollow of his spine, embracing his vulnerability and offering comfort. He moaned softly as her fingers traced a path down the hard ridges of his pectorals and midsection before settling at his waist.

Inhaling the clean scent of the cotton, she caught a pleasant muskiness permeating his citrusy cologne. The moment she sensed it, her body flushed with heat, and she experienced déjà vu—she had comforted him before. But that was impossible.

The memory faded as quickly as it came, leaving a deep sadness in its wake. Cara swallowed, slightly shaken. Hoping she wasn't being too forward, she said, "You can share your story with me."

Simon moved her hands from his waist to his soft lips and kissed them, then twisted to face her. Tucking her into his chest, he whispered, "I'd like that." The intimacy of the moment drew her inexplicably closer to him. If he trusted her enough to confide his story, she would guard it like a precious jewel.

Nestling her hands in the small of his back, she tilted her head to capture his gaze. "Sometimes it's better to touch someone when you have a hard story to tell."

His lips quirked into a sad smile. "That's a nice thought." He tucked her head beneath his chin and tightened his muscled arms around her. Resting her cheek beside his beating heart, she waited.

He cleared his throat. "My family and Calliope's were close. We grew up together. But by the time we were adolescents, our friendship had grown into more." He chuckled softly. "Of course, she had been way ahead of me, knowing what she wanted. Being an inexperienced adolescent male, I didn't realize what was happening between us at first. But when other suitors began to show interest, my feelings awakened. Our families couldn't have been more pleased, always hoping we would... *marry*. Then it came time to choose a career, and she followed me into... what I do."

Cara interjected. "Private security?"

"Yes. I mentioned there weren't many women in my line of work. Calliope was one of the few. In hindsight, I'm not sure if she would've chosen to do this if it hadn't been for me. The job can be dangerous. As a female, I think her family preferred her to choose a teaching career."

Cara frowned. "That's a bit sexist. I admire that she pursued a career she wanted." God knew Cara had dealt with her fair share of sexism as a result of her career choice, but never from her family.

"Maybe, but she had her own mind. We'd been together a few years as a couple when our relationship started to strain. I loved her, but I yearned to explore the world, while she was content to remain in Europe, close to her family. We fought about it the night before...." Simon trailed off, the muscles in his throat shifting against her hair before he continued, "My team had a perilous assignment, guarding a high-profile target being pursued by some rough people. We gathered intelligence that indicated the situation could escalate, so I called in reinforcements. Calliope wasn't supposed to be there that night. For safety reasons, we were prohibited from working on assignments together. But as it turned out, her team was the only one close enough to respond."

He sighed deeply. "It was an ambush. All hell broke loose. We worked in pairs, and my primary role was to protect the target while my partner protected me. Almost immediately, my partner was wounded and couldn't signal when an attacker came at my back. Calliope saw what was happening and left her formation to protect me. Her partner tried to hold off the enemy alone." He paused, and his body tensed.

"Saving me, Calliope left her back exposed... I... watched as she was killed. Helpless...," he said in a deep, gravel-filled voice. Anguish rolled off him in waves. Cara stroked his back in soothing circles and stayed pressed against him.

Simon cleared his throat and continued in a hoarse whisper, "I couldn't save her. Eight went in. Six came out, barely making it with our lives. After I told her family, I decided to take a break for a while. I moved to the United States after her funeral."

Cara's heart hurt for his loss. Her situation with Kai seemed insignificant in comparison. She gazed up at him as he turned his head and brushed the back of a hand across his eyes. Cupping his cheeks, Cara gently turned his head. "Look at me," she whispered.

Unshed tears brightened his gaze as he met her eyes. Guilt, shame, anguish, she tasted it all.

Cara tenderly held his face in her hands. She didn't need to be a therapist to recognize the guilt he carried. "Her death wasn't your fault, Simon," she said, addressing the root of his pain. "It wasn't your fault."

Her words hung between them.

Surprise sparked in Simon's gaze, and then his mouth took hers. Simon's need washed over Cara in a warm wave, igniting her nerve endings with a fiery passion. She abandoned herself to his kiss.

When they broke apart, he wound his fingers in her hair and pulled her into his heaving chest. "Cara," he said in a husky whisper, scooping her into his arms. Carrying her, Simon strode down the hall and into a bedroom illuminated by the faint glow of a picture light over an Impressionist landscape hanging above the headboard.

Simon lay Cara on the king-sized bed and lowered himself over her, hovering on his elbows. He dipped his head and nibbled the soft skin on her neck, sending a shiver along her skin.

A sudden whiff of his pleasant scent assaulted her senses, triggering a clenching low in her belly. She wanted — no, she needed — to touch him. Overtaken by blind desire, Cara brushed a palm down the front of his jeans, and her lips parted in surprise.

He moaned and rolled onto his back.

She lifted the waistband of his shirt and slipped her hands beneath the worn cotton. Brushing her fingertips over his abs, she was surprised at the smooth, silky texture of his skin. She bent to kiss a path down the peaks and valleys of his hard stomach, but he gently captured her wrists, lifted them to his lips, and kissed them.

Shifting his position, he propped himself on his elbows above her. Blue fire burned in his eyes. "I want you so desperately that I can barely breathe. But I don't want my past to overshadow our first time. You deserve better. Understand?" he pleaded, brows furrowed.

Her brain stuttered to a halt. *What?*

Then she understood and nodded, at a loss for words. His passion and honesty moved her. Cara had only slept with two men, and even though she had just met Simon, she would've gladly added him as her third. Despite her body wilting in disappointment, her respect for him deepened.

Staring from above, his gaze earnest, he whispered, "Would it be okay if we just lie here for a few minutes?"

Smiling, she extended her arms, inviting him to rest on top of her.

His lips quirked to the side. "I didn't want to crush you." In a blur of motion, Cara sat on top of Simon, her legs straddling his hips. There was no mistaking the hot, hard ridge resting against her core through their jeans. She instinctively slid along its contour.

He choked out a laugh, his fingers grasping her waist. "Stop, or you might kill me."

She slid back on his thighs, breaking contact. Coquettishly catching a lip between her teeth, she reached for the leather tie at the base of his neck. "May I? I want to see you with your hair down."

He gazed upward with a look of naked vulnerability. "I thought you already had." Emotionally, maybe. He lifted his head and whispered, "Go ahead."

She tugged, releasing the dark golden waves onto the pillow.

He snuggled her closer and kissed her gently at first until it gave way to something hungrier. His fingers trailed down the length of her back. Cara melted beneath his touch. She was exactly where she wanted to be. She wanted this—she wanted him—tonight or in the future.

Simon pulled his lips from hers, his gaze taking on a quiet resolve. "We need to rescue to fish. It's still on the counter."

She conceded with a nod and rolled onto the edge of the bed.

Bracketing her between his muscled thighs, he whispered into her hair. "Thank you." Then he rose behind her, hoisting her to her feet. "Let's have that meal I promised you."

Cara sighed and saluted. "Your sous chef reporting for duty, sir." Next time, the only thing she wanted to be underneath was Simon.

Chapter 32

CHAMUEL

Greene Street Loft. New York City.

COMBING FINGERS THROUGH his hair, Chamuel cringed as he followed Cara out of his bedroom. He had laid bare the raw edges of his pain for Cara to see, unexpectedly sharing Calliope's story and opening ancient wounds. He felt exposed and wanted to kick himself for not removing Calliope's portrait last night after he'd invited Cara to the Met. Then again, he had no idea they would end up here, and in truth, the painting had been there so long he hadn't given it any thought. So, again, he found himself stringing together factual statements, though not all pertinent, to satisfy Cara's inquiry on Calliope's portrait without lying.

Chamuel also hadn't told Cara the whole story about the night Calliope died. He couldn't. Not without exposing his identity, and that wasn't happening tonight. No. Chamuel wanted to relish the evening, filling it with happy memories. Souvenirs to sustain him when he was shackled to a wall in an Angelorum prison, short of a miraculous solution.

He mentioned eight going in and six surviving without explaining the second casualty. Calliope's death had gutted him, but his shame came from losing his target: Mina, the Soul Seeker in his Trinity. The Dark Ones used Calliope as a distraction to weaken his attention on his charge.

Their ploy worked, and he failed both females.

Unable to trust himself to protect anyone again, he removed himself from Trinity rotation and sought atonement through the denial of female companionship in honor of Calliope's sacrifice.

Then, he'd met Cara.

One hundred years of celibacy had surely been enough recompense, had it not? Though he feared each step he took with Cara put him dangerously close to repeating history.

Still, he could barely believe Cara had released part of the century-old burden he carried. Maybe he could heal, and perhaps history didn't have to repeat itself.

Either way, he was falling for Cara. Hard.

Her palm running over his erection beneath his jeans had nearly broken his self-control. The male in him hadn't wanted to stop her, but the gentleman in him had to. He'd spoken true. He didn't want Calliope's death to overshadow their first time together. But that paled in comparison to the real reason.

By kissing Cara, he'd already violated Angelorum law, and he couldn't go further while this falsehood existed between them. He had to give her a choice. Had the truth existed between them, damn the fish, he would've spent the entire night pleasuring her in every way imaginable — and there were many. God knows, he'd been an excellent student when it came to Sensual Pleasures, and there are some things you never forget.

When they reached the kitchen, he did his best to lighten the mood. "Music?" he asked.

Cara beamed. "Yes, please."

Chamuel tucked his hair behind his ears. As a rule, he didn't cook with his hair down, but Cara seemed to like it, and he wanted to please her. He grabbed his phone, picked contemporary hits from his music app, and paired the device to the speakers mounted throughout the loft.

Music played in the background as they chatted and prepared the meal.

Cara watched from the center island for the most part. Her glowing gaze followed him around the kitchen, making his heart sing. Food was love for Chamuel, and he wanted to show Cara how much he cared.

Then, true to his word, Chamuel gave her some simple tips on using his chef's knife, which she used to cut a lemon to garnish the fish. Her earlier hesitancy when he mentioned knives alarmed him. Michael was assigned to give her weapons training, which she would need even with a Guardian. Her protection meant everything to him. Now, more than ever.

As the meal cooked, he retrieved a bottle of wine from one of his two wine towers. "I know fish requires a white, but would you mind a red?" he mused, standing in front of the open refrigerator, content in his fantasy bubble and relaxed enough to forego formality.

She shrugged. "Sure. I'm not one to stand on ceremony."

Chamuel grinned. Her cheerful and easy manner delighted him. He selected a bottle and two glasses from the bar and quickly removed the cork.

Gaze sparkling, Cara raised her glass. "To new beginnings?"

He tapped his glass to hers. "I'll drink to that." His chest ached with the knowledge he was living on borrowed time. Hopefully, their beginning wouldn't be followed by a swift, unhappy ending. He shoved the thought aside and grabbed the fish timer. "Take your wine and grab your coat. I want to show you something."

Raising a curious brow, Cara temporarily set down her glass and retrieved her outerwear.

"Come," Chamuel said, leading her past his bedroom and opening a door at the end of the hallway. They ascended the stairs. At the top, he opened the metal door and flicked on the lights to the roof deck.

Cara gasped. Eyes wide, she placed a hand to her chest. "Oh, my God. This is *yours*?"

His heart swelled with pride at her delight. "Yup. All mine. One of the perks of buying the top-floor apartment."

Cara's awe-filled gaze roamed over the deck and the city beyond as her breath crystallized in the night air. "Simon, this is stunning. If it wasn't so chilly, we could've had dinner up here."

Hearing his alias from Cara's lips left a hollow ache in Chamuel's chest. What hadn't bothered him earlier today became an unwelcome reminder that this wasn't real—that *he* wasn't real. Which only made him want this more.

Tonight, he would cling to the fantasy. Real life could wait until tomorrow.

Impervious to the cold, Chamuel set down the fish timer on a planter and followed Cara toward one of the fountains. He wrapped his arms around her from behind, carefully balancing his wine. He reveled in her warmth along his front. Burying his face in her hair, he inhaled her scent laced with notes of wildflower and let himself dream.

"We will when the weather gets warmer," he said wistfully, and thought of parties they could host in the summer's warmth, time they could spend together relaxing in the sun and tending the garden—

A thought occurred to him, sparking a glimmer of hope. Once Cara learned the truth, they could pause their relationship until the Trinity assignment ended and then resume without fear of reprisal. That could work.

The timer rang, jarring him back to reality.

Cara turned in his arms and stared up with hopeful green eyes. "Can we come back later?"

He didn't want to disappoint her. "Whatever you want. For now, how about we rescue the fish?"

Chamuel packed up his mental folly as he followed Cara downstairs. Beyond a few stolen moments, they had a gauntlet to run before coupledom was a viable option, and with Cara's Calling closing in, he couldn't wait much longer to share the truth.

After a candlelit dinner, Chamuel persuaded Cara to watch a movie, not wanting her to go. Settling on the large sectional, they lay spooned. Cara snuggled into him, his arms securely around her.

They chose a new action thriller on Netflix.

Before he pushed play, he took her hand and whispered. "Cara, the call I received in the museum earlier? I have an assignment this week, but I'd like to see you again." Of course, Cara *was* the assignment. Constantina put him on notice but gave no details — per usual. "I don't know my schedule. Can we play it by ear?" He kissed her palm, waiting for an answer.

"We'll make it work," she said, gazing up at him. "If you're free on Friday night, I'm having drinks with my friend Sienna. She'd love to meet you. Join us?" she asked with a look of expectation.

He kissed her nose. "I'll do my best."

Before the introductory credits finished rolling, she was snoring softly. If Chamuel could freeze time with her melded to him, he'd gladly stay this way for eternity. Punishment be damned.

Chapter 33

KAI

Country Day School. San Jose.

OUTSIDE THE ONE-STORY ranch-style building, Sara's preschool teacher, Miss Jessica, stood with Sara and a small boy, her arm resting gently around the children as they waited with backpacks slung over their little shoulders.

"Daddy!" Sara dropped her burden and launched herself into Kai's waiting arms.

Still shaken from his discovery, Kai had driven like a madman to San Jose until he hit heavy traffic before the highway exit, which slowed his progress to a crawl.

He had texted the kind-eyed young teacher, but still offered her a sincere *mea culpa*. "Miss Jessica, I'm so sorry I'm late." Kai was glad Sara wasn't the only one waiting, though it didn't lessen his guilt.

Miss Jessica smiled warmly. "Not a problem, Dr. Solomon. Sara was keeping Tucker company until his mother got here."

Hearing his name, the boy snuggled closer behind Miss Jessica's legs.

The teacher smiled at Sara and clapped. "Big news. Sara did fantastic on her reading test today."

"Miss Jessica put two gold stars on my paper, not just one." Sara beamed with excitement over her accomplishment.

"Wow, that's amazing," he said, mustering some enthusiasm and setting his daughter on her feet. Retrieving Sara's discarded backpack, Kai slung it over his shoulder and tipped his chin at the teacher. "Thanks again, Miss Jessica. We'll see you tomorrow morning."

Tucker peeked around Miss Jessica's legs, and Kai gave him a wave. "See you, Tucker."

Kai buckled Sara into her booster seat in the back of the A6 and headed home. He half-listened to Sara jabber about her day filled with lost lunchboxes, projects involving crepe paper animals, and allergy-free chocolate chip cookies brought to class to celebrate a student's birthday, while he reviewed what he'd learned from Tom's notes and formulated a slew of questions.

Where did he go from here? Did he continue his work at Forrester as if nothing had happened? Did he look for an independent lab and try to replicate the work? Did he ask for a transfer?

For the first time, Kai almost regretted making the discovery. With this knowledge came a responsibility he wasn't sure he could fulfill. Why him? Why was it so important that he made this discovery? All of it made his brain cramp.

When he pulled into the driveway, pain slammed into his skull like a runaway freight train. White pinpricks clouded his vision as the car slid to a halt. Steadying himself on the steering wheel, he thought of Melanie's extra meds in the house.

Taking deep breaths, he muscled through the unbearable throbbing behind his eyes, eased from the car, and stumbled to Sara's side.

When he opened the door, she sat trembling, her eyes wild. "Daddy, we need to go!" She reached for the handle and tried to shut the door.

He held tight on the other side, confused. His head felt like a bomb ready to explode. "What? Why?"

"Monster!"

Kai shivered. "What monster?"

"The one in the house." She whimpered, her corn-silk blonde hair falling around her face.

Taken aback at her words, he glanced at their quiet split-level. The security system would have notified him if someone breached the residence. Now wasn't the time for monsters under the bed. He desperately needed the migraine meds. "Don't worry, I'll protect you," he mumbled, unbuckling her from the car seat and lifting her out.

"No! Luke!" she squirmed from his arms and ran headlong down the narrow pathway beside the house toward the backyard gate. Kai swore under his breath.

Luke? Who the hell is Luke?

Then he remembered. Sara mentioned his name the night she'd crawled into the bed with him.

"Sara!" Kai staggered after her as fast as the pressure in his head allowed.

The gate banged shut behind Sara.

Glass shattered, and Sara released a piercing scream. His heart jumped into his throat, and he crashed through the gate into a scene that froze him in place.

Sara crouched between a tree and the side fence a few yards away, safe from the fray.

Kai's attention snapped to the scene playing out in the center of the yard. Between the back patio and the swing set, a large man dressed in black, carrying a sword of blinding light, circled a ten-foot-tall horned demon with talons, cloven feet, and scaly, blackish-red skin. The beast's glowing red eyes locked onto the man. Talons out, it snapped its needle-sharp teeth.

Neither man nor beast took notice of Kai or Sara.

The air wavered around them as the demon swatted at the man with talon-tipped fingers. Molten waves of heat rolled toward Kai, who stood rooted, gaping in stunned disbelief.

The man and the demon continued their circular dance, the demon taking random swats and the man dodging the attacks.

Then, in a blink, the man transformed into a white blur and rammed the sword into the demon with a blinding flash. The monster let out an agonizing roar, then disintegrated into black ash.

The scene fell silent. The man was gone.

Kai's headache disappeared. He stood, jaw hanging open, and stared at the empty backyard.

"Daddy!"

Kai turned toward Sara, and a fist slammed into his face, knocking him to the ground.

Sara screamed.

Kai scrambled to get to his feet, but a hard kick landed in his side, knocking the wind out of him and doubling him over on the ground. He groaned, the pain in his head replaced with agony in his face and gut.

Through a swelling eye, he saw a man he didn't recognize grab Sara from behind, her feet kicking empty air. Panic seized him as he was pulled roughly to his feet. Hands closed around his throat from behind and squeezed, constricting his airway.

Kai struggled, clawing at his attacker while Sara screamed in the other man's arms.

"Where are Peyton's notes?" asked a cold, controlled voice.

"I don't have them," Kai choked out through gritted teeth and scratched at the cold, unyielding flesh circling his neck.

"That's unfortunate."

"Daddy, they have our angel!" Sara cried.

The man who'd fought the demon was pinned inside the arms of a much larger man who stood over seven feet tall and didn't look human.

Kai's eyes widened when he saw the woman with raven-black hair who stood beside them, and it all clicked into place.

"Emily." Her name slipped through his bared teeth.

A cloth with a sweet, cloying smell covered his mouth and sucked him into darkness.

Chapter 34

KAI

Undisclosed Location.

KAI SURFACED INTO consciousness and wished he hadn't. His senses awakened to the pulsing mass above his shoulders, the cold ground beneath him, and the damp, earthy smell of a subterranean room. He opened his eyes in the semi-darkness and stared at a wall of iron bars in an underground prison cell.

Beyond the bars, oil lamps hung at intervals, casting dim shadows along the walls and illuminating the hall enough to make out empty cells across the way. He was alone.

Hands secured behind his back, he shivered on the concrete ground and fought back a wave of nausea. It took him a minute to inventory his extremities, testing them one by one to diagnose potential injuries. Besides a chill and stiffness from dozing on a concrete slab with bound hands, he was in reasonable shape.

He closed his eyes and dug into his memory to recall what happened. The scene from the backyard came crashing back. Kai's eyes popped open, and panic sent his heart racing. What had they done with his little girl? He had to find her.

Gritting his teeth, he strained against the ties, which only served to dig deeper into his skin.

Think! He took some calming breaths to focus. Summoning his willpower, he slowed his rushing thoughts and engaged his analytical mind.

Kai struggled into a seated position. The throbbing in his head intensified with the elevation change, followed by an urge to vomit. He gave himself a moment for the pain and nausea to pass, then checked his back pocket with a zip-tied hand for his cell phone.

As expected, it was gone.

He assessed his situation.

He was alive, so he had a chance. Check.

His abduction was related to Tom's death. Check.

Emily and The Foundation were behind his kidnapping. Check.

They needed the vaccine notes. Check.

He had what they wanted in his head, and they had his daughter. Double-check.

Given their track record, he and Sara would be expendable once he gave them what they wanted. Probable check.

He had to buy some time. Miss Jessica would miss Sara at school, but how long would it take her to report Sara's absence? Melanie didn't arrive home from China until the weekend. Between the fifteen-hour time difference and her flight tomorrow, she would only miss one call—not enough to raise much suspicion. His anxiety peaked with their dim prospects for rescue and the time it could take before anyone started looking for them.

Damn it.

Multiple pairs of footfalls echoed in the passageway.

Kai's adrenaline surged, and he rose awkwardly to his feet as his kidnappers came into view.

A sharply dressed man of average height with jet-black hair that brushed his suit jacket led a small entourage, including the oh-so-familiar raven-haired woman who had been the bane of Kai's existence for the last year and two massive men who hung in the shadows.

Keys jostled. A door cut into the bars opened. The man, an ebony cane in one hand, stepped inside with Emily on his other arm. He sized up Kai with cold, black eyes.

Kai's gaze snagged on the V-shaped scar on the man's cheek before landing on Emily, who examined her nails, looking bored. He knew he'd hated that bitch for a reason.

Kai glared at her and growled low in his throat, "You."

Emily gave an exaggerated pout and shrugged.

The man leaned on his cane, shook his head, and *tsked.* "No need to blame my consort, Dr. Solomon." Letting her go, he moved closer to Kai.

"Who are you?" Kai bit out.

The man smirked in amusement and said in a smooth, slightly accented voice, "You're the Messenger—you tell me?"

WTF? Kai frowned, wondering if the drug had scrambled his brain. "What?"

A look of surprise lit the man's hard eyes. "Ah, I see...." He tapped a finger to his lip and squinted. "You don't know. Very smart, Sandra was."

Mystified, Kai kept his face blank. *What the hell is he talking about?*

The black-haired man paced with his cane, his gait betraying a subtle limp. The large ruby topping the cane caught Kai's eye.

"Dr. Solomon, we've waited patiently for you to lead us to Dr. Peyton's work. We started to lose hope." The man hissed on his s's, sending a shiver along Kai's skin.

He drew up close to Kai and shot him a piercing look. "We're disappointed you are no longer in possession of what we seek. However, I've heard you have a near-perfect memory. Let's hope you remember the contents of the lab notes…your precious Sara's life may depend on it."

Kai stared him down. "Where's my daughter?"

"She's quite safe."

"I want to see her," Kai growled.

A malevolent grin spread across the man's face. "Dr. Solomon, you're hardly in the position to make demands." He waved a hand as if shooing away a pesky insect. "You'll see her in due time. For now, why don't I tell you what you'll do here as our guest?"

Kai gritted his teeth and projected a composure he didn't feel, having determined it was better to shut up and listen.

"First, allow me to introduce myself." He placed a hand on his chest and bowed slightly from the waist. "My friends call me *Le Feu*, and I hope, Dr. Solomon, you and I will be friends."

Kai flinched. Like a puzzle, all the pieces locked into place, and his knees went weak. *Shit.*

Cara's dream.

Le Feu regarded him shrewdly and smiled. "Ah, I see my reputation precedes me."

Kai's stare hardened. "Not exactly." He didn't know jack about him, only that Le Feu's name was associated with Kai's death dream, and in turn, Tom's killing. But Kai kept that to himself.

Le Feu sniffed and leaned on his cane. "No matter. Shall we get started? I'm sure you have many questions, and there's so little time to do much. Consider yourself a guest of The Foundation." He swept a hand in front of him. "My apologies for the harsh accommodations. You'll be moved to more comfortable quarters in our state-of-the-art laboratory upstairs. I believe you'll be quite impressed with what we have to offer, but make no mistake—the lab is more secure than this cell."

Le Feu glanced over his shoulder at the two enormous men, who stepped from the shadows. "Chaos and Destruction will be your personal bodyguards."

Kai recognized their inhuman faces… or rather, face. They were identical twins, standing over seven feet tall with skin that held an unnaturally white pallor. They'd never be mistaken for human in a crowd. One of them had captured the man Sara called Luke in his backyard the night before.

Icy energy radiated from the creatures, chilling the air and raising gooseflesh on Kai's arms under his jacket—a sharp contrast to the malevolent heat radiating from Le Feu. Kai's body didn't know whether to sweat or shiver.

"Let me get to the point. You have five days to create the vaccine that we need."

Kai blanched. "Five days? Are you *nuts*?" Even with the notes and a clear roadmap, Kai anticipated that the vaccine would take at least a couple of weeks, if not months, to develop.

Le Feu's eyebrows flew up. "I'm many things, Dr. Solomon, but crazy isn't one of them. I'll remind you, there's a lot at stake…your daughter's life for one."

Kai returned to a healthy state of fear. "Why only five days?"

"Because that's when you become bait for the fish we've cast our net to catch. We've been waiting for sssso very long," he said, with a snakelike hiss and a hungry gleam in his eyes.

Kai swallowed when he spotted the man's forked tongue and stuttered, "Wh-who's that?"

Le Feu shifted his weight on his cane and raked Kai with a glare. "You really don't know, do you?"

Kai said honestly, "No. I don't."

Le Feu chortled and glanced at Emily. "This is going to be so much fun," he said, wearing a smile filled with malevolent glee, and returned his attention to Kai. "Why, your precious Cara Collins, of course."

Kai felt like he'd been gut-punched. "What does Cara have to do with any of this?"

Le Feu winked at him. "You'll see. I wouldn't want to spoil the surprissse. For now, Chaos will escort you to the lab, where I'll allow a brief visit with your daughter." He tapped his cane on the floor. "Then tick-tock. Time to get to work."

Kai's heart pounded, reeling from what he was expected to do, and kicking himself for not telling Cara about his discovery. Kai blurted, "What if five days isn't enough?" He had to know.

A spark leaped from Le Feu's finger and landed on Kai's chest, burning a hole in his shirt. Kai winced and touched the searing spot.

Le Feu frowned and gave Kai a menacing glare. "I require a couple of human sacrifices, Dr. Solomon. Your wife and daughter would do nicely. I'm sure you understand the need for us to provide a strong incentive for your success."

Kai snapped. "Who the hell are you?" he yelled.

Coal-black eyes blazed at Kai. "*Who* I am is unimportant. It's *what* I am that should concern you."

The hairs on Kai's neck stood. "If I give you what you need within five days, then what?" Kai wanted to know his options.

"Then you all get to leave, unharmed."

Kai was immediately suspicious. "How can I be sure?"

Le Feu looked him straight in the eye. "You can't."

"What about Cara?"

Le Feu shook his head. "Oh, I'm afraid she's not mine to release. We have other plans for her."

"You bastard!" Kai gritted and launched himself at Le Feu. Chaos caught Kai in a vicelike grip, chilling him to the bone.

Le Feu stared and said dryly, "I dare say that's impossible, given my lack of parentage."

Emily, who hadn't said a word since she entered the cell, swept her gaze over Kai. "Ta ta! I'll let Kristi know you've decided to take a little vacation," she said, wearing a satisfied smirk.

"I hope you rot in Hell, you evil bitch!" He spat after her.

"Been there, done that, and have the T-shirt," she said in a breezy sing-song and walked out at Le Feu's side.

When they disappeared from sight, Chaos turned Kai roughly and removed his bindings. Relieved, Kai rubbed his battered wrists to get circulation back into his hands.

"Come with us," Chaos breathed in a hollow, inhuman voice that brokered no dissent.

Gooseflesh rose on Kai's arms, and he followed Chaos as Destruction hemmed him in from the rear.

Tom's words echoed in his head: *Ishmael is not one hundred percent human.* In less than twenty-four hours, Kai had seen a lot that fit into that category.

He didn't need to suspend his disbelief. He believed every word.

Chapter 35

CHAMUEL

Fifth Avenue. New York City.

CHAMUEL SAT CLOAKED on a park bench across the street from the penthouse, where Cara was safely ensconced inside. Constantina had put him and Michael on high alert. They were sticking close to Cara, making it next to impossible for Chamuel to see her alone as *Simon*.

Chamuel had been on duty 24/7 since Cara left his apartment, which felt too quiet without her. He relocated temporarily to Penthouse B next to Cara's—part of the Angelorum's real estate portfolio. He wanted to be as close to her as possible for her protection and his sanity.

During the long hours of surveillance, the urgency of his situation grew. He needed to reveal himself to Cara before this went further, and he had to put their relationship on hold until they completed their Trinity mission. Though the right decision, the thought put knots in his gut. If her feelings were as strong as his, he hoped they could face the consequences together. Not that he would ask her to lie. He'd never do that.

The Guardianship would surely eject him, but perhaps he could petition the High Council to mitigate his prison sentence. He had one favor he could call in. Regardless, he was prepared to make any necessary sacrifices. But would she accept him once she discovered who he really was? That was the question tormenting him.

His phone vibrated in his pocket, pulling him from his thoughts.

"Michael?"

"Hi, Chamuel. I sense you nearby. Thanks for the tight surveillance. I just spoke with Constantina. She said Isaac is still investigating the drop in dark energy around New York City. They want us to remain vigilant, but have temporarily reduced the threat level. Also, Constantina predicts Cara's Calling will be soon."

Chamuel palmed his face. Precisely why he needed to get to Cara while he still had a chance. "Yeah, I spoke to Isaac, too," he replied gruffly. "Let me know if you'd like to move around."

Michael heaved a breath. "Thank God. I thought maybe I'd take Cara out after lunch. We're going stir-crazy locked inside the penthouse." He snorted. "Chloe's the only one who's been out since Wednesday night, thanks to the dog walker. Anyway, I have my monthly class for adults with disabilities tonight."

"What time?"

"Class starts at eight-thirty. We finish around ten. Cara's going to keep her plans with her friend Sienna for drinks downtown."

Chamuel's pulse quickened. He had his opening. "I've got her."

"Thanks. See you." Michael hung up.

Chamuel rested his elbows on his knees, weaving his strategy, when a pretty dog with a narrow head and sleek body poked his knee with a wet nose.

"Chloe? What are you looking at, girl?" asked the young girl holding the dog's lead.

Chamuel realized the dog was Cara's and that she could see him behind the veil.

He looked into the canine's expressive brown eyes, staring up at him, and petted the whippet's soft, narrow head. Chloe jumped up and landed a wet kiss on his nose with her delicate pink tongue.

He chuckled, brushing a hand across his face.

"Chloe, what are you doing, silly girl?" the girl cooed. "There's nothing there." The dog walker gently tugged on Chloe's lead, but the dog wouldn't budge.

Chamuel smiled, ruffled Chloe's ears, and whispered in the angelic language. The dog cocked an ear, gave his hand a reassuring lick, and shocked Chamuel with a telepathic response, *"Cara, safe."* Then, she turned and followed the dog sitter in a graceful trot.

Huffing an astonished laugh, Chamuel shook his head. Sometimes surprises came in the most unexpected packages.

Chapter 36

CARA

Fifth Avenue Penthouse. New York City.

CARA ENTERED THE kitchen with their Thai take-out as Michael ended a call. "Lunch!" she said, holding up an open cardboard box with white bags like a prizefighter who'd won a heavyweight championship. She was starving from their workout and couldn't wait to dig into her favorite cuisine: Pad Thai, green papaya salad, and blood orange iced tea. But even her favorite meal couldn't compare to the high Cara had since leaving Simon's apartment two days ago.

Life seemed so much brighter since she met him, and after each gushy text they exchanged, her spirit filled with happy promise. Probably all the oxytocin that was running through her bloodstream. Best of all, Cara had barely thought of Kai since meeting Simon. She hoped the stars aligned, so he could join her and Sienna for drinks later.

Besides mooning over Simon, Cara occupied her time training with Michael in Constantina's absence. For security reasons, they'd used the upstairs meeting room instead of the Brooklyn dojo. Michael moved on to basic weaponry, satisfied with Cara's newfound proficiency in basic self-defense and kickboxing. They put in a full day with blades before collapsing yesterday, and completed another entire session before lunch.

Claustrophobia was setting in.

As Michael retrieved plates and Cara unbagged their lunch, Cara's cell burst into Simon's ringtone, Katy Perry's *"Teenage Dream."* Her stomach fluttered with excitement, and she snatched her phone from the countertop.

"Hi," she said, grinning wide.

"Hi, back," he said in a deep, sexy purr. "If your offer still stands, I can join you and your friend, Sienna, for drinks."

She did a little dance but said calmly, "That would be great. She's dying to meet the guy who stole her friend, leaving me in her place."

He chuckled. "I hope that's a compliment."

"In Sienna-speak, yes, most definitely." Cara hoped for a little alone time with him after seeing Sienna. "We're meeting at nine o'clock at the Standard Grill in the Meatpacking District."

"I know it," he said. "How is nine forty-five? That will give you some time alone with your friend."

"Perfect!" She lowered her voice to a whisper, feeling a goofy glow bloom on her cheeks. "I can't wait to see you."

"The feeling is mutual. Until later?"

"Yes, until later."

She tried wiping the sappy look from her face before glancing at Michael. "I wish you were coming tonight. I'd love to introduce you to Sienna and Simon."

Leaning a hip on the counter, Michael swiped a hand down his face, leaving an unhappy frown, and folded his arms over his chest. "I'm going to say something you're not going to like."

Cara's mood dampened, and she met Michael's hardened gaze. "What is it?" she asked, bracing herself but suspecting she already knew.

"This thing with Simon? It's not a good idea."

Cara's hackles rose, and she nearly growled. "That's a little judgy."

He rolled his eyes heavenward and sighed. "That's not what this is about, and you know it. Your Calling could happen any second, and you need to be focused and ready, or—"

"Or people could die. Yeah, yeah," Cara interrupted, waving a hand. Anger rose in her chest. "I get it. I'm not going to do anything to compromise the mission ahead, but I'm not—and I repeat, *not*—going to walk away from the first thing that's given me a shred of happiness since Tyler ripped out my heart after Kai." She shook a trembling finger as her roiling emotions came to a crescendo. "Not you, not Constantina, not anyone, is going to take this from me!" Tears gathered in her eyes. She spun on her heel and stormed from the kitchen.

The doorbell buzzed as she stomped through the foyer. She wiped away her tears and opened the door. "Hey, Gonzalo." She feigned a smile at the uniformed doorman, a white-haired Argentinian man in his late sixties. Her canine companion stood obediently at his side.

"Here you go, Miss Collins. The dog walker said Chloe did well." He handed Cara the lead.

Cara thanked him, closed the door, and unclipped Chloe's lead, leaving it on the table beside the door. Needing some space, Cara went to the living room and curled up on her comfy couch from Perry Street. Chloe leaped up and curled into a warm ball behind Cara's knees.

She hated throwing a tantrum like a two-year-old, but the pressure was getting to her, and Simon gave her an outlet to blow off steam.

But Michael was right. She needed to focus, and her thoughts of Simon were consuming her attention. Yet…she wouldn't, couldn't, let him go.

Chloe made one of her contented sounds and burrowed her head further into the nook behind Cara's knees.

Cara's eyes drifted shut, only to pop open a second later when a disembodied voice whispered through her mind, *"He loves you."*

Cara bolted upright off the coach, unsettling Chloe, who yawned, stretched her long limbs, and closed her eyes to nap.

Pulse racing, Cara searched the empty room. Where was that voice coming from? Was this place enchanted or something?

Michael ambled in a second later.

"Did you hear that?" she asked, her tone accusing.

Michael instantly fell into a fighting stance, scanning the room. "Hear what?"

"Calm down, Chuck Norris." She passed a hand over her face and mumbled, "Nothing threatening. Forget it."

He blew out a breath and straightened. "Hey, I'm sorry." His gaze held regret. "I didn't mean to upset you. I'm sure Constantina will warn us if your relationship with Simon becomes an issue. But be honest, you've been distracted. It shows in your training."

She couldn't argue and nodded. "I know, but I'm only human, Michael. If the Angelorum wanted the perfect savior, they should've chosen someone else." A few tears escaped, but she refused to back down. "I won't apologize for wanting…love."

She took a step to leave, but Michael grabbed her wrist. "Wait." His gaze softened, and he whispered, "I wouldn't ask you to do that." Tipping his head toward the kitchen, he said, "Let's eat lunch before it gets cold, and then, we'll take the afternoon off and do something fun."

Cara brushed the dampness from her cheeks and gave him a side-eye. "Really? I thought I needed to stay focused."

He huffed. "You may have been distracted, but you still kicked ass. I cleared our little field trip with Chamuel while you got our take-out from the doorman."

She sighed and followed him back to the kitchen.

They went shopping, of all things. But Michael's words haunted her all afternoon. Worst of all, Cara hated that he was right.

CARA ARRIVED AT the Standard Grill on time and before Sienna. Cara loved the buzzing energy in the Meatpacking District, especially on Friday nights. Between the Grill, the beer garden next door, and the club at the top of the adjoining hip-and-chic Standard Hotel, a whole evening's worth of entertainment possibilities existed within one tiny cobblestone block.

The familiar surroundings grounded Cara for what could be her last night with Simon and her only chance to introduce Sienna to Michael, who promised to join them after class. Not her most creative plan, but it's all she had.

Cara scored a barstool at the front bar. Not wanting a repeat of her night out with Sienna, Cara ordered a glass of Cabernet Sauvignon and waited.

Sienna arrived fifteen minutes late and beelined her way through the crowd, squeezing past a couple who were jealously eyeing the empty barstool Cara guarded. "Carissima! How are you?" Sienna gushed, taking her seat and exchanging a peck on the cheek. "I can't wait to meet your guy! When is he coming?"

"Half an hour. Michael might stop by, too," Cara said, taking a sip of wine and laying the groundwork for her "Michael + Sienna = Love" campaign. "You'll never guess what Michael and I did this afternoon."

Sienna waggled her eyebrows suggestively. "Should Simon be worried about your new martial arts instructor?"

Cara knocked Sienna's shoulder playfully. "Stop. I'm screening him for you. So…guess what we did."

Sienna waved the bartender over, cupped a hand to her mouth, and shouted "Malbec" when he came within earshot. Then she sighed, "Oh my God, are we in high school? Fine, what did you do?"

"Get ready…"

Sienna rolled her eyes. "I'm ready, all ready."

Cara clapped gleefully. "We went shopping at Neiman-Marcus. His idea." If Cara knew one thing about Sienna, it's that she loved guys who appreciated fashion and loved to shop as much as she did.

Sienna raised a perfectly arched brow, threw a twenty on the bar, and picked up her drink. "*Really?* He shops without the threat of water torture? That *is* interesting. What did you buy? More importantly, what did *he* buy?"

Cara circled a hand in front of her new Helmut Lang black knit sweater with an asymmetrical neckline and cutouts. "His selection. When he shows up, you can ask him about his purchases yourself."

Sienna ran an appraising eye over Cara and nodded her approval. "I'm impressed." She added dryly, "Are you sure he likes women?"

Cara frowned. "I'm sure. Not that he's on the market any more than you are, but I think you'll like him. Even as a friend."

Constantina's ring tone—doo-wop classic, "Earth Angel"—chimed inside Cara's purse. Cara groaned. "Sorry, I need to take this. Be back in a sec." She left Sienna at the bar and slipped onto the sidewalk. Chilly air hit her skin through the cutouts on her sweater. Hugging herself to stay warm, she answered on the fourth ring. "Constantina?"

"How are you faring, dear one?" A stiffness in Constantina's tone set Cara on edge.

She shivered and stamped her feet. "I'm fine. Are you coming back soon?"

Her mentor hesitated. "I expect so. Can you manage a trip to the farmhouse in Connecticut for a few days?"

Cara recognized her question as an unrefusable request and gave the only acceptable answer, "Of course."

"Take Michael with you, and if she is willing, your friend Sienna," she said.

Cara's brows shot to her hairline. "Sienna?" Why on earth would Constantina want her to bring Sienna? That was like inviting the press to a closed meeting in the Oval Office.

"It may not make sense now, but I promise it will," Constantina said, then mumbled, "*Eventually.*"

Cara blinked. She hoped her mentor knew what she was doing because nothing about this request made sense. "All right. I'll ask her." Cara wondered how hard she'd have to sell Sienna. On the upside, this played perfectly into her matchmaking campaign.

Constantina filled her in and said in parting, "Leave as soon as you can tomorrow morning. Journey forth in peace and love, dearest Cara."

"And you, Constantina."

Cara's hand fell to her side when the call ended. She had a bad feeling about this, compounded with crushing disappointment. She sighed. So much for spending time with Simon.

She entered the heated bar and slid onto the stool beside Sienna, thankful that the circulation was returning to her limbs. "Are you open to taking a road trip?"

Sienna narrowed her eyes suspiciously. "What kind of road trip?"

Cara grabbed her wine, preparing to stretch the truth. "The owners of the Connecticut house called. They want me to check the place out for a few days. Would you be able to get away? I know it's short notice, but I thought I'd ask Michael too." Earlier in the week, Cara had told Sienna about her elite property management gig, which had elicited nothing more than an "interesting career choice" from her best friend.

Sienna stared, unexcited.

Cara sweetened the pot. "There's a luxury spa five minutes away. The owner left us a couple of vouchers." That wasn't *exactly* true, but a phone call would secure the freebies.

Her friend's eyes lit with interest. "Did you say *spa*?" Tapping a finger to her lip, Sienna appeared to give it some thought and said, "OK, I can get away until Tuesday."

"We need to leave early tomorrow morning." Cara winced. Sienna wasn't exactly a morning person.

Sienna frowned. "How early?"

Cara scrunched her nose. "Eight?"

"*Argh.*" Sienna dropped her head in her hands. "Fine, as long as you supply the Venti Starbucks with no expectation of coherent conversation until ten."

Cara *squeed* and threw her arms around Sienna. "Love you, Senny!"

"I might be jealous," a deep, male voice said from behind.

Cara's heart skipped a beat, and she spun on her stool. "Simon!"

He leaned in, touching his lips to hers in a quick but satisfying kiss. Simon winked as he pulled away. Turning to Sienna, he offered his hand. "I'm Simon. It's a pleasure to meet you, Sienna."

Sienna stared, awestruck, her hand lost inside his.

Cara couldn't contain her grin. "It's rare to see Sienna speechless."

Sienna shot Cara a look. "Well done, you." Her attention returned to Simon, and she cocked her head. "Our little Cara has lived a nun-like existence far too long. Can you help her with that?"

Heat surged over Cara's cheeks. "Thanks, Senny. Let me take a second to crawl under the bar."

Simon huffed a laugh and placed a warm hand on Cara's back. "I've lived a bit of a monastic lifestyle myself lately." His dazzling gaze met hers, and she flushed at his warm adoration.

"I can't imagine why," Sienna muttered under her breath. "You're even hotter than she claimed."

Simon's expression softened. "She said I was hot?"

"She did," Cara replied on her own behalf and leaned in for another kiss.

Sienna snort-laughed. "You two need a room."

"Quite possibly," Simon responded with a hearty laugh, then glanced at their nearly empty glasses and called over the bartender. He bought them a round of drinks. When they were delivered, he raised his glass in a toast.

Beaming, Cara touched her glass to his, and Sienna followed suit. Their glasses clinked. "To new friends and life's possibilities," said Simon.

After some light banter, Sienna asked, "Speaking of new friends. Carissima, what time is your friend Michael coming?"

Simon choked on his wine, coughing into his hand and turning beet-red.

Alarm spread through Cara. "Are you all right?" she asked, setting her glass on the bar and preparing to perform the Heimlich maneuver, but Sienna beat her to it and slapped his back a few times.

"Are you sure you're okay?" Sienna asked. Trading a look with Cara, she mouthed, *"Was it something I said?"*

Cara tasted Simon's panic, attributing it to the choking.

Shaking his head, Simon forced out, "Went down the wrong way." When he caught his breath, he said, "My apologies for the interruption. I believe Sienna asked when your friend is coming."

Cara glanced at her watch. "In about an hour."

Simon visibly relaxed and said to Sienna, "Cara mentioned you were recently in Paris...." The conversation flowed easily from there.

Forty-five minutes later, Simon glanced at his phone and squeezed Cara's shoulder, his gaze filled with regret. "I'm sorry. I have to go. It's work."

Cara's heart sank; her hopes were dashed for the rest of the evening.

Simon smiled at Sienna. "So lovely meeting you. I hope to see you again soon." He leaned in, kissing each cheek, European-style. "May I borrow Cara for a minute?"

Sienna's gaze glowed with approval. "You're quite the charmer. Great meeting you, too. Send her back sometime tonight." She held up her wine glass. "I'll be fine until then."

Simon led Cara outside to exchange good-byes.

When they reached the sidewalk, he drew her into his arms and rested his chin atop her head. "I'll be away for a few days." He dipped his head and gave her a reassuring kiss. "I'll miss you."

Cara sighed with a half-smile, rested her cheek against his chest, and melted into the firm contours of his body. She wished their night didn't have to end here. "Me too. I have to go to Connecticut. Looks like our next date will have to wait."

He slipped her from his embrace and took her hands in his. His gaze sobered, and his throat bobbed. "I have to tell you something."

Cara instantly picked up the lemony chords of nervousness surrounding him. She frowned, her euphoria plummeting. "What's the matter?" she asked and braced for bad news.

He looked away and swore under his breath.

"Is everything OK?"

He pressed his lips together and heaved a sigh. "There are things you don't know about me," he whispered, his gaze taking on a new intensity. "Things I need to tell you...so we can have a future."

Cara relaxed, excited that he wanted a future, but afraid of what he had to tell her, so she blurted out the worst thing she could think of: "Are you a terrorist?"

His head jerked in surprise. "No, of course not."

She gave an exaggerated shrug. "With a lead-in like that, what else would I think?" She snapped her fingers. "Wait. Are you married?"

He gave a low chuckle. "Definitely not."

She wrapped her arms around his waist, reclaiming her position against his chest. "Whatever it is, we'll work through it."

Simon hugged her tighter and whispered, "Promise me something?"

Her face against his beating heart, she said, "Okay."

"If you learn anything I haven't told you myself, promise you'll come to me first and give me a chance to explain?"

Her pulse quickened with sudden concern. What hadn't Simon told her? "Is it something bad?"

Simon hesitated. "Not bad, per se, no."

"OK…I promise."

He kissed the top of her head and released her. "Thank you. That means a lot. I'm sorry, I have to go." His vivid blue gaze held a mix of regret and longing. "We'll talk when I return."

Cara hugged herself in the absence of his warmth and toed the ground. "See you soon?"

"Maybe sooner than you think." He winked, then crossed the street, disappearing into the night.

Cara turned to go inside, hoping she hadn't agreed to something she'd regret or set herself up for yet another heartbreak.

Chapter 37

CHAMUEL

Washington Street. New York City.

CHAMUEL SWORE UNDER his breath, having hoped for more time. But after Cara mentioned Michael had planned to meet her and Sienna at The Standard Grill, Chamuel had to cut their night short. The last thing he needed was his Trinity Messenger exposing him. Zeke would take his watch in T-minus three minutes. Truthfully, his evening plans had been ruined by Constantina's call before his arrival.

"I tried reaching Michael, but he's not answering his phone," Constantina had said, *"I'm sending Cara and Michael to Connecticut with her friend Sienna."* Implying that Chamuel would accompany them.

He knew better than to ask why. In their long history, Constantina never offered details about orders. Either because she wouldn't or couldn't.

Cutting his time short with Cara was disappointing, but postponing their discussion could prove catastrophic. He had planned to take her to his loft and tell her everything to mitigate the risk that she would accidentally discover his identity. Instead, he was forced into his risky Plan B, securing her promise to come to him and give him a chance to explain if everything went pear-shaped, which hinged on his implied request for silence.

At least he had a few precious moments with her, maybe his last as Simon. Their time together had opened Pandora's box of emotions and longing he hadn't expected, fueling a newfound resentment that it had to end.

Chamuel was still cursing his luck when a faint wisp of Nephilim energy tickled his aura. A low growl rose from his throat. *The rogue.*

This time, he wouldn't let him get away. He'd lure him out.

Chamuel picked up his pace and headed toward Pier 54 and Little Island, a park on the Hudson River. It was March. The park would've closed a few minutes ago.

The Nephil's energy followed from a safe distance.

Chamuel crossed the West Side Highway toward the towering, semicircular archway made of iron girders, a facade from a former pier shed for ocean liners that once occupied the space. The archway loomed ahead like a skeletal ghost leading to Little Island's South Bridge. Just beyond the entrance would be a more private area, covered in shadows, with traffic to muffle any sounds of a struggle.

Ducking into the shadows, Chamuel felt the energy behind him. He moved quickly onto the dark pathway. Chamuel cast off his suit jacket, cloaked, and unfurled his wings through slits in his dress shirt. He sliced through the air, on a collision course with the other Nephil.

Chamuel tackled his stalker, connecting solidly with the other male's body behind his veil of invisibility. Chamuel retracted his wings before they slammed into the asphalt and rolled to absorb the impact. The back of a blond head, snow-white plumage, and a white tunic came into view as their veils connected.

"Who are you?" Chamuel snarled, gripping the rogue securely from behind. In answer, the Nephil retracted his wings with a swift whoosh, the coarse edge feathers slicing across Chamuel's shoulders as the rogue landed a reverse head butt to Chamuel's face. Stars danced across Chamuel's field of vision, and he lost his grip.

The rogue hopped off him and broke their connection, disappearing.

Chamuel rolled and jumped to his feet. Blood trickled from his nose, mixing with the blood soaking the ribbons of his torn shirt. Still dazed from the blow, Chamuel didn't expect the next punch to his jaw.

Using the Nephil's energy as a beacon, Chamuel shot out, connecting a jab to the male's side. He heard a grunt as their veils intersected, the male flashing into view and disappearing too fast for Chamuel to glimpse his face.

The rogue's fist connected with Chamuel's left cheek with so much force that he was knocked off his feet. The wisp of energy disappeared into the night as Chamuel lay prone on the asphalt, groaning and dizzy.

Lucifer's Hell, the bastard had a nasty right hook.

Chamuel touched the back of his head and winced. His fingertips came away sticky with blood. He slowly got to his feet.

Who the hell was that asshole, and what did he want? If the rogue had wanted to kill him, he'd had his chance.

Nothing about this Nephil's behavior made sense.

Though he'd give him one thing, the rogue was a worthy opponent.

Chapter 38

CARA

Greenwich Farmhouse. Connecticut.

BLESSED SILENCE. Cara sighed, luxuriating in the early-morning quiet with her legs tucked beneath her on one of the shabby-chic couches in the living room, her loyal hound curled in a ball beside her. Michael and Sienna had yet to stir upstairs. *Thank you, Sweet Baby Jesus!*

Why on earth had she thought Michael and Sienna would be a match? Cara hadn't fully recovered from yesterday's nonstop bickering. They'd been like oil and water from the moment they met, which had *not* been on Friday night.

Michael had never made it to the Standard Grill after his train from Brooklyn broke down, trapping him in the subway for two hours. She wished he had. Maybe one of them would've volunteered to stay behind, and her sanity wouldn't be at risk.

The fireworks had started within minutes of Cara picking up Sienna, who hit Michael's hot button with a snide comment about his shirt and the type of men who wore them, which set him off like a Fourth of July fireworks display. Michael zapped back a snarky reply, questioning how she'd know, since she obviously shopped at Target. Sienna retorted that he was a fashion moron and spouted her epic credentials.

From there, it devolved into verbal ping-pong, making the ninety-minute trip to Connecticut excruciating and leaving Cara wishing for earplugs and a referee whistle. Anything to stop their grousing.

Relief came the moment they turned onto the private road and drove up the circular driveway. The wooded lane opened into an impeccably landscaped clearing, revealing a majestic gray-shingled house with white trim and a wraparound front porch. The view stunned them into silence. "Farmhouse" seemed quaintly conservative for a cross between a mansion and an estate better suited for catching ocean breezes in the Hamptons than hidden among the woods in Greenwich.

Cara's reprieve had only lasted until room selection, when Sienna flew past Michael and dropped her bags in the center of his chosen room, commandeering it for herself.

Too bad they couldn't funnel all that tension into something more...*productive.*

Cara petted a sleeping Chloe, savoring the lull. Michael and Sienna's antics had compounded her stress. The turbulence of the last couple of weeks left Cara feeling like she was in a dryer stuck on the spin cycle, knowing that any minute, all hell could break loose. Maybe literally.

Despite the chaos, she was happy she'd met Simon even though it was the worst possible time to start a relationship. *Relationship.* The word sparked hope for the first time in years. She smiled faintly, then remembered the last few minutes of their conversation on Friday night.

What did Simon need to tell her?

Cara wished she had the opportunity to learn Simon's mysterious secret before Constantina pulled her away on this hellish trip with Michael and Sienna. For now, Cara trusted whatever Simon had to say would be alright. As for her best friend and Trinity Messenger, Cara hoped her mentor knew what she was doing.

Cara's stomach growled. She glanced at her phone. 7:15 a.m.

Watson & Haskins had taken the liberty of opening the house and stocking the residence with food for their arrival. Common sense suggested making breakfast here, but she needed a break from this place. Besides, she really wanted a latte. Sienna was good for another two hours. Michael, a self-confessed Sunday sleeper when off duty, probably the same. She could easily walk the mile and a half into town and be back before her houseguests awoke.

The best part? If they were asleep, they couldn't knife each other while she was gone.

Cara rose and walked softly to the front door. Chloe wagged her tail in anticipation as Cara put on a knit hoodie and stuffed her phone and other essentials into her pockets. They slipped outside, down the drive, and onto the private road. Chloe approached their walk with gusto, towing Cara behind her.

Cara assumed Chamuel lurked nearby on some invisible perch. His presence had been so unassuming that most of the time she forgot he was there. She chuckled. Did he hang out on the roof and fly after her? Did he sleep? She'd have to ask Constantina. Regardless, he'd better be on his toes to keep pace with her enthusiastic hound.

Less than five minutes later, Cara turned a corner onto Main Street with Chloe and headed for the dog-friendly café she spotted the day before.

The table umbrellas were open for outside seating, and several souls were already enjoying the warmer-than-usual, sixty-five-degree morning.

As they reached the planters bordering the seating area, Chloe pulled sharply, wrenching the lead from Cara's grip and running pell-mell toward a table where a guy sat, wearing a black leather jacket, jeans, and a baseball cap, pulled low over his eyes.

"Come!" Cara said, issuing the command with her best pack leader vibe. Chloe ignored her.

Cara rolled her eyes, wanting a refund on those dog training classes, and bolted after her crazy canine, who startled the guy from his breakfast by planting her front paws into his lap and bathing his lips in wet kisses.

Cara lunged for Chloe's collar. "I'm so sorry!" Cara said, pulling Chloe away as she whined, tail whipping side-to-side and straining to break free.

"It's all good. Let her go," the guy said with a good-natured laugh, running a hand over his mouth. Cara released Chloe's collar but kept a firm hold on the leash. He scratched behind Chloe's ears, still chuckling, "I haven't been kissed like that in ages." Chloe adoringly licked his hand.

Cara's cheeks heated. "Thanks for being so gracious. This wanton hussy is Chloe. She usually reserves that kind of greeting for her most ardent admirers." Cara dropped to a knee beside her dog and cradled Chloe's face in her palms. "Do you guys have something to tell me?"

He laughed. "I usually prefer my women on two legs rather than four...."

From her lower vantage point, Cara glanced up, getting a full view of the guy's face beneath the hat. She tried not to gape. Holy wow. A pair of killer blue eyes peered from beneath the brim. She caught a glimpse of blond hair, suspecting it was pulled back, with some of the length hidden beneath the hat. Maybe late-twenties, he had cheekbones that could cut granite, an easy, dimpled smile, and movie star white teeth.

His gaze met hers, warm and inviting. "I'm Brett," he said, offering a hand.

Rising, she shook his hand. "Cara."

Brett motioned to the empty chair in front of him. "Would you ladies like to join me for breakfast?"

Cara glanced at his plate. Nothing remained but a half-eaten slice of toast. "You sure?"

He held up a coffee mug, wearing a sexy side smile. "I'm nowhere close to done."

Why not? After yesterday, she welcomed some level-headed company. Chloe disappeared beneath the table as Cara took the white plastic chair opposite Brett, who leaned down and gave Chloe another pet.

Cara narrowed her eyes. "It's like she knows you." Her hound was a great judge of character and must've picked up the same positive energy as Cara.

Glancing beneath the table, he said with a cocky grin, "I'd never forget such a beautiful girl," then adding in a conspiratorial whisper, "Dogs just seem to like me."

Cara smiled. "You must be all right then."

The waitress walked over. "May I get you something?"

Cara ordered a low-fat latte, an egg-white omelet, and toast. The waitress tipped her chin at Chloe. "I'll bring some water and a couple of dog biscuits."

Cara beamed at her. "That'll buy you a friend for life."

After the waitress left, Cara glanced around. "Lots of early risers in Connecticut. I thought Chloe and I would be the only ones here this early on a Sunday."

Brett put a hand to his heart and feigned rising. "Would you like me to go?" he teased.

She sniffed a laugh. "I didn't mean it like that. I live in the city, where no respectable New Yorker has breakfast on a Sunday before ten o'clock. Probably why they invented brunch."

"Ha! You live in the city? Where?" His eyes sparked with interest, and his disarming smile put her at ease. They spent the next ten minutes comparing notes on neighborhoods, the best places to eat, music venues, and their favorite attractions.

Brett lit up as he spoke, recounting a disastrous breakfast he'd had on his last visit. An animated storyteller, he gesticulated with his hands. A silver ring on his finger glinted in the light and caught her eye, triggering a déjà vu. Like she knew him or had been here before.

Half-listening, she examined him more closely. His dimple gave him a boyish charm when he smiled, contrasting with the hip style of his leather jacket, concert tee, and studded belt. Even seated, he looked tall, a little over six feet. He had a light tan, which brightened his blue eyes. Masculine enough, his face had a fine, sculptured bone structure with full lips, high cheekbones, a nice nose, and an angular jaw line.

No doubt, Brett was incredibly appealing, and the third attractive guy she'd met in less than two weeks. Unlike Michael, who felt more like a brother, Cara would've been interested in Brett if she hadn't met Simon. He had a Kai-like quality that drew her in. Possibly the source of her déjà vu?

"Earth to Cara…" Brett leaned forward and snapped his fingers.

Jolted from her thoughts, she flinched. "I'm sorry—what did you say?"

His lips kicked to the side, and he crossed his arms. "You were checking me out, weren't you?"

Cara flushed. That's exactly what she was doing.

Brett poked a finger at her. "Busted!" Then he threw back his head and laughed. "Confession. I might've done the same while you were talking sense into Chloe."

"You did?" His admission surprised her.

He waggled his eyebrows in a comical, rather than salacious, way. "Absolutely…I hope that's okay to admit. My filters? Not the best, but I promise, I'm totally harmless."

Cara tried suppressing a smile. "I'm flattered. Really."

Leaning forward, he whispered, "I'm flattered, too." He turned a rosy hue beneath his tan. For a split second, he *did* remind her of Kai.

Her pulse quickened, a seed of attraction growing between them. Brett had a magnetic pull she couldn't explain. She thought of Simon, and her heart rate slowed. He's the one she wanted, but that didn't diminish her ability to find Brett or anyone else attractive. Did it?

Brett cleared his throat and grabbed the notebook, a pen stuck in the wire spiral, lying beside his plate. "I've been alone for the past couple of days, working, so I'm kind of losing it. I hope I'm not coming across too intense." His gaze reflected worry, and he said more softly, "I really enjoy your company."

Cara found his candor refreshing and his company equally as enjoyable. She smiled warmly. "Thanks. Same here." She appreciated his attention. Before Brett and Simon, she hadn't realized how invisible she'd felt.

The waitress returned with Cara's breakfast and a bowl of water and a handful of dog treats for Chloe. She refreshed Brett's coffee and moved to the next table.

"So, what are you working on?" Cara asked, glancing at Brett's notebook and tucking into her omelet.

Brett fingered the spiral binding, hesitating. "Songs. I'm writing some new material."

Cara was intrigued. "You're a songwriter?"

He shrugged but said nothing.

Aside from Sienna, who dressed some elite entertainers, Cara didn't have any friends in the arts or music. "That's impressive. I admire anyone who can write. I'm more of a math girl. Probably why I went into investment banking." She paused and waved her fork. "I mean, why I *use to be* in investment banking," she said and nibbled her toast.

"Really?" Brett arched an eyebrow. "You must be incredibly smart. Why *used to be*?" His stare held intense interest as he sipped his coffee.

Cara gave a whimsical shrug. "Let's say I'm still figuring out my next chapter." True enough.

Brett set down his mug and leaned in. "You ever get to San Francisco?"

Cara thought of Kai. "I have a close friend who lives there. It's been a couple of years, but I hope to visit soon. Why?"

"I live there. Maybe we can meet up," he said, meeting her gaze. The taste of his vanilla hope skated over her tongue, and the thought of Brett living so far away unexpectedly gutted her. She'd probably never see him again. Which was crazy. How was it possible to feel the loss of someone you had just met?

Cara cleared her throat. "What brought you to Greenwich?"

He wrapped his hands around the mug. "I spent summers here as a kid with my aunt and uncle…he's gone now, though. Passed away when I was in college. I'm just here for a long weekend this time while my aunt is in Europe. It's my safe space when things get out of hand with work. Gives me time to think," he said softly and gazed at her apologetically. "Sorry, I'm rambling. I'm not sure why I'm telling you all this. What about you?"

She tasted charcoal loneliness. Her heart squeezed. Putting her training for remote healing into practice, she sent a gentle wave of energy to clear the feelings away, along with the silent thought, *"You're fine."*

Brett's eyes widened, and he sat up straighter.

As if nothing had happened, Cara smiled inside and said, "I leave Tuesday, but I have a place close by and expect to be here…more," Cara said, unsure of her future commitment to the Connecticut property.

They chatted until an alarm on Cara's phone broke the silence. Cara flinched and checked the time. Over two hours had flown by, and it was almost ten o'clock. She needed to get back.

"Everything okay?" Brett asked.

Cara smiled apologetically. "I need to go."

Brett flagged the waitress for the check. When it came, they both grabbed for it, but Cara got there first. Brett's warm hand covered hers. The touch of his skin sent a spark of awareness through her.

"Let me," Brett whispered, staring at their touching hands before meeting her gaze.

She sucked in a breath. "On one condition."

He arched a brow. "Which is?"

"Promise to call me next time you're in town so I can return the favor?" She doubted it would happen, but who knew what the future held?

"Deal." He gave her another dimpled smile and lifted his hand from hers.

Taking the pen, Cara ripped off a corner of the check and wrote her number. For a moment, she felt disloyal to Simon for giving Brett her number, but instinctually, it felt right.

Brett accepted the tiny slip. "Hey, I'll do you one better. I'll program you into my phone." She tasted a second wave of vanilla as he tapped her info into his cell and created a new contact.

"What if I want to take you up on your offer tomorrow before I leave?" Brett asked, his gaze warm and hopeful.

She snorted softly, wishing she could and knowing she couldn't. "Only if you don't mind a crowd. I'm here with two friends. I snuck out for coffee while they were sleeping."

He sighed, deflating. "Next time, then. It was great meeting you, Cara. Chloe, too." He glanced beneath the table.

Cara followed his gaze to where Chloe was curled up, sleeping on top of his motorcycle boots.

Cara palmed her face. "Has she been on top of you the whole time? I'm so sorry."

"For what? She's toasty on the feet." He grinned.

Chloe awoke with a start and jumped up. She surfaced and bestowed one last kiss on Brett's face and returned to Cara's side. Brett left cash for the waitress, and when they stood to leave, he inched closer and entered her personal space, his gaze heating. Cara's cheeks heated, and her pulse accelerated. He dipped in, his lips hovering over hers. Her breath caught as he veered to the side, brushing a kiss over her cheek.

Did he almost…kiss me?

"Look forward to next time," he whispered and stepped away.

"Me too, Brett," she said, her hand sweating on Chloe's leash, an unmistakable chemistry sizzling between them.

They traded parting smiles and left the café, heading in opposite directions. As Cara and Chloe walked up Main Street, Cara wondered what the heck just happened and why her hands wouldn't stop trembling.

Chapter 39

CHAMUEL

Connecticut.

CHAMUEL'S HANDS CLENCHED at his sides, jealousy searing his innards, as he watched Cara and Chloe at the café with that blond boy. Cloaked on the café's roof, he eavesdropped on their conversation.

Witnessing the flirtation between Cara and the guy was like a knife to the heart. He almost jumped out of his skin when she handed him her number, and the boy nearly kissed her, swerving from her lips at the last second. Chamuel wanted to punch him in the face and stake his claim.

He couldn't bear someone getting in the way of his relationship with Cara or tarnishing the magical time he'd spent with her. But she was human, and that came with its own set of issues—like competition from human males.

As Chamuel watched Cara and the guy walk in opposite directions, a familiar energy approached. Noah, a long-time friend and one of Isaac's Tri-State guys, laid a hand on Chamuel's shoulder to connect their veils and establish communication.

"What's up, brother?" Chamuel asked.

"I see your charge met mine," Noah replied.

Chamuel frowned. *What the hell?* He stabbed a finger at the recently vacated café table. "That kid with the baseball cap?"

"Yeah. Just for the weekend. He's West Coast. Constantina called in a favor. Brett King, big rock star, ducked out from his tour for some incognito R&R."

Chamuel didn't see that one coming. *That angel sure gets around,* he thought sarcastically. Then again, she was a master at orchestration. Still, the news did nothing to calm the roiling misery in his gut. "Since when do we provide security for entertainers?" he asked, trying not to sound petulant.

"He must be important to the Angelorum if he has security this early. He's on a plane Monday to rejoin the tour."

Brett got into a red Mercedes coupe and drove off in the same direction as Cara, beeping as he passed her.

"I'd better go." Noah gave him a crooked smile. "By the way, we miss your cooking at the House. Later, bro." Noah dropped his hand, unhooking their veils, and flew after the red sports car.

Is that why Constantina hauled them to Connecticut? For Cara to meet the blond rock star?

Chamuel had a bad feeling about this. Clues were mounting. Constantina managing Cara's training personally was enough of a red flag. Now, having Cara in contact with a future Trinity member? This had the stink of something big and messy packaged in a web of dread. But that didn't lessen Chamuel's hurt or feeling of betrayal.

Chapter 40

CARA

Greenwich Farmhouse. Connecticut.

GRAVEL CRUNCHED UNDER Cara's shoes, her thoughts clinging to Brett and their encounter, as she and Chloe walked up the circular drive. Blue sky framed the dignified gray farmhouse, where Cara caught sight of Sienna and Michael arguing on the wraparound porch.

For a heartbeat, Cara wondered if they'd been waiting for her. Two more steps and…nope. This had nothing to do with her. Cara picked up her pace, hoping she wouldn't need yesterday's referee whistle, and climbed the stairs with Chloe.

Jaw set, Sienna stood, arms folded across a form-fitting gray top, skinny jeans tucked into high boots, and a purple fur vest that would've frightened small woodland creatures. Michael faced her, hands planted on his hips, wearing an Armani button-down over a fitted tee, tailored jeans, a black belt, sockless Gucci loafers, and his hair expertly tousled. They looked like two runway models about to brawl.

"Hey, guys," Cara said, aiming for breezy and landing closer to brittle.

Sienna flicked a glance her way. "He's pissed because I figured out his little secret."

Michael's cheeks burned with anger and embarrassment, the tastes comingling on Cara's tongue.

"Secret?" Cara asked.

Sienna shook her iPad. "Meet Mr. Times-Square-Billboard—Calvin Klein, circa five years ago. Knew he looked familiar."

Cara's head snapped to Michael. Okay, that was unexpected but not a stretch. Why keep it quiet?

"Him," Sienna added with a scoff. "Do you believe it?"

Michael gave her a dirty look. "What do you mean, *him*?"

Sienna's gaze dipped to his crotch, then back up with a *humph*.

A new taste—chocolate heat—licked Cara's tongue along with the subtle scent of pheromones. *Oh.* Attraction sizzled beneath all the hostility.

Maybe she'd been right after all. Regardless, this idiotic sparring had to stop.

"You two are exhausting," Cara said and spun a finger. "Take whatever this is upstairs and get naked, because I could slice the sexual tension with a machete."

They froze, staring like tulip-munching deer caught in floodlights. Five silent seconds. Then —

"I could never be with someone so vapid," Michael said.

"What is this? The vocabulary section of the SATs?" Sienna shot back, foot stamping. "You wouldn't know what to do with me anyway, *pretty boy!*"

The words landed like a slap. Michael went white and rigid. He stepped in close, eyes flat. "Don't. Ever. Call me that. Again." The cinnamon sting of shame flooded Cara's mouth, hot and jarring.

Sienna flinched. Michael brushed past and disappeared into the house, the screen door slapping shut behind him.

Cara sighed. Maybe that wasn't her best idea.

Chloe trotted to the door and whined. Cara let the dog inside, then took a seat beside a sullen Sienna on the sun-warmed cushion of the wicker settee.

"You, okay?" Cara asked, taking in Sienna's lighter-than-usual pallor and jittery fingers.

Shoulders hunched, Sienna shrugged, clutching the iPad. "Whatever."

"You're attracted to him."

"Don't." Her voice wobbled. "It wouldn't matter if I were. He hates me."

"He doesn't." Not with all that chocolate heat and pheromones. Cara squeezed her shoulder, knowing her friend well. Behind Sienna's barbs was a soft, insecure heart. "Hypothetically: if he were into you?"

"He's not." A beat. "Besides, he's got a major stick up his ass." Unable to meet Cara's eyes, she got up and walked inside, the screen door banging.

Cara shook her head and followed. Ah, well. They were adults. They'd figure it out, hopefully without drawing blood.

The farmhouse greeted her with its cottage charm, polished floors, and a hint of lavender. Sienna had collapsed onto the couch in the living room, flipping a magazine with unnecessary vigor. Michael hovered at the doorway, miserable and trying not to be.

"I'm sorry," he told Cara under his breath. "I know she's your best friend, but she makes me insane. Why did Constantina want us to bring her?"

"I promise, there's a decent person under all that purple fur and prickle," Cara murmured back. She lifted a brow. "Calvin Klein, huh?"

He managed a wry half-smile. "Ancient history. I don't model anymore. Please don't hold it against me." Confidence sat on him like armor, but underneath, everything felt raw. Painful.

Cara touched his forearm, the muscles tensing. A whisper of cinnamon lingered. *You, okay?* she asked with her eyes.

His gaze shuttered. "I'm fine." The lie tasted bitter. Now wasn't the time. She nodded and let him have it.

From the couch: "If you're waiting on an apology, don't hold your breath," Sienna announced to the room, then winced and pressed a hand to her temple.

"Come on, Senny. Can we call a truce?" Cara asked gently and drew closer, alarm rising at Sienna's ashen skin, shaky hands, and shallow breath.

"I'd be in a better mood if the *GQ*-escapee hadn't distracted me before breakfast," Sienna said.

Cara wanted to kick herself. How had she missed it?

Low blood sugar.

Cara said to Michael, "She's hypoglycemic. Hangry doesn't quite cover it. Beastly is more accurate." Michael's gaze softened with a pitying glint. At least Cara could fix this. She said to Sienna, "Want me to make you something?"

"Make it edible if you're feeding the beast," Sienna muttered.

"Egg whites, scrambled. Toast. Coffee with milk and two sugars?" Cara said, reeling off Sienna's go-to breakfast on the way to the kitchen.

"Make it three," Sienna said without looking up.

In the bright, white kitchen, a stainless-steel Viking stove gleamed with a fake potted orchid (Bless Claudette!) on the windowsill beside it. While Michael fiddled with the coffee machine, Cara separated eggs, slid toast into a slot, and reached for a skillet.

"Allow me," Michael said, taking the pan in a white-knuckled grip and giving it a batter's swing. "If I don't cook with this, I might throw it at her." He grabbed olive oil. The igniter clicked, and flame kissed metal. The domestic clatter seemed cleansing.

"She gets under your skin," Cara smirked.

He kept his eyes on the skillet. "More than you know." After a beat. "Why did you tell her I wanted to meet her?"

Really? "Because taking a guy to Connecticut that I just met—while technically having a boyfriend—needed a cover story." She huffed. "I'm doing the best I can with the whole lying to friends-and-family thing." Cara hated this part of her new situation the most.

He squeezed her arm. "Fair point. I'll do better," he said, low. "Promise."

"Thanks." She wished she could say the same for Sienna. "I'm going to sit with her. You okay solo?"

"I hate cooking. Doesn't mean I can't," Michael said, pouring the egg whites into the pan, "Despite what I said in truth training."

Back in the living room, Sienna had gone quiet, scrolling on her phone.

"Michael's making your breakfast," Cara said.

Sienna's head snapped up, horrified. "You're leaving him alone with my food?"

"Be nice," Cara said. "Or at least civil." Cara shook her head and wandered to the windows overlooking the grounds, wishing she'd already met Chamuel. Then, maybe she'd have an ally and some backup dealing with her best friend and Trinity Messenger. At his age, he might have some wisdom to impart. Guaranteed he'd been around the block a time or ten.

Michael arrived, interrupting her thoughts. He carried a mug in one hand and a plate arranged like a magazine spread in the other — egg whites, toast, a butter pat, and a parsley sprig for garnish. *Parsley?* Cara hid a smile. *He cares.* Setting them down, he backed away as though feeding an angry mountain lion.

Michael suddenly stiffened, expression flattening. Then he shot over to her at the windows, eyes wide. "Your Calling," he whispered. "It's coming."

Cara's skin prickled. "Now?"

"Get ready… three… two… one…*now*."

The ceiling vibrated before a column of light crashed through.

Light speared Cara's crown, the force rooting her heels to the floor as the Flow's energy surged through her in a pulsing stream. Holy fire spread through her veins and shot from her pores, blowing Michael off his feet. The room hummed like a tuning fork, the floorboards whined, the air pulled tight as piano wire. Behind the energy's whoosh, Chloe's nails scrabbling on wood, and Sienna gasped. Then the room fell away as harmonious music rose, the braided voices lifting her spirit like a feather in the wind.

Cara surrendered to the blinding light whirling in and around her. She floated, her body below her, tethered by a silver cord. Humanity fell away. Joy filled her soul with weightless resonance. Knowledge was hers, boundless and unending. Love and awe consumed her. A figure emerged. A face that was every face, changing, tender, and unbearable to look into, gazed upon her. *You have been chosen,* the angel spoke through song. *Do you accept your place as a servant in this Trinity?*

Constantina spoke true; Cara had planned this moment before her first human breath. How could she have ever doubted herself? Her answer was a prophesy fulfilled, but only a small step in the journey ahead. *I accept.*

The angel raised luminous hands. *Blessed be your journey. Hold holy your Center Stone.*

The silver cord retracted. Spirit reunited with flesh. Twin golden threads struck Cara's crown, rattling her teeth. The threads intertwined, spinning as one, and accelerated in a kinetic frenzy until they exploded in a soft molecular rain beneath her skin, each drop a note. Kai filled her mind. Not a picture; a frequency. He was everywhere, in every cell. He was an inseparable thread of energy pulsing inside her. The music crested. The angel pinwheeled to a star and winked out. The light withdrew through the ceiling, and Cara hit the floor.

"Cara." Michael's voice, close and urgent. Fingers snapped. Cara's eyes fluttered open. Sienna hovered, color back in her cheeks. Chloe pressed her muzzle to Cara's shoulder with a soft whine.

The room's edges returned, and Cara's newfound knowledge slipped from her grasp. She managed a raspy, "Help me up." They lifted her. Her body was an unnecessary weight that carried sharper senses, transforming how she perceived energy: Michael, a warm chord in her sternum; Sienna, a steady metronome; Chloe, a bright, devoted pulse.

Sienna pointed at the ceiling, mouth opening and closing. "What—the—hell—was—that?"

Cara looked at Michael. *A little help?*

Brow arched, he spread his hands. *It's your show.*

"Oh, for Pete's sake," Cara muttered and folded Sienna into a hug. Calming energy flowed through her palms into her friend, and Sienna's tremble eased, breath evening.

"What did you do?" Sienna asked, eyes glassy with wonder. "I feel…great."

"Remember those Reiki treatments last year?" Cara said, rolling her sore neck. "Like that, but on steroids." Then she took Sienna's hands, her voice softening, "I need you to do something for me."

"Anything."

"You can't tell anyone what you saw. Not this or anything else you learn. It could get us killed."

Sienna blanched, nodding. "I promise."

Cara turned to Michael. "Kai is our Center Stone."

He dipped his chin, expression grave. *Not surprised.*

Sienna blinked. "Center what—"

Cell phones chimed. Cara grabbed hers while Michael strode out of earshot to answer his, leaving a bewildered Sienna.

Cara headed to the bank of windows, her pulse quickening at the displayed caller. "Melanie?" A scream cut through the line. Cara swallowed hard. "Has something happened to Kai?"

"They're gone!" Melanie keened. "Taken—Kai and Sara—"

Panic iced Cara's spine. "Who took them? What do they want?"

"I don't know." Hiccupping sobs. "They called. Don't want money. Said Kai has missing lab notes. They need them, or Kai and Sara will die. He sent them to someone. Did he send them to you?"

"No." Cara pressed a hand to the window's cool glass. She had no idea what Melanie was talking about. If Kai sent her a package, it would've gone to the West Village apartment. With a forwarding lag, who knew? "Where are you?"

"Home."

"Hold tight. I'll be there. Tonight." Cara ended the call with shaking fingers. The floor seemed to list as she ran toward Michael. "It's Kai," she told him, voice small. *The dream.* She hadn't been all wrong. But she prayed she hadn't been all right, either.

Michael said, "I know. Constantina just called. The Dark Ones have him and his daughter. She's arranged a plane—thirty minutes—Westchester County Airport. We need to move."

Cara buckled with relief.

Sienna cleared her throat behind them, and Cara spun.

"What about me?" Sienna said, arms crossed, chin up.

"Constantina wants us to bring her," Michael said to Cara, not thrilled. "Despite my vote to send her home."

"Screw off, Michael," Sienna snapped and gave him the finger.

Cara grasped her head. "Oh my God! Stop it. Both of you. I can't take this right now. Please, for the love of Pete, just give it a rest."

"You're right," Michael said, looking sheepish, and to Sienna, "I'm sorry."

Sienna nodded and grabbed Chloe's leash. "I'll go pack." Chloe followed Sienna up the stairs.

Michael's phone buzzed. He glanced at the text. "Chamuel. He'll meet us at the plane."

Cara's eyes burned. "If anything happens to them before we get there—"

"Hey." Michael pulled her into a hug. "Chamuel is already talking to the Bay Area Guardianship. We'll have a plan by the time we land."

Cara sighed into his shirt and slipped from his embrace. "I thought we were forbidden from revealing ourselves to outsiders. Why bring Sienna?"

Michael blew out a breath. "Seems insane to me, too, but we'll have to trust Constantina." Far be it from Cara to question the wisdom of an angel.

"Will I finally meet my elusive Guardian?" Cara asked.

Michael shrugged. "You've accepted your Calling, and we have a mission. No reason for him to cloak." Michael glanced at his watch. "Pack fast. I'll meet you out front."

They loaded the car in a flurry. Cara locked up as Sienna returned from a quick walk with Chloe.

Michael closed the trunk and dug a slip of paper with the flight details and his phone from his pocket. Sienna walked by and snatched the paper from Michael's fingers. "I'll navigate," she said and turned beside the front passenger door, palm out. "Phone."

He hesitated like he was handing a toddler a grenade, then surrendered it.

They drove toward the airport in relative peace. In the backseat, Cara petted Chloe and watched the Connecticut landscape roll by in a green blur, focusing on the steady thread of energy beneath her skin.

As long as it was there, Kai was alive.

Chapter 41

CARA

Westchester County Airport. New York.

TWENTY MINUTES LATER, they arrived at Westchester County Airport and, bypassing security, headed straight to the hangar and the Angelorum's private Gulfstream G650. A faster ride, per Michael's explanation, than flying commercial. Chamuel had texted Michael that two Tri-State Guardians — Isaac and Ezekiel — would accompany them.

As the bags were loaded, Cara milled around on the tarmac with the others awaiting permission to board. Sienna kept Chloe on a lead at her side and stayed out of Michael's way, which gave Cara freedom to focus on Kai and wrap her head around her Calling. Constantina had prepared her, but some things had to be experienced. If channeling the Flow was awe-inspiring, her Calling was indescribable. The experience was beyond her limits to explain, though she'd emerged understanding she was far more than flesh and blood. How that helped her, she didn't know.

Sienna interrupted her thoughts. "Incoming...."

Cara flinched, following Sienna's line of sight.

At the far end of the tarmac, three tall, well-built men dressed in black and carrying duffel bags approached, dusters flapping as they strode with purpose. Cara squinted, the sun's angle obscuring the Guardians' faces. Meeting the elusive Chamuel had lost its luster since Kai's abduction. The niceties could wait. All she cared about now was the rescue. Cara resumed pacing, anxiously awaiting the all-clear to board the plane.

Michael caught Cara midstride. "How are you holding up?"

"Overwhelmed. Anxious. But okay." No signs of a panic attack, thank God. Good thing. She was about to board a small plane and fly cross-country.

Gaze empathetic, Michael squeezed her shoulder. "Understandable."

Sienna stared over Cara's shoulder and let out a low whistle. "Holy hotness. Wait — " She narrowed her eyes. "Carissima, what's *Simon* doing here?"

Cara's head whipped around, and her brain stuttered to a halt.

What the hell?

A scowling Simon led the formation, blond hair secured at his nape. Flanking his left side, a dark-haired Guardian—the boyish, disembodied head from Central Park—and on his right, a Guardian with a spiky, blond brush cut.

Cara took in their uniforms, synapses firing. Tight tactical tee. Black cargos. Duster. Steeltoed boots.

The subway.

Not possible.

Simon said he was on an assignment.

Was she *his assignment?*

Was Simon…

Chamuel?

Oh, my God.

Realization hit like a gut-punch. Their time together replayed in a rapid montage as betrayal shredded her insides.

No, no, no!

Chamuel. The only male on the planet she wasn't allowed to be with….

Bile rose in the back of her throat.

After wasting nine years loving a man she couldn't have, how could he do this to her? How could he lie and offer what he had no right to give? Blood pulsed through her ears in a deafening roar, her anger bubbling to rage.

Michael extended a hand. "Chamuel, I'd like to introduce—"

Hands fisting, Cara stalked past him, stopping inches from her Guardian, who stood like an imposing granite statue. This wasn't the man who charmed her over dinner at Raphael's but the intimidating warrior she'd first spied on the subway. How had she missed what was now obvious?

Staring up into his impossibly beautiful angelic face, she unleashed her wrath. "Private *fucking* security! Really? Was this a sick joke to you?"

Chamuel's jaw clenched. "Never," he whispered, body rigid, vivid blue eyes simultaneously piercing and pleading. "I can explain."

"Explain what? That you lied to me?" she snarled, tears pooling in her eyes. "Is *this* what you wanted to tell me on Friday?"

Michael froze in shocked silence. *Cara, is this…?*

Simon. She bit.

"Yes," Chamuel answered in a regretful whisper. "I'm sorry."

"Fuck your sorry," Cara ground out. She was done here.

Blistering Chamuel with a glare, Cara spun on her heel and stormed up the stairs onto the plane. She entered the empty cabin. The Gulfstream carried thirteen passengers comfortably, not to mention opulently, but, right now, the state of New York — much less this plane — wasn't big enough for her and Simon. Chamuel. Whatever the hell his name was.

Dropping onto a leather bench seat, Cara disintegrated, tears spilling from her eyes, her heart imploding.

Chloe ran through the cabin door, leaping up and laying her muzzle on Cara's leg with a soft whine. Sienna arrived a few seconds later, slightly out of breath. "What the hell was *that*?"

When Cara didn't answer, Sienna sat beside her and wrapped an arm around Cara's shoulders. "Carissima, tell me what happened out there?"

Cara wished she could. How to explain the man she'd fallen for *wasn't* a man, but a mythical half-angel with wings? His words over dinner, *"And…I might be older than you think."* Understatement. He was older than her grandfather. God, she might be sick. Overlooking his age was one thing, but he was her goddamn Guardian! He was forbidden. Holy crap, she'd broken Angelorum law. Constantina would have her head.

Cara covered her face with her hands, silent tears soaking her palms.

"Cara? Honey?" Sienna gently shook her.

Not knowing how much she should reveal, Cara leaned against her best friend, swiped at her cheeks, and told the factual truth. "Simon isn't who he said he was. He lied to me."

Sienna stroked her hair. "I'm sorry, sweetie. Maybe you guys can work this out."

Cara bristled. "Are you taking his side?" She tried pulling away, but Sienna squeezed tighter, resting her cheek on Cara's hair. "Not at all. But trust me, Carissima, the way he looked at you on Friday night? There was love in his eyes. And just now? He was devastated out there. There may be more to the story. That's all I'm saying."

If it were only that simple. Cara returned Sienna's hug, feeling guilty but glad that Sienna was here. "I'm sorry you got wrapped up in this mess."

"Hey, that's what friends are for…Helping with messes." Sienna patted her back. "Let's focus on Kai. Simon can wait. He's not going anywhere. And if he helps save Kai?" Sienna shrugged. "Maybe give him some grace."

Cara sniffled, slipping from Sienna's embrace. "I really liked him, y' know?" More than liked. She'd fallen hard for the lying bastard. Damn him for stealing her heart and betraying her trust.

"I know," Sienna said, gaze soft, pulling a tissue from her bag for Cara. "It's not over until it's over."

Whatever. As long as Chamuel's actions didn't impact the rescue.

If anything happened to Kai, not even Heaven could help her Guardian.

CHAMUEL

HEART LODGED IN his throat, Chamuel watched Cara disappear through the open plane door. Pain and regret nearly cracked him open. Isaac's and Zeke's shocked energy buzzed from behind, but they wisely stayed silent.

Plan B had backfired. Spectacularly.

After exacting Cara's promise on Friday, he still expected her anger, but not her explosive public display. He'd hoped she would grant him an opportunity to explain before passing judgment.

In his mind, that implied silence.

Shame on him for his miscalculation.

A century of celibacy might have honed him as a warrior, but it stunted his finesse in mating rituals. A more experienced male would've given Cara a choice before their first kiss, rather than making the rash decisions of a pubescent Nephil waiting for his wings to sprout.

An experienced male would've never succumbed to Cara's allure.

That said, he'd never regret their time together. She'd given his world color for the first time since the tragedy. Short-lived though it might've been, he had tasted peace, happiness, and *love*. The thought of losing her gutted him, but he had no right to lay claim. He never did.

Now, he had to pay the price and ensure Cara didn't.

"So, I see you've *met* Cara," Michael stated, jerking Chamuel's attention to his Trinity Messenger, who stood, arms crossed, making no attempt to hide his judgment.

"Obviously," Chamuel snapped, regretting the response the instant it passed through his lips. This wasn't Michael's fault. Chamuel had sworn to protect his Trinity, but his actions had caused harm and discord. He didn't need to add more friction with Michael. He sighed. "I'm sorry, Michael. You don't deserve my anger."

Michael scowled. "Let's finish introductions on board."

Chamuel glanced at the plane and nodded absently.

Michael followed his stare and raked a hand through his hair. "Let's focus on the task at hand, shall we? We'll deal with the fallout of *that* later." *Seriously, what the fuck were you thinking?* Michael hurled over their bond.

Chamuel shot the Messenger a withering glare. Not causing waves didn't include accepting a lecture, especially not from a human who hadn't been on the planet as long as his favorite skillet.

Michael took the hint and led them to the plane.

Dread pooled in Chamuel's gut as Isaac and Zeke followed. Best friend or not, the Tri-State leader would mete out an ass-kicking for this when they were alone, and that was only the beginning.

AFTER TAKEOFF, Chamuel sat cemented to his seat. He'd taken precautions after Cara's Calling to shut down his part of the Trinity communication bond until they could speak. But that was out of the question now. He'd already consigned his brothers to providing witness testimony at the Tribunal hearing sure to come. No need to offer more ammunition.

Chamuel ground his teeth. Had Constantina known this would happen? *Probably.* But why?

Isaac tapped his shoulder. "Cham?"

"Not now," he growled under his breath. He couldn't do this yet.

Isaac's fingers dug into the back of Chamuel's neck. Bending, he whispered, "We can do this the hard way or the easy way. Your choice." Chamuel snarled low and reluctantly rose, following Isaac and ducking behind the curtain into the stateroom between the cabin and the cockpit.

Isaac passed an agitated hand over his buzz cut, fixed Chamuel with an icy-blue glare, and bit out, "For all that's holy, what were you thinking?"

Chamuel ground his teeth. He wasn't taking a lecture from Isaac either. Not yet. He turned to leave. Lightning fast, a forearm caught Chamuel's windpipe in a chokehold from behind, Isaac's breath warm on Chamuel's ear. "You'll stay here until I give you permission to leave."

"I'm in charge of this mission," Chamuel said through clenched teeth. Eyeing the tight space, he considered a throw-down, but having sparred with Isaac since puberty, he ruled it out. His chances were only a hair greater than fifty-fifty in the best of circumstances.

"Technically, but you're compromised. You put me in this situation, so you owe me the respect of hearing me out. Got it?" Isaac's grip loosened, and his voice softened. "Can I let you go?"

Chamuel closed his eyes and nodded in frustration.

Isaac released him and stepped away. "I love you like a brother and want nothing but happiness for you, but how the fuck did this happen? You're her *Trinity Guardian*, for Heaven's sake." Isaac's icy blue gaze shifted from exasperation to anguish, "I have to report you. Do you know how that makes me *feel*?"

Chamuel swept a hand over his face. "Listen, can we agree to deal with this after the mission's over? I've got this." Despite everything, he wouldn't let the situation with Cara interfere with his assignment.

Isaac grimaced. "We don't have much choice. I'll take care of Zeke. And that's another thing. That kid worships you." Isaac shook his head. Suddenly, his head jerked up, eyes frigid. "She didn't seduce you, did she?"

Chamuel's hackles rose, and he glowered at Isaac. "No. She didn't seduce me. This isn't her fault."

Isaac raised an eyebrow. "I know it's been a while. Why didn't you take my advice?"

"Stop, just stop, *I*," he said, falling back into familiarity. "This wasn't about breaking my celibacy, which is technically still intact. If that's all it was, nothing would've happened."

Isaac pressed his hands to his head, then pointed to where Cara sat on the other side of the curtain. "But of all the asinine choices. You had to choose the *one* person on earth forbidden to you? Not only that, she screwed you over out there!"

Chamuel's anger erupted, and he grabbed Isaac's collar. "She didn't know because I didn't tell her. This is my fault. Mine. Not hers."

Isaac wrenched himself free and wilted. "Damn it. You're in love with her."

The curtain parted, and Michael poked his head in. "Can we talk?"

Chamuel waved Michael in, the curtain closing behind him.

"Chamuel? Or would you prefer Simon?" Michael asked, brow cocked.

Ignoring the barb, Chamuel answered with the same weariness settling into his bones, "When I'm off the clock, Simon. Otherwise, Chamuel."

Michael lowered his voice, "I've asked Cara and Sienna to relocate to the front of the plane. We'll take the seats in the back for more privacy. Zeke's waiting there."

Chamuel steeled himself and followed Isaac and Michael through the cabin. Cara had reclined in her seat, eyes closed and earbuds in, listening to music. He wasn't the only one blocking their bond. Her energy was a dead zone, and seeing her felt like a self-inflicted knife wound.

The four of them settled into two pairs of facing seats separated by a table. Michael cleared his throat, passed his gaze between them, and started the briefing. "Dr. Kai Solomon is the Center Stone of this Trinity. Cara dated him in college, and they share a strong emotional and spiritual bond. This mission is pivotal. Not only do we need to rescue Dr. Solomon and his child, but we need to ensure his discovery stays out of Achanelech's hands."

"What discovery?" Chamuel asked.

"A vaccine using Nephilim DNA that can transform soulless humans into a Nephilim army with your strength and powers."

The rogue. A chill slid down Chamuel's spine.

"Holy hell," Zeke muttered beneath his breath.

Michael continued, "We believe the final battle is approaching."

"In Angelorum terms, that could still mean decades," Isaac said with a dismissive wave.

"True," Michael said, "But the *prophecy* is nearer than we think."

"You know this, how?" Isaac asked gruffly.

Michael tented his hands and leaned in. "Dr. Sandra Wilson and Dr. Tom Peyton were part of a special Trinity, an insertion orchestrated by the Angelorum, to pave the way for Cara's and Kai's success. Sandra and Tom worked on a genetic project called Firefly and discovered the DNA's true origin," Michael explained.

Chamuel's brow furrowed at the unprecedented move, which flew dangerously close to violating the Angelorum's non-interference rule. "Why the insertion?"

"The Trinity Stones willed it to counteract the Dark Ones' advanced knowledge of Cara's coming and to keep the balance."

So, not the Angelorum, but the eyes and ears of Heaven. Not good. The anomalies were piling up. The rogue. An insertion. Constantina's involvement. Achanelech's surprise visit after keeping a low profile for the last few decades. Something big was afoot.

"That explains why Achanelech and the Sentinel were sniffing around Cara, but how did they find out?" Chamuel asked.

Michael shook his head. "Unknown. But we have intel on the Sentinel. She's Achanelech's consort, Emanelech, the Ice Demoness."

Isaac's eyebrows rose. "So, he found himself a mate."

"Not recently. They've been associated for the last century, give or take," Michael said.

Even that prideful prick had a better relationship track record than him, Chamuel thought sourly. "Besides the insertion, what was so special?"

"Nothing about this Trinity was typical. Sandra was a civilian Three Hundred Class scientist with special gifts," Michael said.

No wonder Chamuel had never heard of her. Based on the Nephilim age classification, Sandra was between 300 and 400 years old, more than twice Chamuel's age.

Michael continued, "She played both Messenger and Seeker. Dr. Peyton was her Center Stone."

Chamuel jerked in surprise. No Nephil has ever been a Messenger or a Seeker in the history of the Angelorum, much less both. "How was that possible? The Messenger bloodlines are strictly human."

"At the request of the Angelorum, she willingly went through the *transformation* to ensure she would avoid detection. Not only was Sandra a scientist, but she had the gift of sight, making her the best choice to orchestrate without interfering with free will or having true Messenger abilities."

Chamuel fought a sudden wave of nausea. The Transformation was a harsh legal punishment and every Nephil's worst nightmare. Sandra had his respect for sacrificing her wings, the source of her strength and longevity. Making him sicker was the knowledge that he, too, might share the same fate.

"Fifteen years ago, Sandra was placed in the outside world to build her credentials and blend into human society with her Guardian mate, Ishmael. Sandra knew this might be a suicide mission when she accepted. She agreed to set in motion a sequence of events to put Cara exactly where she needed to be to fulfill her destiny." Michael's stare intensified. "That's not all."

Chamuel waited for the punch line.

"Sandra's given name was Hope, Daughter of Eae." The angel's name hit Chamuel like a bucket of ice water, the implications cascading through him like a raging river.

"Now shit's starting to make sense," Isaac whispered to Chamuel over their Guardian frequency, but Chamuel was too stunned to reply.

Eae.

Constantina.

That raised the stakes exponentially.

Chamuel's head swam. "Why, Cara? Why now?"

Michael shrugged, hands clasped on the table. "Think about it. Science has finally made it possible with the advances in genetic engineering. Research is less expensive and quick to replicate. It's advanced rapidly over the last two decades, especially with the introduction of artificial intelligence. This is the first time in history this *could've* happened."

Chamuel felt like a Luddite. "Go on."

"The Dark Ones murdered Sandra and attempted to recover their work from Tom. Sandra ensured they couldn't. They failed and murdered him, too. Sandra orchestrated a plan to pass the discovery to Dr. Solomon and only him. It's taken him over a year to discover the package she and Dr. Peyton arranged before she died. We suspect Kai has been under surveillance since he took over the project."

Chamuel agreed, but he was also certain that of Lucifer's thirteen Dark One lieutenants, Achanelech was leading the charge and personally responsible for Hope's murder. Retribution for the centuries-old destruction Eae and Leo, her soulmate, perpetrated against him, destroying his demon twin and leaving Achanelech with an unhealing limp as a perpetual reminder that he was bested. "What was in the package?" Chamuel asked.

"A key to a post office box containing all the lab notes on how to make the vaccine." Michael centered his gaze on Chamuel. "We believe this is a trap…to capture Cara. Given what the Dark Ones already know about her, we assume they're aware of Cara's relationship to Kai and expect her arrival. The demonic energy that dropped off the grid on the East Coast reappeared in the Bay Area, signaling they didn't need to waste resources in New York. Basically, we're walking right into their hands."

Chamuel's brow deepened with worry. "If they have the research, why do they want Cara?"

"The same reason Sandra sacrificed herself, and why Constantina is training Cara." Michael took a deep breath. "If you haven't guessed it already, Cara is the First of the Holy Twelve."

Chamuel pressed his eyes shut. *Of-fucking-course, she is.*

"Son of a bitch," Isaac mumbled beside him while Zeke let out a low whistle.

"I'd consider extra backup for the rescue given this development," Michael said.

As comprehension seeped further into Chamuel's consciousness, his shoulders stiffened. Constantina had chosen him for reasons that were now clear. She didn't only need a warm body she trusted, she needed a battle strategist. Any hope of their Trinity ending with this completed mission evaporated, along with his chances of a relationship with Cara and escaping punishment. At best, he could delay it.

He swallowed, recognizing the monumental burden that sat on his shoulders beside his massive screw-up with Cara.

Michael snapped his fingers to get his attention. "There's more. Sandra's mate Ishmael disappeared before she died. We believe the Dark Ones have him."

Chamuel exchanged a glance with Isaac, who gave an imperceptible nod and said, "There have been other incidents." Isaac told Michael about the recent Boston occurrence, then shot a look at Chamuel. "Also, the Sentinel escaped with the help of a rogue Nephil. Chamuel has encountered his cloaked presence a couple more times since then. We thought there could be a traitor in the Guardianship, but we couldn't find a registered energy signature besides Chamuel's at those times and places. Is it possible the Dark Ones already succeeded in making their own Nephilim?"

Michael shook his head. "Not likely, no."

"Does Cara know about any of this?" Chamuel asked.

"No. Only that Dr. Solomon is working on a highly confidential project. Nothing more." Michael locked eyes with Chamuel. "In my opinion, we should refrain from giving her too many details."

Chamuel couldn't tell if Michael spoke to him as Cara's Guardian or as the man who loved her. Not that it mattered since the answer would still be the same. "Agreed. It will only cause her more anxiety," he said, hoping he wasn't making another monumentally stupid decision.

"Do we know when Kai and his daughter were taken?" Isaac asked.

"According to Watson & Haskins in San Francisco, Kai retrieved Sandra's package last Monday. We also checked with the daughter's school. The teacher confirmed that Kai picked her up around six o'clock on Wednesday, but the next morning, someone called to report a family emergency that required Sara's absence for the rest of the week. So, about four days. Since no one raised the alarm, their disappearance never hit the news."

"If this is Achanelech's doing, chances are, they're still in Northern California. They shouldn't be that hard to find," Chamuel said, hoping he was right. Issac nodded his agreement.

"Finding them will be easier than getting them out alive," Michael said and glanced at his watch. "We arrive in San Jose within the hour. We'll learn more once we speak with Kai's wife." He stood, indicating the meeting was over. "I'm going to check in on Cara. See you on the ground."

Chapter 42

KAI

Undisclosed Location.

KAI FOUGHT A yawn and prepared another sample. Since entering the lab, he had worked continuously, snatching a few hours of sleep every eighteen to twenty hours. Unable to tell whether it was night or day from his underground prison, Kai used the timer on one of the lab machines to track his five-day countdown. He'd need every second to finish the vaccine, and time was running out.

Le Feu hadn't exaggerated. The lab had everything Kai needed, including a state-of-the-art, AI-assisted genetic sequencing machine. Kai's work took on a new pace and direction with Tom's comprehensive notes filling his knowledge gaps. He knew precisely which gene pairs to focus on and which chromosomes to study.

Best he could tell, the vaccine transformed human DNA to mirror the donor's DNA, highlighting two specific characteristics: longevity and rapid healing.

Even though no bacterium or virus was involved, Kai used the same technology as non-DNA-based vaccines for delivery into the body and replication, with one exception. If his calculations were correct, replication would start immediately after the injection, reaching saturation in the body within one hour rather than one month.

The process wouldn't be pretty, but it would be fast.

He yawned and pushed through his exhaustion. Sara's safety depended on his success. He'd spoken with her earlier over the closed-circuit video system for his daily allotment of five precious minutes. Seeing her little face and messy hair on the screen gutted him. Tired and confused, she appeared otherwise unharmed.

"Are you all right, sweetheart?" he had asked, holding his breath.

She bobbed her head. "I'm not scared." She had held up half a white bread sandwich and reassured him, "Don't worry, Daddy. The peanut butter and jelly is really good, and I have an apple for dessert."

He nodded, a lump rising in his throat. He was terrified of what would happen if he failed to produce the vaccine. Steadying his voice, he'd said, "You're very brave. I'm so proud of you. Mommy would be proud, too."

She'd averted her eyes at the mention of Melanie and looked as if she'd wanted to say something but decided against it. Instead, she said, "I love you, Daddy. We'll fight the monsters together." Anxiety rippled through Kai at something buried in her tone before the video monitor went dark.

That was hours ago.

Now, Kai hunched over a lab table and examined his samples. A voice spoke out of nowhere, *"Dr. Solomon, can you hear me?"*

Kai's head flew up, startled. He spun, looking for the voice's source, and found himself alone. "Where are you?"

The voice echoed inside Kai's head. *"Please, don't speak aloud. I can hear you through your thoughts. Think what it is you want to say."*

Kai frowned. *Am I losing my mind?*

"No, Dr. Solomon, you are mentally fit," the voice replied matter-of-factly.

Kai squelched a nervous laugh at the literal interpretation and rolled with it. This wasn't any more insane than what had already happened this week.

"Who are you?" he asked silently.

"I am Ishmael. We've been waiting for you."

Kai's subconscious released Gladstone's words into his thoughts, *"Ishmael is the key, and the key is Ishmael."*

"I see you've received Sandra's message. Good. We have little time. We can only communicate because Chaos and Destruction have left the premises. Their close proximity interferes with telepathic communications and neutralizes some of our power. A rescue attempt will be made for you and Sara within the next twenty-four hours. When they come, tell them I'm here, below you, in a deeper dungeon with the others...We're with your daughter, Sara."

Ishmael had Kai's full attention. *"Is Sara safe?"*

"Yes. My brother Luke is with her. He apologizes for failing to protect you and Sara from the Dark Ones and for killing the demon in front of one so young."

Kai recalled the scene in his backyard and the man with the shining sword. The one who'd transformed into a white blur. The man who wasn't quite human.

"What are you?" Kai asked anxiously.

"I am of angelic origin, Dr. Solomon," Ishmael said. "Please let them know there are ten of us in all. Some of us are injured and weaker than others. But you have my word that we'll do everything possible to protect your daughter."

Overwhelmed with gratitude, tears pooled in Kai's eyes. "Thank you," he whispered.

"One last thing, Dr. Solomon. You must not let Le Feu get the vaccine. Once he has it, he will kill us all, including you and your family."

"But he said he'd let us go if I succeeded." Kai felt foolish the moment he thought the words.

"You know too much, Dr. Solomon. Mark my words. He doesn't intend to let you live." The voice paused. "The twins are returning. I must go. Journey forth in peace and love, Dr. Solomon."

Ishmael was gone.

Kai had anticipated Le Feu's betrayal and already had a plan. Now, all he had to do was escape. Kai created two versions of the vaccine. One he would inject into the three test subjects, which would degrade in less than a week. He would hide a syringe of the second—the actual vaccine—in his sock and smuggle it out during the rescue.

The door of the lab opened, jarring him from his thoughts. He glanced up, and his heart stopped. A tide of emotions swept over him with the shock of recognition when the familiar blonde woman walked into the room.

But he knew from the cold, blank expression on her face—this wasn't his wife.

Chapter 43

CARA

San Jose Airport.

SUN AND MILD temperatures warmed Cara's face as she disembarked in San Jose, where three black Escalades met their private flight on the tarmac.

Cara hung back as the driver, a tall, dark-haired Latino man dressed in the same tactical gear as Simon, exited the lead car. Simon and Isaac strode over to greet him while Michael, Ezekiel, and the new Guardians collected the luggage and loaded their suitcases and duffel bags into the waiting vehicles.

Cara avoided Simon for most of the flight. Seeing him made her heart hurt, and her blood boil. She had difficulty thinking of him as the same Simon she dated last week—the Simon whose lips and touch she craved. The Simon who had given her a glimpse of happiness. Simon, a man who didn't really exist. Though in her mind, it was Chamuel who wasn't real. This man would always be Simon to her.

Simon extended his hand and placed it on the huge man's shoulder in a formal Guardianship greeting. "Raphael. It's been a long time, my friend. Thank you for assisting."

"Chamuel, it's more of an honor than a duty to assist you, brother," he said warmly and turned to Isaac for a proper greeting.

Simon tapped his phone screen. "I texted you and the others the address. "We'll ride in the lead car and brief you on the way." Then he signaled Michael with a wave. "Ride with us."

Accompanied by Chloe and a reserved Sienna, Cara silently brushed past the Guardians, relieved to escape to the next car in line.

Thirty minutes later, the Escalades pulled up outside Kai's home. Simon, Isaac, Raphael, and Michael exited the first car and approached hers.

A knock sounded on the back passenger window, and the black-tinted glass lowered to reveal Simon.

Cara's cheeks flushed, and her anger surged back, but her resolve wavered when she heard the deep, familiar timbre of his voice and remembered the feel of his body pressed against hers. Damn him. She kept her expression impassable.

His vivid blue eyes held yearning and resolve, "Cara, bring Chloe, please," he requested gently.

Confused, she glanced at the sleeping dog curled at her side. Not trusting herself to speak, she gave a silent nod. Regardless of how she felt, he was in charge of this operation, and if nothing else, she trusted him to do his job. Cara roused Chloe, clipped the lead to her collar, and exited the door facing the street. They met everyone on the sidewalk.

Simon addressed her, "Since you know the wife, you and Michael take the lead."

Cara approached the house with Chloe and Michael, while Isaac, Raphael, and Simon followed behind.

The front door was ajar behind the screen.

Cara's senses bristled as she rang the bell and called out, "Melanie, it's Cara!"

"Come in," said a familiar voice.

Cara crossed the threshold, and Chloe's hackles rose.

The dog's energy flared into a protective shield, and a deep growl rumbled in Chloe's chest. Gums peeled back from her teeth, Chloe reared back, barking viciously, ready to attack.

Melanie shrieked and cowered, shielding her face with her arms.

Perplexed, Cara held the lead with both hands, struggling to control her near-rabid canine. Blue lasers shot from Chloe's eyes and landed on Kai's pretty, blonde wife, revealing rotting flesh beneath the light. Cara screamed, gooseflesh covering her body.

Holy freaking hell!

Michael gripped Cara's shoulder to steady her.

Melanie released an inhuman shriek, her mouth morphing into an unhinged maw with rows of sharp teeth. A flash of white flew past Cara's peripheral vision. *Were those wings?*

Simon materialized behind the demonic Melanie, his hand wrapping around her throat.

A high melodic note passed through Simon's lips, and Chloe calmed, but her lasers held fast on Melanie. Simon spoke to the Melanie-creature in the same otherworldly language Constantina had used during training.

"What's happening?" Cara hissed to Michael.

"He's questioning her," Michael said. "She's not what she seems."

Well, duh. Melanie looked like a rotting corpse a few seconds ago.

The demon choked out a response to Simon's questions while trying to wrench his hand from her throat. The sound she expelled wasn't her voice but a legion of demonic whispers that sent a chill through Cara.

Cara shivered. "Is Melanie one of the Dark Ones?"

"Not exactly," Michael said, keeping his gaze pinned on the scene in front of them.

Simon snapped a hilt from his belt, the blade flaring into existence. In one swift movement, he plunged the blazing dagger into Melanie's chest. She crumpled to the ground, motionless.

Cara's eyes went wide. "Did you kill her?"

Simon's gaze flashed to hers. "No. She's unconscious. Happens after an exorcism. That demon had been riding shotgun for almost a year," he said calmly.

Cara glanced at Melanie lying on the floor. She looked like herself again. "Will she be okay?"

"She should be," he said, then glanced at Raphael. "Have your team take Mrs. Solomon to the clinic."

Raphael nodded. "Done."

Simon's gaze returned to Cara. "At least now we won't be feeding information to our enemies," he said, all business.

Cara grabbed his forearm as he strode past and glanced at Chloe, who looked up with big, expressive brown eyes and blinked. No lasers in sight. "How did you know about Chloe?"

Simon's lips twitched as he stooped to ruffle Chloe's ears. She jumped to lick his chin. "Good job," he whispered, then rose and said to Cara, "I figured it out last week, when I met her during my surveillance."

"But, wh-what is she?" Cara stuttered, glancing at her dainty little whippet.

Simon smiled wryly. "She's an Angelorum Sentinel...She hunts demons," he said, and strode out the door.

Chapter 44

CARA

San Francisco.

CARA STARED OUT the Escalade's window as they wove through downtown San Francisco. Michael sat on the other side of her whippet Sentinel, who was fast asleep in an exhausted ball between them. Cara tried to process what she'd witnessed at Kai's house—demons, blue lasers, a flash of wings behind Simon. On the positive side, the excitement helped to dull her emotional pain.

Sienna leaned over Cara's seat from the third row. "Carissima, who are all these hot men? Do they work for Simon?" Sienna asked in a low voice, her eyes trained on the light-skinned black man with long braided hair sitting behind the wheel.

The driver let out a stifled snort. If Cara wasn't sitting on the passenger side, she might've kicked the back of his seat. The Guardian's riveting emerald-green eyes caught her gaze in the rearview mirror, wearing an amused expression that said: "I can't wait to hear this."

She narrowed her eyes at his reflection and glanced at Sienna. "Not exactly. They work for the same *private security* organization as Simon, but for different people." The half-truth felt like chalk on her tongue, but she and Michael had agreed they wouldn't reveal unnecessary Angelorum details to Sienna unless Constantina cleared it.

"Hmm…I wonder if they'd be open to making a calendar," Sienna purred. "I shouldn't be the only one enjoying the view."

Michael rolled his eyes and snapped, "Are men all you ever think about?"

"I could ask you the same question," she retorted with a glower.

Michael whirled on her. "God, you're such a bitch!"

Sienna growled and lunged, nails out like a feral cat.

Cara dove between them and pushed Sienna back into the third row. "For the love of Pete! Will you both stop, already!"

The Guardian in the front seat burst out laughing. "Play nice, children, or I'm going to stop the car and make you walk," he said with a thick West Indian lilt. "Pretty One, you shouldn't let him get to you. But, to be fair, you shouldn't poke fun at the gentleman's preferences."

Michael gazed out the window and smirked with vindication.

"And you, sir," the driver said to Michael, "shouldn't fault a woman for going after what she wants. You might profit from her example."

"Ha!" Sienna barked at Michael. The side of his face flushed, and he shifted uncomfortably. Cara tasted his embarrassment.

"Thanks for that shot of wisdom, uh…?" Cara paused, fishing for a name.

"Call me Jade, Miss Cara," he said, his lilt warm and inviting. Jade caught her eye in the rearview mirror and winked. Cara appreciated what Sienna said about the view. She wasn't wrong; Jade had flawless skin and pleasing features.

Like Simon. God, she was so stupid. Constantina had told her about the Guardians' angelic characteristics. So far, all the Nephilim she'd seen were breathtaking by anyone's standards.

"It's nice to meet you, Jade. Sorry for the *disturbance*," Cara said, not having to see Michael's tense frown or Sienna's pout to feel their roiling energy. Despite acting like a pair of two-year-olds, their anger still had an undertone of chocolate heat.

"No problem. Let me know if there's anything else you need, princess," Jade said. Given the last couple of weeks, Cara hoped "princess" was an endearment and not a title she wasn't aware of.

The SUVs turned into a Marina District neighborhood.

"Nice place," Cara mumbled to Michael as the Escalade pulled up in front of a blue, ultramodern three-story house. "Someone's residence?" One glance told her that he hadn't recovered from his dust-up with Sienna.

Michael nodded. "Constantina thought a private safe house would be less conspicuous than the Bay Area Guardian facility," he said with forced nonchalance, his arms still bolted across his body.

The ultramodern structure sat among traditional row houses. A glass picture window, constructed from smaller square panes, spanned two stories along the front and right sides of the house. A roof deck, surrounded by glass panels, crowned the structure, while the ground-floor façade featured a stainless-steel double garage door and a front entrance.

The Escalades filed one by one into the private lot on the side of the house—a true luxury in San Francisco.

"Thanks, Jade," Cara said, catching the Guardian's eye as they exited the SUV.

He gave her a bright, white smile. "Good luck. You might need it."

True, that. Cara sandwiched herself and Chloe between Michael and Sienna as they followed Simon, Isaac, Raphael, Ezekiel, and the others into the house and up the stairs to the first floor.

The house's interior was as modern as its exterior, and contained a two-level open floor plan. The kitchen ran along the right wall with a long island separating it from the spacious living room on the left. Stairs behind the kitchen led upstairs to the second-floor loft space, edged in an open railing like a ship's deck. Every wall was painted white, with splashes of color from oversized artwork and upholstered accents on the super-modern furniture.

Cara cocked her head. Was that a guitar mounted on the wall of the dining room?

"Cara," Simon said from behind. She spun to face him. He wore a mask of professional indifference, which she appreciated. What went down between them would have to wait until after they rescued Kai. He said evenly, "You, Sienna, and Michael can take your bags up and use the two upstairs bedrooms. My team and I will use the lower levels." His gaze lingered on her for a second before he turned and headed toward the living room with Isaac, where they intended to set up their command post.

Chloe tugged on her lead, wanting to follow Simon, so Cara unclipped her, and she trotted off to join the men.

Et tu, Chloe?

Grabbing their bags, Cara stepped between Sienna and Michael for their climb upstairs in case one of them got the overwhelming urge to toss the other over the second-floor railing.

Simon called from the living room when they reached the top, "Cara, Michael, meet us down here in twenty minutes?"

Cara nodded and headed into one of the bedrooms with Sienna, while Michael unloaded his stuff in the room beside them.

Twenty minutes later, Cara and Michael entered the living room, bursting with Guardians dressed in standard-issue black. Crowding on the L-shaped sectional and filling every chair, the overflow sat on the floor. Only a love seat behind Simon remained conspicuously empty.

Cara recognized Isaac, Zeke, Raphael, and Jade with six other seated Guardians—ten of the largest, most beautiful, and culturally diverse men she'd ever seen in one place. Simon made eleven. Thank God, Sienna was reading on the roof deck, out of eye line to all that rippled muscle.

Simon waved her and Michael over. "Brothers, I'd like to formally introduce you to my Trinity." Simon nodded toward her, then Michael. "This is our Soul Seeker, Cara Collins, and Michael Swift, our Messenger." Then, he gestured to the love seat. "Please, sit."

Rather than sitting beside her, Michael sat on the floor and winked, leaving a place for Simon. She glowered at him. *"Traitor."* He shrugged.

Simon cleared his throat. "Let's do introductions. Please give your name and house affiliation," he said and lowered himself beside Cara. She wanted to jump out of her skin at the same time her traitorous body warmed at Simon's nearness. Thinking of Kai and their mission, she set aside her discomfort.

"I'll start." The dark-haired Guardian leader stood and gave a slight bow. "Welcome to San Francisco, Collins Trinity. I'm Raphael, Son of Peliel. I lead the Bay Area House, and this is my team," he said with a cordial smile, gesturing to the males seated around the room.

Cara perked up, remembering the naming conventions Constantina had taught her: Guardians taking their mother's angelic name and Trinities using the Soul Seeker's surname.

Raphael returned to the sofa. Jade rose next.

Jade bent at the waist, a mischievous glint sparkling in his emerald eyes. "Princess and Sir," he said, addressing them, "I'm Jade, Son of Arella with the Bay Area House. Glad to be of service both in battle and in dispensing wisdom."

"Whether you want it or not," said the gruff, rusty-haired Guardian sitting beside Isaac.

Jade winked and sat down. "Gabe hates that I'm always right."

Gabe answered with a loud snort.

"Brothers…No bickering in front of our guests," Raphael said, shaking his head like he was scolding school children.

Zeke, the baby-faced Guardian she'd met in Central Park, stood up next. He wore a rakish smile that lit his warm brown eyes. She liked his playful energy. Unlike the other Guardians, who had no visible tattoos, Zeke had intricate tribal designs radiating from his black T-shirt sleeves to his wrists. He gave a wave. "Hey! Glad to be here to help with the rescue and to kick some demon ass." He tipped two fingers at Isaac. "I'm with the East Coast Tri-State House. Oh, yeah. Ezekiel, Son of Itqal, but call me Zeke."

Isaac gave him an icy glare and muttered, "Remind me to send you back through diplomacy training," as he rose to face Cara and Michael.

Behind him, Zeke caught Cara's eye, and the corner of his mouth tipped into a mischievous smile. *"He's such a stick in the mud."*

Cara flinched at Zeke's voice in her head. He winked.

Simon glanced between them and glared at the young Guardian. *"Stop flirting with my Soul Seeker, Zeke."* Cara stiffened at Simon's telepathic intrusion. She resented the reprimand, which was clearly intended for both of them.

Zeke shrugged it off, wearing a look of mock innocence.

Isaac glanced over his shoulder at the young male, shook his head, and resumed, "Isaac, Son of Heiglot, and leader of Tri-State House. Your Trinity has our full commitment to this mission."

Issac took his seat beside Zeke as Gabe lumbered up. He was burlier than the rest of the Guardians but equally muscled. He pawed at his rust-colored ponytail, a few shades redder than Cara's hair, tightening it behind his head. His eyes, the same color green as hers, caught her gaze and warmed. "Cara, please accept my apology for my rude behavior earlier." He cast a brief glare at Jade. "I'm Gabriel, Son of Iahmel, and I'm also a member of the Bay Area House. I'm here to get down to business and find our prisoners." He jerked his head toward Jade, cracked his large knuckles, and said, "Any of these guys get out of hand, you let me know. I'll take care of 'em for you."

"I've got that covered," came Simon's chilly response.

Cara bristled at his possessive tone and sent him an irritated scowl before smiling at Gabe. "I appreciate that." Gabe glanced between her and Simon. His eyebrow twitched, and the corner of his mouth tugged into a small smile. Raising his hands in surrender, he sat down.

By the time all the introductions were made, they'd met: Sun, Son of Urpaniel; Jophiel, Son of Harudha; Christian, Son of Jariel; Camael, Son of Liwet; and Isiah, Son of Mehiel.

Simon leaned forward, his thigh accidentally brushing hers. She edged away, his salty hurt skating over her taste buds. Cara wanted to scream. *He was hurt? Really?* Enduring enough torture for one day, she slipped to the floor beside Michael.

Without missing a beat, Simon said evenly, "Raphael, please share your update before I explain our plan."

Raphael retrieved a tablet from the coffee table and cleared his throat. "We've done a refresh on Achanelech's properties and known associates. He's gotten smart, creating new holding companies over the years, but I've shortlisted some possible locations. I've also pulled building plans, architectural drawings, and permits—not that they'll tell the whole story. But it's a start."

"The guy on the subway has Kai? Who is he?" Cara whispered to Michael.

"The Demon King of Fire. Also, goes by Le Feu. He seems to have a stake in Kai's latest genetics project at Forrester—" A wave of nausea hit Cara, and she sank her fingers into Michael's shoulder, interrupting him.

Heart pounding, she switched to their frequency. *The dream I had. Le Feu kills Kai! We need to find him!* Then it clicked into place—Tom's death in the Forrester parking lot and the notebooks Melanie mentioned on the phone.

She'd forgotten her telepathic link to Michael included Simon, when he chimed in, "*We will find him before that happens.*"

Simon stood up. "Thanks, Rafe. What are the final numbers for our mission?"

"Two teams of five are on their way. They'll meet us at the site once found. The other local teams are otherwise engaged and can't get away." He rubbed his brow, looking worried. "Before we spoke in the car, I'd hoped that would be enough."

Simon's brow furrowed. "Barely. We could use more backup."

Raphael scrubbed a hand down his face and got to his feet. "I put in a call to Angel Benitez down in LA. No response yet."

Murmurs and looks of discomfort spread throughout the West Coast Guardians. Gabriel popped to his feet and glared at Raphael. "The *Exile*? Benedictine and his degenerate retiree Four Hundred Class have no place in Guardianship business."

"Sit down, Gabe," Raphael said through clenched teeth, goring Gabe with a withering stare until he lowered himself onto the sofa.

"But—"

"Don't question my authority!" Raphael snapped, the living room pulsing with his irritation. Gabriel's mouth clamped shut. He sat in a red-faced, stormy sulk.

"Let me be clear," Simon snarled at the team and scowled at Gabe. "I don't have time for bullshit Guardianship politics. I don't care if he and his Nephilim have two heads and bark at the moon once a month. We need all the help we can get." He glanced at Raphael. "When will we know if they're coming?"

"Don't know. It might take Angel days to return my call. If he calls at all."

Cara wondered who Angel was and why he was exiled.

Hands on his hips, Simon shook his head. "Then we can't count on them. That means we're twenty-one strong. Michael is a trained fighter, so twenty-two." He calmed and asked Raphael, "How many listening devices do we have?"

"Six. One for each rescue team of four, and an extra for the two-person explosives team."

"What are they for?" Gabe asked after exchanging quizzical looks with Zeke and Sun.

Michael whispered to Cara, "Guardians typically depend on telepathic communication during missions, just like we do in our Trinity. Not devices. It's like asking them to use scuba gear on dry land."

Simon addressed the sea of puzzled faces. "We've been investigating Guardian disappearances during Trinity assignments over the last year or so. A common theme in the Seeker interviews has been unexpected interference in telepathic communication on our frequencies. Ishmael was taken by the Dark Ones under similar circumstances. We believe these incidents are related. Since our communication is based on our ability to bend the laws of physics, the most likely possibility is that we're dealing with something supernatural in nature. Our enemies won't anticipate the use of modern technology to communicate as we would telepathically. Raphael secured state-of-the-art listening devices used by US Special Forces teams."

The Guardians' expressions changed from confusion to interest.

Raphael removed a small two-part device from his pocket and handed it to Simon, who set it on the coffee table and removed his hair tie. Simon's hair fell loose and touched his shoulders. He seated the earpiece beneath his hair.

Simon's loose hair warmed something low in Cara's belly. Her body obviously hadn't gotten the memo.

Simon smiled wryly at Isaac, "Except for this guy, who prefers his hair short and prickly, wearing our hair down will conceal the devices." He picked up the other piece on the table. "The receiver is small enough to hide on our belts. It's also on a closed frequency that can't be accessed by anyone outside our teams. We'll keep the communications booster outside the perimeter in one of our vehicles."

Lots of head nodding and discussion ensued, all of it positive.

"Now, we need to figure out where they're holding Dr. Solomon and his daughter," said Simon. "You all have your search assignments from earlier. See Isaac for the flight roster. Thanks, Brothers. Dismissed."

The Guardians hoisted themselves to their feet and broke into individual conversations.

Simon lowered his voice and said to her and Michael, "Hang back, so I can fill you in."

The doorbell rang, and Simon waved at Zeke. "Can you get the food? I can hear your stomach growling from here."

Zeke gleefully rubbed his hands together. "Don't need to ask twice." His heavy boots echoed across the hardwood floor as he headed toward the stairs. He yelled back, "For the record, I'm disappointed we couldn't strong-arm you into cooking for us, bro."

Simon flushed. "Another time."

Zeke's voice rose from below a few moments later. "Guys, a little help down here? There's enough food for an army. We might need a hand truck," he said, muffling a laugh.

Jade grabbed one of the Guardians in the living room, and they went to his aid.

As the Guardians dealt with the food, Simon glanced between Cara and Michael. "We'll search by air in one-hour bursts so that we can grab sleep and reserve our energy for the rescue. We need to fuel up before we fly, so the first patrol will leave right after we eat. I suggest grabbing food with the rest of us to keep your strength up. Our goal is to find the location before dawn and move in while it's still dark. So, get some sleep."

Cara shuddered as the rescue became a reality.

Simon rested his fingers on her shoulder, sending an annoying jolt of excitement over her skin. "Cara, when we find Kai, you'll come with Michael and me. Zeke will round out our team of four. As the Seeker, you're attuned to Kai's energy. You'll lead us to his precise location. We need to bring our A-game to make it out of there in one piece. This will be high stress, so trust in your training."

Cara met Simon's gaze for a split second and swallowed. She appreciated his straightforward approach. She prayed she wouldn't have a panic attack. Kai and Sara's fates hung in the balance, and she couldn't let them down. Taking in a deep breath, she lifted her chin. "I'll do my part."

Simon gave her shoulder a final squeeze. "Good girl." Then his gaze found Michael, "See Isaac in the command center. He'll give you an assignment and share the finer details of our rescue plan. I'll see you both later." With a departing nod, he strode toward the kitchen to join the other Guardians, as Zeke and Jade spread food containers on the kitchen island.

Cara relaxed, now out of Simon's orbit. Being close to him only made an already complicated situation more complicated.

Michael clasped her shoulder and peered into her eyes, his gaze searching. "This can't be easy. You, OK?"

"I'm fine." Meaning functional. She nodded at the men staking out places to eat around the island and the wall banquette. Competing scents of meat, fish, and chicken awakened Cara's hunger. "I'll meet you over there in a few minutes. Gird your loins. I'm going to get Sienna."

Michael snorted and mumbled, "I'll grab my codpiece."

Cara headed upstairs, chuckling at the visual. She opened the exterior door to the roof deck and walked into the cooling evening. Party lights illuminated the deck, creating a festive atmosphere.

Scrolling on her phone, Sienna sat on a plush lounge chair facing San Francisco Bay and the iconic rust-red Golden Gate Bridge, visible in the distance over the rooftops.

Cara sank onto the chaise lounge beside Sienna. Resting her head on the bright-blue cushion, Cara enjoyed a moment of reprieve. "It's so beautiful up here." San Francisco was one of Cara's favorite cities, but this time, there wouldn't be dinner at her favorite restaurant, The Slanted Door, located in the Embarcadero Ferry Terminal.

The spectacular view brought back memories of Simon's roof deck, and disappointment draped over her like a wet blanket. Another reminder of the joy he'd stolen. For a moment, Cara missed her old life.

"I'm sorry for dragging you into this," Cara whispered, gazing up at the darkening sky.

"You owe me a spa day," Sienna joked. "Wait, make that two. The extra one is for putting up with that insufferable prig, Michael."

Cara snorted a laugh. "Deal." Rolling her head to the side, she looked at Sienna and confessed, "The food's here, along with more rescuers. Counting Michael, twelve hungry men are downstairs eating as we speak. We should probably stake out a meal before they devour them all."

"Ugh," she said and waved a dismissive hand. "Whatever possessed you to think I'd like Michael?"

Cara *tsk-tsked.* "Come on, Senny. Be nice. If you stopped picking on him, you'd figure it out."

"Forget him." Sienna waggled her eyebrows. "Tell me about the other guys."

Cara rolled her eyes. "They're here to work. I know that wouldn't normally stop you, but they're knee-deep in rescue plans." She failed to mention that Guardians typically limited their partners to members of the Angelorum, but if Sienna wanted to give it a go, Cara wouldn't get in her way. Better than watching her harass Michael.

"We'll see," she said in a sing-song and sprang from her lounge chair.

They descended the stairs into the din of a packed kitchen. Guardians sat wedged around the banquette and on stools at the bar, chatting, eating, and occasional laughter.

Sienna pulled Cara aside and whispered, "O-M-G! I've died and gone to Hottie Heaven."

Smirking, Cara whispered, "Just remember to behave."

"I'll do my best, but no promises."

They approached Michael at the counter, who stood by the remaining food containers. Spotting them, he asked, "Chicken, beef, fish, or vegetarian?"

"Fish," Cara said. Michael handed her a container.

Sienna stared openly at the male smorgasbord. "Beefcake. Sorry, beef."

Michael rolled his eyes, snorted, and shoved a container at her, marked "Beef."

Narrowing her eyes, Sienna ripped the white container from his grasp and stomped off to the island, where she sidled up to Jade. Sienna turned on her signature smile. "Is this seat taken?"

Jade grinned and motioned to the stool. "Be my guest, Pretty One."

"Let the games begin," Cara whispered to Michael.

Michael scowled and snatched a food container. "She's unbelievable," he said in a tone betraying his annoyance. "I put out food and water for Chloe. No interest. She's working the room for table scraps."

"Not surprised. The little hussy." Cara chuckled, spotting the canine in question beneath the table, nosing Simon's knee for some of his meal.

The burly red-haired Guardian, Gabe, ripped a piece of chicken off the bone, and his hand disappeared under the table. Chloe sniffed at it, delicately took his offering, and ate it.

"You're just encouraging her, Gabriel," Cara shouted over.

He shrugged, gave Cara a broad smile, and winked. "I hear she's a Sentinel, Miss Collins. That makes her part of the team. Gotta keep her fed like the rest of us."

Cara shook her head and watched the little beggar score more Guardian handouts. She gave Michael a side-eye. "Did you know?"

Michael shifted on his feet and hedged, "Not exactly…But I suspected something was up the night I met you. I heard a telepathic voice that wasn't yours. Something about making healthy babies."

Cara's head whipped around, and she nearly dropped her meal. She remembered. At the time, she thought Michael and Sienna would make a lovely couple and received a random thought in return: *They would make healthy babies.*

"That was *Chloe?*" she asked, incredulous.

Michael shrugged. "Had to be," he said and eyed her warily. "Do you know what she meant?"

Not wanting to enlighten Michael, Cara deflected, setting down her food and placing a hand on her hip. "And you didn't think to tell me?"

He snorted a laugh. "Tell you what? That your dog speaks telepathically? You would've thought I was out of my mind."

"Probably. Damn…you're right." Sighing, she glanced at Chloe. "All this time, I thought she was just a charming little dog who liked men."

Car's skin tingled with awareness, and she caught Simon gazing at her from the banquette. She couldn't bear the closeness and gave Michael a pleading look. "Come eat on the roof deck with me?" she begged.

Michael glanced at their Guardian. "It will have to be quick. I need to meet with Isaac."

Halfway up the stairs, Simon called from below, "Cara, try to get a couple of hours of sleep, so you're ready when we need you."

Cara grimaced and glanced over her shoulder, feeling a mix of gratitude and resentment. "I will. Thanks." Now she understood why the Angelorum had their rule. For situations exactly like this.

Chapter 45

MICHAEL

Safe House. San Francisco.

"I THINK SIENNA is attracted to you," Cara said, her declaration freezing Michael mid-chew as he sat astride a chaise lounge beneath the deck's party lights. *Is Cara delusional?*

Michael had the overwhelming desire to spit his rice onto the plate. He grabbed the bottled water beside his chair, took a swig to help him swallow, and choked out, "Why would you say that? She's thrown herself at every guy we've met since leaving the city. Besides, she thinks I'm gay," he mumbled with no small amount of aggravation. Not to mention her uncanny knack for pressing his personal hot buttons and clawing at his self-control every chance she had.

"She doesn't think you're gay," Cara said matter-of-factly, setting aside her food. "I know her better than I know myself sometimes. Despite her crazy behavior, the fact that you're the only one in the room she's *not* throwing herself at tells me everything. The fact that she drives you so nuts should tell you something."

"Yeah—to stay as far away from her as possible," he growled, digging his heels in.

"Really?" Cara's gaze bore into him. "Then, why did you take over cooking her breakfast after you found out she had a glycemic attack?"

"You said you can't cook," he muttered in a lame attempt to defend himself, poking at the rice with his fork. Just because he and Sienna didn't like each other didn't mean he couldn't feel sorry for her or want to do something nice, did it?

Cara tapped a hand to her chest. "For the record, I *can* make eggs. Look at me, Michael."

He gazed up into her scowling face and stormy green eyes that brokered no bullshit. She huffed. "OK, explain the insane amount of estrogen meets testosterone in a warm, dark chocolate explosion I taste whenever you two take a run at each other. There's enough chocolate-y sexual energy there to power the Golden Gate Bridge and add twenty pounds to my hips."

Her words hit like a blow to his solar plexus and held a shred of truth he wanted to avoid. "I don't know what you're talking about," he said, spearing some broccoli and popping it into his mouth.

Cara swished her tongue in her mouth and pointed. "Liar."

Michael swallowed, stared at his plate, and stayed silent. His face flushed with heat. No way. That couldn't be true. Sure, Sienna was beautiful. Anyone with eyes could see that, but almost every second he was with her, he wanted to wring her neck. How did that translate into sex? Sex implies trust, and he sure as hell didn't have that with Sienna. Quite the opposite. But he couldn't deny she'd gotten under his skin, and that scared the shit out of him.

He reluctantly dragged his gaze to Cara.

She raised a brow. "Sienna may not have said 'thank you,' but I know she appreciated you making her breakfast."

Sienna did thank me. Privately. In her thoughts. But he couldn't tell Cara that without revealing his other abilities. Abilities he had no intention of disclosing to anyone. Ever.

He was still pissed at himself for breaking his own rule, dipping into Sienna's mind like that when he'd set down her eggs, expecting something awful. Instead, he heard words of gratitude. He forgave her a little then. Too bad it hadn't lasted.

Cara touched his arm. "I know it's none of my business, but I care about both of you, and it kills me to see you at each other's throats. Honestly, I think there's a spark buried beneath all the conflict."

Michael entertained the possibility that Cara had an infinitesimally small point, and a strange thrill grew in his chest. He eyed Cara. "You really think she doesn't hate me under all that venom?"

Cara wore a smug smile. "I'd take the odds."

He glanced at his watch and flinched. "I need to go. Isaac's waiting." All the talk about Sienna had derailed him from asking Cara about Chamuel. What a cluster. Michael could kick himself for missing the similarities between Cara's description of Simon and Chamuel. Probably, because he never expected their Guardian to do something so extreme. "Hey, before I go…I'm sorry Chamuel lied to you. I know you didn't know who he really was. You deserve happiness."

He swung his leg over the lounge and rose.

"Thanks." Cara grabbed his forearm. "Michael, maybe I shouldn't tell you this, so please keep it between us." She hesitated. "Don't let Sienna's rough exterior fool you. A lot of what she puts out there is a defense mechanism from a traumatic childhood. We both suffered from severe anxiety attacks in high school. That's why we're such good friends. I think…" Cara took a breath and pushed on, "I think the reason she baits you is to avoid being rejected by someone she wants. Does that make sense?"

He swallowed and nodded. What Cara said about Sienna's childhood resonated with him. He could relate to childhood trauma more than anyone would ever know. So, it wasn't personal with Sienna. His issues were the barrier, not hers.

Cara stood with him, ready to go.

"I appreciate you telling me about Sienna," he said, and hoped he remembered this next time Sienna pushed his buttons. He pointed to Cara's container. "Want me to take that?"

She handed him her garbage. "Thanks. I'm going to get some rest."

Michael left Cara upstairs and took the empty containers to the kitchen.

Low-pitched banter filled the living room where the Guardians had reconvened. Catching Chamuel's eye across the room, Michael said telepathically, "*Roof deck is clear when you're ready.*"

Chamuel nodded.

Michael walked past Sienna, who sat alone at the island, moping and mindlessly poking her food with a fork.

He had a moment of gleeful delight that she'd struck out with Jade. Giving her his back, he smirked. "Why so glum?" he asked, attempting polite conversation as he disposed of the garbage into a black trash bag.

"Do you think I'm pretty?" Sienna asked in a dejected whisper behind him.

The question caught Michael off guard. He froze and tempered his snark. "You sure you want my opinion?"

"You think I'm useless and unattractive, don't you?" Concern echoed in her biting tone.

Pretty wasn't her problem, bitchy was. Michael swept a hand down his face. "Yeah, right. You're a hag," he said sarcastically, turning to face her. "You can't be serious."

Head dipped, her long, jet-black hair fell in a curtain around her face. Her shoulder shook as fat tears spilled from her eyes into the uneaten food.

Michael panicked. Had he made her cry?

Bottled emotions burst forth like an angry genie trapped in a lamp and unleashed his eight-year-old self, crying alone in the woods. His brain reacted instinctively—he wouldn't let that happen to anyone. It didn't matter that he'd just spent the most uncomfortable few days of his adult life with Sienna or that an hour ago, they would've gladly thrown sharp objects at each other. She needed him, and he would do whatever it took to comfort her.

Michael dropped the bag. In four steps, he was around the island and at her side. He pulled Sienna from the barstool, draped an arm protectively around her delicate shoulders, and searched frantically for someplace private. Spotting a door behind the living room, he led her into a small recording studio and closed them inside.

For the first time, Michael wondered who owned the house. He hadn't given much thought to the guitar mounted on the dining room wall, but seeing the studio and line of platinum disks hanging on the wall, he assumed the owner was in the music industry.

He squinted and caught the vaguely familiar name *King Metaljam* on one of the plaques.

Michael led a sobbing Sienna to a small couch and sat beside her. "Shh," he soothed, resting his chin on her head and inhaling the scent of jasmine and rose petals that clung to her hair.

When her crying subsided, he tipped her chin so he could meet her eyes. "Why did you say that out there?" he asked gently. "I've never said you're unattractive or useless. Have I?"

Sniffling, she dabbed at her eyes with a dinner napkin and whispered in a shaky voice, "You must think it, though."

He brushed a piece of her silken hair behind her ear. "I've never thought that. You're smart and…beautiful. Why are you really crying? It can't be what I said in the kitchen. What's the matter?" He wanted—no, he *needed*—to know what upset her. Granted, she'd been a total pain in the ass, but her vulnerability snuck past his defenses and resonated with the broken pieces he hid from the world.

She wrung the napkin in her hands. "I feel so useless here. There's nothing I can do. I'm usually the one who takes care of Cara. Now, I'm just a burden." She looked up at him. Spiky wet eyelashes surrounded sky-blue eyes. "I'm sorry for the way I've treated you, Michael. Cara was right. You're a good person. It's me who's horrible."

Her apology touched him. Regret echoed inside his chest. Maybe he wasn't the only one who always needed to be in control. He pulled her closer and tucked her head against his shoulder, pressing his face into the heady scent of her hair. "Your moral support means a lot to Cara. You're her best friend, and she loves you."

As he held Sienna, her petite frame felt good in his arms, awakening something raw and primal inside him. She'd driven him crazy these last few days, but maybe Cara wasn't entirely wrong about the energy between them. He'd spoken the truth when he said she was beautiful and smart. If he'd been completely candid, he would've added sexy. Here, like this, there wasn't a man in his right mind who wouldn't fall under her spell.

Leaning back, he glanced at her downturned eyes and lush lashes. "You better now?"

She nodded and then lifted her gaze, chin tilting up. Michael's gaze drifted to Sienna's full lips, and on instinct, he leaned in and kissed her. The touch of her lips unleashed a heated passion that had been building since they'd met. He deepened the kiss, his tongue parting her lips, exploring, and tasting. White-hot desire ignited inside him, searing a path through his veins straight to his groin.

"Michael…," she moaned, curling a hand around his neck and drawing him closer. Her kiss turned demanding as her free hand traveled along the hollow of his spine and turned his body to tinder under her touch.

He met her head-on, running his fingers through the length of her silky hair before gathering her tightly into his chest. His body reacted with throbbing excitement, triggering his internal alarms and ripping him from the moment. Adrenaline shot through him with the sudden urge to flee. He jerked back and planted his hands on Sienna's shoulders, pushing her gently away to create distance between them.

Gazing at her, he panted and struggled for a graceful exit. "I'm sorry. I shouldn't have taken advantage of you like that."

She stared in naked confusion, her lips pleasantly swollen from their kiss. "What do you mean?"

His heart thumped wildly, and he swallowed hard. "I don't want to take advantage of you when you're vulnerable."

"I don't think that." She shook her head, and her small voice clawed at his chest. He wanted to soothe her, not hurt her.

"We should go," he whispered, wrestling with feelings he shouldn't be having.

She wiped at her eyes. "Okay."

Grasping her shoulders, he kept his eyes locked on hers. "Please don't misunderstand. I wanted to kiss you, but I need to get back outside." It was the truth. He *did* want to kiss her; the problem was, he wanted to kiss her until he forgot his own name. And he couldn't ever let that happen. "We'll talk later," he said, the lie tasting bitter on his tongue.

Taking Sienna's hand, he led her upstairs to the room she shared with Cara. Avoiding Cara's quizzical stare when he deposited Sienna inside, he left without a word.

Damn, Cara, for being right.

His encounter with Sienna rattled him deeply, awakening feelings that terrified him. His hands shook so badly, he had to use the stair railing as he descended.

Coward, he chided. She'd never want you if she knew the truth. No one would. Halting midway down the stairs, he squeezed his eyes shut, wishing he could erase the last thirty minutes. Sienna would never be a good candidate for his "friends with benefits" approach to dating. Instinctively, he knew she'd want more than he could give. She deserved it.

"Are you all right?" Michael's eyelids flew open at Chamuel's concerned voice. His Trinity Guardian frowned at the base of the stairs.

Michael swallowed and nodded, not trusting his voice even in a silent reply.

Chamuel waved a hand. "Join us in the command center before I leave with the next patrol."

Chapter 46

CHAMUEL

Safe House. San Francisco.

CONCERN SPARKED IN Chamuel when he saw Michael frozen, his eyes closed, in the middle of the staircase. He'd witnessed Michael and Sienna's earlier exchange in the kitchen before they disappeared into the recording studio.

Had he not been on his own emotional rollercoaster all day, Chamuel might've missed Michael's pain. He suspected Michael's state of mind had something to do with Sienna, which baffled him, considering their apparent dislike for each other. Had that changed?

Chamuel noticed a mild tremor in Michael's hands when he met him at the bottom of the stairs.

"I'm fine," Michael said, his voice barely a whisper.

Chamuel swept a hand over his face and gripped Michael's upper arm. *"Come with me."*

"I said I'm fine," Michael gritted, twisting out of Chamuel's grasp.

Chamuel threw up his palms and stepped back.

Michael clutched his head with his hands. "I'm sorry. I…Let's go to the kitchen."

Chamuel followed Michael around the island. A black garbage bag lay crumpled on the floor, forgotten. Chamuel planted his hands on his hips. "Listen, Michael. You don't have to talk. But I need to know if I can depend on you. Our Trinity has taken some blows today, most of them from me. Regardless, I can't jeopardize our safety or the safety of our teams. We need to pull ourselves together."

Michael crossed his arms and averted his eyes. "I'm sorry, I didn't mean to snap at you. I won't let you down," he said wearily.

Chamuel nodded, feeling as tired as Michael looked. So much had to go right in the next few hours. "That's all I need to know. Thank you," he said and turned to leave.

"Do you love her?" Michael asked silently from behind.

He spun to face his Messenger and glared at the judgmental tone. *"From the second I laid eyes on her,"* Chamuel said, not that it was any of Michael's business, then strode from the kitchen as he said over his shoulder, "Meet us in the living room when you're ready."

Chamuel reached the sofa, huffing with frustration and feeling disgraced.

Isaac glanced up and cocked a blond brow. "You, okay?"

Chamuel paced, taking deep breaths. "Yeah. Fine." He hated the entire situation and how it had unfolded. He felt like he was trapped in Hell.

"Cham—"

He held up his hand. "Don't, okay. Just don't."

Isaac fixed him with a hard stare. "Trade places with me. I'll take the next patrol with Zeke." Chamuel and Zeke had drawn the short straw, having to split three vectors between the two of them due to the odd number of Guardians.

A low growl rose from Chamuel's throat. He didn't need Isaac coddling him.

"Yo! You ready?" Zeke entered the living room, and Chamuel rounded on him.

Zeke took a giant step back. "Whoa, Cham! Take it easy, man. What's going on?"

Chamuel blew out a breath. He wanted so desperately to punch someone. Michael's question blew the lid off the calm he'd been fighting to keep since Cara's explosion outside the plane. He should probably worry more about himself than anyone else. He'd get people killed if he didn't pull his shit together.

"I've got this one," Michael told him silently and joined them at the command post. "It's my fault. I overstepped."

Chamuel was grateful for the diversionary tactic.

Isaac gave them an ice-cold frown and drummed his fingers on the table beside the laptop. "If you gentlemen are done sparring, I'd like to give you your vectors." Chamuel and Zeke reached into their pockets and handed over their cell phones.

Heavy boots sounded in the upstairs hallway. Jade, Gabriel, and Raphael appeared at the top of the stairs. They were dressed in tight black jeans and fitted black T-shirts made for flying.

"Anything?" Isaac yelled up.

"No, mon," Jade said as he reached the bottom of the stairs and shook his head, his long ponytail of black braids swishing from side to side. "Just some random dark activity north of here by Napa. Not what we're looking for."

Raphael swiped a hand down his face and collapsed onto the sofa. "Nothing notable between here and the Nevada border." He looked past Chamuel's legs. "Hey, Gabe, grab me some water and a sandwich from the fridge while you're over there."

"Bring enough water for everyone," Isaac yelled over.

Gabriel grunted. "Guys, I only have two hands."

"Stop cryin' like a big baby," Jade said with a good-natured chuckle and headed toward the kitchen to help.

"Watch it, Jade." The rust-haired Guardian slammed the refrigerator door. "Or, I'll clip your wings while you sleep."

"*Tsk-tsk.* What's the matter with you tonight? You have another midair collision with a turkey vulture?" Jade grabbed half the bottles and sandwiches from Gabe's hands and headed back to the living room.

Chamuel gulped down a bottle of water—enough to hydrate him but not enough to need a mid-flight piss.

Isaac cleared his throat. "Michael, after Cham and Zeke return, I'll need you to take over for me at the command center while I fly with Raphael's guys." Then he eyed Raphael. "Your team's back on at midnight, so get some rest. Hopefully, we don't need more than two 'rinse and repeat' cycles per team."

Chamuel tried to shake off his nasty mood and said to Zeke, "Let's go."

"Ready when you are, Boss," he replied with a cocky grin.

"Here's your vectors," Isaac said and returned the cell phones into Zeke and Chamuel's outstretched hands.

"Keep the blue blob within the purple lines, and you're good to go."

Chamuel took a quick look at his flight plan and shoved the phone back into his pocket. He and Zeke headed to the stairs.

"I'll see you off," Michael said.

"Be my guest." Chamuel took the stairs two at a time. He passed Cara's room on the way to the roof and ignored a pang of longing.

Zeke burst through the door onto the deck. Chamuel followed and halted. He couldn't help it; he had to know. "How's she doing?" he asked Michael.

Michael's gaze held empathy rather than judgment this time. He gave Chamuel's forearm a reassuring squeeze and said gently, *"About the same as you, my friend. Fly safe. I'll make sure she's ready later."*

A lump formed in Chamuel's throat. He nodded and joined Zeke at the far edge of the deck. Given the deck's narrowness and their wingspan, they had to take off one at a time.

"I'll go first," said Zeke. "See you later."

Simon stepped back to give him room.

Zeke's wings slipped out and unfurled with a muted *whoosh*. Zeke flapped the powerful appendages in preparation, and thousands of feathers—some soft as silk, others sharp as knives—shimmered on top of a powerful bone-and-membrane understructure, giving his wings a deceptively harmless and majestic appearance. Then Zeke crouched, leaped, and vanished behind a cloak of invisibility after a few wing beats.

Chamuel pushed thoughts of Cara from his mind, let loose his wings, and headed southeast in search of Dr. Kai Solomon.

Chapter 47

CARA

Safe House. San Francisco.

CARA LAY IN the queen-sized bed, thinking about Simon as Sienna slept soundly beside her—thanks to a Xanax. Cara sighed. Maybe Sienna had a point. Maybe she needed to hear Simon out. She'd promised him that much at The Standard Grill, hadn't she? But that wouldn't change the fact that, because of Simon, she'd broken the Angelorum's one sacred rule before she had even accepted her Calling!

What puzzled her was how he had managed to deceive her when everything he told her had rung true. Then again, he probably knew about her training and how to subvert it.

God, Simon had been so perfect. He made her forget about Kai. *Gah!* She smacked the pillow and wanted to strangle him all over again for putting them in an impossible situation.

What the hell was he thinking?

She peeled back the covers and tiptoed out of bed. Closing the door softly behind her, she padded down to the cavernous living room.

She spotted Isaac camped out on one of the modern sofas at the Guardian command post. He looked up from the computer on the coffee table as she entered the room.

"Is Simon back from patrol yet?" she asked.

Isaac's ice-blue gaze drilled into her, displeasure written all over his face. "He just went downstairs for a shower and some sleep."

She bristled, not in the mood for anyone else's judgment, especially since she was the injured party. "Thanks," she mumbled and continued toward the rooms downstairs before she could talk herself out of it. This probably wasn't the best time to confront Simon, but it definitely wasn't the worst, and it might be the only time they had before the rescue.

"I wouldn't do that if I were you," Isaac warned.

"Lucky, you're not me," she ground out and descended the stairs.

She tracked Simon's energy to the right door and knocked softly after a moment's hesitation.

"Come in," a deep male voice called from inside. His tone held ease, which told her he hadn't detected her coming. Shame on him. She took a deep breath and walked inside.

A T-shirt dropped from his hands. He froze, standing bare-chested and wearing a look of surprise. His hair lay in loose waves around his shoulders, framing his handsome face. "Cara…," he whispered. Emotions softened his features, transforming him into the man she loved.

She hated that all it took was a look to steal her breath. Her gaze traveled to his pectoral muscles, and she wanted to scream when she saw the red Guardianship sigil inked over his heart. Had she glimpsed the tattoo the night she tried to seduce him, she would've known he was a Guardian.

Her jaw tightened. *Is that why he deflected my advances?*

She raked her gaze over his carved torso down to clearly defined six-pack abs and ridges along his hips that disappeared into the top of his black jeans. His body was like a work of chiseled marble, more beautiful half-naked than fully clothed, which only angered her more. Another taunting reminder of what she wanted and couldn't have. The injustice infuriated her, and it was all his fault.

Simon ignored her assessing gaze and swallowed. "Cara, you shouldn't be here."

Balling her hands into fists, she paced like a caged tiger, realizing she had acted prematurely. She wasn't ready to hear him out. The anger and heartbreak were still too raw. "I shouldn't *be* here?" she gritted out, her eyes boring into him. "You're damn straight. *I shouldn't be here!*"

He cringed like she'd struck him.

"You know what pisses me off the most?" She shook a fist. "That I spent the last nine years of my life in love with a man I could never have. You were the first person who made me forget him…You gave me hope! You let me fall in love with you." Her face reddened, and she stabbed a finger at him. "You…the only person on this goddamn *planet* I'm forbidden to have! Why would you do that?" Her voice escalated until tears of frustration spilled down her cheeks.

She hadn't meant to cry, but once she said the words, she couldn't stop the tears. Concealing his identity from her was one thing, but he'd stolen her chance for happiness—just like Kai and Tyler before him. She deserved to love an attainable man.

Simon stepped toward her.

She retreated and hissed, "Stay away from me."

Simon's expression twisted in pain, his gaze beseeching. "Cara, please. I wanted to tell you. I planned to tell you Friday night before Constantina called. This lie has been eating me up inside since we met." He drew in a breath, and his gaze grew brighter. "I fell in love with you the moment I saved you from the demon, and I've been agonizing over what to do ever since."

Cara's heart lurched at his admission. But then, it hit her like a runaway freight train. *He. Would. Never. Age.* She froze and whispered, "When did Calliope die?"

His brows knit in confusion. "Why does that matter?"

"Tell me!"

His face went slack, his gaze dimming. Then he said in a defeated whisper, "December 1889."

His words landed like a blow.

She stalked back and forth on the carpet, rubbing her temples. "How could this relationship have ever worked? When I'm ninety years old, you'll be a young two-hundred-something and look like a fresh thirty-two! People will think I'm your great-grandmother. It's impossible…it was over before it even started," she mumbled and stopped mid-pace to glare at him. "Is it Simon? Or should I call you Chamuel? Congratulations. I've never felt so manipulated!"

Hurt registered on Simon's face and in his energy. But his spine straightened in a show of dignity. When he spoke, his voice was low and steady, "Everything I've told you, everything I feel for you is real and true. My given name is Chamuel, but my chosen name is Simon. I'm a man as much as I'm Nephilim. I'm the man who gave you his love. I *am* Simon. For you, I'll always *be* Simon."

When he looked at her, unshed tears glistened in his eyes. "I would've given everything I had to be with you, and that's a lot for a Nephil and a Guardian in my position."

He picked up the T-shirt and shook it at her as a tear broke free and rolled down his cheek. "Do you even know what that means? I'm facing one hundred years in prison for just kissing you. I'm sorry if that sacrifice wasn't worthy enough of your love. And maybe you're right. Maybe this should've never happened."

She stood, shocked and immobile. Tears froze in her eyes.

Prison for one hundred years? She hadn't known that was the punishment. Her heart nearly cracked in half.

"You need to leave now, Cara," he said, his voice cracking on her name. He stalked into the bathroom and closed the door. She didn't move until the shower turned on. Burning with shame, she left Simon's room. Tears spilled unchecked down her cheeks and blinded her as she ran.

CHAMUEL

CHAMUEL LOCKED THE bathroom door and turned on the water, refusing to let her rip away his last shred of dignity. He leaned against the bathroom wall, his legs no longer able to support him. He slid down and sat, resting his head in his hands. He knew Cara was angry, but he had hoped they could work something out after Kai's rescue.

When he no longer heard her footfalls running down the hall, all his pain and frustration broke free, and his body shook with uncontrollable sobs. He hugged his knees, hot tears splashing onto his arms. He hadn't shed tears like this since Calliope's death.

Cara rejected him tonight for more than hiding his identity. She'd rejected him as a Nephilim male. He didn't see that coming. Didn't she understand the punishment he'd have to endure for violating the law? He'd have to relinquish his wings *after* he spent one hundred years in prison. Her human life would have long since ended, while he would continue to live in shame for the rest of his.

How could I have been so stupid?

Her words had shattered his hopes for happiness. She might as well have ripped out his heart to justify the unbearable pain. How could she value his love so little? His stomach clenched violently. He lunged forward and made it to the toilet just in time to throw up his last meal.

Collapsing onto the floor, he wiped his mouth with the back of a hand and then hoisted himself to his feet and shed the rest of his clothes. His body and soul naked, he walked into the hot shower, wishing he could wash away the pain as easily as the dirt on his skin.

Maybe it's for the best, he rationalized. Regardless, he screwed up royally, and he would spend the rest of his life paying for his mistake.

Chapter 48

CARA

Safe House. San Francisco.

CARA THREW OPEN the door to the roof deck and ran outside, her sobs echoing in the dark. Fog and her teary vision muted the twinkling lights on the Golden Gate Bridge. She leaned against the glass railing, wishing she'd never gone to Simon's room, wishing she'd never gotten a taste of love with yet another man she couldn't have.

The temperature had dropped sharply from earlier, and she shivered in the chilly night air.

"Need a shoulder to cry on?"

Cara froze. She swiveled her head to pinpoint the voice. The orange end of a cigarette glowed at the far end of the deck, punching a hole in the night. It shimmered and crackled as the smoker inhaled.

"Who's there?"

"Why don't you come on over and find out?" he teased. "I promise I don't bite…hard, anyway." He chuckled at his own joke. When she hesitated, he added warmly, "Just kidding. Come over and keep me company. I'm just relaxing over a beer and a smoke after my patrol with Chamuel."

She hugged herself tightly, sorry she hadn't grabbed a sweater in her haste, and wandered over toward the glowing cigarette. As she drew closer, the angle of the light through the deck's bathroom window illuminated a man sitting astride one of the chaise lounges, his legs spread wide and his boots resting on the deck.

Zeke patted the lounge next to him. "Have a seat."

She sat, pulling her legs up beneath her.

He reclined on the lounge, crossing his feet at the ankles as he took another drag on his cigarette. He was shirtless like Simon had been earlier, and his dark hair hung loosely around his tattooed shoulders. He had a red sigil similar to Simon's on his rippled chest, along with the ink on his arms and torso.

"Aren't you cold?" she asked, squeezing her gooseflesh-covered arms tighter.

He glanced at her with a rakish smile. "Nope. I don't feel heat or cold like you do. I'd give you my shirt, but it's covered in bug splatter." He winked, and his smile grew wider. "If you weren't Cham's girlfriend, I'd offer to warm you up."

Her cheeks flushed. "I'm not his girlfriend." *Anymore*, she added silently.

"Semantics." He smirked. "Either way, if I lay so much as a finger on you, Cham will hack it off and feed it to me."

He pulled the towel Sienna had left earlier from behind his back and handed it to her. "Here, wrap this around you. It should help."

Cara nestled inside the towel. It was warm to the touch and did the trick at chasing away the cold.

Zeke picked up a beer bottle from the other side of the lounge chair and tipped it at her. "Want one? They're in the fridge under the bar."

She rubbed her face with the back of a hand, ridding her cheeks of leftover dampness. "Tempting, but no, thanks."

He took a long slug from the bottle. "You don't know what you're missing."

Eyeing his cigarette, she said, "I'm surprised you smoke."

He held the cigarette in front of him and contemplated it. "Bad habit. I blame it on an old girlfriend. She turned me on to smoking. At least I don't have to worry about lung cancer."

Cara couldn't contain her surprise, assuming Nephilim were above human vices, and asked, "A Nephil girlfriend?"

His face scrunched, and he looked at her like she'd sprouted a second head. "In suburban Connecticut? Are you kidding me? There are maybe fifty Nephilim females in my entire class, and most of them live somewhere in Europe, Asia, or South America. Not to mention, they were snapped up as mates long ago by the older guys. No, to answer your question. A *human* girlfriend." He threw his butt on the deck and sat up to ground it out under a boot heel.

Taken aback, Cara said, "I thought Nephilim preferred their own kind."

He scoffed. "Yeah, if they want to stay celibate. Speaking of…The sun and the moon must rise and set on you for Cham to have broken his celibacy and violate the only sacred law we have."

Cara flushed at the mention of Simon's name. "He's celibate?"

He raised an eyebrow, and his lips kicked to the side. "Don't know. You tell me."

Her face grew hotter, and she shrank inside the towel.

"Well, based on your reaction, I guess he still is. Let's put it this way: he hasn't gotten laid since before I was born. Rumor has it, he's been celibate since the freaking Victorian era. Lots of pent-up demand there." He chuckled.

Cara wasn't sure if she should be offended. Zeke sure was irreverent. If anything, she found him refreshing.

"Tell me about..." His Guardian name stuck in her throat. "...Chamuel."

Zeke lit another cigarette and took a long drag. "He's good people, Cham. I've known him my whole life. I'd say he's like a brother, but he's more like a father. Both he and Isaac." He sat up and leaned forward. "Mind if I ask a question?"

"Sure."

He fanned a hand over himself and teased, "Why the heck would you pick an older-than-dust Nephil when you could have one like me in his sexual prime?"

She laughed at his mock earnestness. "I can't believe you asked me that."

He chuckled warmly, then stretched his legs and recrossed his boots at the ankles. "Made you laugh, though," he said with a sweet smile and took another drag.

"Just be careful not to offer yourself like that in front of my friend Sienna," Cara warned. "She might take you up on it."

He released a loud snort. "I doubt it. She's got her sights set on your Messenger."

Cara sighed. "I wouldn't hold my breath. I've given up. They nearly shed each other's blood a dozen times over the last three days. I'm getting tired of body-blocking for them."

"Don't be so sure. Twenty minutes in a dark closet would be life-altering for those two if they'd just get out of their own way." Zeke took a last drag and tossed the butt over the side of the deck.

The thought of Michael and Sienna in a closet brought a smile to her face. She had to admit talking to Zeke helped, even if she felt like she was hanging out with someone's hot younger brother. "Don't take this the wrong way, but you look about seventeen. I'm having trouble thinking of you as more than jailbait."

His eyes flashed. "Hey, I'll have you know that I shaved over forty years off my driver's license to match my perceived age."

She smirked. "So, how old are you?"

He turned his head on the cushion and suppressed a grin. "Don't you know it's impolite to ask a guy's age?"

"Yeah, right. That's my line."

"Sixty-three, if you really want to know."

"You look good for your age," she said dryly, reminded again of the Human-Nephilim age conundrum. "You were telling me about Chamuel...."

He held up his beer. "You sure you don't want one?"

She shook her head.

"Listen, Cara. I might be a smartass and act like an immature idiot, but I'm not stupid. Cham loves you, and Isaac almost kicked his ass on the plane because of it. Believe him, Cara. And please don't hurt him. He deserves better than he's allowed himself. He's never stepped over the line for anything or anyone before. Give him a chance."

Cara swallowed, feeling chastened. She let out a nervous laugh and brushed a finger under her eye to trap an escaped tear. "I don't know how to get past this, Zeke. We exchanged words before I came up here. He probably hates me now."

"Apologize and *make* it work." Zeke sat up and swung his legs over the lounge to face her. "I'll admit, you screwed the pooch when you outted him like that at the airport. Isaac will have to report him, but I won't. As far as anyone knows, I saw nothing, and I know nothing. The law is stupid. If you love each other, you should be together."

She hugged the towel more tightly around her. She had to make this right. But when? How?

"I think Isaac hates me, too."

"Nah. His bark is worse than his bite. Don't let his frosty exterior fool you. He inherited it from his mother. She's the angel of snowstorms. That said, he's Cham's best friend and super protective of him. They've been tight since Calliope and Mina died."

Cara's head popped up. "Mina? Who's Mina?"

Zeke cringed and lifted his beer. "One bottle, and I'm spilling everyone's secrets."

"Who's Mina?" she asked again, her heart suddenly pounding in anticipation.

He swore under his breath and took a deep breath, followed by a long slug of beer. "Mina was the Soul Seeker in his last Trinity. She was killed the night Calliope died. The Dark Ones used Calliope to divert Cham's attention away from Mina, killing her. He never forgave himself for their deaths. It's the reason he took a voluntary vow of celibacy as penance."

Cara's heart dropped, and she covered her mouth to catch her gasp. Squeezing her eyes shut, she shoved down the rising bile.

Zeke cleared his throat. "While I'm airing everyone's dirty laundry, if you haven't figured it out yet, Calliope was Isaac's sister."

His words were a slap in the face. What an idiot she'd been. What a selfish, stupid idiot. Simon—Chamuel—took a chance on her, and she'd failed him—badly and inexcusably.

THUD!

Cara flinched at the noise.

Sun stumbled and collapsed in a heap on the other side of the deck.

"Sun!" Zeke moved in a blur across the deck and lifted the Guardian to his feet. Cara left her towel and stumbled on one of the chairs before finding her footing and making her way over.

Sun's chest heaved, sucking in air as he draped his arm around Zeke to stand. He tried to speak, his lips forming shapes, but no sound came out.

"Calm down. It's okay," Zeke said evenly.

"F-found...in...warehouse," Sun sputtered through gasps. "Found...Dr. Solomon."

Excitement ripped through Cara. He found Kai!

"Cara," Zeke said sharply, straining under Sun's dead weight. "Go downstairs and tell the others. Have someone bring up food and water."

Cara nodded and ran for the door. She screamed over her telepathic link. *"Simon! Michael! Sun found Kai!"*

Chapter 49

CARA

Menlo Park.

CARA HELD ON tight and stared at Michael's headrest from the backseat of the Escalade while Simon broke land speed records. Zeke sat beside her with his eyes closed and his arms folded across his chest, pretending to sleep.

"Meet us at the closest rendezvous point," Simon said into his Bluetooth headset.

Simon and Isaac set two rendezvous points: one for the three warrior teams and a second, closer location for the rescue teams, from which they would transport non-Nephilim charges in or out of the attack zone. That's where Simon was headed and where the warrior teams would fly before infiltrating the warehouse.

Cara looked down at the black uniform Raphael had given her. She hadn't questioned how they'd found one small enough. He'd also offered her a small blessed dagger, like the one Michael had used to train her, but she'd refused it. She might've rethought her decision if she knew it would've come in handy to cut the tension in the car.

There was no outward evidence of their argument other than Simon's rigid shoulders. Worse, his energy had disappeared completely, like he'd dropped an iron shield around himself to keep her out. Not that she blamed him. She'd done the same on the plane.

She couldn't meet Simon's gaze after their argument and her discussion with Zeke. She hated that she'd hurt him with her shameful attack. Her anger melted away after realizing Simon's actions resulted from poor decision-making rather than outright betrayal. He had risked so much to be with her, and she had thrown it back in his face. She owed him a huge apology. But that would have to wait.

Simon pulled the SUV into the shadows and parked. He stared at the windshield. "Zeke, Michael, can you step outside for a minute?"

She gave Zeke a panicked look. He poked her leg, winked, and got out of the car. She was tempted to follow. Being alone with Simon unleashed a swarm of manic butterflies in her gut. She couldn't handle any more confrontation, not when they were so close to rescuing Kai.

He turned off the ignition, and the dim overhead light went on.

One blue eye caught her gaze in the rearview mirror, and he cleared his throat. "Can I count on you tonight?" he asked evenly.

His question unnerved her. "Yes. Can I count on you? I can't even feel your energy right now." Her words sounded more accusatory than she intended.

He slammed his palm on the steering wheel. "This isn't about us, Cara," he snapped. "The life of every person going in there tonight is on me." Both eyes now visible in the rearview mirror flashed an angry blue. "I've made enough mistakes for one week, and I can't afford to make any more."

His stinging comment drew tears to her eyes. She couldn't stop herself from biting back. "So, I'm a mistake now?"

He sighed and turned in the seat. His face crumpled, losing some of its anger. "Don't put words into my mouth. I just need to know I can rely on our Trinity…that I can rely on *you*."

"So, I don't end up like Mina?" she whispered, her lip quivering.

A look of shock and pain washed over his face, and his eyes shone like she'd never seen before. "Who told you about Mina?" he whispered.

Then it struck her—she could die, just like Mina. Simon could die tonight trying to protect her. Kai and Sara could die tonight if she failed. Out of nowhere, her lungs heaved, and the SUV caved in around her.

No air. I'm not getting any air. Cara's eyesight tunneled as she clawed at the door handle and rolled out of the SUV. Landing on her feet, she sucked in the cool night air, trying to mine it for oxygen. And then she took off, running blindly in the dark.

"*Cara!*" Michael screamed silently.

"*I've got it,*" Simon growled in her head.

Whoosh! Two massive arms hooked her beneath the armpits and lifted her into the air. The wind whipped through her hair as Simon positioned her crossways beneath him and sheltered her against his warm, muscular chest. Air rushed beneath her, reminding her of an amusement park ride gone off the rails.

"*What the hell was that about?*" Simon asked, his wings flapping above them.

THUNK! His feet hit the flat asphalt roof, and he set her down on one of the low warehouses nearby. Leaning over, he rested his hands on his knees and breathed heavily, his brilliant white wings aloft behind him.

Cara's eyes widened. His wingspan had to be at least eighteen feet. Even in the dark, it was dazzling. Then he straightened, and in the blink of an eye, his wings furled and disappeared behind him.

The adrenaline rush hit her immediately, freeing up her breathing. Even though panic no longer held her oxygen hostage, she could barely speak from her acute ordeal and the shock and awe of flying in his arms. "I…couldn't breathe…panic attack…like the day in the subway when I first saw you…Have to get my mind off of it."

Simon's brow softened. He lunged over, taking her into his arms. His lips crushed down onto hers, exploring and tasting her until the anxiety drained from her body. Her body reacted instantly, circling his lean waist with her arms and pulling his pelvis tightly against her belly. A shock of heat filled her. She hadn't realized how much she'd wanted to touch him until she cried out in relief.

His fingers cupped the sides of her head, holding her in place against his lips.

She broke away, breathless. "They can't see us, can they?"

His eyes blazed with blue fire, and his voice was husky. "Cloaked." He covered her lips with his and deepened the kiss until her lungs begged for air in a good way.

Slowly, he pulled away. "Why didn't you tell me?" he whispered, holding her against the hard planes of his pectorals.

She laid her ear against his beating heart and inhaled his musky scent mixed with citrus. "I've had the attacks under control for years until that day in the subway. This is the first one since then." She looked up and caressed his cheek. "I'm sorry for what I said before. I didn't mean it, and I hate that I hurt you. Know that I'll protect you with my life in there."

"I would expect no less." He tucked her head under his chin and kissed her hair. "I won't let you end up like Mina. I promise it on *my* life."

Before she could utter the "I love you" on the tip of her tongue, he stepped away.

"We need to go. We'll talk about everything later when we have time." He looked over the edge of the building and beckoned her with a hand.

She reared back. "We're not jumping, are we?"

A wicked grin touched his lips. "Payback's a bitch." He snatched her into his arms and leaped off the roof. She screamed the entire two seconds it took to touch the ground.

She punched him in the arm when they landed, her face beet red. "Don't ever do that again!"

He eyed her warily. "Then don't run off like a scared rabbit."

They walked back to join the others, Cara's lips still plump from their kiss. Simon instantly became engrossed in last-minute tactical details with Isaac and Raphael, who had arrived while they were away.

Cara joined Zeke and Michael by the SUV.

"Are you okay?" Michael asked with concern in his eyes.

She nodded and averted her gaze, afraid that her eyes would give too much away. Zeke smirked at her when Michael turned his back, nodding an "I told you so."

Over the next few minutes, the soft landings of Guardians were heard just outside their line of sight. Men walked into view, wings retracted and ready for battle.

Simon called over to her, Michael, and Zeke when everyone arrived. "Cara, we need you to help us find Kai within Achanelech's lair to finalize our logistics."

"I'm ready. What would you like me to do?" That would be the easy part. She'd been attuned to Kai's energy ever since she'd accepted her Calling.

"Focus on the warehouse and give us an energy read. Reach out and find Kai's exact location," he said.

Cara thought about a technique Constantina had suggested that would strengthen her abilities. She extended her hands. "Simon, Michael, join hands with me. I want to leverage the full energy of our Trinity."

They join hands. While daisy-chained together, Cara would use them as conduits to amplify her power. Reaching out slowly, she pulled energy through all of them. The effect was immediate and jolting as the Flow filled her and opened her third eye.

Eyes closed, she pushed outward with her mind as Constantina had taught her. "Based on the number of black energy voids, I'm counting well over a hundred soulless entities on the main level. They're gathered on the north side of the building, probably in the amphitheater. But I don't feel Kai on that level." The architectural drawings showed three sublevels beneath the ground. She'd explore them one by one.

Cara pushed her third eye's vision into the first sublevel and hit paydirt. Excitement shot through her. "Kai is toward the center of the building, one floor down. He's alone." Cara's gift wasn't meant for finding humans outside her Center Stone, but Sara carried Kai's DNA, so Cara should be able to find her.

Cara dove down another level, and her heart leaped. "Next level down. There's energy like Kai's. Sara!" Then, golden energy pulses of various intensities sprang up around Sara. Cara squeezed Simon's fingers. "I feel others...Nephilim. Some are injured or near death."

Emotions rushed like a flash fire through the Guardians at the mention of their brethren among the captives. Cara heard their telepathic chatter, their voices overlapping as they all spoke at once.

"Sun, didn't you feel them?" Gabe growled.

"I only felt that shitload of soulless," replied Sun defensively.

"Maybe Ishmael's with them," said Isaac.

"Who do you think is down there?" Christian asked.

Simon's hands still joined with hers and Michael's, he said aloud. "That's why we'll be wearing the listening devices to communicate. Something is preventing our natural form of communication."

He dropped Cara's hand, and the Guardian's mental chatter abruptly stopped.

Simon paced. "I'm surprised and thankful that Cara picked them up, even if we couldn't. Yet, I felt them when she did."

"Simon?" Cara spoke up behind him, wanting to share her hypothesis.

He turned. "What is it?"

"When you let go of my hand, I stopped hearing the Guardians in my head. I think between us…," she said, moving a finger in a triangular motion between her, him, and Michael. "When we share energy, we link *all* our gifts."

Simon froze mid-step. "You heard us speaking behind the veil of silence on our Guardian frequency."

"Yes. Everyone spoke at once when I mentioned the Nephilim."

Michael chimed in. "I heard them too."

Cara released a tense breath. "There's more. When I dropped Simon's hand, something else became visible, as if Simon's energy had cloaked it from our vision. There are two ice-cold spots close to where the Nephilim are being held. Not your garden-variety energy. Whatever it is has a much different footprint than the soulless or any of us."

Simon's expression darkened. "Is the energy active or static?"

This time, Cara only used Michael as a conduit. Holding his hands, she quickly swept through the floors. Her voice shook. "Active. They've moved to Kai's floor."

Simon nodded. "Thanks. That gives me a few ideas."

He turned to the Guardians. "Follow me. Raphael and I will run each team through logistics one last time."

Cara stayed behind with Michael. A wave of exhaustion hit her, buckling her knees.

"Whoa, are you okay?" Michael caught her in his strong arms and pulled her into his chest.

She shook off the dizziness. "Sorry. Channeling that much energy took a bit out of me. I'll be fine. I just need a few minutes." Taking a deep breath, she stood firmly on her own. Constantina warned her that using her gift would always come with a price, but that she'd build her tolerance over time.

One by one, the teams deployed, taking flight and cloaking. When everyone else was gone, Simon and Zeke approached her and Michael.

Simon wore a sober expression. "Are you ready?"

Cara nodded, ignoring her nervous stomach.

"Zeke will take Michael. Cara, you're with me." Simon glanced at Zeke and tapped his ear beneath his flowing hair. "Zeke, hook up our veils as soon as you get there so I can give you an update from the inside team."

"You got it." Then he grinned at Michael. "Nephilim Air Flight 201, now departing. All aboard." Zeke hooked his arms around Michael, and they disappeared from sight.

Simon put an arm around Cara and drew her into the warmth of his body. He tipped her head up and cradled her jaw gently in his palm.

"Before you ask, we're cloaked," he said softly. He passed his thumb gently over her bottom lip and held her gaze. His lips descended on hers with hungry desperation. Melting into him, she inhaled his scent, wanting to lose herself in the firm contours of his body, but something wasn't right. His kiss, tender and passionate, told her what he wouldn't. This would be their last.

He slowly retreated, and his energy slipped like sand through her fingers. "Time to go," he whispered.

Swallowing a lump in her throat, she numbly allowed him to turn her in his arms and position her for flight.

He tucked her securely against his chest with an arm above her breasts and another low on her hips. His wings unfurled and billowed behind him like sails filling with air. He crouched low, then launched them into the sky with a few powerful wingbeats. Even with his body pressed to hers, she had never felt so alone.

Chapter 50

CONSTANTINA

Safe House. San Francisco.

CONSTANTINA ENTERED THE safe house and met Chloe at the top of the stairs, where the little dog stood quietly, wagging her tail in greeting. Constantina knelt and smoothed the Sentinel's wrinkled brow, then signaled for Chloe to give her report.

Chloe's gentle voice spoke in the angelic tongue, her message a wispy breeze in Constantina's mind. *"Demon gone. Chamuel keep Cara safe."*

Constantina beamed at Cara's loyal companion. *"Well done, dearest girl. Stay with Sienna, and protect her until the others return."*

Chloe licked Constantina's hand, then trotted off and climbed the stairs on silent paws, returning to her watch.

The roar of motorcycles in the distance grew louder.

Raphael's call hadn't been enough to summon her old friend, but at her request, he'd been more than happy to assist. He had secured this residence — that of his current charge — in exchange for a favor.

The doorbell rang a few minutes later as rumbling Harley-Davidsons filled the street. Constantina smiled. The Avenging Angel's Biker Club had arrived.

She glided downstairs to open the door.

A tall, burly, and attractive Hispanic man with a shock of dark hair stood on the threshold wearing biker leathers and a cocky smile.

Her eyes lit up at the sight of Angel Benitez — the leader and Avenging Angel referred to in the motorcycle club's name. Extending an arm, she placed a hand on his shoulder in a traditional greeting and used his proper angelic name. "Benedictine, it's been a long time, dear one."

He returned the formal gesture, then swept her into a bear hug and squeezed her tightly. "Eae, so good to see you. I figured this was Guardian business when I got Raphael's message. But you know I'd only do this for you. Must be big to take you out of hiding."

If he only knew. "You don't like the name Constantina?" she asked with a demure flutter of lashes. He was one of the few she allowed to use her angelic name. Unlike the Guardianship, Council rules dictated that descended angels use their given names during their earthly lifetimes to show respect for their human form.

He smiled, his teeth glowing white in the low light. "You'll always be Eae to me," he said with genuine affection over the escalating engine noise.

She tapped her ear and pointed outside. "Would you mind dropping a veil of silence to avoid unwanted attention?"

"Anything for you, angel." He winked and snapped his fingers. The street went silent.

Angel patted her shoulder as they ascended the stairs to the living room. "I appreciate you taking care of Brett in Connecticut. By the time Adela called to tell me little brother had vanished, he was already on a plane—the little bastard," he said with an affectionate growl.

She smiled. "Isaac was more than happy to assist at my request, and, in return, I thank you for arranging the use of Brett's beautiful home as our safe house."

He waved a hand. "*Da nada.* He's used to renting it out when he's gone. He's got some time before his tour ends."

"By the way, Cara made contact with Brett while he was in Connecticut," she said. Exactly as she intended.

"Really?" He wore a look of surprise for only a second, then threw back his head and laughed. "You're already ahead in this celestial game of chess we're playing, aren't you?"

She shrugged. "Maybe for a move or two, but I take nothing for granted…What are our numbers outside?" she asked.

Angel pursed his lips and squinted at the ceiling. "We're about sixty strong," he said and shook a finger at her. "You got yourself in some bad shit, *mija.* I figured you'd need extra muscle, so we're picking up another forty on the way."

She couldn't argue his point and nodded gravely. "That should do."

Angel, standing in heavy boots and riding leathers, eyed Constantina's velvet cloak. "I hope you have something to ride in befitting an 'Angel Who Thwarts Demons,'" Angel said, air-quoting her divine origin.

"What do you think?" she said, wearing a sly smile, and slipped off her cloak, revealing a black Guardian uniform and weapons belt. She discarded the cloak on the nearest chair.

Angel's head bobbed in approval. "You make one badass demon slayer." Then he rubbed his hands together in anticipation and gave her another white-toothed grin. "Let's get this show on the road, mija. I'll leave my ride here. We'll be more comfortable on Brett's Harley."

She followed him downstairs to the garage. Angel grabbed an extra helmet and motorcycle jacket Brett had stashed in the locker at the bottom of the stairs and handed them to Constantina. The stainless-steel garage door ascended to reveal bikers packing the street. Angel kick-started the bike—the engine rumbled to life beneath him, and Constantina hopped on the back.

Angel rolled the bike out and signaled for Paco, his second-in-command, to follow. They took off with the club in formation behind them. Constantina was eager to join Chamuel and the others. They needed the backup, and she couldn't afford to be late.

Chapter 51

CARA

Menlo Park.

THEIR FEET HIT the ground with a soft thud thirty yards from the two-story warehouse. Simon held her hand and whispered to someone through the earpiece in what she now recognized as the angelic language. *Either that or he's talking to himself,* Cara thought.

Zeke and Michael suddenly appeared. Michael's hand rested on Zeke's shoulder, and Zeke's hand clutched Simon's forearm to connect the veils.

"Isaac's team disabled the alarms on the side door around the corner," Simon said.

"We'll go first and give an all-clear," Zeke said.

Simon said something unintelligible to the person listening on the other end of his earpiece and then said to Zeke, "Good. The next checkpoint is inside."

"See ya in a few." Zeke dropped his hand, and he and Michael blinked out.

Cara swallowed past a dry throat. As much as she wanted to save Kai, she couldn't shake the dread plaguing her. Only a few cars were parked out front, giving the building a deceptive air of desertion, though she felt the soulless army inside. Were they workers or assassins? Apparently, Achanelech employed both. Raphael confirmed a legitimate business ran at this location.

Floodlights mounted on the building illuminated the entrances, while the rest of the perimeter remained shrouded in darkness. When they were close enough, Simon snugged them against the side of the building, and they crept along the outer wall. Damp mist hung in the night air.

They rounded the corner. Cara gasped. Two men stood guard with assault rifles. Simon shoved her behind him, covering her with his body. "Don't move," he said. Her heart pounded. Cloaking wouldn't protect them from a spray of automatic gunfire.

She poked her head around his elbow in time to see Michael appear, ninja-like, behind the man on the left. He struck, twisting the man's arm with lightning speed until it popped. The guard screamed. His weapon dropped to the ground as the second man lifted his. Zeke appeared, knocked the assault rifle from the guard's hands, and stabbed him in the chest with a glowing dagger.

Cara covered her eyes and heard a sound like sugar pouring from a five-pound bag. She looked through her fingers and expected to see a body crumpled in a bloody heap. Instead, a pile of black sand lay on the cement.

Zeke spun. The dagger was gone, a blinding sword in its place. He sliced the sharp blade across Michael's target. The body blazed and disintegrated into a second pile of black sand.

Zeke picked up the large guns, hesitated, then shrugged and tossed them behind the bushes. He grabbed Michael, and they disappeared. The door creaked open.

Cara rubbed her eyes. "Where are the bodies?"

"Angelic weapons disintegrate the soulless. Less of a mess. Same with demons, except they turn into black ash."

"I thought the soulless were human?" she squeaked.

"They *were*...Once their soul is gone, they're susceptible to our weapons."

She glanced at the bushes. "Why didn't Zeke take the guns?"

"We can't cloak guns, only angelic weapons or something blessed like the dagger Raphael gave you." Cara didn't mention she'd left the dagger behind.

Michael poked his head out the door, cutting off her opportunity for further questions. Glancing in their direction, he waved them inside.

Simon whispered into his earpiece, then paused to listen. "Let's go."

When Cara stepped through the door, the unmistakable taste of tar coated her tongue. Malevolence filled the place.

She clung to Simon's hand as they worked their way around the first floor with Zeke and Michael. Décor obviously wasn't a high priority. The place had as much charm as an old garage with gray cinder-block walls and worn industrial carpeting. Offices lined the first-floor perimeter, surrounding a cafeteria, a large amphitheater, and a cavernous warehouse.

Red light dots shone from the security cameras. Cara released a breath after they passed beneath one without setting off an alarm.

They worked their way inward to where Kai was held below them. After-hours security lights lit their path as they searched.

As they drew closer, Simon put a finger to the earpiece, then reached toward Zeke and Michael's energy to connect their veils. "The staircase is around the corner to the right. Raphael and his team passed the lab and are heading to the prison to find Sara and the Nephilim."

Simon disconnected the veils, shutting down communication and taking the lead with Zeke and Michael following.

"Where is everyone?" Cara asked, unsettled by the eerie silence. For all the bodies located inside the building, shouldn't someone be milling around?

He slowed. "It's a trap. Say the word, and I'll take you out."

Of course. "No, I'm in." She wouldn't abandon Kai.

"Atta girl." He squeezed her shoulder and met her gaze. "I should've told you. I don't want any more secrets between us."

"I appreciate that."

Simon gave a small smile. "Let's find Kai."

Shoving aside her nerves, Cara tuned into Kai's vibration and used it as a GPS. They found the center stairwell. Gray metal stairs led the way down. Kai's energy grew stronger as they exited the staircase. Simon reconnected the veils.

"Behind that door," Cara said, pointing.

"Got it," Zeke said, separating the veils and disappearing.

A few seconds later, Zeke uncloaked, appearing with Michael, and hovered over the electric door lock. Placing a device beside the keypad, he punched in a series of numbers.

The lock popped and released as a deluge of black energy assaulted Cara's senses, and armed soulless flooded the hallway from both directions.

Chapter 52

CARA

Le Feu's Warehouse.

UNCLIPPING TWO HILTS from his belt, a sword blazed to life in each of Zeke's hands. Simon shoved her and Michael through the doorway into the lab. "Michael! Keep Cara safe!" he said and slammed the door.

Cara stumbled in the darkness, her heart pounding. Michael's fingers grazed her arm to signal his position while the melee ensued outside. Scanning for dark energy, she came up empty, but Kai blazed like a beacon across the lab. "Kai?" she whispered.

The overhead lights snapped on, bathing them in fluorescent light. Cara squinted in the sudden glare. Equipment surrounded them in an extensive laboratory. An exhausted-looking Kai stood across the room, wearing a white lab coat. Behind him, a tattooed thug dressed in a black leather vest held a knife to Kai's throat.

Cara swallowed hard. She hadn't picked up dark energy because, *duh*, the thug was human with an intact soul.

Tattoo sneered and jerked his arm tighter around Kai's neck. "Well, well, Doc. Your little friend arrived right on time."

Kai gritted his teeth but said nothing.

Cara avoided Kai's gaze and glared at Tattoo. Her mind raced. Had Kai already given them what they wanted, or was he just bait? She shoved down her panic and channeled the outward calm she used with irrational clients experiencing unexpected market downturns. "What do you want, and how can I help?"

Tattoo chortled, raking his gaze down her body. "My list is long, but it's not about what I want. Our master, Le Feu, would like a word."

Cara glared and said evenly, "If Le Feu wants me, let Dr. Solomon go."

The thug jerked Kai backward. "I have a better idea. Why don't I slit his throat and watch him bleed?"

Kai's eyes met hers, then shifted to a point behind her. She read his signal too late.

"Michael! Watch out!" she screamed through their Trinity link as meaty hands grabbed her from behind. She got a whiff of her attacker's cologne, and the heavy floral notes made her nose twitch.

A loud thump sounded on the other side of the door, followed by a blood-curdling scream. Cara let out a violent sneeze.

Kai used the distraction. He trapped Tattoo's knife-hand in a wrist lock, shoved his hips back into Tattoo's groin, and spun beneath his arm, wrenching it at an unnatural angle. Tattoo let out an agonizing wail, the knife clattered to the ground, and Tattoo collapsed on the floor.

Nice work, Kai! Cara thought, torn between shock and admiration. Beside her, Michael was a whir of motion, releasing deep grunts with every blow. A bone snapped, and the guy holding Michael screamed and dropped into a heap.

Michael launched an attack on the man holding Cara.

She stumbled clear of the two men and shouted a warning, "Kai!" as Tattoo lunged for Kai's legs. Kai hit the floor with a hard clunk, and Tattoo jumped on top of him. He landed a punch while Kai did his best to block the next few from his position on the floor.

"And this is for smashing my nuts!" Tattoo croaked, ready to return the favor. No way he'd make Kai a eunuch on her watch.

Cara dove onto Tattoo's back, hooked her arm around his neck, and squeezed with all her might.

"Bitch!" Tattoo gasped, clawing at her arm before reaching back and grabbing a fistful of hair. Cara's eyes watered, and she saw stars as he used his hold to flip her over his shoulder. She screamed, landing on her back, the wind knocked out of her.

Tattoo loomed over her, a nice-sized clump of auburn hair hanging from his fingers. He tossed the strands, straddled her, and locked his hands around her throat. "If we had more time, I'd teach you to show a little respect," he leered, saliva stretching between his lips. He planted his thumbs on her throat.

She caught a panicked look in Michael's eyes when he spotted them. His opponent seized the opening and swept Michael's legs out from under him.

She had no plans to die today. She'd thank Michael later for teaching her fifty ways to break a chokehold. Clamping her chin down, she shifted her hip beneath her, ready to monkey paw Tattoo off her, when the door burst open with a battle cry.

Hands from above ripped Tattoo off her. He went flailing twenty feet across a table, sending lab equipment crashing to the ground before he landed in a crumpled pile on the other side.

Simon sailed after him in a white flash. Fists *thunked* on flesh amidst screams and the sickening crunch of cartilage.

Cara flinched and crawled to Kai. "Are you okay?" she asked, rubbing her throat.

He sat up, hooked an arm around her, and pulled her close. "Thank God, you're okay."

She inhaled his warm, familiar scent mixed with a few too many days without a shower and returned his hug. Then she helped him to his feet and checked him for injuries. His face had started to bruise, but he was fine.

A few more karate *hi-yas* and Michael stood, panting, over the men lying in writhing mounds at his feet.

Simon reappeared, wiping blood from his hand onto his pants. "Let's go. Zeke's outside. Isaac's team went down to free the others. Stay behind me."

Simon paused at the heavy metal door and pushed it open a crack. Holding a finger to his lips, he motioned them to take cover beside the door. Then Simon whispered into the silent hallway, "Zeke?"

Michael hovered beside Cara while she held Kai's hand, her gaze glued to Simon and the door.

Silence.

Simon drew a hilt from his belt, stepped through the opening, and stumbled backward, "Sphinx" hissing from his lips.

The icy wall of energy hit Cara as the door flew open and an enormous humanoid with hair and skin the color of white marble snatched Simon off his feet, immobilizing him. Simon released an ear-splitting screech like nothing Cara had ever heard. The Sphinx clamped a hand over Simon's mouth, squelching the noise, while a scowling Simon struggled against the creature's grip until his body went limp.

Simon's energy disappeared.

"Simon!" Cara's telepathic cry hit muffled silence. This icy being must be at the heart of the Nephilim's communication problem. Her pulse quickened; this thing was one of a pair.

Before Cara could react, rough-looking soulless men streamed through the open door, guns raised. Her heart sank as they were all grabbed and marched into the hall.

And there it was. The creature's twin, carrying Zeke, limp as a ragdoll, banded beneath its arm. Zeke's feet dangled uselessly like Simon's, and he wore the same frustrated scowl behind a mitt–sized hand covering his mouth. Facial expressions seemed to be all they could control.

Simon's Sphinx spoke to Cara in a hollow, inhuman voice. "If you fight us, your Nephilim will die." Like she had a choice.

"Come," said the other Sphinx, carrying a pissed-off Zeke, as it took the lead. Armed soulless herded her, Michael, and Kai behind them, while Simon's Sphinx hemmed them in from the rear.

They trudged up the stairs in silence. Cara hoped the other teams had gotten an earful from Simon's communication device and sent backup.

On the off chance that the Sphinx had only blocked Guardian communications, she called Michael. *"Michael? Can you hear me?"* She waited for a response…nothing. Again, *"Michael?"*

Nothing. *Shit.*

Cara reviewed her long lesson on the Flow. The Trinity channel she shared with Simon and Michael was attuned to their energy, and only they could access it. But there were other channels. The Guardians had an entire spectrum to themselves, and there were channels based on proximity — like the one Zeke used to tell her Isaac was a stick in the mud at the briefing. Intent was all it took for access. Staring at Michael's back, she called again, trying a different frequency, *"Michael?"*

Another voice answered. *"Cara, how are you doing that?"*

Her lips parted in surprise. *"Kai?"* she asked, remembering her discussion with Michael in Central Park. Only Universal Receivers could pick up conversations without intent. The opposite of Michael, a Universal Sender, who could send messages to anyone regardless of distance. Even so, with the Sphinx close by, why could she reach Kai but not Michael? Maybe because he was her Center Stone? Whatever. She'd figure that out later.

"Yup. I heard you shout the warning to Michael and the big guy, Simon. Who are these people, and how did you get mixed up in all this?"

She suppressed a smile. *"They're friends. We came to get you and Sara out of here. You wouldn't believe the rest if I told you."*

Kai snorted. *"You'd be surprised what I'd believe after the last few days. You were right about Le Feu. He used me to lure you here…I think he wants to kill you,"* he said after some hesitation.

If Le Feu wanted her dead, she'd be dead already. She was more worried about Kai. *"We knew it was a trap walking in."*

"They have Sara. She's in the dungeon with someone named Ishmael and ten of his brothers."

That explained the Nephilim she sensed at the rendezvous point. *"Did Sara tell you that?"*

"No, I heard Ishmael's voice in my head yesterday, just like I hear yours now — which, for the record, freaked me the hell out. Seems he could only communicate when those big creepy fucks, Chaos and Destruction, were out of range."

She was right. The Sphinx twins blocked Nephilim and Trinity communication. Obviously, she'd found a loophole, but that didn't explain why Kai could hear her. To her knowledge, Center Stones had no special gifts.

"*Cara, did you get the notes I sent you?*" he asked with sudden urgency.

Melanie's question about the notes came rushing back. "*No, but I bet I know where they are. I moved. Long story. That's what Le Feu wants?*"

"*Yes, an equally long story… Mel is one of them,*" he said, his words laced with disgust. "*They brought her to the lab yesterday. I can't believe she'd do this to me…to our family —* "

Cara wished she could give him a calming touch. "*It wasn't her fault. I'll explain later, I promise.*" Cara knew well how Kai processed what he considered betrayal. This would be hard enough for Melanie, but losing Kai over it would be unfair. Still, one less piece of bad news to break.

They arrived at the open doors of the Amphitheatre, and the Sphinx twin holding Zeke stepped aside. One of the soulless guards dug his fingers into Cara's upper arm and propelled her through the doorway ahead of the others.

Soulless filled the seats; their black energy sucked at Cara the deeper she went inside, the taste of tar thickening on her tongue enough to gag. On the stage below, a sharply dressed man and an attractive, raven-haired woman sat on a dais in a pair of high-backed throne chairs.

Cara recognized them immediately.

The subway creep with the V-shaped scar and the Sentinel.

Chapter 53

CARA

Le Feu's Warehouse.

"THAT'S LE FEU on stage with Emily, The Foundation's rep at Forrester," Kai said silently as he was pushed through the doorway after her. That's not all she is, Cara thought dryly.

The Sphinx and soulless shuttled the rest of their party into the amphitheater, every seat filled with soulless hunters, and locked them inside. The goons holding her and Kai shoved them downward on the center steps before jerking them to a halt midway to the dais.

Le Feu's voice boomed from below. "I see our Angelorum guests have arrived with our trusted scientist. Just in time for the *festivities.*"

Like a flock of predatory birds, the hunter's heads turned in unison, their leering gazes fixing on her and Kai. Tendrils of black energy slithered like boa constrictors, probing Cara for vulnerabilities. She threw up a shield with a simple protection prayer, dulling the tarry taste and sickening urge to vomit.

A child's low whimpering sounded from the dais behind the floor-to-ceiling theater curtains, sending a chill over Cara's skin. Two minions parted the velvet drapes, and another rolled a wooden platform onto the stage. Kai's daughter lay on top, heavy ropes binding her hands and feet to the platform.

"Sara!" Kai screamed and struggled to escape his captor.

"Daddy!" Sara shouted, her small limbs wriggling against the bindings.

Caressing his cane's ruby top, Le Feu glowered at Kai. "Dr. Solomon, unless you'd like me to plunge a knife into your daughter's beating heart, I'd suggest you both be quiet." Kai froze beside Cara and paled as Sara cried softly, staying otherwise silent.

Cara swallowed hard, trying to figure out what to do. Where the hell were Isaac and the other teams? Even with them, they were woefully outnumbered. Whatever little she could do to raise their chances of getting out of here alive, she'd do it.

Think, think, think!

An idea sparked. She may not be able to fight her way out, but she could buy time, if only by distraction with a cheap parlor trick.

Gathering energy into her chest, she shot it through her pores into her captor, blasting him backward into the startled crowd. "Let her go!" she thundered.

"Holy shit!" Kai mumbled over their bond, staggering with his goon from the blowback.

"I see you've had a good teacher," Le Feu said dryly, his penetrating gaze uncomfortably warm.

"The best," Cara said, hoping to live long enough to make Constantina proud. "So, why did you want a word with me? Need someone to manage your portfolio? Or," she gestured to the hideous 1970s décor. "Some decorating tips, perhaps?"

Le Feu scowled. "Don't play with me, girl. You know exactly why you're here."

Cara crossed her arms. "Actually, I don't. Why don't you enlighten me?"

Le Feu chortled. "So, that's how you want to play it? Fine." He rose from his chair and paced. "Since your education appears to be lacking, I shall do just that—enlighten you. If it were up to me, you'd be demon food. But it's not me who is so deeply interested in you, but the Morning Star. You see, you're a pawn in an angelic game of chess, albeit the winning piece."

She shook her head and *tsked*, hoping to keep him talking. "Dude, I'm an investment banker. The only thing I can help anyone *win* is a better return on their assets."

"If that was all you could do, you'd be dead," Le Feu said blandly, his gaze boring into her. "Where shall I begin? What do you know?"

Cara glanced at her nails and shrugged. "That you're pathetic, soul-sucking fallen angels who use soulless humans to do your dirty work. How's that?"

Le Feu's eyes bulged. "I will not tolerate disrespect! I promised to deliver you alive, not necessarily unharmed. But the rest of your friends are expendable."

"Cara, tone it down. Are you trying to get us killed?" Kai's voice echoed in her head as Achanelech shoved a wave of fire toward Michael. Ignoring Kai, Cara shot out an arm, casting her energy into a bright, sparkling shield. The fire hit and dissipated. Fatigue washed over her, signaling the dwindling of her energy reserves from flexing her nascent skills.

"Nicely done," Le Feu said through gritted teeth. "I wonder how many it will take to drain you dry." He had a point, and they both knew it. She needed more training to develop endurance. At best, she had one more tactical block in her.

Cara scowled. "Go ahead. Tell your story." Just as he knew she'd depleted her energy, she knew his pride burned to showcase his genius.

With a conciliatory smile, Le Feu resumed pacing, cane tapping, free hand tucked into a pants pocket. "True, we were cast down to this chunk of rock, but you know what they say, 'Better to rule in Hell, or in this case—on earth—than to serve in Heaven'...or rot in one of its prisons. But I digress...."

He stopped to face her. "Rather than leave well enough alone, three hundred do-gooder Hosts followed us and formed the Angelorum. They were gifted with a small, sanctioned army of Nephilim, while we were left to fend for ourselves. So, we create the army you see here," he said, sweeping a hand around the Amphitheatre, then graciously nodded to his Sentinel. "And, thanks to my lovely consort, Emanelech, we have the Sphinx, her personal ice minions, who have proven quite effective against your Nephilim."

After a dramatic pause, Le Feu continued, "We've coexisted with the Angelorum for over two thousand years. The prophecy says there will be—pardon the pun—a fight 'til the death, between us, casting the others back to where they respectively belong and allowing the other party the freedom to rule, so on and so forth. Your birth, Miss Collins, was the start of that prophecy. You are the First of the Twelve, the ringleader who will lead the battle of the righteous, which is why the Morning Star is so anxious to speak with you."

Le Feu's gaze shifted to Kai. "Thanks to Dr. Solomon, we hope to gain a competitive advantage, as they say. We will use his genetically engineered vaccine to create our own Nephilim. If his formula fails? No mind. We have others working on the project." He shrugged, nonplussed. "You see, Dr. Solomon has already delivered the one thing the others cannot—*you*."

Tinkling laughter echoed from the shadows in the back of the Amphitheatre. "I see the sin of pride still drives you. You shouldn't congratulate yourself just yet, Achanelech."

Le Feu's head shot up.

Cara's heart soared as Constantina stepped from the shadows, a sword shimmering in her hand. Her mentor's blonde hair was pulled into a tight ponytail, her demeanor hardened and battle-ready.

Achanelech's gaze filled with distaste. "Eae. It's been too long," he said, his tone mocking. "Thought you were in hiding. To what do I owe the pleasure of this visit, *O Angel Who Thwarts Demons?*"

Cara blinked. She'd never thought to ask Constantina's angelic name.

"Not long enough, apparently, and I don't bring pleasure to demons," Constantina said blithely, wearing a bland smile.

Le Feu rolled his eyes and head along with them. "Must you always be so…*literal*?" he spat with a look of disdain.

"I think you mean *honest*," she retorted.

His hand twitched on his cane, and he bit out a snide reply, "Since we are being *honest*, lose any children lately?"

Cara silently gasped. Constantina had lost a child?

Her mentor's small shoulders tensed, her fingers flexing around the sword's hilt. "Might I ask you the same question?" Her gaze bore into him with the precision of an ice pick.

His face reddened, and his forked tongue darted out with a hiss. "Unlessss you have an army behind you, Eae, I doubt even you can take me by yourself." He tutted and gestured toward Simon and Zeke, still bound by the Sphinx. "Your Guardians won't be any help. Not to mention, you're surrounded by my minions who are more than capable of taking down a *human*, angelic or otherwise."

Constantina gave a soft snort. "Must it always come down to violence with you? There are other ways."

She slowly descended the steps toward the dais.

"Stop!" Le Feu bolted across the stage, his leathery black wings unfurling behind him. "Unless you want me to spill the precious blood of your First."

"We both know that would be unwise," Constantina said evenly.

Black fire lit Le Feu's eyes. "There's one thing you're right about, Eae—there are other ways." In a blink, the ruby top slid from the cane, revealing a serrated dagger, and held the glinting blade to Sara's cheek. "Dr. Solomon, you have a choice. Cara or Sara? Funny, the similarity of those names. Are their lives equally as interchangeable?"

Cara gasped.

Kai looked at Cara, horrified. "He can't ask me to make that choice."

"Oh, but I just did." The blade's tip drew a drop of blood, and Sara's whimpering grew louder.

Le Feu's face darkened. "Choose, Dr. Solomon."

Kai's face was panic-stricken. *"I can't choose,"* he whispered through their bond.

"Choose your daughter, Kai," Cara replied softly as a man grabbed her from behind and rested cold steel beside her jugular, setting off a fruitless tussle between Simon and the Sphinx.

She'd be defenseless if she used her energy again, so she'd have to do this the old-fashioned way. Heart racing, she grasped the man's knife arm and twisted into him. She kneed him in the groin as she pulled his arm back and forced him to the ground with a shriek of pain. She smirked and sank her fingers into the pressure point on his neck that Michael had shown her, rendering him unconscious.

"Stupid girl!" Le Feu said, flinging the dagger at Kai with inhuman force.

Time slowed as the blade traveled end over end. Cara screamed and launched her body into the knife's path.

"NO!" Simon roared above her.

Agony tore into her side as she fell with a hard *thunk*, slamming her ribs into the stairs as her head bounced off another tread.

"Cara!" Kai yelled.

Cara's cheek rested awkwardly on a cold stair. From her vantage point, she saw Gabriel appear behind Kai's captor with a blazing sword. Black sand collapsed to the floor. Then Kai was kneeling beside her. Relief consumed her.

"*I'll always love you, Kai...,*" she whispered telepathically and surrendered to the darkness.

Chapter 54

KAI

Le Feu's Warehouse.

KAI'S FOOTING WAS tenuous on the steps, so he couldn't replicate Cara's self-defense move to disable his captor. He'd never thought his three years of judo during high school would pay off as well as it had in the lab. Straining helplessly against his captor, he watched in stunned horror as Cara launched her body between him and the blade.

"NO!" screamed Simon, the big guy from the lab, his limbs useless in the Sphinx's stranglehold.

The knife struck Cara, and she collapsed onto the steps. Blood flowed rapidly around the hilt of the blade. *Holy shit.* Had the blade nicked her heart?

The doors burst open, and the stage curtains parted. Over one hundred winged angels stormed the Amphitheatre. Kai trusted they were the good guys. Still, he had to blink a few times to process the sight, then shouted for Sara.

In a blur of white wings, an angel with long, black braids scooped her up and flew out the door to what Kai hoped was safety.

His captor screamed, his grip loosening from Kai's neck. Twisting away, Kai spotted a huge red-haired guy who plunged a shining blade into the guy who had restrained him. Kai's brain barely registered the body disintegrate in front of his eyes, or the battle raging around him in a swirl of wings, blinding swords, screams, and rushing sand.

"Cara!" Kai dropped to his knees in a spreading pool of blood. Heart pounding, he reached for solutions. Cara had saved him from having to choose between two people he loved, but if he didn't act quickly, the result would be the same. Taking a deep breath, he reeled in his panic.

"I'll always love you, Kai…," Cara whispered in his head as her eyes slipped shut and she stilled.

Out of thin air, two huge men with swords appeared behind the Sphinx who held Simon and drove their weapons home, freeing him. Simon was at

Kai's side and on his knees in two strides. He pulled Cara into his lap and cradled her. Agony twisted Simon's features as Cara's blood soaked his clothes.

"We need to get her out of here," he said with hoarse desperation.

"No," Kai snapped. Moving her would be a death sentence. Hating the idea, he only had one option. Kai removed the syringe from his sock, shrugged out of his lab coat, and shoved it at Simon. "Put pressure on the wound."

Taking the white coat, Simon glanced at Michael. Six angels with blinding weapons retracted their wings, joining Michael and creating a circular wall of protection insulating them from the fray.

A bloody aerosol mist escaped Cara's lips, which meant the knife had pierced a lung. Kai leaned in and put an ear to Cara's chest, confirming his hypothesis. He had to work fast before she bled out.

"Give me access to her chest," Kai demanded.

Simon acted quickly, repositioning her on his lap.

Kai slammed the vaccine syringe into her heart, the fastest delivery into her bloodstream. He calculated the healing rate and circulatory regeneration for her body mass. The dosage was for a two-hundred-pound man. He didn't know if more was better, but he'd find out in less than three minutes. He had even less time to remove the knife before her tissue healed around it.

Jaw tense, Simon asked, "What can I do?"

They locked gazes. "I need my hands free for CPR. Put pressure on the wound, and on my count, pull the knife out on three. Understand?"

Simon nodded stoically and grasped the jeweled hilt firmly with one hand while preparing to apply pressure with the other.

"One, two, three!"

In one smooth tug, Simon slid the knife from Cara's chest.

Kai said a silent prayer—to a God he didn't believe in—then held Cara's wrist, feeling for a pulse. It was weak but there. He touched an ear to her heart, monitoring the thready beat as it faded to silence.

"Put her down flat!" he instructed Simon. Terror filled Simon's eyes as he moved her with lightning speed.

Kai started CPR with a single-minded focus.

I will not let you die. I will not let you die. Cara, please don't leave us, please don't leave me. I'm so sorry.

He counted off his compressions and filled her good lung with air. Using his sleeve, he brushed perspiration from his brow and coppery blood from his lips without slowing.

Come back, Cara! Please don't leave me.

Her pale skin grew whiter, her eyelashes resting in delicate crescents on her cheeks. Kai vowed not to quit until she came back or he died of exhaustion. Rivulets of sweat ran down his sides beneath his shirt as he mindlessly counted, compressed, and blew breath through her blood-covered lips.

He checked his watch. Over three minutes.

He checked her pulse. None.

Please, God, don't let her die. Help me save her. Don't leave me, Cara…I'll always love you, too. I'm so sorry.

Kai's vision blurred, and he kept going.

CARA

A YOUNG WOMAN stepped from the warm, loving light. "Welcome, my sweet girl."

Cara's heart surged. "Grandma?" she asked breathlessly. Cara was only four years old when Grandma Hannah died, an old woman by then. Here, she looked like she'd stepped from the wedding photo kept on her father's desk in their New Jersey home.

The smiling woman nodded and took Cara's hands in hers. "What a lovely woman you've become. I'm so proud of you. We all are."

Cara glanced around the bright, loving mist that shrouded everything but them. "Is this Heaven?"

Hannah squeezed her hands. "Not quite. We're on the Bridge, just outside."

As if staring through a glass floor, Cara glanced at the scene below and the silver cord tethering her to the body lying beside Simon while Kai performed CPR. Their love tugged at the cord, trying to reel her back. With a shy glance, she said to Hannah, "I can't stay. They need me."

Hannah's smile held a heavenly radiance. "That's why we're meeting here. There's no going back once you pass through Heaven's gates, and your time has not yet come. For now, you must follow your soul's journey, trusting in yourself and who you are to guide you." Hannah glanced down. "Know, too, that he holds a piece of your soul, which you gave willingly. You're destined to be rejoined. Look inside, then see him."

Cara's heart stuttered. Who did she mean? Kai or Simon?

The glimmer of knowledge she had found during her Calling returned. She waited a beat and looked inward, seeking an answer. Like a key unlocking a treasure chest and exposing the riches inside, she *remembered*.

Hannah smiled. "Now, you understand…You are a Soul Seeker, but the soul you truly sought was your own."

Her surprised gaze found Simon. A glistening seed lay within him, beside his heart. He was the *One*. He had *always been* her soulmate. Her soul's seed, a beacon to find him. Cara's gaze shifted to Kai, their connection now clear. Theirs was a debt, now repaid, sealing their loyalty to one another. The truth of it, setting her free.

Cara hugged her grandmother. "Thank you."

"Return to them," Hannah said, returning the hug. "But, remember. You must discover who you were *before* this life. Your true essence. He who holds a piece of your soul is the key to your self-discovery. Godspeed, my dear."

"Will I remember this?" Cara asked with a final squeeze.

"When it's time," Hannah said, wearing an enigmatic smile.

"I love you," Cara said.

"I love you, too. We shall meet again."

Cara closed her eyes and fell into blackness.

KAI

BREATH BRUSHED KAI'S cheek. Pressing an ear to Cara's chest, he found a heartbeat. Tears of relief rolled down his cheeks. "She's back."

Simon's broad shoulders slumped, but he carried the haunted look of a man who had stared into the abyss.

The bleeding had stopped. Kai glanced at Simon and rose. "You need to get her out of here while I find my daughter."

Simon touched his ear and smiled weakly. "No need. Your daughter is safe. She's waiting at the rendezvous point."

Kai's knees buckled in relief. "Thank you."

Simon's gaze filled with gratitude as he gently scooped up Cara, cradling her to his broad chest. "No. Thank *you* for saving Cara. I couldn't have lived if anything had happened to her."

Kai nodded, lips pressed together. "I feel the same," he said, catching the love shining in Simon's gaze when it fell on Cara, raising a pang of jealousy in Kai's chest. Cara hadn't mentioned she was dating, much less had fallen in love.

The fighting was over, leaving the floor covered in thick black sand. Sword-wielding men with white wings milled around the packed room, but there was no sign of Le Feu, Emily, or the Sphinx twins.

Michael broke into the circle. "Kai, Simon, the place is set to blow. We need to go. Now!"

Kai looked at the bloody knife. Rather than leave it behind, he wiped the blade on his discarded lab coat and stuck it into his belt. He'd keep it as a reminder of what he'd almost lost.

His composure regained, Simon led them to the nearest exit and into the pre-dawn air.

"Zeke," Simon yelled to a large, dark-haired guy who looked barely old enough to drink. "Take Kai."

Majestic white wings unfurled behind Simon's and Zeke's backs. Kai's eyes widened, and he stepped back. He hadn't made the connection that Simon was one of *them*. That might explain why Cara hadn't told him about her new boyfriend. He planned to have one hell of a conversation with her when this was over.

"You got it," Zeke said.

A winged man with a short, blond military haircut appeared. "Cham, I'll take Michael."

Simon nodded, his expression pained. "Thanks." Then to everyone, "Let's go."

Zeke tapped Kai's shoulder. "OK, dude, here's how we roll." Zeke provided a quick explanation, then crossed his arms over Kai's body from behind. "Don't be embarrassed if you barf. Happens a lot the first time."

Kai's stomach roiled on takeoff with the first jerking wing flaps, but after that, the ride smoothed. Air raced beneath Kai as they flew at an exhilarating speed beyond anything his imagination could generate. At least he didn't vomit.

Dawn was breaking when they landed ninety seconds later at the rendezvous point. The hundred-plus angels from the amphitheater were milling around motorcycles and waiting SUVs. Not a wing visible among them.

Kai caught sight of Sara immediately. She sat on one of the Harley-Davidsons in front of a man with long braids, the same man who snatched her from the stage. "Sara!"

She turned and saw him. "Daddy!"

The man placed her on the ground, and she ran toward him.

Kai swept her into his arms, overwhelmed and thankful. He peppered her face with kisses and hugged her tight.

She giggled. "Daddy, stop squeezing me. I can't breathe."

"I'm sorry. I'm just glad to see you."

She nodded sagely. "I know. The angels protected me." She pointed at the man who rescued her. "Jade let me sit on his motorcycle until you got here."

Kai traded a grateful nod with the man, who gave a slight bow.

Simon landed with Cara in his arms, retracted his wings, and approached the SUV where the blonde woman, Eae, waited.

Kai followed with Sara perched on his hip.

"Dr. Solomon saved her, but she needs medical attention," Simon said and glanced at Kai.

"I'm not sure how long it will take before she returns to consciousness. Give her a sedative and keep her out for a couple of hours to help her heal," Kai said and looked at Cara. For the first time, he thought about what he'd done. He saved Cara, but at what cost? She was the first test subject for the actual vaccine. "I don't know what's going to happen next," Kai confessed in a whisper.

Constantina placed a hand on his arm and another on Simon's. A peaceful wave rolled through Kai, relaxing him. "We'll take care of her, dear ones. We'll take Cara to the clinic with Ishmael and the other rescued Nephilim. All will be well."

Simon placed Cara gently on the backseat and kissed her forehead before turning to Kai. "Come with me."

Sara on his hip, Kai followed.

A group awaited, and a man named Raphael introduced them both to Angel Benitez, aka Benedictine, the Avenging Angel's Motorcycle Club leader. Simon arranged to meet the other team leaders at a safe house in the Marina District to debrief.

The team broke apart and headed to their vehicles. Kai and Sara jumped into the same SUV as Simon. Kai kept Sara on his lap, refusing to let her out of his grasp. Not only had Kai walked away with the lives of those he loved, but he discovered something he never thought possible—a belief in a higher power.

The roaring motorcycles left the warehouse complex first, followed by an SUV motorcade.

"I'll drop you at the clinic on the way," Simon said, his face stoic and unreadable as they entered the freeway.

BOOM!

Kai flinched, hugged Sara tighter, and glanced behind them. In the distance, a mushroom cloud of fire engulfed Le Feu's lair and everything inside.

Chapter 55

CHAMUEL

Angelorum Clinic. San Francisco.

CARA LAY PALE and unconscious in a hospital bed. Chamuel sat beside her, holding her hand. He brought their clasped fingers to his mouth and brushed his lips over her knuckles, closing his eyes and savoring her skin. Kai came in earlier to draw blood, monitoring changes from the vaccine. So far, so good.

When the door opened, Chamuel expected Kai, not Constantina.

She smiled at him, love lighting her gaze, and placed a gentle hand on his shoulder. "My son. How are you faring?"

Though they'd spoken several times since Chamuel's Trinity assignment started, many years and at least one incarnation had passed since they'd been in the same room, and Eae had addressed him as her progeny. Their connection felt good, though he wished he didn't feel like such a failure upon their long-overdue reunion.

He laid his hand over her much smaller one. "Mother, I trust you know what's transpired?"

"Yes, my love. Isaac told me. Do you love this woman?"

"With all my heart," he replied.

"There will be consequences."

Simon faced her, hoping to see an ally and not an accuser. "I would give anything...." He cleared his throat, his heart aching. "Even my life for hers."

Constantina's soft features conveyed neutrality. "I believe you. You have grown much since Mina and Calliope's deaths. If Cara feels the same...we shall see what can be done."

He held her gaze. "Let me go before she wakes. Put Isaac in my place. He's the only one I trust to guard her. You can take me to the Tribunal. I'm prepared to stand trial."

Constantina frowned. "Chamuel, if you love Cara, why would you choose to run from her?"

Rising to his feet, he scrubbed a hand over his face to erase the anguish written there. "Mother, don't you understand? I've compromised the safety of my Trinity. I couldn't save her. If Kai hadn't been there, she'd be dead like Mina, and I would've lost not only another Soul Seeker but the First of the Holy Twelve." The memory of her almost dying in his arms wrecked him. He'd gladly fall on his sword to keep her safe.

Constantina showed no surprise. If anything, she seemed to anticipate the request. "We must make our choices and take accountability for them. But I think you should wait until she wakes and let her choose."

He wanted to scream in frustration, hating his weakness. "Didn't you hear me? I *failed* her."

Constantina said patiently, "Please, sit down."

He did as he was told and awaited the lecture sure to follow.

Her voice softened. "My dear son, don't confuse Cara's fate with yours. Did you consider that your failure might be the exact thing needed to fulfill her destiny and for you to end up in her arms? There are no coincidences, Chamuel. Look closely, and you'll see." He had forgotten her kindness, wisdom, and how much he loved her, even when she berated him.

"In my humblest opinion, it would be wiser to wait and face the Tribunal with Cara at your side," she concluded.

What she said made logical sense, but after what Cara said to him last night in his room, he had come to his own truths. She had made him feel like half a man, which, in fact, was precisely what he was. He was male but not a man. He wasn't human.

He was a Nephilim.

An abomination.

When kissing Cara on the roof to ease her anxiety, he prepared for her to push him away. By then, he had already decided to leave after the rescue. Her passion and willingness had surprised him, but it hadn't changed his decision. Their last kiss, before flying to the warehouse, was his goodbye. Because he finally understood the value of what he had stolen from her.

He was ashamed of his selfishness, pursuing her without considering the consequences. He could not give her a normal human life, and he could never give her children. In the unlikely event he ended up with a suspended sentence, he vowed to put as much distance between them as possible to keep her safe and to give her the chance to find a human male who could provide all the things he'd so boldly taken.

Someone like Kai, if he were not already mated.

Unshed tears glistened in his eyes. "Please, let me go," he begged. "I only came here to see her one last time."

Constantina released a defeated breath. "Chamuel, free will is yours. Far be it from me to interfere. I've already given my opinion. You're free to go if that's your wish. But if you leave, you leave behind a chance for redemption. You'll be at the mercy of the Tribunal alone."

He felt her disappointment, but it paled in comparison to his own. "Redemption isn't meant for someone like me...," he said softly and lowered his head. A hot tear slid down his face.

His mother laid a cheek on his head and stroked his hair. "That is where you're wrong, my sweet and loving son," she whispered, her breath warm and comforting. "I named you Chamuel, dear one, because your fate is tied to matters of the heart. You deserve love. You've paid dearly already in this lifetime. I hope you'll reconsider and have faith in our Cara." Releasing him, she glided toward the door.

Wrapped in his own worries, he'd almost forgotten to acknowledge what he'd learned on the mission. "Mother."

She stopped, a hand resting on the doorknob, and glanced over her shoulder.

"I'm sorry for the loss of your daughter, my sister Hope. I didn't know."

She smiled sadly. "Her sacrifice paved the way for your Trinity's success. Honor her well. Journey forth in peace and love, dearest Chamuel," she said and left without awaiting his response.

Chapter 56

CARA

Angelorum Clinic. San Francisco.

"CARA? CARA, WAKE UP," urged a masculine voice over the beeping heart monitor. Swimming to consciousness, Cara's eyelids fluttered open to fluorescent ceiling lights.

"Bright," she croaked, clamping her eyes shut. Her mouth felt like she'd brushed her teeth with sand and forgotten to rinse.

"Her vitals look good," said a female voice. "Turn off the lights over the bed…Cara?"

Cara slowly opened her eyes. Michael, Sienna, Kai, and a doctor wearing a white coat with a nametag reading "DR. JESSICA STONE" crowded around her bed. Cara's gaze landed on Kai. "You're okay."

Kai's eyes glimmered with emotion, and he grabbed her hand. "Yeah. Sara and I—you were amazing."

Her memory was foggy and fragmented. The last thing she remembered was liberating Kai from the lab. "I don't remember."

Kai squeezed her hand. "We almost lost you."

Sienna piped up. Her red-rimmed eyes told Cara she'd been crying. "Kai's being modest." She leaned over Cara and whispered, "Kai saved your life, Carissima. You scared us to death. Please don't do that again."

Michael stood behind Sienna, his hand protectively on her back. When Sienna straightened, she leaned into him, taking comfort.

Cara's lips twitched into a smile. She'd dig into that one later. She scanned the room for the one face she needed to see. "Where's Simon?"

An awkward silence gripped the room.

Michael cleared his throat. "He was here before you woke up, but he's been called away." The bitter taste of Michael's lie passed over Cara's tongue.

Panic gripped Cara's chest. "That's not true."

Michael bowed his head and sighed. "He petitioned Constantina to relieve him from duty. He's gone."

Something primal snapped inside her. "No!" She reached for the handrail and pulled herself up. She needed to tell him she loved him and that he needed to stay and never leave her.

Michael stepped around Sienna, his eyes widening in alarm. "What're you doing?"

"I have to find him—" She swayed, a wave of dizziness attacking her equilibrium. Concern filled her friends' faces. She loved them all, but she needed to see Simon.

"*Shh.*" Michael gently pushed her back against the pillow.

"I want to speak with Constantina," she demanded.

"She'll be here later. Why don't you rest?" Michael glanced at Kai, who nodded at Dr. Stone, who adjusted the IV, and Cara drifted to sleep.

SHOUTS AND A hospital cart's squeaky wheels cut through Cara's drug-induced haze. Simon. Angels fighting. Pain. Something was wrong. Simon was weak. She wanted to wake, but sleep sucked her back into its clutches like quicksand.

CARA BOLTED UPRIGHT and gasped, aware that time had passed since sensing Simon. Her head swam with the sudden shift in elevation. The heart monitor was gone, and only a saline IV bag remained tethered to her arm. She swung her legs over the side of the bed, thinking only of getting to Simon and healing him. She grabbed the IV bag's tall, mobile trolley and used it as a crutch.

Michael walked in. "Whoa! What are you doing?"

She tried to stand, heart hammering. "What happened to Simon?"

Michael took a deep breath, rested his hands on her shoulders, and lowered her back onto the bed. "I'll tell you. Just sit down."

He sat in the chair beside her bed. "Cham...*Simon* joined Raphael's team to search for a second hideaway that Ishmael told them about. Simon took a couple of bullets while he was in the air. One of his wings was torn in the fall. He's in surgery now."

Cara gasped. "Will he be all right?"

Michael's gaze shuttered. "They're optimistic," was all he said.

Tears welled and spilled over. "I need to see him when he's out of surgery. Michael, I made such a huge mistake. I love him. He needs to know that. He needs to know that I'm sorry."

Michael leaned in and gathered her into a warm embrace. "It'll be okay," he whispered, "I promise." Sweet truth.

When Michael released her, she worked up her courage to ask, "Is he in trouble? You know, for dating me?"

Michael's lips pressed into a grim line. "I don't know."

Her heart sank. Even if she told Simon everything, he still would have to stand before the Angelorum High Council and answer for his crime. For loving her. The thought of his imprisonment sent her over the edge. Whatever it took, she'd make sure he wouldn't stand trial alone. "Is Constantina here? I need to speak with her."

Michael nodded solemnly and headed for the door. "I'll send her in when she finishes with Dr. Stone. Hang in there."

"Wait. How's Sienna?" Cara asked.

Michael offered a guarded shrug. "She's fine. Just worried. She went back to the safe house."

Calling up more courage, she crossed her fingers and asked, "So…things are better with you and Sienna?"

He smiled softly. "Let's just say we've called a truce and leave it at that."

Cara had hoped for more, but she was satisfied with any steps that got them closer—in Zeke's words—to twenty minutes in a dark closet.

By the time Constantina arrived fifteen minutes later, Cara was free from the IV and energetically rummaging through a bag of street clothes from Sienna.

"You're looking well, dear one," Constantina said with a warm smile. "Apparently, the vaccine has accelerated your healing beyond even your own powers."

"What do you mean?" Cara asked, laying out the clothes Sienna had chosen—a pair of jeans and a clingy top surely chosen to peddle Cara's "breast-ware," as Sienna called it.

"Your Kai. He injected you with the Nephilim vaccine he developed as you lay dying from Achanelech's knife. Had Dr. Solomon not thought so quickly, we would've lost you. But we are unsure of how the vaccine will change your body chemistry beyond the healing, so we are monitoring you closely." Her smile widened, and she clapped her hands. "That solves at least one mystery."

"What mystery?" Cara asked, only half-listening.

"Your lifeline in the Trinity Stone showed a baffling color hybridization we'd never seen before—a shift from human to Nephilim."

Cara's eye twitched. Wait, what? Never mind. She had a more pressing matter. "Can we talk about that later? I need to speak with you about Sim—Chamuel."

Constantina's smile dampened slightly. "Of course."

They sat, Cara on the edge of the bed and Constantina in the chair.

Taking a deep breath, Cara dove in. "Chamuel is Simon," she said, tears threatening to return as she spoke the words. "I know our relationship is forbidden, but I didn't know his real identity until we were leaving for San Francisco. Is he really going to jail for a hundred years for kissing me? If so, what can I do to stop it?" she blurted and held her breath.

Constantina took her hand and said softly, "I know what happened between you and my son."

Cara's jaw dropped. "Chamuel is your *son*?" She hadn't seen that one coming.

"He is. From a prior incarnation." Constantina's gaze searched Cara's. "My question is this — what would you sacrifice to save him?"

"Everything. My life, if necessary," she said without hesitation.

"The ultimate gift is the sacrifice of one's life for another," Constantina said, giving Cara's hand another squeeze. "Asked the same question, he gave the same answer."

"He said that?" Cara's heart leaped.

"He did," Constantina said, dipping her chin. "Would you be willing to spend the next three hundred years by his side?"

"What do you mean?" Cara asked, perplexed. She'd be lucky to give him the next sixty years if he wanted her after what she said.

Constantina beamed. "According to Dr. Solomon, the vaccine imbues Nephilim characteristics, such as longevity, into the host DNA. Minus wings, of course."

Cara blinked, the implication of Constantina's revelation sinking in. "Wings?" she repeated dumbly, flexing her scapulas, as if that were even a possibility.

"Correct," Constantina said, nonplussed. "The original scientists removed the genes for wing development. They were unsure if the human body could handle the transformation, and if it could, they wanted to prevent Achanelech from developing his army."

Which made sense, but the idea of transforming humans into Nephilim boggled her mind. She'd need Kai to explain what that meant, fully understanding she should be losing her mind about now. Instead, a shiver of excitement rolled through her at the possibilities. "I'll live as long as Simon?"

"We believe so," her mentor replied, "which is why you should petition the High Council to sanction your bond, if you're willing. I know you'll have at least one vote."

Cara's heart soared with relief, and she hopped off the bed. She would do whatever it took to save Simon. "Thank you! Can I see him now?"

Constantina eyed Cara's hospital gown, then the outfit on the bed. "May I suggest a change of clothing first?"

CARA POKED HER head into Simon's room, where he slept in a hospital gown, sheet pulled to his waist. His hair, free of its tie, framed his impossibly handsome face on the pillow.

She gasped at the sight of his snow-white wings, folded at his sides, one swathed in bandages. Feathers of all sizes shimmered in a dazzling array of textures. Stepping inside, she approached the bed and sat beside him.

Unable to resist the allure, she skimmed her fingertips over the glittering plumage. His feathers were as soft as they looked. Delighted, she glided her fingers over a wider expanse, luxuriating in their silky smoothness, only mildly disappointed she hadn't inherited a pair. She had so many questions.

Constantina whispered from the doorway, reminding Cara she wasn't alone, "You know, it's quite personal to touch someone's wings." Cara jerked her hand back and impishly glanced at Constantina, who chuckled softly and closed the door.

Making a mental note to brush up on Nephilim etiquette, Cara took Simon's hand in hers. Asleep, his lush lashes lay in golden fans against his smooth cheeks, giving his face a youthful innocence, nothing like a commanding Trinity Guardian.

Simon. Chamuel. It didn't change how much he meant to her. Still, she'd hurt the male she'd fallen in love with, and he's the one she needed to address.

"Simon, it's me, Cara," she whispered, determined to get this out, even if only as a dress rehearsal for when he awoke. "I'm sorry for what I said and for not giving you a chance." She paused, a lump forming in her throat. "I love you, Simon…I don't want to lose you. Please, don't go." Running her fingers lightly over his forearm, she traced his veins and smiled softly, "You know, the day I first saw you in the subway, I thought you were some sexy Viking god. Since then, whenever I'm near you, I want to —"

"Take your clothes off?" he said, eyes closed, a smile growing on his lips.

Cara flinched and flushed with embarrassment. "How long have you been awake?"

He opened an eye, dipped his head to see her, and chuckled. "Since you walked in."

She *tsk-tsked* and pinched his arm.

"Ouch! That wasn't very nice from someone seeking forgiveness," he said, rubbing his skin without losing his teasing grin.

She fought a smile with a pleading look. "Please, let me finish?"

His gaze softened to a warm, blue flame, and he enveloped her hand in his. "If you must."

Sobering, she continued, "I didn't understand how much you've risked to be with me, and I won't let you face it alone. No matter what. Forgive me?"

Lifting her hand to his lips, he kissed her palm. "I forgive you," he whispered, then waggled a brow. "Want to make it up to me?"

"You're making this too easy," Cara said with a shy grin. "I expected to grovel more than this."

"Life is too short to grovel," he said, warm gaze fixed on hers, as he scooped her up. She let out a girly squeal as he placed her astride his waist and pulled her close. Her hair cascaded around their faces from above, giving them a curtain of privacy, their faces inches apart, his fingers warming her hips.

She stared into his extraordinary eyes and whispered, "I love you, Simon. Promise you won't leave me?"

The corner of his lip twitched. "If that is your wish, I promise."

She lowered her lips to his, sinking into the exquisite heat of his kiss. Simon's arms flexed, pressing her to his body, warm and rock solid beneath her. A low moan rose from her throat as he took no quarter, drinking her in and exploring her mouth with sensuous hunger. Her body heated with awareness as he reacted beneath her, hardening and thickening against her core.

Breathing hard, he caressed her cheek. "You are my heart. On my life, I won't leave you."

"I want you," she breathed, her voice husky. The feel of him so close was too much to handle. She ached for him in a way she'd never had for anyone else.

He tucked a strand of hair behind her ear; his half-lidded gaze was dark with desire. "I want you more than I can breathe, but I'm—"

The door opened, and Isaac strode inside.

"*...expecting Isaac,*" Simon said, finishing through their bond, his gaze apologetic.

Isaac's startled gaze widened, and he pulled up short. "*Uh*—shit. Sorry, Cham. I expected you to be alone." Then, he pointed a finger between them and raised a brow. "Let me guess. Change in plans?"

Cara cleared her throat and gingerly crawled off Simon, who rolled to his side and strategically covered himself with a wing.

"Yup. Change in plans. See you at the Tribunal."

Isaac passed a hand over his face and smirked. "That was the shortest Guardian assignment in Angelorum history."

Cara's gaze snapped to Simon. "Isaac was going to take over for you?"

Simon sighed. "He still might. Let's see what the Tribunal decides."

Backing up, Isaac raised his hands and snickered. "I'm going to pretend I never saw this. You lovebirds have fun, but don't get too cozy. This place is crawling with people who want to see you."

When the door closed, Simon spooned her into his chest, encircled her in his arms, and kissed the top of her head.

Cara let out a frustrated snarl. "*Grr*…We don't have time, do we?" Her body was too heated, her skin too tight. Her desire for him was like a primal hunger she needed to satisfy. She'd never felt something so powerful. Had the vaccine amped up her hormones? Not that she was complaining. But no denying, the thought of making love to Simon unleashed a whole new side of her.

Simon nibbled her neck and said in a husky growl, "Not a fraction of the time I need to properly satisfy you. But, I promise," he whispered into her hair. "The first opportunity of guaranteed privacy, we'll be together — if it's the last thing I do."

"Deal." She sighed, not knowing if she could wait that long. God help the Tribunal if they got in their way. Well, at least there was one thing she *could* do. Raising a brow, Cara assessed Simon's bandaged wing as heat gathered in her palms. "Before anyone else barges in, let me fix that wing."

Chapter 57

CARA

Angelorum Sanctuary. France.

THE ATTENDANT LEFT her room at the Angelorum Sanctuary, and Cara reclined on the bed beside a discarded book she had tried reading to kill time. In a few hours, Simon would face the High Council Tribunal. Though not charged, Cara would stand by his side.

On the plane to France, Constantina briefed them on the nuances of Tribunal proceedings. Cara hadn't been pleased to learn she and Simon would be kept in isolation when they arrived at the Sanctuary until after the hearing. Their Trinity link would be blocked while on Sanctuary grounds. But Cara enjoyed a challenge. They'd found a loophole while on the place. No one said they couldn't send energy pulses, but so far, her attempts had failed.

They would see only their Council-assigned attendants until the hearing. If the Tribunal decided in Simon's favor, they would be mated in a blessed union. If not, they would spend the next century apart, the thought of which made Cara queasy.

Cara rolled off the bed and paced, feeling like a caged tiger.

She had barely glimpsed the secret underground city before a transport whisked them from the station to the High Council's complex. They had traveled in a windowless van from the airport to a secret above-ground structure that connected the surface transit station to the underground city below.

Cara had gotten only the briefest glimpse of the angelic, fairytale city, which lay beneath a rock dome sky and looked like a cross between the Emerald City in *The Wizard of Oz* and a nineteenth-century European village. Since then, Cara had seen nothing more than marble hallways that connected her bed chamber within the residential section of the Council's complex to a private dining room. Granted, the complex had all the amenities of a fine hotel, but she was anxious to explore the city.

Arm crossed, she paced the short length of the room, wishing Michael had been allowed to accompany them. Instead, Michael, Sienna, Chloe, and Zeke had stayed behind when they landed in Westchester.

A smile danced on her lips, thinking of the flight home from San Francisco. Miraculously, Michael and Sienna's truce had lasted. Cara hoped they would get their "twenty minutes" someday.

A knock at the chamber door startled her. Cara opened it to find Constantina on the other side. "There's someone who wants to see you, dear one," she said.

Cara frowned. "I thought I wasn't allowed any visitors?"

Smiling, Constantina clasped her hands. "We made an exception."

"Who is it?"

"Why don't you come and find out?"

Constantina didn't need to ask twice. Short of Attila the Hun, Cara would meet with anyone to escape the room. She followed her mentor through the windowless hallway and down a circular staircase. Cara didn't press Constantina for details, since stealing gold from Fort Knox would be easier than getting Constantina to ruin a surprise.

They stopped at a large ornate door off the main hall. Cara didn't know what to expect inside.

"Your guest awaits." Constantina opened the door, ushered Cara over the threshold, and closed her inside.

Cara stood in a vast, white-walled gallery, where works of art covered the walls. Then she spotted Kai, dressed in white, admiring a painting.

Oh my God! The dream she had on her birthday.

Kai turned. A smile lit his face, and she ran into his embrace.

Cara had barely seen him since the rescue. Between sorting out family issues and studying the effects of the vaccine on her DNA, he'd had his hands full. But he had promised to visit soon—she just hadn't realized it would be this soon.

Happiness swelled inside her. She'd heard several versions of how she'd saved Kai and how he'd saved her, none of which she remembered. None of which mattered. Everyone was safe, and that's all she cared about.

Cara hugged him tight and inhaled deeply. His warm scent mixed with the familiar white birch of the Calvin Klein scent she'd first given him in college.

Kai shifted back. Holding her at arm's length. He frowned, his gaze intense. "I'm sorry I had to leave after the rescue."

She reeled him back into the hug. "It's okay. Thank you for saving me."

"Cara, if it wasn't for you, I wouldn't have been alive to save you. You saved us. I don't know what I would've done if either of you had died," he whispered with a final squeeze before stepping away.

His words warmed her, but she didn't understand why he was here and not with his family. "How are they? Melanie and Sara?"

He sighed. "They're fine, thanks to you and the rest of the crew." Then, his gaze lit, and he grabbed her hand. "I remember what I was going to tell you in the dream that night."

Her heart stuttered.

Looking away, he swallowed before meeting her gaze with glistening eyes. "I'm sorry I doubted your loyalty all those years ago. I never meant to hurt you. What happened between us in college was my fault. I should've trusted you, but I let my self-doubt get in the way. I screwed up, and it cost us an opportunity to be together. I was an idiot. Forgive me?"

His longing tugged at her heart, and a weight lifted from her soul. With his words came a new understanding of why she'd been so drawn to him. Their souls were bonded through a mutual promise, now fulfilled. They had saved each other in more ways than one.

Tears welled in her eyes. "There's nothing to forgive. Everything turned out exactly as it should have."

He embraced her again and rested his face against her hair. "I'll always love you, Cara. Thank you for being such a good friend and always being there for me."

At that, tears trailed down her cheeks, and she hugged him harder. She'd waited forever to hear those words. Even though his forgiveness wouldn't lead to what she had imagined so long ago, the words were just as healing. Because of Kai, she had a life and another chance to love.

"I'll always love you, too," she whispered.

He kissed the side of her head. "Simon's a lucky man."

She pulled away, brushing her fingertips beneath her eyes. "I have to go. Wish us luck. Are you staying for a while?"

"Not this time, but I'll be back. Constantina offered me a job."

Cara's eyebrows shot up. "*Really?*"

He grinned. "Someone I care about needs a personal physician, and the Angelorum needs a lead researcher on Nephilim DNA. I believe I'm uniquely qualified."

A wide smile burst across Cara's face. "Thank you."

His blue eyes twinkled. "Good luck. I'll see you soon."

She tasted the truth in his words and knew he meant it.

Chapter 58

CARA

Angelorum Sanctuary. France.

CARA ENTERED THE back of the Tribunal chamber behind her attendant, who pulled her to a halt with gentle pressure. Lavender and sage wafted from candles flickering in sconces beside the door, taking Cara back to her lessons with Constantina in the penthouse meeting room. This room had the same painted ceiling and quiet serenity.

How far Cara had come, and how she'd fallen.

Here she faced judgment from twelve elaborately and colorfully robed members of an angelic protectorate. Eleven of them sat inside an elevated, crescent-shaped enclosure suspended above the floor. Constantina sat among the eleven. One level lower, the High Council Leader, Angelis, gripped the lectern inside an ornately carved octagonal pulpit that jutted into the center of the room. He couldn't be more than forty with his conservatively cut gray-peppered hair and wire-rimmed glasses. He looked more like a banker than an angel.

From Cara's vantage point, she saw Isaac, wearing an accuser's white robe with blue metallic threads, standing in the center of the floor facing the Tribunal, his attendant at his back.

Angelis gave Isaac a kind smile and nodded. "Thank you for your testimony, Isaac, Son of Heiglot. That will be all."

Simon and his attendant entered through a doorway along the back wall, on the opposite side of where Cara had come in. Like her, Simon wore the robe of the accused — white with red metallic threads. Simon's gaze fell on her and warmed. He sent a tiny energy pulse that caressed her skin, and she volleyed one back. Though it didn't do much to quell her nerves.

Dismissed, Isaac walked from the center of the room with his trailing attendant. He glanced at Cara, giving an apologetic smile as he passed. Guilt and regret gnawed at Cara for her planeside outburst, wishing she could take it back. Because of her, Isaac had been forced to testify against his best friend. For that, she was deeply sorry.

After Isaac exited, she and Simon were ushered to the center of the floor. Their attendants retreated, leaving her facing the High Council at Simon's side. Close enough to touch him but prohibited from doing so, Cara clasped her hands tightly and kept her spine rigid to calm her nerves.

Angelis cleared his throat. "Before I ask either of you to present, we've selected some events from the Flow."

"What?" Cara blurted without thinking.

Angelis cocked his head and glanced quizzically at Constantina, who explained, "Besides energy and communication, the Flow acts like a cosmic video recorder, storing every moment of history on earth."

Cara swallowed hard. This wouldn't be pretty.

The lights dimmed, and a 3-D, life-sized holographic film sprang to life in the open air above them. In the scene, Cara lay cradled on Simon's lap, unconscious, after the demon attack in her apartment. His large hand hovered over a lock of her hair while he wore an expression filled with wonder.

Cara's breath caught, and warmth spread through her chest. She hadn't known that happened.

The image faded, replaced with another until the 3-D snippets flashed by in a continuous stream of intimate moments: Simon's arms securely around her after catching her fall in Raphael's; Simon's hand creating the looping script of the note inviting her to dinner; her hand in his over the dinner table at Raphael's; their first explosive kiss at the jazz lounge; standing in his arms viewing the Rubens at the Met; her head tucked beneath his chin as he told her about Calliope; their kiss outside the Standard Grill; her exposing him at the Westchester airport. All their special moments were played for everyone to experience. Her vision blurred, and she bit her lip to keep it from quivering as all hope drained from her.

How will Simon ever be pardoned for this? She tasted Simon's bitter lime fear, his energy reflecting hers. She brushed at the escaping tears with her fingertips, wishing for a tissue.

When the clips ended, Angelis cleared his throat. "Cara Collins, you may speak first." Simon's encouraging energy pulsed at her side. She wanted more than anything to touch him. Instead, she wrung the sweat from her palms and suppressed an urge to scream.

"What can I say? You've seen it all," she whispered. When Constantina had coached her, she hadn't mentioned the possibility of a blow-by-blow from the Flow.

Angelis's voice was kind. "Those are only clips; they cannot possibly tell the full story. The Flow is not privy to your thoughts or intent, my dear. That's what you must tell us."

Cara swallowed and told her side of the story, sticking to thoughts, feelings, and intent.

Simon followed and presented his side.

After they pled their case, they were taken to separate antechambers while the Council debated their fate behind closed doors.

Two of the most painstaking hours of Cara's life passed — sitting alone with only fear to keep her company — before she and Simon were led back onto the floor of the Tribunal chamber to hear the verdict.

When she returned to Simon's side, tension radiated through his rigid spine, shoulders, and grim expression.

The Council filed into the chamber and took their seats in the boxed enclosure while Angelis proceeded to the pulpit. He unrolled a parchment scroll and cleared his throat.

"I address you both: Cara Collins, Soul Seeker of the Collins Trinity and First of the Holy Twelve; and Chamuel, Son of Eae, and Guardian of the Collins Trinity.

"You have been called forth today to address a violation of Angelorum Law. The law in question prohibits romantic involvement between Trinity members. More specifically, it prohibits the assigned Nephilim Guardian from pursuing a romantic attachment with the human Soul Seeker or Messenger within the Trinity. The purpose of the law is to prevent emotional attachments that create biased judgment and jeopardize the success of the mission and the safety of the Trinity members. The Angelorum's history is rife with Trinity mission failures and numerous deaths, underscoring the need for such a law. Every failure gives the Dark Ones more power to tip the balance.

"The oath of the Trinity Guardians requires them to put the needs of the Trinity before their own, since their purpose is singular to our world. They are created to protect and defend. To do that effectively, they are endowed with humanity and human emotions, rendering them fully capable of succumbing to the trappings of romantic love.

"To prove guilt, we examine intent, which can start with a look or a caress. Though not all intent is acted upon, the line for judgment starts with a kiss."

Ice water rushed through Cara's veins as she thought of the clips from the Flow. She'd hoped Simon had exaggerated when he said he could be sentenced to one hundred years in prison for just kissing her.

"Punishment for the violation of this law is as follows: revocation of membership within the Guardianship; forfeiture of the benefits associated with the post of Guardian; removal of the Guardianship Mark; mandatory separation from Trinity members; one hundred years of mandatory imprisonment within Sanctuary complex without visitation; and after the sentence, removal of the wings."

Each punishment layered on top of the next drove the air slowly from Cara's lungs until the crushing weight of Angelis's words settled fully in her chest. She struggled for oxygen in ragged gasps.

Can't breathe! Cara's fingers clawed at her throat, unable to get enough air. Woozy, her vision narrowed, and the horizon flipped. Eyes rolling back in her head, she lost control of her knees. Strong fingers gripped her as she slipped backward into pitch-blackness.

"CARA? CAN YOU hear me, dear one?" Cara roused to find Constantina's ocean blue eyes, laced with worry, staring down at her. Cara lay on a sofa in the antechamber outside the Tribunal chamber. They were alone.

Cara sat up, and the charges came rushing back. She'd done this to Simon. Guilty sobs ripped from her lungs. "It's my fault."

Constantina pulled her into her arms, smoothed her hair, and soothed her, "*Shh.*"

Cara breathed in Constantina's soothing lavender scent. "He doesn't deserve that," she choked out and whimpered, swiping a hand across her tear-streaked face. "Please don't let that happen."

Constantina kissed Cara's forehead. "*Shh.* The verdict has not yet been read. Have some faith, dear one," she said, removing some tissues from her Council robe and handing them to Cara. "Take a minute, and then rejoin the Tribunal."

Cara sat up. Hand quaking, she dabbed her eyes and blew her nose. "I love him, Constantina. I can't do this without him."

Constantina nodded and smiled kindly. "I know." She moved to leave.

"Why me, Constantina?" Cara blurted, caving in to her self-doubt. "Why was I chosen to be the First of the Holy Twelve? My anxiety makes me…weak."

The petite woman returned and placed a hand over Cara's heart. "The answer's right here. When I said to have some faith, I also meant in yourself." With a parting smile, she left, robes swishing behind her.

Cara hoped she wouldn't let everyone down. Taking a deep breath, she returned to the Tribunal to be with Simon.

Simon's chest heaved, his crystal-blue eyes filling with relief when she returned to his side. She mustered a wan smile then faced the Council.

"Welcome back, Miss Collins," Angelis said without judgment and dipped his head in greeting. "May we proceed?"

Her cheeks flushed. "Yes."

"All right, then. We, the Council, believe this case is not a simple violation. As such, we have taken mitigating circumstances into account and sought guidance from the Trinity Stones."

Cara stood straighter, wondering if that was better or worse. She would take Constantina's advice and have faith.

Angelis paused, his gaze shifting between her and Simon until it settled on her. She swallowed and clamped her hands together in a white-knuckled grip.

"The Trinity Stones revealed, Cara Collins, that you were destined since birth to be mated to one of your own kind."

But she and Simon were not the same kind.

She swallowed hard and held her breath, aching to touch him but not daring to do so. His energy shifted to apprehension beside her.

Angelis rolled the scroll forward and continued reading. "The anomaly within your Trinity Stone revealed a transformation from human to Nephilim." He gave her a brief glance. "A recent development, as I understand. As such, your destiny shows a Nephilim bonding."

Relief washed over her, and she released her breath.

Lowering the scroll, Angelis's gaze fell on Simon. "Chamuel, Son of Eae, would you willingly bond with Cara Collins, a fellow Nephil?"

"I would," Simon said, his deep voice cracking. Hope rippled through her.

Angelis pursed his lips and turned to Cara. "And you, Cara Collins, would you willingly bond with Chamuel, Son of Eae?"

"I would," she said, wanting to leap with joy.

Angelis gave a slight nod and continued, "It was clear to the Council from the beginning that for the Twelve to succeed, we, the Council, would be challenged to allow some rules to be broken." His gaze hardened on Simon. "Admittedly, we didn't expect it to be so soon or in violation of so sacred a law."

Simon dipped his head.

"Look at me, Chamuel. When they call, we answer to our destinies, and yours required breaking the law to be with Cara. That, in itself, takes courage. Our esteemed Council member, Constantina, who birthed you in a prior incarnation, chose you for this role. She has spoken on your behalf. In addition, we heard testimony from Isaac, Son of Heiglot. We would be violating our own rules if we were to orchestrate or interfere with destiny. Free will is yours. This was clearly your choice and your destiny."

Next to her, Simon's energy took a positive turn.

"Still, after much deliberation over our law's nuances, we've decided this violation cannot go unpunished."

Simon's energy flagged, and Cara tightened her spine to compensate for the weakness in her knees. She chanted to herself: *Breathe. Inhale. Exhale.*

Angelis said, "Chamuel, Son of Eae, we, the Council, hereby remove you as Guardian of the Collins Trinity and place you on furlough from the Guardianship until further notice."

Angelis paused as Constantina descended the staircase to stand beside Angelis in the pulpit. He handed her the scroll. "Dear ones, Angelis has agreed to let me deliver the remaining verdict." She smiled at Simon. "Chamuel, my son, you will retain your Guardianship Mark and membership since it is expected you will someday return. As for mandatory imprisonment...."

Cara stood perfectly still. Her legs and lungs were frozen in fear.

"The Council unanimously voted and agreed to accept your self-imposed celibacy, which lasted well over one hundred years, in place of mandatory imprisonment. We believe you've paid enough. Furthermore, we have chosen to sanctify your bond with Cara. The strength of your love and the mutual willingness of your sacrifice have proven you both worthy."

Air rushed from Cara's lungs in relief, and she almost fainted again, but this time from exhilaration. She thought of her conversation with Zeke on the roof. He hadn't exaggerated; Simon *had* been celibate since Calliope died.

Constantina rolled the scroll and turned to Cara. "Is that acceptable, dear one?"

She nodded vigorously, too excited to speak.

"My son, there's one more thing. The Trinity Stones revealed that you are the Second of the Holy Twelve."

Simon gasped, and her head whipped to the side. His jaw hung slack.

"The Trinity Stones predict that those attached to the Twelve will draw their power from love. But be warned, this will be an innate vulnerability for the Dark Ones to exploit."

Cara raised her hand before she could stop herself.

Constantina smiled. "You may speak, Cara."

"But...but...I thought the Twelve all belonged to Trinities...."

The smile spread on Constantina's face, and she winked. "I don't recall mentioning they had to be a *current* Trinity member...Do you?"

Constantina returned the scroll to Angelis and stepped back. Angelis beamed at them. "We, the members of the High Council, bless you to journey forth in peace and love. This hearing is adjourned."

Cara stood, incredulous. Simon's energy spiked before he took her hand in his.

Catching Cara's eye, Constantina nodded.

Cara bowed her head in thanks. Then, she turned to Simon, her gaze locked on the crystal-blue pools of the man she loved, and her soul leaped with joy.

"Let's go," he whispered, clutching her hand tightly. They walked swiftly to the chamber's exit. When they were far enough away, Simon gave her a smile, and they broke into a run.

Chapter 59

CARA

Angelorum Sanctuary. France.

FIVE MINUTES LATER, Cara and Simon opened Simon's chamber door, panting for breath and giddy with relief. They received a few disapproving stares as they raced through the High Council wing to Simon's guest room, but neither cared. They were free, and that's all that mattered.

Simon's lips hitched in a crooked grin. "I believe it's customary to carry one's mate over the threshold," he said, scooping her into his arms like she weighed nothing and carrying her into the room.

Cara giggled. Arms circling his neck, she enjoyed the hard press of his body. His mouth was dangerously close. Craning her neck, she nipped his lower lip. "Silly tradition, but I'm not complaining."

A low chuckle rumbled in Simon's chest. He kicked the door shut and gently set her on her feet.

She stood banded in Simon's warm embrace. "I can't believe it's over," she said, still processing the verdict. Words failed to express her relief, joy, and buoyancy of spirit. Still, she had to ask, "How do you feel about not being my Guardian anymore?"

Simon shrugged, his glowing gaze trained on hers. "I can keep you safer as one of the Twelve."

Cara cocked a brow and asked, "Did you know you were one of the Twelve?"

He choked out a laugh. "Hell, no! I didn't even know you were the First until Michael told me on the flight to San Francisco." He slid his hands down her sides and rested them on her hips. "The irony? If I hadn't broken the law, I don't think I'd be the Second."

Cara pondered that for a moment. During training, Constantina had been vague on how and when the Trinity Stones would reveal the Twelve. But she had been clear on one thing—the connection between free will and destiny. Simon had chosen her freely, connecting his destiny to hers, and there wasn't anyone she'd rather have at her side in love or battle.

That left ten more people to find.

She leaned into his rock-hard chest and teased, "Rulebreaker."

He huffed a laugh and kissed her nose. "Takes one to know one."

She glanced at their robes, then at the king-size bed covered with a fluffy duvet, and batted her lashes. "Well, sir, I believe it's time to collect on that promise you made in the hospital." Which seemed like a frustratingly long time ago.

His gaze heated, and he whispered, "Hold that thought," and swept her into his arms.

She squeaked at finding herself cradled to his chest and gave his chin a light nip. "You're taking the 'sweeping me off my feet' thing a bit too literally." Chuckling, he deposited her on a settee in the sitting area and beamed like an eager schoolboy. "Wait here. I have something for you."

Cara kicked off the ceremonial sandals as Simon disappeared inside the walk-in closet. Reemerging, Simon cradled a small antique ring box in his palm.

He dropped to a knee beside her and opened the small gold-embossed leather box. Inside, a stunning antique engagement ring sparkled on a blue velvet cushion.

She gasped and stared at a large, cushion-cut diamond surrounded by sapphires. "It's beautiful," she said in a breathy whisper.

He caught her gaze, his eyes shining. "This was Constantina's. She thought you'd like it." Cara's heart warmed.

When Cara discovered her mentor was Simon's mother, she understood why Constantina had entrusted him with her safety. Not to mention, Cara was thrilled to have Constantina as her future mother-in-law.

Cara offered her hand to Simon. Rather than slipping the diamond onto her finger, he closed the ring inside a fist and bowed his head. Alarm pulsed through her as she stared at his crown. "What's the matter?"

"I know you told the Tribunal you would bond with me, but that's not the same as me asking. I want to ask…more than anything." He lifted his gaze, his expression pained. "I'm sure Constantina told you…I cannot give you a child." His throat bobbed in a swallow. "I'll understand if you reject my offer in favor of a fertile human male."

Her heart squeezed. Simon's willingness to sacrifice his happiness and put her before himself touched her deeply.

She shook her head vigorously. "I might not be fertile either after the vaccine," she blurted, having spent zero time processing the implications of Kai's lifesaving measures. Giving it now only a passing thought, she concluded she'd take alive and childless over dead any day. Besides, they had many hurdles to overcome before considering parenthood, and as much as she liked the idea of having kids, she wasn't entirely committed to the idea.

Tears gathered in her eyes, and she gently cupped his cheek. "All I want is you."

He kissed her palm. Eyes glistening and voice hitching, he asked, "In that case, Cara Collins, would you agree to marry me in a human bonding?"

Happy tears slid down her cheeks. "Yes."

A few weeks ago, she never imagined something like this was possible—that she could fall in love and move past Kai, and that both things could feel right.

Simon wiped his cheeks and slipped the ring onto her finger. "I'm honored to be your intended mate."

Cara stared at the glittering ring, and the weight of those last weeks crashed down. Her throat tightened, and she shuddered. "I almost lost you."

He brushed a wave of hair from her face. "I'm right here, and I love you with all my heart." Leaning in, he touched his lips to hers, and the heat bottled up since the hospital broke free.

In a frenzied rush of lips, tongue, and teeth, they met, hands hungrily gliding over each other's soft curves and hard planes under the white fabric.

Simon pulled back, panting. "I believe...I owe you...a night of exhausting passion."

"Promises, promises," she taunted.

"I always keep my promises," he said, his voice a low rumble. Scooping her up, he strode to the bed and gently laid her down, then slid onto the duvet beside her.

Cara rolled to her side, eyed his robe as he rested on his back, and bit her bottom lip. She ran a finger over the buttons. Her stomach fluttered with nervous anticipation. She agreed to marry a man she hadn't seen fully naked. A healthy curiosity flared regarding the muscled landscape and the—*ahem*—tantalizing endowment she's encountered in the hospital beneath the white robe. "May I unwrap you?"

His brow rose, and the corner of his mouth hitched. "Like a present?"

"Exactly."

"Please. Unwrap me." He cradled the back of his head in a hand and rested his gaze on her, fighting a grin.

Cara undid each shiny button and peeled the robe apart. Underneath, he wore only black boxers. Her lips parted at the sight of all that smooth, rippled muscle. "You're practically naked."

He chuckled deeply and shrugged. "I slipped on the boxers while I was in the closet getting your ring. I was instructed not to wear anything beneath the robe."

"Who told you that?" she blurted, thinking about the knit dress beneath hers.

His eyes widened into innocent blue saucers. "My attendant."

She squinted. At the Tribunal, his attendant was male. "Wait. That guy?"

His lips kicked into a teasing grin. "Nope. A *woman*," he said, slowly drawing out the word.

Wait, what? Cara blinked. "Another woman saw you naked?"

He rested a hand on his stomach and laughed in a deep, rich baritone. "She birthed me, so, yes, she's definitely seen me naked."

Cara's jealousy fled, and her expression flattened. "Constantina," she muttered and pinched his arm. "That was mean."

"You should've seen the look on your face," he chided, still laughing. Then he rolled her on top of him, so she straddled his waist, and he kissed her nose. Her hair cascaded around them in an auburn curtain. "You should know, I only have eyes for you," he said, his lips still tilted in amusement. "Constantina must've been confident the Tribunal would fall in my favor. She was preparing me to consummate the bonding promise if I was freed."

Cara blinked, the feel of his arousal growing beneath her. "So, you're saying Constantina served up her son—naked—on a proverbial platter?" Heat rushed to her cheeks at the thought of Constantina asking Simon to ready himself for seduction. That was nothing, if not progressive.

"Constantina is both pragmatic and direct." His smile crinkled the corners of his warm, glowing eyes. "To ease your mind, she only gave instructions. She didn't watch me dress."

Cara snorted softly, "Well, that's a relief." She bit her lip and moved her hips along the hard ridge tightening between her thighs.

He moaned and narrowed his eyes, his hands drifting to her hips. "I believe you were disrobing me."

"I believe I was," she said in a throaty whisper and slipped a hand behind his neck to free his hair. She tossed the leather tie aside and combed her fingers through the thick golden waves, spreading them in a halo on the pillow. Then cupping his cheeks in both hands, she pulled his lips to hers, kissing him with hot abandon.

His fingers traveled along the curve of her spine before grasping her waist and pressing her closer. Rotating her hips, she ground into him, eliciting a low growl from his throat as he arched his head back, and his fingers tightened around her waist.

In one smooth move, he shifted her beneath him and knelt above her, the flaps of his robe falling open. She traced her fingertips over the red lines of his Guardianship Mark and down his muscled torso until they skated over the boxers straining to cover his rock-hard arousal.

"If I have to wait for a second longer, I might lose my mind," he breathed and kissed her deeply while removing his robe and tossing it to the floor.

Hovering above her, he pulled her to a sitting position, making quick work of her buttons, and slid the white cotton garment from her shoulders. He cast it to the floor and buried his nose in the delicate skin at the base of her neck. Inhaling deeply, he left a trail of sizzling kisses. His hair brushed over her in feathery touches as he explored her throat, sending shivers over her skin.

She moaned and swayed into him, her core tightening. Her fingers clenched his bare biceps as she surrendered herself to his sensuous ministrations. He peeled off her dress and added it to the growing pile.

Lowering her to her back, he unclasped her bra one-handed on the way down.

A bout of butterflies gripped her, and she slapped a hand over the bra to keep it in place. "Wait…" she whispered. "I'm a little nervous…it's been a while." Five years to be exact.

He slid down beside her and stroked her hair with a free hand. "Would it make you feel better to know that I'm nervous too?" he asked gently.

She nodded, suddenly feeling like a shy teenager awaiting her first kiss.

"As the Council mentioned with appalling clarity, I've been celibate for more than a hundred years." He raised a teasing brow and confessed, "I might be a little rusty."

Relaxing, she sighed, released the bra, and fluttered her lashes. "I believe you were disrobing me?"

"I believe I was." His eyes brightened, and he slid the bra straps along her arms, fully releasing her breasts. The bra arced in the air and disappeared. Hooking his thumbs under her panties, he slid them off, and she lay naked before him.

Simon's breath caught, and his gaze roamed over her curves, hungry yet reverent. "You're even more beautiful than I'd imagined," he whispered and trailed his fingers lightly along her neck to her chest, passing his thumbs over the center of her breasts and raising her nipples to stiff peaks under his circling touch. Her core heated and clenched. Any shyness she had fled.

Cara closed her eyes and moaned.

He released a low growl, and his mouth descended to her breast, hot and needy as he sucked and pulled at the sensitive peak, grazing it gently with his teeth before moving to the other.

She wound her fingers in his hair as he set her skin on fire, and her hot center pulsed with need. His tongue moved lower, circling her navel and blazing a trail of nips and kisses over her stomach and along her hipbones. Grasping her thighs, he opened them, giving himself full access to her heated core.

She wanted him with every fiber of her being. It wouldn't take much to send her over the edge at this rate.

He gazed at her, half-lidded, his powerful arms bracketing her thighs. "I've dreamt of tasting you since the night we met," he said, close enough to her core that his breath caressed her sensitive flesh.

"Oh, God," she breathed, her body clenching and wanting. She needed him more than she needed oxygen.

The hot tip of his tongue connected with the sweet, plump bundle of nerves, and she arched with a soft cry. She dug her fingers into his broad shoulders as he tasted her in slow, sensuous circles. Licking and probing, he pushed her to the sweet brink of orgasm.

"You're so ready for me," he said, running a finger along her wet skin, then sinking it slowly inside her. Sensation rippled through her. Another finger penetrated her, and her back bowed. Sliding and rotating his fingers in tandem, Simon massaged her from the inside. "So beautiful..." he whispered, his gaze transfixed on her parted lips and ragged breathing.

He rested his head on her inner thigh as the pressure built low in her belly. The sweet sensation of his fingers gliding in and out was driving her wild. As she headed towards release, he swirled his tongue over her swollen center until an orgasmic wave took hold, and she shattered, coming in pulsing waves around his fingers. His fingers stilled, and he kissed her inner thigh until the orgasm subsided.

As she lay gasping for breath, he returned his tongue to her sweet spot and resumed his exploration deep inside her. A second orgasm gripped her, hard and fast. She clasped the bed covers, and her hips jolted off the bed. "Simon!" she cried out as she cratered under sensation overload. When her body stopped quaking, he crawled up to lie beside her.

She laced her fingers in his and kissed his knuckles. "That was so...incredible." She was amazed at the ease with which he'd turned her into a satisfied boneless heap.

"That's just an appetizer," he whispered and nuzzled her neck. "I promised neither of us would be able to move afterward...As I said, I always keep my promises."

"Can't wait...for the main...course," she gasped and eyed his black boxers.

He took her into his arms and kissed her, the faint smell of her on his lips. "We have all night."

Taking a moment to recover, she propped herself on an elbow and trailed her fingers to his waistband. She inched down his boxers. "There's only one thing left between us."

An amused smile touched his lips. "Are you sure you're ready for the big reveal? I don't want to scare you, but Nephilim males tend to be a little...*bigger* than an average human male."

Cara's breath caught, even though she knew that from a few stolen touches. In truth, she was both intrigued and a little apprehensive.

"Don't worry." He caressed her shoulder. "We're trained well from adolescence in the art of Sensual Pleasures. The coursework is required before we enter the Guardianship. Nephilim-Human relations are covered thoroughly." He waggled his eyebrows. "Some of us even pursue advanced electives."

Cara snorted a laugh, not wholly surprised given the Angelorum's uncanny sense of pragmatism. If what she'd just experienced was any indication, she was one lucky woman. She flashed a teasing grin. "How advanced did you get in your studies?"

"Very." He winked.

That was good enough for her. She pulled his boxers down the rest of the way, releasing him in all his uncut glory. True to his word, he was well-endowed, long, thick, and totally hairless.

When Constantina had told her Nephilim genetically lacked body hair beyond eyebrows and a full head of hair, Cara hadn't given it much thought, other than the time they must save on shaving. But she had to admit, she found Simon's smooth skin and hairless sex incredibly appealing.

Simon rose to his knees and knelt before her like a piece of living sculpture.

Cara couldn't help but stare, caught between wanting to drink in his beauty and devour him. "Oh my...you're truly breathtaking."

He placed her hands on his chest. "Claim me," he whispered.

Heat rushed through her veins. She gently danced her fingertips down his cheeks. Her lips met his skin, and she kissed a trail along his jaw and up to his lips. Kissing him deeply, she ran her fingers through his golden hair, cradling his head in her hands.

His erection strained between them.

She moved her lips lower to his neck, breathing in his clean and citrusy smell. He let out a soft groan, his fingers caressing her bare shoulders as he steadied himself on his knees.

Pulling back, she ran her hands across his broad shoulders and over his chest, taking in smooth skin over hard muscle beneath her fingertips. Her hands traveled to his rippled back and lower over his well-sculpted backside. His physical attributes, while undeniable, were mere icing on the cake. It was the strength of his heart and kind soul that fueled her desire for him.

She slid her palm down his hot length, circling her fingers at the base and gliding them up the smooth skin in a firm stroke. He thickened in her grasp, parting her fingers, which could no longer contain his girth.

He tightened his grip on her shoulders, a hiss escaping through his teeth. "Not yet…please," he whispered hoarsely and shut his eyes, gritting his teeth to maintain control.

Her mouth watered as she gazed at the solid, thick length of him in her hand. The large, glistening head called her name. She lowered her mouth to heed its call and hoped he forgave her.

SIMON / CHAMUEL

SIMON'S EYES ROLLED back behind closed lids, his groin tightening almost painfully with the need for release. His heart pounded like a freight train ready to career off the tracks. If Cara stroked him or grazed his sensitive head, he was done for. He had to pinch himself a couple of times while his tongue explored her delicate contours to tone down his excitement.

The wildflower scent of her desire filled his senses along with her heady taste, both ambrosia to his aching soul. And the sounds she made…oh, those sounds. He wanted her more than anything he ever remembered wanting. Her body was soft and deliciously pliable, as much as a Nephilim-born woman, easing his concerns that he might hurt her.

Her fingers had paused around his throbbing length.

He took a deep breath and opened his eyes just as her hot mouth engulfed his tip. The sensation shot straight to his brain.

An impassioned cry ripped from his throat as her tongue bathed him in white-hot ecstasy. He clamped his hands on her shoulders as his balls contracted into two hard lemons, and his length kicked in her palm, expanding to capacity and filling her mouth.

"Please, not yet…" he croaked and summoned every shred of willpower he possessed. Gently, he slid from her heavenly mouth into the brace of cool air. "Feels…too good."

She licked her wet lips. "I couldn't help myself. You looked so delicious," she purred, her wide, green eyes meeting his gaze as she rose onto her knees. She caressed his face, her finger sliding over his lip before she kissed him. Tucking a piece of hair behind his ear, she pulled him to her, her tongue exploring his mouth with urgency.

He circled her waist in his arms, pulling her closer, his erection trapped between them. He reveled in the sheer bliss of her naked, creamy skin against his.

Through a half-lidded gaze, she said in a sultry whisper, "Make love to me, Simon."

"With pleasure." He laid her gently on the bedcovers and savored the sight of her. He held back his desperate desire to bury his length inside her. First, he needed to give her more pleasure and assure her readiness.

Cara was his first human woman, more delicate than a female Nephil. If he caused her pain, it would shatter him.

Leaning over her, he caressed the round globes of her breasts, thumbing the beautiful pink buds and rolling the tips between his fingers until they puckered and begged for his tongue.

Cara moaned beneath him, arms above her head. Her moans released something primal within him, and he lowered his mouth to her breasts. Swirling his tongue around a sensitive peak, he sucked and pulled, dancing from one nipple to the other until she writhed beneath him.

"Simon," she begged, jutting her hips up to meet him.

"Let me taste you again," he whispered hoarsely and grazed his fingers down her belly to the triangle of soft, curly hair the color of autumn leaves at the juncture of her thighs. The feel of it against his fingertips fascinated him.

He parted her thighs and plunged his tongue into her wet heat. She cried out, arching into him as he massaged the tender stem of her sex with his thumb, careful not to cross the threshold from pleasure to pain. His tongue moved to her core while he slipped two fingers inside her. His training led the exploration to find her most intimate pleasure spots. He read her micro-reactions, mapped them, and committed them to memory for when he pleasured her with his sex.

"Simon!" she cried, burying her hands in his hair as her body pulsed around his fingers with an intense orgasm.

He grappled with his control as he pleasured her, his body ripe for release with the movements created between his erection and the bedcovers as the foreskin unsheathed his swollen head.

His hands cradled her backside as he drank at her wet center, swallowing her essence as she bucked in the throes of pleasure. Her wildflower scent triggered a powerful déjà vu. Suddenly, the sensation of her felt powerfully familiar. The thought that struck him the night he caught her in his arms returned. He was sure he recognized her. Not her human form, but her...soul.

She panted beneath him, and he did one final test as she rode his fingers in a pulsing wave. He took a breath and slipped a third finger inside her. She accepted it readily, and relief swept through him.

"I want you...now," she said in an urgent whisper. Grasping his biceps, she pulled him toward her.

Kneeing her thighs wider apart, he positioned himself over her. His erection tapped his stomach, more ready than he cared to admit.

She gazed at him with hazy desire and wrapped her legs around his hips, opening her most intimate part to him. The glistening pink petals sent a siren's call, inviting him inside.

Hovering over her, he aligned himself with her entrance, took a deep breath, and slowly pushed inside. The feel of her wet heat surrounding his shaft sent a shock wave through his senses. His jaw tensed, and he pushed deeper into her clasping embrace until he was sheathed halfway.

She winced beneath him. He froze. Fear shot through him, and he started pulling out. "Am I hurting you?"

She shook her head, dug her nails into his glutes, and pulled him into her. His eyes burst wide open as he sank to the hilt. The velvet friction inside her set his nerve endings crackling in sweet overload.

"Cara..." he growled.

"Simon," she whispered and caressed his cheek. "I won't break." She gave him a sexy smile and slapped his ass. "Make love to me."

He blew out a relieved breath, rolled his hips, and moved with intentional strokes. The feel of her almost brought tears to his eyes. The pressure building low in his pelvis was already unbearable. His ab muscles bunched with each thrust as he picked up his rhythm. Pushing deeper with each thrust, he sought her pleasure spots, rubbing his length over her swollen core with every stroke as he held back his pleasure.

Leaning in, he kissed her deeply, her tongue rising to meet his. He balanced on an elbow and held her in place against him, his hand supporting the small of her back. Her nails traveled the length of his to his backside. A shiver rippled through him.

Her sweet moans accompanied his rhythmic thrusts. As he increased his tempo, Cara moved in tandem. Every stroke held the heat of his passion and his absolute wonder as the tight embrace of her sex worked to unleash a powerful release that threatened to blow him apart. But he'd die before denying her a perfect first experience.

"Oh...Simon!" Her body arched into him, and her fingers dug into his backside. Her wet heat seized him in a snug, pulsating grip that milked his length.

His vision blurred, and his heart pounded so hard he heard the blood hammering through his eardrums. He pistoned with deep, penetrating strokes.

Then her hand cupped his balls and squeezed with gentle pressure.

A bellow ripped from his lungs as his entire body jerked and spasmed in release. His length pulsated wildly as he rode his orgasm before turning to satiated mush.

Panting and breathless, he rolled onto his back. Still buried deep inside Cara, she moved with him. Her strained breaths joined his as she lay covering his heaving chest.

Her green-eyed gaze filled with deep satisfaction. "That…that was beyond incredible," she said and rested her head against his pounding heart.

He wrapped his arms around her; their skin fused from head to toe. Happiness engulfed him for the first time in well over one hundred years, sweeping away the guilt, sorrow, and restlessness that had defined him. More than happiness, Cara felt like his home. And he would never leave her again.

He stroked her hair as she lay on his chest with her arms draped around him. "I love you," he whispered.

She raised her head and touched his face with her fingertips. "I love you too."

Maybe Constantina was right. Perhaps he deserved redemption. Because, for the first time, he felt worthy enough to stand at Cara's side.

He ran his fingers along Cara's spine, keeping her body melded to his. He thought again about the déjà vu and the familiarity he felt while making love to her. He had to know if he was right—if he recognized her soul. Hopefully, she wasn't too tired to indulge him.

"I need to ask you something," he whispered.

She glanced at him with sleepy eyes. "What is it?"

He shifted them into a sitting position, his length still happily seated in her warmth, and pulled the duvet around them. He pressed his forehead to hers. "The night I caught you in my arms, I experienced what we call 'soul recognition.' At first, I didn't think it was possible. Now, I wonder if that's what drove me to break my oath and why the Council let us off easy. Will you help me answer that question?"

She gazed at him with trusting eyes. "Just tell me what to do."

Chapter 60

CARA

Angelorum Sanctuary. France.

CARA'S SCALP TINGLED as she reclined beneath the duvet with Simon kneeling over her. "Is soul recognition like finding a soulmate?" she asked.

Simon's expression turned pensive. "Yes and no," he said after some hesitation. "When two humans meet, they sometimes have an instant affinity with each other, like they've known each other their whole lives. There's a good chance their souls have already met. So, it's similar in that sense, but not all affinities are love interests."

Cara nodded, thinking of her relationship with Kai—and how she now understood they were soulmates of a different kind. Their destinies were linked through a debt repaid by saving each other. "So, you think we've met before?"

He held out a hand, palm up. "I think we've *loved* before."

A tingle traversed her spine, and she placed her hand in his. "What's the difference between a soulmate and a soul recognition?"

He pressed her hands to his heart. His gaze softened, and he whispered, "I think we share a piece of the same soul."

Simon's words resonated like hundreds of tiny bells, and an elusive flash of her grandmother taunted her. "How do we do this?" she asked, feeling a connection to the memory evading her.

He brushed a kiss over her knuckles and released her hand. "First, I need to tap into my angelic side, then we'll join our energy. That should create a conduit to give us a peek behind the veil that separates Heaven and Earth—and allow us to connect at the soul level."

She eyed him skeptically. "You sure that's going to work? It sounds very, I don't know, *impossible*."

His lips turned up in a cocky grin. "Not if you trust my third-year Angelology textbook."

She snorted a laugh. "Silly me." Then again, the man had wings. Her definition of 'impossible' had recently expanded its borders. Why not a little astral projection to Heaven?

He kissed her nose and winked. "I'm going to call my power. Ready?"

As ready as she'd ever be. She nodded.

Above her, he closed his eyes, and a gentle breeze filled the room. A glow grew beneath Simon's skin, and light radiated outward until it surrounded him in a halo of white light. When he opened his eyes, they shone in an unnaturally bright blue, and his wings unfurled with a light whoosh behind him. His brilliance forced her to squint.

When he spoke, his voice held a booming, otherworldly timbre, "This will only work if we're joined." He positioned his body between her thighs and rested on his elbows, his wings creating a downy-white canopy above them. "Grab my shoulders, and call your energy."

She inhaled sharply and said a prayer to summon what now she fondly called her Pillar of Power. In answer, golden light slammed from the heavens through the top of her head, circling her heart and exiting her palms into Simon.

Her light eclipsed his, and her lids closed.

His lips touching hers, they shared a heady breath, and a breezy current swiftly carried her away.

JOYOUS LAUGHTER RANG out like a thousand tinkling bells. Opening her eyes, she sought the sweet, melodic sound and realized she was the source. She ran headlong through a meadow of wildflowers in every color of the rainbow. A clear, blue sky and several suns filled the day with warmth. She ran swiftly, dodging nettles, so they didn't snag the white tunic billowing around her bare legs.

"You can't outrun me forever, my love," a masculine voice teased behind her, which only fueled her happiness and elicited more blissful laughter. The thrill of the chase made the capture so much sweeter. Her spirit was light, and happy tears gathered in her eyes.

Though she desired to be caught, she delighted in not making the catching too easy. Spending the afternoon with him in their meadow made her heart burst with joy. There were so few days like this when they could set aside their duties and escape to the Elysian Fields to languish in each other's arms. But today was special.

Her heart would leave Heaven shortly on his next earthly assignment, and nearly a century and a quarter would pass in his time before they could reunite. So, she wanted today to be memorable. Not that he would remember, Layela would see to that on her behalf, but she would have those memories until she, too, departed.

Time meant little here, but she needed more of it to find a suitable replacement to fill her post before her rebirth. She had to be highly selective, given the importance of her position and the challenges that lay ahead. Darkness threatened entrance through Heaven's Gate, and she could not, would not, let that happen.

Strong arms encircled her from behind and lifted her off her feet.

"I have you," he whispered, his breath tickling her ear, and put her down.

Her joyous laughter swelled as she faced him and threw her arms around his neck. "That you do, my love." The energy of his soul burned brightly across Cara's eyes, his beauty undeniable. She recognized Simon immediately in the vision…but his name wasn't Chamuel then, and hers was not Cara.

She absorbed his loving gaze. "You have me forever."

His hungry lips came down on hers, his arms tightening around her. She melted into his warm embrace. His hands traveled over her curves with urgent, reverent touches, and then he swept her into his arms. The desire in his eyes betrayed his heart. He lowered her onto a bed of crushed wildflowers before he collapsed on his back beside her. The suns warmed her face as they lay enjoying their loving rays.

He rolled to his side and traced a fingertip over her brow. She caught his gaze and lost herself in the loving pull of his sky-colored eyes. Her body craved to couple with him, wanting nothing more than his body as an extension of hers.

They exchanged smiles, shed their white garments, and spread them on the wildflower mattress. He positioned himself between her thighs, and her laughter mixed with tears as she wrapped her legs around his waist and pulled him closer. His muscles tensed, and he joined with her.

She released an ecstatic cry, her senses reeling with the exquisite feel of him moving inside her. Her heart exploded with the moment's perfection. Birds chirped in tandem with the hum of heavenly music as he made love to her for the last time in their meadow.

He stilled, and she opened her eyes at the abrupt stop. He stared down at her, smiling, tears streaming freely down his cheeks. "Promise you'll find me?" he asked in a hoarse whisper, looking for reassurance.

She ran her fingers through his soft hair. "On my soul, I will find you." She could do something to assure it, but that required a ceremony and consultation with the Well of Souls. His scheduled rebirth would leave no opportunity for such things after this visit. Either way, she was the sole decider.

She hesitated, deciding to face any consequences for her actions, then placed two fingers to the bare skin over her heart and sank them into her chest. They reemerged a moment later, holding a pearl of light. She held it up to show him and then pressed the pearl into his chest until it disappeared beneath his skin.

"Now, I will always be with you, my love."

"And, I will love you forever and a day," he said, his mouth once again finding hers as her body shattered into pure sensation. Her eyes fluttered shut, and her cries joined his in pure, unbridled waves of rapture. She lost the fading syllables of her bellowed name as a breeze carried them away.

CARA'S HEART STUTTERED, the rapture following her. She opened her eyes. Simon smiled above her, his blue eyes shining and his cheeks wet. "You kept your promise."

She brushed a piece of blond hair stuck to his damp cheek behind his ear. "Forever and a day, my love." She recognized the glow in his crystal-blue eyes and remembered their deep love.

The memory flash that had evaded her solidified. "I remember!" she said on a breathy exhale, recalling her visit to the Bridge with Hannah and looking down at her body. She remembered the silver cord and the piece of her soul shining like a pearl of light beside Simon's heart that bound them for eternity—a beacon for her to find him. It all made sense now. Then, she shuddered. There were consequences for what she did, but she had no idea what they were.

"Remember what, my love?" he asked, caressing her cheek.

"I died in the warehouse. I saw my grandmother, Hannah." She gently cradled his face, her voice cracking, "I came back for you."

A tear fell from his eye. "Thank you," he said and placed a hand on his heart. "I will treasure and protect this piece of you, always." He sealed his word with a kiss.

Her heart rejoiced at his words, but a thread of worry tugged at her. Something Hannah said about finding out who she was.

He rested his forehead on hers. "What is it?" he asked gently.

Cara debated telling him, but this moment had far greater importance. There was always tomorrow.

"It's nothing," she whispered and kissed him. Then, once again, he swept her away, and the world receded around them.

Chapter 61

CARA

Angelorum Sanctuary. France.

"WHAT CAN I do to convince you to come back to bed?" Simon asked in a deep, sexy growl.

Setting down the brush, Cara glanced at Simon in the mirror and grinned. "You're insatiable, you know that?" She'd thrown on one of his T-shirts, which hung like a dress to her knees, in a lame attempt to discourage him.

He eyed her with a mischievous smile from where he lay on the bed, propped on an elbow, naked as the day he was born. "I have over a century of celibacy to make up for."

She chuckled and resumed detangling her bed head with the brush. "I think we've made a lot of progress over the last few days, don't you?" They'd put a nice dent in their celibacy streaks, the pleasant soreness at the juncture of her thighs a reminder of their progress. "Besides, we need to pack."

Constantina had encouraged them to travel while they still could. According to her, they had a small respite before gathering the rest of the Twelve. *Thank you, Sweet Baby Jesus.*

To celebrate their engagement, they planned an impromptu vacation for the next few weeks to visit their favorite places. Thanks to Simon borrowing a vacation home from one of his fellow Guardians, they would start in Monaco. From there, they would return to the States and tour the Grand Canyon.

Her phone pinged with a new text. She picked it up where it lay face down on the dresser. Surprise widened Cara's eyes, not only at who texted and why, but at the late hour in New York. Shawna Jones, a former colleague, had banded together with the other impacted Cabot employees and taken the recording of Rick boasting about the questionable dismissals at the Christmas party to a law firm. They were serving papers for a class action discrimination suit against Cabot Investments when the firm opened in the morning.

Cara smiled. There was justice in the world.

"Everything okay?" Simon asked.

"Karma biting my old boss, Rick, in the backside," she said mildly and returned Shawna's text, offering any assistance they might need. "Shawna and the others are taking them to court."

Simon chuckled, familiar with the power play she made the day she resigned.

A soft knock sounded on the door.

Cara cleared her throat and pointed at him.

He gave her a mock frown and covered himself with a sheet.

She opened the door a crack.

It was Constantina. Cara missed their training sessions and had to get used to seeing her mentor wearing High Council robes.

"Sorry to disturb you, dear one. I want to show you something before you depart with Chamuel," Constantina whispered.

Cara gave her a sheepish smile and pulled at the T-shirt. "Give me five minutes?"

Constantina gave a knowing smile. "Of course. I'll wait down the hall."

Cara shut the door, and Simon enveloped her from behind. His body pressed to her, his groin twitching against her spine. "So, what does Constantina want at this early hour?" He nibbled her earlobe, sending a shiver over her skin.

She turned in his arms and rose on tiptoe to plant a warm kiss on his lips. "You can't stand this close to me looking that delicious, or I'll never leave."

He cocked a wicked eyebrow. "Until later, then?"

"Count on it. But for now, I suggest clothes, lots of them."

Clicking his tongue, he strolled to the bathroom. "Fine." She drank in his muscled glutes as he disappeared through the doorway.

She quickly changed into form-fitting black slacks, a clingy T-shirt that would make Sienna proud, and low-heeled sandals.

"I'm going for a workout," Simon yelled from the bathroom. "Then I'll pick up the keys to Yves's villa. Do you mind leaving before lunch?"

"Sounds perfect," she said.

He poked out his head. "Another kiss before you go?"

She met him halfway and indulged in one last kiss. "I love you," she said, wearing a satisfied smile and feeling like the luckiest woman alive.

He kissed the top of her head. "I love you more. Better go. You don't want to keep Constantina waiting."

CONSTANTINA

CARA STOOD WIDE-EYED beside Constantina and stared into the Trinity Pool. Constantina trained the magnifier on the cluster of Trinity Stones that made up the Holy Twelve and stepped aside to show Cara. Below, the smooth, triangular stones shimmered in a kaleidoscope of colors, pulsing with life and destiny.

Cara pressed her face to the viewer and drew in a breath. "They're dizzying to watch. Do they really speak to you?"

Constantina squeezed Cara's shoulder. "When you're ready, they'll reveal secrets to you, too. But with secrets come knowledge, and in turn, great responsibility. Like Semyaza and his Watchers before us, the lure to share too much will always be present. Good is a choice, but temptation lies close, even for us. We reside within the Sanctuary walls and maintain our distance to help resist the power our borrowed humanity affords us. We're not immune to sin. Like Lucifer, we can Fall."

One of us already has, Constantina thought, the eleven faces of her fellow High Council members flashing through her mind. She needed to root out the traitor in their midst. Whoever betrayed her and Hope would continue unless they were stopped. Until that happened, she trusted no one on the Council, not even Angelis.

Frowning, Cara asked, "Why are you showing me these now?"

Constantina smiled wryly. "I've been remiss in your education, as Achanelech so bluntly pointed out."

Cara released a frustrated growl. "What did he say? I still don't remember much from that night. Kai thinks it could be a side effect of the vaccine."

Small mercy. "Not to worry, dear one. At some point soon, you will. Whether or not you remember Achanelech's word makes them no less true. Our encounter with him was only the opening salvo, a skirmish in a far larger war. In all his prideful puffery, Achanelech tipped his hand, as they say. He planned to ensnare you for Lucifer, and I doubt Dr. Solomon's abduction will be his only attempt. We must prevent that from happening. He was right about one thing: you are the most important piece in this puzzle. Still, you will need Chamuel and the others to succeed. We must gather the Twelve and ease them into the knowledge as time and destiny dictate. Our work begins again soon."

"Speaking of Kai, I do remember one small thing," Cara said, her gaze sharpening on Constantina with complete clarity. "In the warehouse, we spoke mind to mind. Is he one of us?"

Constantina squelched her surprise with a controlled smile. How unexpected, fascinating, and yet unsurprising, given Kai's parentage. Sharing what she knew would be prohibited had Cara not shared this premature revelation. What Constantina hadn't mentioned to Cara in her initial training was that the Holy Twelve were not guaranteed to follow the rules of traditional Trinities. Hence, Chamuel's place as the Second…and Kai's Messenger blood.

"He is," Constantina conceded. "When the time is right, he shall know. For now, and for Kai's safety, that truth stays between us, all right?"

"Of course." Cara placed a hand over her heart and met Constantina's gaze with intense resolve. "In the antechamber at the Tribunal, I asked why I was chosen. Now, I think I know. I promise not to let you down."

Constantina cocked her head, pleased. "I never doubted you. But I'm glad you no longer doubt yourself."

Cara embraced Constantina in a tight hug, encircling her in loving energy. "Thank you for everything."

"Enjoy your time with Cham—Simon," Constantina said, stumbling over her son's chosen name. *"I'm not renouncing my birth name, Mother,"* he'd said, *"Just adding a new one. Cara says that I will always be Simon to her."*

"Journey forth in peace in love, dearest Cara."

Cara's arms fell away. "And you, Constantina."

Constantina sighed, watching her soon-to-be mated daughter exit through the door at the end of the catwalk above, glad that true love had prevailed. She hoped *this time* her son and his soulmate would succeed.

She returned her gaze to the cluster of the Twelve in the Pool. Now, they would gather the Wanderer's children.

Their next mission clear, Constantina too, left the sanctuary.

CONSTANTINA UNLOCKED HER private rooms with a scrolled key and entered, halting with a gasp.

A tall mountain of a male, head bowed and hands clasped at his waist, stood waiting in her receiving room. His long, white hair was gathered and secured at the nape of his neck, the silky length hidden from view.

"Ishmael?" The Nephilim Guardian's name spilled from Constantina's lips, and she arched a quizzical brow, more confused than alarmed at the sight of her daughter Hope's mate standing before her. A smile grew on her lips, and affection stirred in her heart as she closed the distance between them.

Once released from Achanelech's prison, he had slipped away before they had a chance to speak.

He glanced up, his pale blue eyes fixing on hers. "My apologies for the intrusion, Eae," he said in a low voice.

So many emotions bombarded her at once. The loss of her daughter, Ishmael's abduction days before Hope's death—a death she failed to prevent. All because she tried to help.

Constantina wrapped her mated son in a hug. Her short stature brought her head to his chest. "I tried to find you after the warehouse."

He circled her in a warm and solid embrace. Looking down to meet her gaze, he gave a solemn nod. "I know," he said softly. "I'm sorry…I had to go back.…" He swallowed, his eyes glassy with unshed tears. His lip quivered, and his voice grew thick. "I wasn't there to save her. I failed you both."

Constantina pressed her eyes shut and shook her head. "No. You did not." She released him and motioned toward a settee and a cluster of chairs. "Please sit, Isa."

He lowered onto the settee. She sat beside him and took his large hands in hers—hands that touched and loved her daughter for more than three hundred years. "Look at me."

His gaze rose to meet hers.

"There is a traitor among us. Someone who betrayed me and betrayed Hope. That is the person responsible for her death. Not you. Will you help me find them?"

His gaze darkened, and his lips pressed into a grim line. "Of course. I remain your loyal servant."

"Good." She nodded and squeezed his hands. "I shall call upon you soon, but for now, I am so very sorry for your loss, my precious son. I thought I'd lost you, too. I'm grateful that you live." As with Ishmael, one year had done little to dull the pain in Constantina's heart over the loss of her daughter.

"Thank you," he whispered, and this time, he reached for her. Her hands disappeared inside his much larger ones. "Hope is not why I'm here. It's something else. Actually, *someone*."

Constantina stiffened, her senses snapping to life with a vibrating tingle. Her pulse accelerated, and she asked in a breathy whisper, "Who?"

His glassy eyes took on a glow, and he whispered, "He lives."

Constantina's heart stuttered. "Who lives?"

Ishmael swallowed. "I told him you would come, but he was already gone when you rescued us."

"Who lives, Isa?" she demanded, her heart pounding as hope blossomed in her chest.

"Samuel."

A hand flew to her chest as she gasped.

Achanelech had lied.
Her son was *alive*.

Epilogue

ACHANELECH

Hell.

ACHANELECH OPENED A swollen eye to survey the blackened lump of demon flesh lying in a heap beside him. He was sure he looked no better. They'd been dumped like demon garbage.

Agony tore through him in unending waves of fire, and he wished hard for an oblivious death, anything to escape the pain and infernal wailing of tormented souls beyond their cell. He didn't want to move, but he had to know if she was gone.

He inched a charred claw across the tar-covered floor toward Emanelech in her dragon-like demonic form. Her leathery skin had burned to flaky, silvery-black ash.

The pain in his throat was unbearable as he forced out her name. "Em," he said in native Hellspeak, the effort akin to swallowing knives.

His demon heart palpitated when he spotted a slight flutter on the black mound. There it was: a slice of blue — her eye, not her demon eye, but her human eye. "Acchie..." she said, but he could barely hear her over the horrific noise surrounding them. "I hurt, Acchie," she rasped, her eye fluttering shut.

"Don't leave me, Em." Pain worse than his suffering flesh ripped through his dead heart.

"Can't..."

"Please," he begged. He couldn't fathom how he'd ended up here in such utter despair. But he knew he couldn't survive it without Emanelech at his side.

"Miss...home," she whispered, this time in human language.

Their Master had done a number on them for their screwup with that Soul Seeker. They'd almost gotten her killed before she escaped, and Lucifer had been less than thrilled with their performance. He'd shown his displeasure for what seemed like an eternity. They'd never be able to survive topside in this state.

His clawed finger caressed her ashy arm, bits flaking off under his touch. "Where, *ma chèrie*? Le France?" he croaked, though his throat was not fit for speech.

"No…Heav…"

Terror gripped him. It was forbidden to mention the "H" word in Hell. She must be delirious from the punishment.

"Em, no. Don't ssspeak," he hissed, his forked tongue flicking between what was left of his teeth. "We'll never get out of here if you do."

Her eye opened in a slit. "Redemp…" He would've paled if he could have.

Redemption? Was she insane? Achanelech wanted to choke her into silence before she condemned them to a permanent residence in Lucifer's wailing wall. Anger bubbled through his veins like red-hot lava. There would never be redemption for them. Ever.

The sigil on his neck twinged, and then the twinge grew into a steady pulse. His children had arrived.

He bowed his head and opened the gateway. The cell filled with a black inky haze.

Oh, the irony. Since Semyaza and the Watchers were condemned to unending darkness during the time of Noah, Achanelech had commanded the disembodied spirits of their Nephilim spawn. And they were here to do his bidding.

*Master…Master…Master…*They spoke, one by one, in the language of Hell.

"Take us home," he whispered in a misery-filled plea.

He had work to do and a score to settle.

Eae would pay for all she'd done to him. He'd patiently waited over a century for her mate Leo to descend from his heavenly perch, but Achanelech would wait no longer. She had more to lose, and vengeance would be his.

Want more Angelorum Twelve?

Dear Reader,

Thank you for entering the World of the Angelorum! If you enjoyed *Trinity Stones*, consider leaving a review on Amazon, Goodreads, or sharing on Instagram or TikTok (#BookTok). Please and thank you! Truly, word of mouth is what helps authors sell books.

The Angelorum Twelve Chronicles is an epic story told across four books, plus a prequel novella, *Hope's Prelude*, which divides the series, reveals secrets, and introduces characters (living and dead) from the first two books. The Angelorum Twelve series is best enjoyed in order. Though *Hope's Prelude* can be read before or after Trinity Stones, it contains spoilers and makes the most sense after *Wanderer's Children (Book 2)*. The prologue in *Trinity Stones* flashes back to the prequel, *Hope's Prelude*, which includes Samuel's story, Sandra & Tom's heroic sacrifice, and the love story with Isa, since they are integral to the Twelve, and they deserve their own story.

If this is your first trip into the world of the Angelorum, I hope you'll fall in love with the characters as much as I did. Each book — including this one — can be read to a satisfying conclusion.

Previews of all the published & preorder books in the series, including the next book in the series, **Wanderer's Children (Book 2)**, can be found on **my website's download page**:

https://lgoconnor.com/downloads/

Heat level: Wanderer's Children is steamier than Trinity Stones.

Hugs & Happy Reading!

L.G.

The Angelorum Twelve Books & Reading Order

*From L.G. O'Connor, award-winning author of **Caught Up in Raine**, comes a 4-book epic angel & demon fantasy series with forbidden and fated love, enemies-to-lovers, found family, and sizzling romance that will leave you wanting more.*

Science and spirit meet in The Angelorum Twelve, an epic angel & demon fantasy. For 2,000 years, the Angelorum—the next generation of angelic Watchers—has maintained the balance of good and evil between humanity and Lucifer's Dark Ones. Both sides have played by the rules...until now. Lucifer has a score to settle and a celestial loophole to seize to restore his rightful place in the final battle of good and evil. Twelve souls will stretch the limits of Heaven and Earth to stop him...

TRINITY STONES, Book One.

There are no coincidences, only destinies to be fulfilled.

Cara Collins is questioning her choices. Between a back-stabbing boss, a non-existent social life, and lingering feelings for Dr. Kai Solomon, a man she can never have, things need to change. After discovering she has the power to restore the gift of youth, the same day she receives an unexpected $50 million windfall, it seems Fate agrees.

Learning she is part of a Trinity, Cara is shaken to discover she can become the angelic weapon needed to defeat Lucifer and his Dark Ones in their quest to conquer Heaven and enslave humanity. Torn between her duty to save the world and the promise of a new love, the timing couldn't be worse.

Cara's unseen Nephilim Guardian, Chamuel, knows he has a problem the moment he sees his new charge. His heart stirs for the first time in over a century for the one female on earth forbidden to him under Angelorum Law. After a chance encounter under his human identity, he's powerless to resist her—regardless of the devastating price he will pay if anyone, including Cara, discovers the truth.

When dark forces kidnap Kai and his daughter, forbidden love, betrayal, and destiny collide, forcing Cara to make an impossible choice to save the people she loves without sacrificing the future of humanity, and playing right into Lucifer's hands.

WANDERER'S CHILDREN, Book Two.

Los Angeles. San Francisco. Chicago. New York. The Wanderer's mission three decades ago: secretly sire children to hide his bloodline, and protect them until their destinies unite to fight the final battle between good and evil.

Duty will call soon to gather the rest of the Angelorum Twelve and prepare them for battle. Before that happens, Cara Collins wants one peaceful weekend with her bridesmaids before her wedding to her former Trinity Guardian. But we don't always get what we want …

Life has changed. Cara's newly acquired Nephilim DNA is wreaking havoc on her body, with an overabundance of pheromones triggering a mortifying outbreak of "insta-love" among her friends that would make Cupid proud. If only she could point her arrow at her Trinity Messenger, Michael Swift, who has been running from his attraction to Cara's brazen best friend, Sienna, the only woman ever to skirt his defenses. Even if he wants a future with her, first, he must confront his tormented past, or risk threatening the future of the Angelorum.

After a chance encounter, runaway rock star Brett King is harboring a crush on Cara, but, infatuation aside, Brett is more than he appears. One of the Wanderer's children, he and his siblings are the key to gathering the rest of the Twelve souls destined to fight in the final battle of good and evil. With the growing threat of Lucifer's fallen angels, Cara has more to worry about than petty jealousy, drunken debauchery, and a bridal shower. An enemy within the Angelorum is determined to see them fail, if a traitor in Cara's inner circle doesn't destroy them all.

HOPE'S PRELUDE, Prequel Novella, Book 2.5.

Save the *One* who will save them all.

Enter the world of the Angelorum for a glimpse into its origins as destinies entwine to deliver us one step closer to battle …

Stolen as an infant by Achanelech, the Archdemon of Fire, Samuel has lived in his kidnapper's dungeons for over a century. Unaware of his angelic origins, he is persuaded to help capture his Nephilim brethren in exchange for a longer leash and a chance to plot his own escape.

While dealing with visions of her death, Dr. Sandra Wilson races against the clock with research partner, Dr. Tom Peyton, and her Nephilim mate, Isa, to develop a vaccine that will save the One.

With Isa ensnared in Achanelech's trap, and the Archdemon closing in on Sandra, it is Samuel who must risk his freedom to ensure the future of the Angelorum … and the mother he never met.

Acknowledgments

A note about the re-release of this novel & series. This epic story holds a special place in my heart. As life and other projects emerged, I was pulled in other directions, but I plan to finish Book of Four Rings (Book 3), which is 75% written, hopefully in 2026. I also plan to conclude the series with Well of Souls (Book 4). I've known from the beginning how every part of this story ends. I love these characters, and it has been great reacquainting myself with the whole crew. I promise, you will get an answer to every open question, including why Cara inherited $50 million. I hope you will stick with us!

I'm grateful for the time I've spent as a She Writes Press author for Trinity Stones, but this book deserved a refresh (new editing and a new cover) and more marketing attention than it received. I started rewriting this manuscript in 2021, between other projects, hoping to re-release it before its 10th anniversary. Ah, the best laid plans. So, after almost eleven years, here is the new Trinity Stones. So, journey forth with me in peace and love!

In addition to my original 2014 critique and beta teams: Joanie Sorensen, Deborah, Cindy, Jenni, and Kisa; the "cross-stitch" beta reading crew (Marilyn, Pat, Lesley, and Eileen); the New Providence Writers Critique Group; and my progression of editors, especially Zetta Brown.

I would like to recognize my 2025 release beta readers, paranormal romance author Carla Susan Smith, and Jill Stedronsky. Thank you all for making this book even better!

About the Author

Photo: Oak & Ivy Photograph

L.G. O'Connor spends her free time spinning fantasy, contemporary, and mystery stories that touch the heart with themes of family, redemption, forgiveness, and above all, hope. An avid reader, she loves books with memorable characters that stay with you long after the story ends.

L.G. is the author of the multi-award-winning romantic women's fiction trilogy: *Caught Up in Raine, Shelter My Heart*, and *Surrender My Heart*, which follows a family of three women who must confront the past to find redemption and second chances. She's also the author of the epic fantasy romance series, *The Angelorum Twelve Chronicles*. L.G. enjoys connecting with readers at book clubs and reader events.

If you enjoyed this book, (please!) leave a **REVIEW or RATING** on **Amazon, Bookbub, Goodreads, #BookTok**, or wherever you purchased the book.

Find/Follow L.G.:

Website & Newsletter www.lgoconnor.com
Bookbub @LGOConnor for New Releases
Substack (@lgoconnor) for her Wellness and Writerly posts

Glossary of Terms and Proper Nouns

(the) Angelorum (pr. n.) All members of the protectorate, consisting of the three hundred descended angels that make up the next generation of Watchers, the Nephilim Guardianship, the human Messenger families, and the human Soul Seekers.

(the) Angelorum Sanctuary (pr. n.) The central headquarters of the three hundred Angelorum Watchers and the Nephilim Guardianship located at an undisclosed underground location in the French countryside.

(the) Angelorum Twelve (pr. n.) The twelve souls who will lead the Angelorum into the final battle against Lucifer, the Morning Star, and his fallen minions, the Dark Ones.

(the) Angelorum Watchers (pr. n.) A group of three hundred angels who approached God after the Great War in Heaven and requested to be sent down to earth after Lucifer and his fallen minions to provide a protectorate to oversee the balance of good and evil as the next generation of Watchers. The request was granted, allowing the angels to incarnate as humans. However, they were allowed to remain "awakened," which would enable them to retain their original angelic identity, their memories of Heaven, and their past lives with each incarnation. They are physically marked by the lack of a vertical indentation above their lip (philtrum). Also known as the Sanctus Angelorum protectorate or *Defensores Contra Malum.*

Calling (n.) Official request by the Angelorum for acceptance into the Angelorum. For a Soul Seeker within a Trinity, it's when the Center Stone of the Trinity is revealed, and the full powers of the Soul Seeker are activated.

Center Stone (n.) Physically, the Center Stone resides in the middle of each Trinity Stone, representing the soul in which the Trinity is tied, and the mission is centered.

Cloaking (v.) Nephilim power. Hiding behind the veil of invisibility. To hide someone beneath a veil requires physical contact. When connected, connected individuals can see and hear one another but cannot be seen or heard by anyone outside the veil.

Dark Ones (pr. n.) Angels cast from Heaven with Lucifer (the Morning Star) after the Great War in Heaven. Their wings were torn from their bodies, so they could never return.

Defensores Contra Malum (pr. n.) Another Latin name for the Sanctus Angelorum protectorate. Translates to the Protectors from Evil within the hidden scripture, the *Book of Human Angels.*

Demon (n.) Disembodied spirits of Nephilim spawned by Semyaza and the first Watchers. Used as Hunters for the Dark Ones. Appear as a black, inky haze before manifesting into their physical form, which resembles a demonic satyr. Members of the Angelorum can feel the demon's presence through the onset of a sudden migraine-like headache and the taste of tar on the tongue. When they die, they turn to black ash.

Divine Visitation (n.) An interlude between one of the Powers and a descended human angel that results in the conception of a Nephilim child.

Enoch (pr. n.) Appears in Genesis, the seventh of the pre-Deluge Patriarchs. Great-grandfather to Noah. Believed to have been taken from Earth to become the angel Metatron. The Apocryphal Books of Enoch attributed to him. Semyaza and the angelic Watchers inhabited Earth during his lifetime, and he bore witness to their sins.

Fallen (pr. n.) See Dark Ones.

(the) Flow (n.) An electromagnetic field that surrounds the Earth and is utilized for communication and the transmission of healing energy.

Guardian (n.) Nephilim warrior. May or may not be actively assigned to a current Trinity. As part of a Trinity, they take an oath to protect the members of their Trinity.

(the) Guardianship (pr. n.) The Nephilim warriors who provide protection for the Angelorum. Guardians can be assigned to a Trinity to protect a Messenger and a Soul Seeker as they pursue their mission.

Hunter (n.) Trackers working for the Dark Ones who hunt and destroy Soul Seekers and other Angelorum members. Can be either disembodied entities or physical, soulless humans.

Irin (pr. n.) Angels assigned to watch the Watchers and record human history on Earth. Also known as the Archivists. They are the librarians for the Flow.

Libre Homo Angelorum (n.) Translated from Latin as the *Book of Human Angels.* A hidden scripture that tells the story of the Angelorum Watchers.

Messenger (n.) A human who can communicate directly with the Angelorum through the Irin. Messengers' telepathic abilities are used in a Trinity to provide communication and guidance. Messenger traits are inherited through the bloodline of their fathers.

Nephilim (n., plural) **Nephil** (n., singular). A being conceived through an angelic divine visitation. The child is half-human, half-angel, and possesses angelic characteristics, including wings, the ability to fly, telepathic communication, the use of angelic prayers, and the ability to speak the angelic language. In addition, the Nephilim cannot procreate and live for up to five hundred years. A significantly improved version of the evil Nephilim of Genesis, created by Semyaza and the disobedient angelic Watchers.

Nephilim class (n.) Every century of Nephilim has a class number. Once a Nephilim turns one hundred years old, they enter the One Hundred Class, and with each subsequent century, they enter the next class. The last class is the Four Hundred Class, which is composed of those who turn four hundred years old and whose lifespan ends before they reach five hundred years old.

Powers (pr. n.) The 9th Order of Angels in Heaven. The great warrior angels are considered the last line of defense for Heaven.

The Prophecy (n.) The prediction is that a final battle would occur between the Angelorum and the Dark Ones, led by twelve souls who have the power to overcome evil and banish the Fallen into the prison where they belong for the rest of eternity.

Semyaza (pr. n.) Fallen angel of apocryphal Jewish and Christian tradition. Believed to be the leader of the angelic Watchers sent to Earth to watch over man.

Sentinel (n.) One who keeps watch and identifies members of the Angelorum and the Fallen.

Soul Seeker (n.) A human who is bound to the soul of another. When the time is right, the Seeker will be Called to partake in the event of the bound soul (Center Stone), which has significance in the balance of good vs. evil. The Seeker is partnered with a Messenger and a Guardian and is the farthest removed from the Angelorum Watchers. Seekers can have healing and/or other abilities.

Soul Separator (n.) An angelic sword used to cast out demons possessing live humans.

Soulless (n.) A human who relinquishes their soul as food for the Dark Ones. The aura of a soulless human is black and cloudy, the same as a demon. When killed, they turn to black sand.

Sphinx (n.) Ice minions controlled by Emanelech. Creatures who stand guard at the entrance into the first circle of Hell. Conjured in the form of twins, Chaos and Destruction. They can block Nephilim and Trinity telepathic communication. They are a force more powerful than Nephilim. There are only two.

Transporter (n.) A suborder of the Powers, the 9th Order of Angels. This type of angel transports souls to their final resting ground, Heaven or Hell. Another name for a Reaper.

Trinity Pool (n.) A pool of white sand containing the Trinity Stones. Each stone represents a Trinity assigned to a current or future event that could tip the balance of good vs. evil. The Trinity Pool is located in the inner sanctum of the Angelorum Sanctuary. The stones in the pool are alive and continually change as the individuals make free will decisions, impacting the outcome of events. They pulse with colorful light and can speak to those who hear them. They are the link between Heaven and Earth.

Trinity Stone (n.) Smooth triangular stones with rounded edges that are sectioned into three parts. Each section represents a member of the Trinity, which surrounds a Center Stone embedded in the middle, representing the soul in which the Soul Seeker is connected, and who will be part of an event that will tip the balance of good versus evil. As free will decisions lock in destinies, secrets are revealed.

Trinity (n.) Three parties joined together by a Center Stone: a Soul Seeker, a Messenger, and a Guardian.

Uriel (pr. n) Archangel and leader of the Powers.

Watchers (pr. n.) Also known as Grigori. Fallen angels who broke their covenant with God by fornicating with human women to create evil half-breed Nephilim, and by sharing mysteries prohibited from humans. The Nephilim were destroyed in the Great Flood, as referenced in the Book of Genesis. The Archangel Michael bound them for seventy generations in the valleys of Earth until Judgment Day.

9 798898 555390 1